THE BOWERS FILES

Praise for
Opening Moves

"*Opening Moves* is a mesmerizing read. From the first chapter, it sets its hook deep and drags you through a darkly gripping story with relentless power. My conclusion: I need to read more of Steven James."

—Michael Connelly, *New York Times*
bestselling author of *The Drop*

"Steven James has created a fast-moving thriller with psychological depth and gripping action. *Opening Moves* is a smart, taut, intense novel of suspense that reads like a cross between Michael Connelly and Thomas Harris. Young detective Patrick Bowers battles his own demons as he uses his intellect and experience to track twisted killers. Full of twists and enjoyable surprises, *Opening Moves* is a blisteringly fast and riveting read."

—Mark Greaney, *New York Times*
bestselling author of *Ballistic*

More Praise for Steven James
and His Award-Winning Novels

"James writes smart, taut, high-octane thrillers. But be warned—his books are not for the timid. The endings blow me away every time."

—Mitch Galin, producer of Stephen King's
The Stand and Frank Herbert's *Dune*

"Fresh and exciting."   —*Booklist*

"Absolutely brilliant."

—Jeff Buick, bestselling author of *One Child*

continued . . .

OPENING MOVES

STEVEN JAMES

A SIGNET SELECT BOOK

SIGNET SELECT
Published by New American Library, a division of
Penguin Group (USA) Inc., 375 Hudson Street,
New York, New York 10014, USA
Penguin Group (Canada), 90 Eglinton Avenue East, Suite 700, Toronto,
Ontario M4P 2Y3, Canada (a division of Pearson Penguin Canada Inc.)
Penguin Books Ltd., 80 Strand, London WC2R 0RL, England
Penguin Ireland, 25 St. Stephen's Green, Dublin 2,
Ireland (a division of Penguin Books Ltd.)
Penguin Group (Australia), 250 Camberwell Road, Camberwell, Victoria 3124,
Australia (a division of Pearson Australia Group Pty. Ltd.)
Penguin Books India Pvt. Ltd., 11 Community Centre, Panchsheel Park,
New Delhi - 110 017, India
Penguin Group (NZ), 67 Apollo Drive, Rosedale, Auckland 0632,
New Zealand (a division of Pearson New Zealand Ltd.)
Penguin Books (South Africa) (Pty.) Ltd., 24 Sturdee Avenue,
Rosebank, Johannesburg 2196, South Africa

Penguin Books Ltd., Registered Offices:
80 Strand, London WC2R 0RL, England

First published by Signet Select, an imprint of New American Library,
a division of Penguin Group (USA) Inc.

First Printing, September 2012
10 9 8 7 6 5 4 3 2 1

PUBLISHER'S NOTE
This is a work of fiction. Names, characters, places, and incidents either are the
product of the author's imagination or are used fictitiously, and any resemblance
to actual persons, living or dead, business establishments, events, or locales is
entirely coincidental.
   The publisher does not have any control over and does not assume any responsibility for author or third-party Web sites or their content.

ALWAYS LEARNING   PEARSON

To Brent,
who believed in Patrick Bowers from the start

"And if ye will not for all this hearken unto me, but walk contrary unto me; Then I will walk contrary unto you also in fury; and I, even I, will chastise you seven times for your sins. And ye shall eat the flesh of your sons, and the flesh of your daughters shall ye eat."

—Leviticus 26:27–29

Dear readers,

I had nightmares writing this book.

Some of the scenes were just too troubling for me, too real. I felt like I was staring in the face of pure evil.

Maybe it's because some of the information I included comes from actual crimes. When we read pure fiction we can reassure ourselves that at least those atrocities never occurred; history, on the other hand, doesn't afford us that option.

For example, pedophile and killer Albert Fish was a real person. So were the necrophile Ed Gein and the cannibal Jeffrey Dahmer. And so are the bank robbers and killers Ted and James Oswald, who are, at the time of this writing, serving two life sentences plus more than 450 years at separate prisons in Wisconsin.

Opening Moves became especially personal to me since, according to Ted Oswald (who was eighteen when he was apprehended), one of their future targets was his high school physics teacher, who'd given him a grade his father, James, didn't like. That teacher was my dad. During the trial, Ted recounted that James "was going to have me build a silencer in front of him [my father] and then shoot him in the belly and watch him barf."

My dad might very well have been one of the Oswalds' future victims if they hadn't been caught by the Waukesha County SWAT team.

When I look at our world, I see it threaded with both glory and horror, with awe-inspiring acts of love and deep furrows of unspeakable evil. Hope and terror spiral around us every day—and within us too, I believe, in our own hearts. This is something Patrick Bowers is discovering for himself more and more in each book, and something I was reminded of once again while writing his story.

I hope that my books never glamorize evil, but instead do the very opposite and tell the truth about how disturbing and pervasive it is in our world. I also hope that, when possible, the stories can point us past the darkness and help us awaken to something better than the nightmares that all too often plague us in real life.

—Steven James
Summer 2012

1997

DAY 1

The Alley

1

New Territories Pub
804 South Second Street
Milwaukee, Wisconsin
11:07 p.m.

Vincent Hayes stepped cautiously into the bar, trying unsuccessfully to still his heart, to quiet his apprehension.

He'd never done this before, never tried to pick up a man.

As he entered, two patrons who were seated at the bar—a Mexican in his mid-twenties and an older Caucasian who looked maybe a few years older than Vincent, around forty-five or so—turned to face him. The younger man had his hand resting gently on the middle-aged gentleman's knee.

Vincent gave the men a somewhat forced nod, they smiled a bit, then turned to gaze into each other's eyes again and went back to their conversation—perhaps a joke that the Mexican was telling, because Vincent heard the other man chuckle as he passed by and then took in the rest of the bar.

Country music played. Nondescript. Some singer he

didn't recognize. The neon beer signs and dim overheads did little to illuminate the nook and crannied pub. Vincent scanned the tables looking for the right kind of man— young, athletic, but not too muscular. The drugs he was carrying were potent, but muscle mass might diminish their effect. Maybe. He wasn't sure. He'd never used the drugs before, but tonight he couldn't risk taking the chance that the man would awaken before he was done with him.

He was looking for a black man.

All around him in the dim light, men stood talking. Most were gathered in groups of two or three. Very few single guys. Vincent was brawny and cut an impressive figure that turned a few heads, but none that looked promising.

Even though he wanted to be alert so he wouldn't make a mistake, he also needed something strong to take the edge off, to help anesthetize his inhibitions. Vincent took a seat at the bar and ordered a vodka.

Yes, yes, of course he was nervous. But there was also adrenaline there. Anxiety churning around violently beneath the surge of apprehension.

Keep your cool. This is not a time to make some kind of stupid mistake.

So far he hadn't seen anyone who fit the bill. Some were too old. A few younger couples were moving in time to the music on the dance floor on the far side of the bar. No single African-American like he was looking for.

He felt the brush of movement against his arm. A slim white guy who didn't look old enough to be here legally drew up a barstool. "Waiting for someone?" His voice was melodic and inviting. Charming might be a better word for it.

Yes, he was the right age, but he was the wrong race. Vincent gave him only a momentary glance. He didn't want to be rude or draw attention, but he didn't want to lead him on either.

"Um. Yes."

"Shame."

Vincent downed half of his vodka.

"Lucky guy," the man said under his breath, but, almost certainly on purpose, loud enough for Vincent to hear.

Get out of here. Try another bar. Already too many people have seen you in here.

Although it was supposed to happen at this bar, Vincent realized it was more important for it to happen than where it did.

"Sorry," he mumbled. He laid some cash beside his unfinished drink, then stood to leave. He'd taken two steps toward the door when he saw the type of man he was looking for: an athletic African-American, sitting alone in the booth near the narrow hallway to the restrooms.

Just like the young man who'd taken a seat beside Vincent a moment ago, this guy looked on the shy side of twenty-one, but Vincent guessed that carding people wasn't exactly at the top of the management's priority list.

He had a beer bottle in front of him, a Lienenkugel's. Almost empty. Vincent ordered two more from the bartender, excused himself from the guy who'd been coming on to him, and carried the two beers toward the booth.

Just get him to the minivan. You're bigger. You can easily overpower him in there.

As Vincent crossed the room, he surreptitiously dropped the two pills into one of the bottles and gently swirled them to the bottom.

When he was halfway to the booth, the young black man looked his way.

Vincent smiled, then, nervous, dropped his gaze.

You can do this; come on, you can do this.

He'd already decided he would cuff him as soon as he got him into the van. Hopefully, he'd be too drugged to fight much or call for help, but Vincent had a gag and duct tape waiting just in case. If he wasn't able to get him to take off his clothes before he cuffed him, he would strip the guy, cutting off his shirt and jeans with the fabric shears when he was done.

And then move forward with things from there.

Almost to the booth now, he waited for the man to say something, but when he didn't, Vincent spoke, trying out the same line the guy had used on him a few moments earlier. "Waiting for someone?"

The black man—kid, really—looked his way, wide-eyed. Wet his lips slightly. "I saw Mark with you. That what he asked you?"

Vincent set down the drinks. "Busted."

"He needs to expand his repertoire."

"I guess I do too."

The young man eyed the beers, and said demurely, "One of those for me?"

Vincent slid the drugged beer toward him, smiled again, and took a seat.

The guy offered Vincent a soft nod, accepted the drink, and held out his hand palm down, a diminutive handshake. "I'm Lionel."

"Vincent." He shook Lionel's hand.

"Mmm. Vincent." It almost sounded like Lionel was purring. "Very European." His eyes gleamed. "A shade mysterious." He took a sip of his beer. "I haven't seen you here before, Vincent."

"I'm . . ." Vincent couldn't think of anything clever or witty to say. "Well, I . . . This is my first time."

"Your first time, what? Here?"

He hesitated. "Yes."

"Or your first time. Period?"

"Yes. My first time. Period."

Lionel looked at him as if he'd just said something humorous. "You haven't done this before. Ever?"

"No." Vincent took a drink as a way of hiding, but also of, hopefully, encouraging the young man to drink his beer as well.

It worked.

When Lionel had finished the swig, his eyes drifted toward Vincent's left hand. Toward his wedding ring.

"You're married."

"Yes."

"Why tonight? Why did you come tonight? Is she out of town?"

The last thing Vincent wanted to do right now was talk about Colleen. "Yes," he said, lying. "Visiting her parents."

"And you decided to try something a little different? For a change?"

"To step out on a limb. Yes." His heart was beating. Thinking about Colleen made all of this harder.

Vincent took another sip from his drink. So did Lionel.

"I don't live far from here," Vincent offered, and then immediately realized that it was much too forward. On the other hand, if his suspicions were right, Lionel was working the place, looking for payment for his companionship, and wasting a lot of time on formalities wouldn't serve either of their interests.

"Really? Where?"

"Not far."

A wink. "Staying mysterious, are we?"

Vincent had no idea how to respond. "I really . . . I'm not sure how to say this. Um, are you, well, are you—"

Lionel laid his hand gently on Vincent's forearm. "I can be whatever you want me to be, Vincent."

It was a long moment before he removed his hand.

"Okay." Vincent said.

Lionel smiled softly. "Okay."

Another swig.

And another.

And although Vincent was anxious to get going, he realized he needed a little time for the drugs to work, so he answered Lionel's questions about where he'd gone to college, UW–La Crosse, and what he did for a living, managed a PR firm. In response, Lionel mentioned that he had a theater degree from DePaul and was an actor "between jobs."

As the minutes passed, the drugs and alcohol started to have the desired effect.

"Lionel?"

"Um-hmm." His voice was wavering, unfocused.

"Do you want to leave?"

"Your place is close?" he mumbled.

"Yes. Let's get you to the car."

No response, just a bleary nod.

So Vincent helped Lionel to his feet and supported him on the way to the door.

2

Apparently, two men leaving this bar—with one of them evidently drunk—was not too out of the ordinary. Nobody paid much attention to them as they left the building.

Vincent could see his breath as he crossed the sidewalk, but the November night felt brisk rather than icy cold and that would be good for Lionel, for what Vincent had in mind for him.

Earlier, Vincent had taken the backseats out of his minivan and it wasn't difficult to help Lionel into the vehicle. Once they were inside, he closed the door and retrieved the handcuffs.

He hoped Lionel wouldn't struggle, but Vincent had been a linebacker in college, still worked out four or five days a week, and was willing to get physical, if that's what it took.

Vincent began to unzip Lionel's jacket.

"What are you . . . ?" Lionel's words were blurred, confused.

"We need to get you out of these clothes."

"I thought we . . . were going . . . to your place."

"Plans have changed." He tugged off Lionel's coat.

Lionel eyed the handcuffs. A look that went past confusion and dipped into fear crossed his face and he tried to wrestle free. He was squirrelly and hard to hold on to, and Vincent was forced to do something he hadn't intended to do—punch him in the face. Lionel crumpled to the floor. "What the—?"

Vincent cuffed his left wrist and when Lionel tried to get up again, Vincent grabbed his head and smacked it hard against the floor of the van. "Don't fight. It'll make it worse."

"No—"

This wasn't going well, not well at all.

Vincent bent over him. "Be quiet, Lionel, or I'll have to do that again. I don't want to, but if I—"

"Help!" Lionel rolled to his side, tried to scramble toward the door, but Vincent snagged his left arm, twisted it behind his back, brought the right arm around as well and cuffed the wrists together. Once he was assured that Lionel wasn't going anywhere, he stuffed a cloth into his mouth and wrapped a few rounds of duct tape around his head to hold it in place. Lionel tried to shake free, to cry out for help, but could hardly make any sound at all.

Vincent hurried to the driver's seat and started the engine.

Get away from the bar. You need to get away from here. Right now.

Sweating, shaking, Vincent turned the key and the engine came to life. He scanned the street, the sidewalks. A couple of men had just left the bar but were headed in the opposite direction and weren't looking at the van. Vincent heard the muffled sound of Lionel trying to call for help, but it wasn't nearly loud enough for the men out-side to hear.

The drugs, they should have knocked him out by now.

Vincent lurched the van onto the street too fast, his heart racing, his mouth dry.

Easy, don't get pulled over. Do not get pulled over.

Eight blocks away he paused in a deserted parking lot, turned off the headlights, and let the engine idle; then he returned to the back of the minivan. The drugs were tak-ing their toll on Lionel. He lay on the floor, barely con-scious.

Quickly, Vincent removed Lionel's shoes, then his socks, then his pants and underwear. The fight had gone out of him and he didn't resist, just stared vacantly at the roof of the minivan.

Using fabric shears, Vincent cut a long slit up each sleeve of Lionel's sweater. He removed it and then went to work on his undershirt.

A few moments later Lionel lay naked and cuffed in the van.

"I didn't want things to go like this," Vincent told him.

Lionel rolled weakly onto his side, curling himself into a fetal position.

Vincent returned to the driver's seat and guided the van to North Twenty-fifth Street, to the alley that ran between a ramshackle two-story house and an empty lot that was surrounded by a rusted six-foot-high chain-link fence. Two stout, brick apartment buildings lay just to the left of the fenced-in lot. The alley was empty. No one on the sidewalk that led past it. No traffic.

However, half a dozen cars were parked along the alley's side of the street, leaving room for snowplows to drive along the other side if the weather took a turn for the worse. Vincent realized it was good that there was a string of cars already there by the curb. It would make his van less conspicuous.

He parked and crawled into the back. "Okay, I'm taking off the gag. But don't cry out or I'll have to hit you again, and I really don't want to do that."

Lionel, if he understood, did not respond. Just lay still and submissive.

Using the shears again, Vincent cut off the tape, tugged it free, and removed the gag. Then he opened the door to the van. "Go," he commanded Lionel. "Get out."

At last Lionel looked at him.

"Go on." He swung Lionel's feet around so they were sticking out the door. "Get out of the van."

Lionel tried to leave on his own, but collapsed onto the sidewalk with a low moan.

Get away, Vincent. You have to get away. This is close enough.

But then the reality: *No! They need to find him in the alley. Or else—*

He hadn't wanted to do this, but now he got out and, supporting Lionel, led him fifty feet into the alley, left him standing unsteadily, but on his own, then hustled back to the vehicle.

But he didn't leave yet.

Once inside the van, he tried to calm himself. He looked around. Saw nothing suspicious. No pedestrians. No movement on the street. Because of the vacant lot beside the alley, Lionel was still clearly visible from the road.

Nervously gripping the keys that he'd left in the ignition, Vincent took a few seconds to catch his breath.

The brisk air seemed to be bringing Lionel out of the drug-induced stupor. He stumbled across the alley, eventually leaning for support against a telephone pole by the fence encircling the lot.

Vincent was about to pull into the street when he saw a police cruiser round the corner and come prowling toward him. Heart hammering, he glanced toward Lionel one last time and saw him drop heavily to the ground beside the telephone pole.

From there he would be visible to the cops if they looked down the alley.

Vincent ducked his head down and leaned across the front seat so he'd be out of sight. An anonymous, empty minivan on a quiet, anonymous street. Well, maybe not an anonymous street, but—

He didn't think the cops had seen him, but it was possible—

No, no, no. You cannot get caught!

The squad's headlights swept across the road, through the windshield of Vincent's van, then toward the alley, toward Lionel.

They see him. They have to see him by now!

The movement of the headlights stopped and Vincent heard one of the police car doors slam shut. Then the other.

Get out of here. If you're caught, everything will fall apart. You can't let that happen. There's too much—

"Hey!" one of the cops yelled to Lionel. "Are you alright?"

Vincent's heart slammed, hammered in his chest.

There was no indication yet that they'd taken note of his van.

They're going to check on him. You can get out of here when they do. You need to go.

Drive.

No, they would follow him. He knew they would. At least one of them would.

Run. You need to run.

Maybe. Yes, leave the van here.

His head was still low, but he heard more shouting from the cops and pictured them hurrying toward Lionel. If they hadn't already started to, in a few seconds they would scan the area. Then they would search the nearest vehicles one at a time. They would catch him if he stayed where he was and follow him if he tried to drive away.

Now. It has to be now. On foot.

Slowly, Vincent edged his head up, gazed toward the alley, and saw both cops leaning over Lionel.

This was it. In a moment they would start looking for anything suspicious. Vincent silently opened his door and slipped onto the street, keeping the minivan between him and the cops. Afraid the door might alert them, he didn't click it shut all the way. No noise.

A dog barked in a yard a few houses away, on the other side of the alley. The cops turned their attention to the sound: "Check it out," one of them said to his partner. While the officers were momentarily distracted, Vincent scurried fifteen feet farther down the road and crouched behind another car.

It would be easier from here. The angle was wrong for the cops to see him. The one who knelt beside Lionel was talking into his radio now, calling for backup.

Go.

Swiftly and without a sound, Vincent went for the next car.

Beyond that there weren't any more vehicles close enough to hide behind, and just as he was wondering if he should try waiting it out here for a few minutes, he heard the sirens. More cops were already on the way.

No, if he stayed here, they'd find him. He either needed to get behind the nearest apartment, which was about twenty-five feet away—but that meant traversing the lawn in plain sight—or make it to the other side of the road and hope the parked cars would block the view as he crossed the street. Then he could disappear into the neighborhood on the next block over.

Which was better?

Hard to say.

Hard to say.

Maybe crossing the road. If he stayed low enough, the cars would at least partially block the view. Less chance of being seen.

Yes, that would work, he could make it. He had to.

The vague sound of distant traffic floated through the chilly night. Nearby, more dogs were joining in barking, but Vincent tried to block all that out.

He took a breath and went for it, dashing across the road as swiftly as he could, but just as he reached the far curb, he heard one of the cops yell, "Stop! Police!"

Go!

As fast as he could, Vincent sprinted into the dark channel between the two houses in front of him.

A quick glance back told him that the cop was in pursuit. Looking forward again, Vincent managed to duck just in time to avoid a clothesline strung up in someone's backyard. He came to a waist-high wooden fence, scrambled over it, and bolted past a driveway and through the night, weaving between the houses to try to lose the cop.

"Stop right there!" the officer yelled. Amazingly, he sounded like he was gaining on him. He wasn't out of breath and it was the voice of a guy who knew he was going to take you down.

But Vincent didn't stop running, there was too much at stake. He rounded another house. If he could just stay out of sight, just—he dodged an abandoned tricycle and barely missed slamming into a jon boat stationed on its rusted trailer beside the home—just get to the next street—

Though he was already almost two blocks from the alley where he'd left Lionel, he could see the flicker dance of the blue-red-blue lights of more squads driving toward the scene.

Vincent angled left and flew past a tumbledown duplex. He didn't see the cop anymore and figured he must have lost him somewhere between the last two houses. He kept running.

By now, some of the porch lights in the neighborhood were snapping on as more people woke up from the shouting, the yelping dogs, the police sirens.

Vincent whipped around the corner of a house.

And almost ran into the cop, a tall scruffy guy, who stood in front of him with his gun raised. "Do not move."

How did he get—?

"Hands up!"

Vincent raised his hands. He needed to get away, there was no other option. "Officer, I'm not—"

"On your knees. Do it."

The guy looked like an athlete. Vincent calculated whether or not he could take him. It might not be easy.

Go for the gun.

That would be tight too. But he couldn't risk being taken in. "Please, Officer, I need to—"

"Now." The cop leveled the gun at his chest.

Desperation swallowed everything. This was it. He had to go for it, had to risk it, had to act now, before more officers got here. He started to bend down as if he were obeying the officer, but then used his bent knee to propel himself forward and lunge for the gun.

Years of college football and weight lifting had made Vincent quick and tough and not afraid to mix things up. He went hard at the cop, snagging his hand and knocking the gun away. Then he balled up a fist and aimed a blow at the officer's kidney, but the guy blocked it just in time.

He deftly grabbed Vincent's wrist, twisting it to control him.

Countering, Vincent threw a hard hook with his other fist, connected solidly with the guy's jaw, but that didn't stop him—he drove his shoulder into Vincent's chest and slammed him to the ground.

Vincent tried to wrestle free but the cop was wiry and strong, and as he rolled to get away, he felt his arm being wrenched behind him to subdue him. Vincent strained fiercely to get away, but the cop twisted his arm more, toward the breaking point.

"No!" Vincent couldn't help but yell. If he didn't get away—

But then he was cuffed and the officer was pinning

him down with his knee, calling for backup. "Do not move," he told Vincent.

"You don't understand—"

"Quiet," the officer said. "This is Detective Bowers." He was talking into his radio. "I'm on the southeast corner of Twenty-sixth and Wells. I have the suspect."

"Please," Vincent gasped. "He has her. If you don't let me go, he's going to kill her. You can't let that maniac kill my wife!"

3

I paused. "Who has her?"

"Some guy—I don't know his name! He broke into our house, told me I had to take a black man to that alley. Please—he said if I got caught, it'd be too late for last rites, that he'd slit her throat. Slit her like a pig." The guy's voice cracked. "That's what he said."

I patted him down. "Where are they?"

"I don't know. You have to believe me!"

No weapons. A wallet. Car keys. A portable phone in his pocket. Not just a pager, an actual portable phone. Though they were starting to become more popular, it spoke of wealth. I removed the items. "What's your name?"

"Vincent Hayes."

A few seconds ago he'd knocked my gun, a .357 SIG P229, away, and now I quickly retrieved it and slipped it into my holster, then held Hayes down firmly.

Assess the threat. Clear the scene.

I scanned the shadows to make sure no accomplices were coming to assist the guy, but the view in all directions was restricted. After evaluating the sight lines, the distance to the nearest intersection, and the spacing between the streetlights, I realized I didn't like our position here at all.

"You said he told you to do it. Did you meet with him?"

"On the phone!"

It was possible for someone to be making something like this up on the spot, but it seemed unlikely. The best way to ferret out a lie is with a follow-up question. "Who are you working with, Vincent?"

"No one." A pause. "What do you mean?"

"Abducting the man in the alley. Who else was involved?"

"No one. It was just me."

"Don't lie to me."

"He made me do it! I swear. Stop wasting time. He's going to kill her if—"

"Where do you live, Vincent?"

He rattled off an address and I radioed it in to get a car over there. I was still holding him down and he was a hefty man, so I was glad that, at least for the moment, he'd stopped trying to roll away.

"No, no no, they're not there—" Then abruptly, he seemed to change his mind. "Wait. You can't go in. If he sees you, he'll kill her! He said no cops!"

There was no question that I needed to check out this guy's story to see if his wife was safe. "Go in dark," I told dispatch. "Possible hostage situation."

Swift, light footsteps approached us. I whipped out my SIG, snapped around, ready, wired. But it was just Sergeant Brandon Walker, the guy we called Radar, entering the circle of light tossed down from one of the streetlights about thirty meters away.

At thirty-seven, Radar was twelve years older than me and was the one officer Lieutenant Thorne thought wouldn't be threatened or insulted partnering with the youngest homicide detective on the force. He'd been right. Radar was a good cop. A good man. A great dad. Even though he wasn't an imposing guy—slim, balding, stuck with a nose that was a little too big for his face— Radar was scrappy and smart, and I was glad he was my partner.

I holstered my weapon, hailed Radar, then asked Vincent, "Why would he kill her?"

"I don't know! He made me do it. Like I told you, he said if I got caught, he'd slit her throat! You have to—"

"You alright, Pat?" It was Radar jogging toward us, weapon out to cover me.

"I'm fine. You hearing this?"

"Yeah."

He arrived at my side.

"Get two cars over here, Radar. I want this guy in a cruiser ASAP so we can talk to him in private."

He was eyeing my face where Vincent had punched me.

"Go on," I told him.

"You sure you're okay?"

Only then did I become aware of the pain emanating from my jaw and pounding through my head. It was hard to imagine that I hadn't noticed it a few seconds ago, but adrenaline does that to you. My index finger ached too; it'd gotten wrenched pretty badly when Vincent yanked at my SIG, and now the proximal interphalangeal joint felt thick, swollen, hard to move. "I'm good. Make the call."

While Radar stepped away to radio the cruisers, I

asked Hayes, "How would he know you did it? Were you supposed to meet him? Call him?"

"He said he'd be watching."

"From where?"

"I don't know."

I scrutinized the area again. "Tell me what happened. Make it quick."

He snatched a breath and quickly recounted the story. "I came home, found blood in the kitchen. He'd taken her. There was a note with a phone number and I called it. He told me I needed to leave a black man in his twenties, naked, cuffed in that alley, that if I got caught or went to the cops, he'd kill Colleen."

"Did he tell you that alley on Twenty-fifth, that specific one?"

"Yes."

That was the alley where, back in 1991, Konerak Sinthasomphone had been found. The teenage Laotian had been drugged and was disoriented, but had escaped apartment 213 when his abductor, a serial killer named Jeffrey Dahmer, briefly left him alone.

When the police arrived, Dahmer convinced the two MPD officers that Konerak was his drunk lover. When the officers returned Konerak, who was still disoriented from the drugs, to Dahmer's apartment, they caught the scent of a terrible smell that Dahmer told them was his aquarium he'd been putting off cleaning—but it was really the decomposing body of a victim Dahmer had killed earlier that week, Tony Hughes. The officers left Konerak with Dahmer, who, within minutes, overpowered him, killed him, and began to eat his heart.

The same alley.

When Konerak was found there, he'd been handcuffed—naked and cuffed, just like the guy tonight. Two months later, when a young African-American man named Tracy Edwards escaped from Dahmer and led the police to Dahmer's apartment, one of his wrists was cuffed as well. He'd fought back when Dahmer attacked him and barely managed to get away in time. Everyone on the MPD knew the story.

I processed everything, made a decision, told Radar, "Send out a call that the suspect got away."

He glanced at Hayes, then looked at me again quizzically. "That he got away?"

"If this guy's telling the truth, as long as he's free from the police, his wife stays alive."

"Got it." Radar went for his radio again.

"Okay." I turned to Vincent. "What's the phone number you found at your house?"

"On my portable phone. The last number I called. I don't remember it." Obviously he was scared, worried, desperate, but he must have been able to tell that I was trying to help, that I wasn't discounting his story, and his straight answers were just what I needed.

I took out his phone and yanked the antenna up. I wished there were a simple way to redial portable numbers, but a quick call to the station, then to the telephone company, got me what I needed.

I punched in the number and let it ring.

While I waited for someone to pick up, the two cruisers I'd requested pulled up to the curb and four officers jumped out. Radar helped them hustle Vincent Hayes into one of the cars.

The phone kept ringing. Still no answer.

Radar returned and I told him urgently, "Have everyone keep their red-and-blues on. I want it to look like we're still searching for the suspect." It wasn't much, and if Vincent was telling the truth and his wife's abductor was watching, or maybe if he was monitoring emergency frequencies, it would already be too late. But it was worth a try and—

The ringing stopped. I waited, but whoever was on the other end said nothing, so I did: "It's done." I kept my voice low and tried to sound out of breath so that whoever was on the other end wouldn't recognize that I wasn't Vincent. "The cops came, but I got away."

No answer.

"They found the black guy," I said.

"Yes."

"You said you'd let Colleen go."

"Who is this?"

"Vincent," I lied. "I did it. I swear. Let me talk to—"

I heard a gasp and then a scream on the other end of the line, and then nothing at all.

"Colleen!" I yelled.

A blank silence, and then a rapid beeping sound. The man had hung up.

I redialed, nothing. Called the station: "Get me a trace on 888-359-5392. Now!"

4

We were unable to trace the call, found no one at the Hayes residence, didn't learn anything helpful from the bartender at New Territories, and when I met up with Vincent at police headquarters in interrogation room 2A thirty minutes later, I had no good news to share with him.

It was possible that the woman I'd heard scream on the phone wasn't Colleen Hayes, and it was also possible that the scream was staged, that no one had even gotten hurt. I found that unlikely, but all too often premature assumptions end up needlessly derailing investigations and I wasn't about to let that happen in this case. Facts need to establish hypotheses, not the other way around.

Right now Vincent didn't need to know anything about someone screaming on the phone.

I found him seated at a metal table bolted to the floor, his hands and feet shackled. If his story was true, he'd been coerced to commit tonight's crimes and theoretically might not pose a risk or need to be cuffed. But he had drugged and kidnapped a young man, resisted arrest, assaulted an officer of the law—in fact I wasn't even sure how many laws he'd broken in the last two hours. We still hadn't confirmed his story. Cuffed was good.

And what about that phone call? Somebody answered. Someone screamed.

"Okay, Mr. Hayes." I took out a notepad and a miniature cassette recorder. "We were rushed earlier when I asked you to tell me what happened tonight. I need you to fill me—"

"Is Lionel okay?"

"Yes. He's still at the hospital. They're keeping him overnight."

On the ride here, the officers with Vincent had grilled him on what kind of drugs he'd given Lionel, how much he'd used, when and how they'd been administered, how many drinks he'd seen Lionel have. "He's okay for now," I said, "but you gave him some pretty potent stuff."

"And you got nothing on Colleen? Nothing?"

"We're still looking for her."

It struck me that he'd asked about Lionel first, rather than his wife.

Vincent was quiet. "Can I have some coffee?"

His request seemed a bit out of the blue, and was possibly a sign of interrogation avoidance, but on the other hand, it's not uncommon for people to act unpredictably during times of intense stress.

Folks have been known to start cleaning their homes while the place is on fire, desperately trying to straighten things up or get the dishes in the dishwasher before leaving. Mothers who've lost their babies will sometimes hold the child to their breast and rock the corpse gently, even kiss its forehead as they would if the baby were still alive, though they would never think to snuggle with or kiss a corpse under any other circumstances.

Before life squeezes us to the limit, we can never be

sure how we're going to respond, so even though I found it odd that Vincent didn't immediately ask any more questions about his wife, I gave him a pass.

"Alright." Protocol called for me to offer him something to eat, which I did, and which he declined.

Outside the interrogation room I found a young female officer whom I didn't recognize. Her name tag: GABRIELE HOLDREN. Slim build. Black hair. Bright eyes. I asked her if she could get some coffee for Mr. Hayes.

"Would you like some too, Detective?"

"No, I never touch the stuff." Grind up burned beans and pour water over them? Drink that sludge? Not my idea of a good time.

While she went for the coffee, I returned to my chair across the table from Vincent Hayes, flipped open my notebook, and started the cassette recorder.

"Mr. Hayes, I need you to tell me exactly what happened tonight. Starting with the last time you spoke with Colleen."

"I talked with her at about seven. I run a PR firm; we're under the gun with a deadline and I told her I wasn't going to be home until at least ten." His voice was balanced. He didn't sound like a guy who was worried about his wife's life being on the line; he sounded more like a man who was discussing his market earnings with his accountant.

I noted that.

"She was at the house when you spoke with her?"

"Yes. Everything was fine; she understood about my getting home late. No big deal. We hung up. I went back to work, came home a little after ten, and, just like I told you earlier, she was gone."

"Tell me about the blood."

"In the kitchen, on the floor. Spots of it, not that much."

The clinical, objective way Vincent was describing everything was starting to disturb me.

I had some ideas about where to take this conversation, but I needed to cover the proverbial bases first.

"Did you notice anything missing?"

"No."

"What was your wife's state of mind? Had you argued earlier? Anything like that?"

"No, she was fine. Like I said."

"How is your marriage, Mr. Hayes?"

"Our marriage?"

"Were you having any problems? Any other romantic relationships either of you were engaged in outside of—"

"No!"

"Mr. Hayes, is there anyone who might wish to harm either you or Colleen?"

"No. No one."

A knock at the door. I answered it and Holdren handed me the coffee for Hayes, then disappeared into the hallway again. I slid the burnt-bean-flavored water to him. His wrists were cuffed, so he lifted the foam cup with both hands as he drank.

"What did you do when you found the blood? Did you call 911?"

He shook his head. "Like I told you before, there was a note there by the phone. I called the number and a man answered. He told me to go to a bar, get the black guy."

"And did he specify which bar?"

"New Territories. I was supposed to try there first.

Find a guy, someone in his twenties, drug him, then drop him off naked and handcuffed in the alley at 924 North Twenty-fifth Street."

"Did you recognize the voice of the man on the phone?"

He shook his head. "No."

"And 911, why didn't you call it then?"

"He said no cops." Hayes's tone made it clear he was getting more impatient. He set down his cup. "I explained all this before."

It didn't bother me that he was getting upset. The more you rattle someone, the more the truth comes out. When people get angry, they stop waffling and hiding things from you and start saying what's really on their minds.

Okay, enough with the stock questions.

"Where did you get the pills?"

"What?"

"The pills you gave Lionel Shannon. Where did you get them?"

"He left them for me. The guy on the phone did."

"Where?"

"Two pills. In a kitchen drawer, wrapped in tinfoil."

I jotted this down, more for show than anything. My memory is pretty good, besides, I always verify everything later from the written transcript of the interviews. "Earlier you told the officers who were driving you here that you gave Lionel a drug called Propotol. How did you know the type of drug if the offender provided the pills for you?"

"He told me."

"On the phone?"

"Yes."

I watched him closely to gauge his reaction to my next question. "Mr. Hayes, do you own a pair of handcuffs?"

A pause. "Yeah. My wife and I, well . . . we're into . . . Anyway, yeah, I used those. He told me to go to the bar and—"

I set down my pen. "Vincent, you live less than fifteen minutes from New Territories—probably closer to a ten-minute drive at that time of night—but we know from talking with the bartender that you didn't arrive there until after eleven o'clock."

"I guess so." He shook his head. "I don't know."

"You just told me you got to your house a little after ten. If your wife's life was in danger, why did you wait nearly forty-five minutes before driving to the bar?"

A switch seemed to go off inside him. Finally, there was passion in his voice again. "You have to believe me! I went as soon as I could!"

"Then what did you do in the meantime?"

"I took the backseats out of my minivan and then drove to the bar. I sat there for a while, trying to get up enough nerve to go in. To actually do it."

It was possible, but it seemed like a stretch. My suspicions were teeter-tottering back and forth.

And why would Colleen's kidnapper tell Vincent the name of the drug?

I couldn't think of a good reason.

Vincent must have sensed my reluctance to buy at face value everything he was telling me. "Listen, he's going to kill her, I know he is!" He tugged violently at his shackles, snapping the chains tight. "You have to get out there. You're wasting time talking to me!"

"We have good people looking for Colleen as we speak, I guarantee you. But the more you can tell me right now about what happened, the better our chances are of finding her quickly." I said "quickly" rather than "alive" because part of me feared it might already be too late for that.

Once again, I asked him to recount the telephone conversation as closely as he could, and he did, but there was nothing new, nothing contradictory, nothing he hadn't already told me. "Mr. Hayes, think carefully. Is there anything else—anything at all—that might help us find Colleen?"

He massaged his forehead roughly with two fingers and a thumb as if he were trying to squeeze out information. "No. Just believe me. You have to find her."

"We will." I hit the STOP button on the recorder and put it in my pocket. I wasn't sure what to think, not anymore. There were enough red flags in his story to keep me guessing, but there was also enough consistency to make it believable. "Until we know more, we have to keep you in custody. I think you know that."

He nodded silently.

"I'll send an officer to take you to your cell."

You never leave anything in the hands of an unsupervised person in custody, so I took the empty coffee cup from Hayes, left the interrogation room, and went to meet with Lieutenant Thorne to fill him in on what we knew.

5

After briefing the lieutenant, I told him, "Here's what we need to do: look for a small piece of tinfoil on the floor of the van. Vincent didn't have it on him when we caught him, and I can't imagine that after he drugged Lionel he took the time to find a trash can and throw out the foil. Have the guys sweep Hayes's house and the bar."

Thorne was a broad, densely muscled man with simian arms. He didn't speak at first, but his eyes did. Inquisitive. Calm. Confident. "You're thinking there might be prints on the foil? Or no foil at all?"

"Yes."

"We'll check the trash cans too."

"Good. Also, dust the handcuffs that were on Lionel. Hayes told me they were his, but we need to find out if there are any prints on them besides his and his wife's."

"Vincent might be lying about the whole thing."

"It's possible. Think about it—if you were the abductor and left the pills behind, wouldn't you have also left the cuffs? If your primary demand required a pair? So either the killer knew Vincent had his own set—"

"Or Hayes is lying. Is working with him."

"We have to stay open to that possibility."

He chewed on his lip for a moment. "It'll take at least two weeks before we can verify that the DNA of the blood in the Hayes kitchen is really Colleen's."

In the wake of the O.J. trial two years ago, it seemed like every defense attorney in the country wanted DNA tests done and there just weren't enough resources in the system to process all that evidence. Every year the field of DNA testing is advancing by leaps and bounds, but it's still exorbitantly expensive, time-consuming, and most crime labs are backed up for months, if not years. They say someday we'll be able to get the results on priority cases immediately instead of two to three weeks later. That would definitely be a game-changer.

"But," Thorne went on, "she is missing, there are signs of a struggle; it sure looks like she was attacked there in the house. The note with the phone number was there, just like Hayes said." A pause. "And you heard a woman scream on the phone."

"Yes, but her identity remains unconfirmed. It might not have been Colleen."

He looked a little irritated. "You always hedge your bets, don't you, Pat?"

"I don't like making bets, I like—"

"Unearthing the truth."

A pause. "I've mentioned that before?"

"Possibly. And why were you and Radar in that neighborhood again?"

"We were in the area following up on a call. A neighbor phoned dispatch, said someone was lurking around Dahmer's old lot. The neighbors don't like strangers around there."

"Yeah. No kidding." He pushed back from his desk,

then rose from his chair. "I'm assigning a task force to this. I can probably get you two or three people plus Radar. You'll be lead."

"Good."

"And I'll get the crime scene guys to finish processing the scene."

We actually had four known crime scenes. "And the bar, the van, the alley."

"Don't worry. We got it." Thorne looked at his watch. "It's coming up on one thirty. I want you on your A-game in the morning. Go home. Get some rest. And put some ice on that jaw. That bruise is gonna be nasty in the morning. I'll see you at nine."

"Call me if—"

"Don't worry, I will."

I have a small apartment.

It's the kind of place you might expect a single guy who's almost never home to have. Sparse furniture. A fridge that's almost always empty except for some leftover Chinese or Thai food and a dozen half-used bottles of condiments. A pull-up bar in the living room. A bed that's almost never made. A few too many dishes in the sink.

Okay, more than a few.

Working on a detective's salary while also taking grad classes in criminology and law studies at Marquette, I don't have a whole lot of time or extra cash floating around for home decorating.

It's my own little balancing act: a professional life that has to be meticulously organized, that consumes most of my time and mental energy; a home life that ends up paying the price. All part of the deal when you sign up for this gig.

I checked my messages and found one from Taci Vardis, the woman I was seeing. She was finishing her residency in surgery through the Medical College of Wisconsin, so both of our schedules were insane and we'd had some difficulties coordinating them lately.

"Hey, Pat. It's me. Um . . . Well, it's kind of late, but if you get in before midnight, give me a call. I'm still at the hospital. I'm looking forward to tomorrow night. Supper." A pause. A sigh. "I can't believe it's been a year since we met. Anyway, I was just thinking of you. Gotta go. Love you. Bye."

Despite the warmth in her voice I caught the hint of something else. A touch of loneliness? I couldn't tell. Even after listening to the message four times, I wasn't able to read exactly what might lie beneath her words.

A little disquieted, but unwilling to call her this late, I grabbed some ice for my jaw and my finger, then took some time to review what I knew about the case. After filling out the paperwork from Hayes's arrest, I read over my notes for tomorrow afternoon's class at Marquette.

With this Hayes case suddenly dropped in my lap, I wasn't sure if I'd make the three o'clock seminar, but we had a guest lecturer coming in to teach a two-week course on geographic profiling and environmental criminology and the topics intrigued me. He'd assigned readings to do before the session began, and as usual, I was behind.

From what I'd read so far of his work, he was using cutting-edge computer models to analyze the timing, progression, and location of serial offenses, and then overlaying that data against the lifestyle choices of the victims and the cognitive maps that both they and the offender formed of the areas in which they lived. The concept of cognitive mapping had been especially interesting to me.

The geospatial-analysis process was still a little fuzzy to me, but ever since the semester began nearly three months ago, I'd been looking forward to hearing Dr. Werjonic talk us through it.

When I caught myself dozing off, I knew it was time for bed. The clock on the wall was a little fast but told me it was almost three, and that was plenty late for me.

As I lay down in bed, I took a few minutes to try and clear my head.

I've never been good at shutting out the images of the crime scenes I see, turning off that part of myself, and all too often the memories plague me in my dreams where I can't fight them off. Tonight, even though I hadn't seen her yet and didn't even know if she was injured, I was afraid I would have nightmares about a dead Colleen Hayes.

But I didn't.

I had nightmares about someone else.

6

In my dream, I'm standing in a forest, bristling pines surround me. Mist whispers through the trees, through the dusk. Ethereal and surreal. Images of past crime scenes are passing before me, layering and overlapping. Blood and broken bodies, the tears of survivors, heartache and terror sketched across their faces.

It isn't like I'm seeing with my eyes; more like a slightly blurred reality sliding slowly across itself somewhere beyond, but also somehow within, my field of vision.

Then the images fade and a cocoon appears, hanging from a branch just a few feet away. The skin is rich and translucent and something inside the cocoon is moving, but as it pushes against the skin, I see that it's not a butterfly, not a moth, but rather a worm encircled with wide black veins. The worm is grayish pink, like a sad November twilight.

I'm aware of reaching for the cocoon, but as I do, it falls to the ground.

However, time moves at a different speed here in my dream and the cocoon drops slowly, slow enough for me to take two long breaths as I watch it descend.

Finally, it lands, moist and alive at my feet, where it

suddenly grows to the size of a bloated python and becomes something terrifying, with bristling teeth and bulging eyes. I back up, but it writhes toward me.

Gray, but veined in black.

As I retreat, sharp branches scratch my back, forcing me to stop, but the grisly creature does not. I kick at its head, but at the last moment it dives into the soft earth.

I realize that the snake, or worm, or whatever it was, might emerge again, might encircle my legs, so I hurry away from that part of the forest. The bare tree branches reach for my arms as I pass and sharp twigs like skeleton fingers claw at me from inside the curtain of evening mist. As I bump into the branches, droplets of water fall from above me onto my neck like teardrops in the mist.

A cocoon.

Birthing a monster.

Burrowing into the earth.

Even in my dream I'm somehow aware that the cocoon and the disturbing creature have some greater significance, some meaning beyond themselves, but I have no idea what that might be.

As I pass through the cool, dewy evening, I sense that I am not alone.

I reach the edge of the forest. A field stretches out of sight before me, open and wild, cleared of the ghostlike fog by a steady prairie wind.

Where I am, I cannot say.

The sun is low.

Dusk is near.

The air deepens to a chill. Something is happening. Something bad.

I want to wake up, but I cannot. Even when I pinch myself, even when I bite down hard on my cheek, I cannot.

Fifty meters away a man appears, stepping out of the bleary mists. He's carrying a shovel and dragging something. A sack. No—

A sleeping bag.

It is not empty.

My heart thumps heavily, unmanageably, inside my chest.

It's a little girl's sleeping bag, pink and embroidered on top with large yellow flowers, but now encircled with duct tape in three careful places.

A tragic, terrible cocoon.

Like the one that gave oozing birth to the worm.

I cannot see the man's face.

The sun pauses on its way to the edge of the world and the man stares long and hard at the earth. For a moment everything in my dream wavers, as if time itself were catching its breath, and then the man takes a few steps farther into the meadow. Stops.

Though I want to approach him, my desire doesn't affect how things play out in my dream and I remain standing there, watching, deeply unsettled because of the sleeping bag and its contents, which I fear I know.

Heartbeat quickening, I watch the man dig, and when the hole is complete, he drives the shovel into the earth beside him and reaches for the sleeping bag.

It sags heavy and sad in his arms. Then he lowers the bag, the tender-child-shaped bundle, into the shallow grave he just dug.

I want desperately to do something, to stop him, but it's a dream and I can only watch.

Only—

He rises again, considers the hole, and then, as the day grows thin and the shadows grow long, he retrieves the shovel and begins to fill in the grave.

I'm aware of a profound sadness because I know it's too late. The child is dead. There's nothing more to be done.

Despite that, a banshee voice screams in my head, telling me to stop him.

And this time I'm able to move.

I run into the field.

The man continues to shovel, and as he does, I race toward him. I know it's a dream, but I sense that still, somehow, he will see, or at least hear me coming.

But he doesn't seem to notice, doesn't look my way.

I wish I could see his face.

He drives the shovel into the pile of dark earth beside the hole and brings the blade up with its mouthful of dirt, tips it onto the pink cocoon. And I hear him singing softly, in a voice surprisingly gentle and loving, a father's voice. Words falling like soft petals to the ground:

"Hush, little baby, don't say a word . . ."

Shoveling in time with the words.

"Daddy's gonna buy you a mockingbird."

Emptying the shovel, driving it into the ground again as I approach.

"And if that mockingbird don't sing . . ."

I'm close now, almost ready to stop him.

But another voice urges me to see what's in the bag.

The dying daylight lands on my face and it feels like the coming night is seeping into me. The cop in me insists on stopping him, but the dream world directs me to the hole instead.

"Daddy's gonna buy you a diamond ring."

I arrive. Look into the hole.

And see the bag move.

Whatever is wrapped inside it is not dead.

"No!" I can hear myself scream.

I go for my SIG but find no gun by my side. I leap at the man to tackle him, but my arms pass through him. He's a ghost to me, even though he's shoveling real dirt onto a living child. He continues his work, oblivious to me. I jump into the hole and reach for the duct tape, to undo it, to free the child.

Dirt is landing on my back. Real dirt. He keeps shoveling. The gentle singing doesn't stop.

"And if that diamond ring turns brass . . ."

I struggle with the tape, but can't find its end, can't get the crying child out.

The girl inside the bag is calling for her mommy to help her. The man doesn't stop his terrible work. More dirt falls on my back, spilling over me and into the hole, onto the girl.

"Daddy's gonna buy you a looking glass . . ."

No!

Frantically, I brush the dirt aside, but suddenly I'm being drawn backward as if a great hand has grasped my neck and is lifting me, dragging me from the scene. I struggle, but it does no good. As the image shrinks, the man shoveling the dirt appears smaller and fainter, his song fading as darkness and distance swallow him. Then the fog around me deepens and the sound of the little girl crying becomes nothing but an echoed memory lost in time.

She was not dead.

No, she was not.

And then I'm awake, my blankets wound around my legs, a tight, tangled cocoon.

A terrible, terrible cocoon.

Sickly light seeps through the curtains. Reluctant sunlight from a day that does not want to be born.

I wrestle free of the blankets and stand, my breathing harsh and heavy.

Somehow, I can still smell the pine trees of the forest, still hear the terrible lullaby: *"Daddy's gonna buy you a looking glass."*

No, I hadn't dreamt of Colleen Hayes, hadn't dreamt of the terrible things that might have happened to her, that might have evoked the scream I heard on the phone. Instead, I'd dreamt of Jenna Natara, a seven-year-old girl who disappeared three years ago—one of the first homicide cases I worked as a detective. When she was found, forensics verified that she'd been buried alive in that sleeping bag after she'd been raped.

The lyrics to that lullaby, from a ripped-out page of a nursery rhyme book, were found tucked beneath Jenna's pillow the night she was taken, after her parents discovered that she was missing. They'd been asleep in the room at the end of the hall when she was abducted.

We never caught Jenna's killer, but the semen found on her underwear led me to tie that homicide to the abduction and murder of another girl, one in my hometown of Horicon, when I was a teenager. I was the one who'd found Mindy Wells's body in the old tree house near the edge of the marsh just outside of town.

Suspects had surfaced and been cleared, nothing solid. No answers.

Those kinds of cases never go away.

Not when they involve children.

It sounds cliché, but the images do haunt you. Never let you go.

Not even in your dreams.

DAY 2

Monday, November 17

The Train Yard

7

At 6:58 a.m. I was doing pull-ups when I got the call.

A dockworker had found Colleen Hayes, unconscious, by a shipping container on one of Milwaukee's piers jutting into Lake Michigan. Her hands had been cut off, heavy-duty plastic ties cinched tightly around her wrists to stop her from bleeding to death.

When I heard the news, I felt ready to crush the phone with my hand. As thankful as I was that Colleen was alive, I was also enraged that this had happened and I told myself that, unlike what had happened to me with the unsolved cases of Jenna Natara and Mindy Wells, I was not going to be haunted by the thought that the man who'd done this had gotten away. I have enough images for my nightmares, and so does the rest of the world—enough victims too.

As I hung up, I wondered if it was a good sign or a bad one that Colleen's abductor had not carried out his threat to take her life. It might mean that he didn't have the stomach for murder. Or it might mean that he enjoyed watching people suffer more than he enjoyed watching them die.

Evil.

Man's inhumanity to man.

I wish I could claim that I've never understood how people could do the unspeakable things that I see in my cases, but there's a part of me that does understand. I think everyone who's honest about his own base, primal instincts has to, at least to some degree, see mirrored images of his own desires in the brutality of others.

It seems to be there, inside of us, from an early age. We don't need to be taught to lie, or to be selfish or cruel or vindictive—we need to be taught how not to. And given the right circumstances, those impulses might rise, might blossom into something dark and uncontrollable.

One time, Taci asked me why I did what I did, why I'd chosen to be a homicide detective. At the time I didn't think she was being completely serious, and I'd said lightly, "To catch the bad guys."

"No, I'm not joking around, Pat." Though her tone wasn't sharp, I could tell she really was being serious. "There's more. I know there is."

Suddenly, unexpectedly, words came to me. Perhaps I'd heard them in a movie, or maybe they escaped from a private, reflective place I wasn't even aware of before that moment, but they came, and they surprised me when they did: "To keep the demons at bay."

"What demons?"

I'd gone to church as a child—my parents had taken me—but I'm not very religious. Still, the word "demons" was the one that'd come to mind. I had to think about what exactly I'd meant. "Um . . . I'm not sure. I just feel it sometimes—the darkness tugging at me. When the things you despise the most about human nature call to you, whisper for you to take a step closer to them. You know what I mean?"

She regarded me quietly. I saw love in her eyes, but also concern. "What things whisper to you, Pat?"

"Dark things." I tried to say it in a tone that told her I preferred to be done with this topic.

But either she didn't catch that, or she wasn't ready to let the subject drop, because she said again, "What things, Pat?"

The things that lead us over the edge.

"The things I see in my cases."

Even though I was closer to her emotionally than I'd ever been to anyone in my life, in that moment that was all I felt comfortable telling her. Her silence indicated to me that it might not have been enough. Or maybe it was too much.

The topic hadn't come up again, but I sensed that the ghost of what I'd said was still there, had somehow crept between us, settled in, found a home, and wasn't about to leave any time soon.

Colleen Hayes might have gotten a good look at her attacker, might be able to identify him, so before going to MPD headquarters for the nine o'clock briefing, the first order of business was paying her a visit at the Milwaukee Regional Medical Center.

I left a message for Taci that I'd be at the hospital, asked if she could meet up with me for a minute or two while I was there, then hopped into my car and took off.

Thinking about Taci.

About evil.

About keeping the demons at bay.

8

The Milwaukee Regional Medical Center lies situated on a sprawling campus now littered with autumn leaves. Only a few of the trees still clung to their leaves, but those had turned brown in the dreary fall and only served to help give the campus a tired, weary feel. It was the biggest academic health-care center in the state, with six different care facilities all on the same campus. I knew it well. I'd been here on a lot of my cases, as well as to see Taci.

Four things concerning the abduction and mutilation of Colleen Hayes were on my mind:

(1) I was profoundly thankful she was alive.

(2) Her kidnapper's choice of the location in the alley showed that he (or they, if there was more than one) had some interest in or connection with Jeffrey Dahmer.

(3) It was impossible at this point to discern her attacker's original intent, whether that was to kill or to maim—or possibly even to let Colleen go free.

(4) Based on the grisly and flagrant nature of the crime, I could hardly believe that this was the kidnap-

per's first offense. The stark brutality of his mutilation of Colleen might actually help us narrow down the suspect pool, might actually help us find him.

Radar was waiting for me when I arrived at the hospital, and he met me at the front door. After asking me about my jaw and my wrenched finger, and after I assured him, honestly, that they were feeling remarkably better, he said, "It's gonna be a cold one today." His eyes were on the spreading slabs of gray clouds blanketing the sky.

"Yeah."

"I wish it would just snow and be done with it."

Wisconsin winters are long enough for me as it is. Besides, I'd been hoping to squeeze in a few more weekends of rock climbing at Devil's Lake State Park over near Baraboo before the snow and ice settled in for the next four months. But I didn't really want to talk to Radar about the weather. The attack on Colleen and the dark residue of my dreams were weighing too heavily on my mind.

"How is she?" I asked.

"Doing pretty well. Considering." He paused. "At least physically."

We passed through the doors. "Has she said anything?"

"Not yet, no. You should know Captain Domyslawski contacted the FBI last night after the abduction. There are a couple agents from the NCAVC coming over this morning."

Oh, great.

The FBI's National Center for the Analysis of Violent Crime was the division of the Bureau dedicated to providing investigative support for tracking and capturing the country's most violent offenders. I hadn't worked with the Feds before, but I'd heard horror stories about doing so, and that didn't give me a whole lot of confidence on how all this might play out. I trusted the officers I worked with here on the force, but consulting with a couple of desk jockeys from Quantico didn't exactly thrill me.

Radar was on the same wavelength. "Let's hope they don't get in the way," he said.

"You read my mind."

There wasn't a gentle way to frame the next question, but it had to be brought up and direct is usually best. "Do we know if Colleen was sexually assaulted?"

"The docs who helped her last night didn't find any evidence that she had been. So at least there's that to be thankful for."

"Yes," I said. "At least there's that."

We found Colleen Hayes's room, showed our IDs to Thompson, the officer in our department who was stationed as a sentry outside it, knocked and, at her invitation, stepped inside. She'd been mute since she was found, so hearing her voice surprised me, but when we entered, I realized it wasn't Colleen who'd called us in after all, but rather the stout nurse who stood beside the bed, checking the IV.

The nurse seemed taken aback when she saw us; perhaps she'd been expecting a doctor on rounds or maybe another nurse. She didn't hide her scowl when we showed her our badges, but she held back from making any sort of a scene, perhaps just to keep from upsetting her patient.

Colleen lay on the bed, her legs beneath a blanket, her arms also tucked beneath it, no doubt to hide the stumps where her hands used to be. She was conscious and was staring away from us at the shrouded window on the south side of the room. With the curtains drawn, there was no view, but I had the feeling she wouldn't have really been seeing it if there was.

Once again I was struck by the horrifying nature of this crime. Without prosthetics she would never again comb her hair, type on a keyboard, flip the page of a book, slip a key into a lock—the little things we all take for granted.

And the big ones.

Like feeding herself. Or caressing her fingers across her lover's cheek.

Radar and I introduced ourselves and took a seat beside her bed.

9

The nurse finished her duties and exited, leaving Radar and me alone with Colleen Hayes.

To me, hospitals don't just smell sickly clean, they also seem to be permeated with the stench of death from those who've died inside them. And—

Man, there was just too much death on my mind today. With the weight of my job and my troubling dreams, the morning already felt heavy, too heavy. I needed to find a way to lighten things up.

But, unfortunately, that wasn't going to happen at the moment.

"First of all, Ms. Hayes . . ." I saw a rosary on her bedside table and was hit with the tragic truth that she would never be able to work her way through the beads again. "I'm very sorry you were attacked. I promise that we're going to do everything we can to catch the man who did this and we're going to put him away."

She was quiet.

"I want you to know that Vincent is alright. He's in—"

"What," she said abruptly, "did he make Vinnie do?" The fact that she was already speaking to us took me aback. Her words were tight with concern, but also sharp with anger: "The guy who sawed off my hands." She paused. "The doctors told me Vinnie is okay, but that he couldn't come to visit me because he's in jail. What did that man make my husband do?"

It was her right to know what Vincent had done and I summarized what'd happened last night concerning Lionel. I didn't mention Vincent's flight through the neighborhood or the fact that he'd physically assaulted me when I was apprehending him, but Colleen stared at the bruise on my jaw and I imagined she was able to put two and two together. I slid my left hand over my right to hide the swollen, discolored finger.

"So my husband is in jail." It didn't sound like a question.

"I understand you must be—"

"You understand what? Exactly?" She glared at me, then pulled her arms out from under the blankets and held them up in front of me. Where her hands used to be were nothing but thick bandages. That was all. "What is it you understand?"

I felt so underqualified to be here. She needed a minister or a psychiatrist rather than a detective. "I'm sorry," I told her truthfully. "You're right. I don't understand. I couldn't possibly."

"And this man . . ." She fumbled to stick her arms under the blanket again. Radar was closer to her than I was and he quietly helped pull the blanket back for her. She finally got her arms beneath it. ". . . Lionel, he's alright?"

"He is," Radar answered. "He's already back home and it doesn't look like he's going to press charges."

She said nothing, looked toward the window again.

I waited a few moments to let her sort things through,

then pulled out my notebook and said softly, "Mrs. Hayes, can you tell us anything about the man who hurt you?"

She took a deep breath but didn't answer. I noticed the tear in her eye and felt even less qualified than before to be here. Thankfully, Radar put one hand on her shoulder, and with the other, he wiped away her tear. He was a married man, had a daughter and a son; I was neither a father nor a husband. He knew a lot more than I did about how to comfort hurting people and I was glad he was here.

Neither of us told her things would be okay; rather, both of us were silent and that seemed to be the better choice at the moment. She began to instinctively reach for her face to dry her tears, but stopped just short of removing her arm from beneath the blanket. I found some tissues, handed them to Radar, and he gently pressed away her tears.

At last she took a deep breath. "He wore a black ski mask. But I saw his skin. He was white. Had brown eyes. I saw that too, before he blindfolded me. After that I only heard his voice."

"Could you tell how tall he was?"

"Big. I'd say over six feet tall." She looked at me. "Kinda like you. And strong too."

"Was there any indication that there was more than one person?"

"No. I mean, nothing that I could tell."

Radar cut in, "Colleen, do you have any idea where he took you?"

"No. I was in his trunk."

Good. That was something. The car had a trunk. The man drove a sedan of some type.

"He never took off the blindfold. My arms were tied up when he did it. I was in a chair. He didn't knock me out when he cut off my hands. I screamed, I just kept screaming. Then he gave me a shot and I fell asleep. I woke up in the hospital like . . ." She let her voice trail off, then stared down at the blanket covering her arms.

I leaned close. "Think about the drive there, Colleen, the time you were alone with him. Could you tell how long you were in the car or how many times he stopped at traffic lights or stop signs?"

She shook her head. "I don't know how many times we stopped or how long we drove. I was too scared. It seemed like forever."

"Did you hear anything unusual—sirens, trains, whistles, alarms, anything? Or notice any odd smells that might help us narrow down our search? Cologne, body odor, anything like that? Maybe he was a smoker?"

She thought about it for a long time. "I smelled yeast. That I remember. It was a little faint, so I'm thinking we were somewhere near the breweries, but not too close."

Wind, temperature, and humidity as well as production schedule would all affect how far the smell of the breweries would have spread. Things to look into.

"That's good," I told her. "Very good. That helps. Anything else?"

"It was cold when he did it, like we might have been out in a garage or something. He carried me there from the car. When I screamed I could hear it echo a little, but it was sort of muted too. I don't know. I can't think of anything else."

"Do you think you could recognize his voice?" Radar asked. She shook her head again.

And then she was quiet and we didn't want to press her, but we also didn't want to leave her alone, so we sat with her for a while even though it meant being late for the briefing at police headquarters. But Thorne wasn't exactly famous for starting his meetings on time and there are some things that are more important than punctuality.

Finally, our police chaplain, Reverend Padilla, who served the force but also comforted the victims of violent crimes, came in. We excused ourselves, left the room, and silently passed down the hallway.

Although we needed to get to the department, before leaving the medical center I called Taci's wing to see if she could meet me by my car. She was in the next building over and by the time I'd made it outside, she was already on the sidewalk that led to the parking lot.

"Hey, Pat." She gave me a quick kiss on the cheek, the kind you might give when greeting a friend. Just a friend.

"Hey."

Radar went on ahead to give us a chance to talk.

Today Taci, a brunette with striking dark brown eyes and a kind smile, wore a cream-colored double-breasted peacoat, cerulean skirt, white tights and modest heels. She looked as charming and attractive as ever.

"I got your message last night," I told her as we started for the car. "But I didn't get in until after one. It was too late to call."

"Our schedules make this hard, don't they?"

"It's been a little rough lately, sure, but things will settle down once your residency is over."

She was quiet. "I heard about everything that's going on. About Mrs. Hayes. All the doctors are talking about it. That poor woman." Her words were marked with deep compassion, one of the qualities that had caught my attention the first time we met. "It's horrifying what happened."

"Yes."

"How are you? Through all this?"

"Focused."

"You're going to catch this guy, aren't you?"

"Yes. I am."

A moment passed. "Pat, I'd hate to be the person you're after."

I hadn't really wanted our conversation to be about the case or about Ms. Hayes, so I tried to lighten things up a little. "You are the person I'm after."

I was sort of hoping she'd say, "You too" or "You already have me" or something along those lines, but instead she looked a little uncomfortable. "Thanks."

This whole conversation was becoming slightly discomfiting.

"Listen," she said. "About tonight. Dinner."

"Yes. Pasta. My place."

"I'm . . . Well, it'll be good. Give us a chance to talk."

With the briefing at the department coming up, I really didn't have a lot of time, but I offered anyway. "We can talk right now." A few flecks of snow began to meander around us. We were almost to my car.

"No. Not in the parking lot."

"There's something we need to talk about in private?"

"No." But then she hesitated and backpedaled a little. "I mean . . . Well. No. Anyway . . ." She gave me another peck on the cheek. Friendly once again. "I'll see you tonight. At seven."

"See you at seven."

Then she returned to the building, leaving me to wonder what exactly she wanted to discuss with me privately tonight on the one-year anniversary of the day we first met.

I climbed into my car.

When I radioed the department to tell Thorne I might be a little late, I found out the meeting was postponed until nine thirty, which gave me a few extra minutes. The alley where we'd found Lionel wasn't too far out of the way, so I decided to swing by and have a look at it in the daylight.

10

I parked beside the alley.

The fenced-in lot bordering it contained the place where Dahmer's apartment building used to stand. Inside the fence, the ground was covered with dry, brown grass and a dusting of gritty snow. The lot looked unremarkable and anonymous, which was exactly what the city of Milwaukee wanted. Bulldozing the building and clearing the rubble had been a way of trying to erase from the city's collective memory what had happened here.

I got out of the car, walked to the chain-link fence, and peered through to the other side.

The cloud-dampened light and flecks of restless snow accentuated the lonely, foreboding mood of this place.

After working as many cases as I have, you realize that you can scrub a floor clean of blood, you can tear out a wall or knock down a building, but tragedies all too often seem to stain the air of these places of death, to rip open space and time and root themselves stubbornly to a specific location.

The invisible, tormented geography of pain.

My thoughts traveled back to hearing about what'd happened just on the other side of this fence, back to the stories about the sixteen young men who'd died at Dahmer's hand so close to where I was standing, and I couldn't help but feel a chill.

The wind was picking up and bit into my face. But that's not what was giving me shivers. My thoughts of Dahmer were.

Even now, three years after he was beaten to death in prison, the shock was still there, fresh and painful in my city.

It was like those stages of grief that psychologists talk about—denial, anger, bargaining, depression, acceptance. Milwaukee hadn't reached the acceptance stage yet. I have my own theory about grief—you get angry, and then you repress it or it swallows you whole. Either it disappears or you do.

But that was just me.

And so, Jeffrey Dahmer.

A psychopath like none in a generation.

He would pick up young men from the bars in this neighborhood on Milwaukee's west end—usually they were African-American, but he wasn't picky when it came to race. He was more interested in looks and physique.

His MO: drug their drinks, get them back to his apartment, handcuff them, overpower them, kill them, eat them. Sometimes he would stuff their corpses into vats. Sometimes he would sleep with the bodies or chop them up and keep the body parts in the fridge and the skulls beside a candlelit altar to Satan in his closet. Sometimes he drilled holes in the heads of his victims while they were still alive and poured acid into their brains, hoping to turn the men into zombie love slaves.

During his trial he pled insanity. And lost.

In the end, he was convicted of fifteen homicides, but he admitted to two more, including one in Ohio. The city of Milwaukee later purchased his estate and all of his possessions were buried in a landfill, the location of which only five people knew—Captain Domyslawski, Lieutenant Thorne, Detective Annise Corsica (who'd led the investigation), and two city sanitation workers I hadn't met who drove the garbage truck and dumped out its contents.

The location was kept secret so the site wouldn't be visited by curiosity seekers or scavenged by souvenir hounds. It was grisly just to think about, but a certain segment of society collects memorabilia from killers like Dahmer and, inevitably, the site where his belongings were dumped would've become a Mecca for people interested in collecting keepsakes of cannibals.

Though by now Dahmer's belongings were certainly covered by a mountain of other trash, I was still thankful that no one had discovered which landfill had been used. Keeping people away would have been an endless, disturbing ordeal for local law enforcement.

I walked to the telephone pole where we'd found Lionel Shannon.

No clues jumped out at me. No sudden revelations came to me.

The snow picked up. The minutes ticked by.

Finally, with the thoughts of what'd happened last night and the things Colleen Hayes had told us this morning circling through my head, I left the alley and drove to HQ for the briefing.

11

The public entrance to police headquarters is on North James Lovell Street. I used the department one on West State Street, just around the corner.

And found the two FBI agents from the National Center for the Analysis of Violent Crime waiting for me just inside the door.

The man: hulking and thickly muscled—bigger even than Thorne, and nearly my height. He had a presence about him that commanded respect and it seemed to affect everyone around us, almost as if he'd brought his own weather system with him into the building.

The woman: petite, with stylish glasses, her light brown hair pulled back into a sensible ponytail. The guy looked about thirty; she looked fresh out of the academy. Both were dressed neatly and conservatively. Most male FBI agents who aren't working undercover seem to be into ties, but not this guy. Black turtleneck all the way. He held a half-finished two-liter bottle of Mountain Dew in one hand, a leather briefcase in the other.

He introduced himself: "Ralph Hawkins, FBI." The words came out in a low rumble, a voice you'd expect from a guy who could bench-press a pickup. "This is Special Agent Ellen Parker."

I greeted them. He passed the bottle of soda to his other arm, then enveloped my hand in his as we shook. "Detective Patrick Bowers," I said. "Homicide. Just call me Pat."

"Ralph."

"And Ellen is fine," Agent Parker told me.

"Good."

A couple of moments later, as we passed down the hallway, she unexpectedly excused herself and walked off alone toward the elevator.

Ralph paused. "Gives us a chance to chat."

Ah. So. Here we go.

I gestured toward the stairs and led the way.

"I understand you're in charge of this case?" he said.

"Yes." I could only imagine what a logistical and bureaucratic nightmare this was going to be if he tried to pull rank and take over. It would have been audacious, but I wasn't ready to put anything past the FBI.

We entered the stairwell. Thorne's office was on the fourth floor. We started up the steps.

Despite his size Ralph was quick and light on the stairs. "There are two ways we can do this. We can either waste time dicking around trying to figure out who's calling the shots, or we can work together to catch this psycho. Your call."

So, he had an attitude and got straight to the point.

My kind of guy.

"Agent Hawkins—Ralph . . ." We reached the second floor. "I have every reason to believe that you're experienced and well qualified at what you do, but I need you to know that I'm going to find this guy and bring him in or take him down and if you get in my way I'll do whatever is necessary to move you aside so I can do my job."

Okay, so maybe it wasn't the ideal thing to say to kick off our working relationship, but I've never been especially known for my tact.

He paused as we reached the third-floor landing. He wasn't out of breath. Neither was I.

I waited for his response. Tried to read him. Couldn't.

Then he took a long, unhurried swallow of his Mountain Dew, finished most of it, and smacked his lips. "Glad to hear we're on the same page. But . . ." I caught the hint of a smile. "How am I gonna get in your way, Detective, when I'm going to be the one way out in front of you?"

"Oh, I don't know. I can be a bit determined at times."

"I'm counting on that." We started for the fourth floor. "Besides, you couldn't move me aside."

"I'm stronger than I look."

He cracked his neck and cords of muscle strained beneath his skin. "So am I." He downed the rest of his soda and tossed the empty bottle into a trash can as we entered the hallway and passed the elevator bay.

And as he strode beside me on the way to Lieutenant Thorne's office, I couldn't help but wonder—if he really was stronger than he looked—just how tough this guy, who was obviously not a desk jockey, actually was.

12

We met in Thorne's office, all of us crammed around his desk on folding chairs.

Six of us were at the briefing: Ellen, Ralph, Radar, Lieutenant Thorne, me, and Detective Annise Corsica, a severe-looking woman in her forties with short, choppy hair, thin lips, and probing, astucious eyes. Annise had been on the force more than twenty years and, to put it mildly, had not been happy when I'd been promoted to homicide detective seven years earlier in my career than she'd been.

I'd seen her exhibit what I could only call incompetence on cases, and the amount of respect we shared for each other was mutual; however Thorne liked her and, apparently, she was on the case.

He kicked things off with introductions and then turned the floor over to Ralph. "I'll let Agent Hawkins explain exactly why we've brought the FBI in on this. It has to do with more than Vincent and Colleen Hayes."

That, I hadn't heard. I directed my attention to Ralph.

"There are two bodies that've been found," he said, "one in Champaign, Illinois, one in Ohio, near Cincinnati. We've been doing our best to keep it under the media's radar—" He glanced at Brandon. "Why do they call you Radar, anyway?"

Thorne answered for him: "He zeroes in on people. Finds 'em. He's got gut instincts like no one else."

It was true. Radar did seem to have uncanny instincts, and that bugged me, not because I envied him, but because I don't trust hunches, gut feelings, intuition. I trust facts and logic, and when Radar's unfounded inferences led to results, it always confounded me.

"Gotcha," Ralph said. "Anyway, we've been playing this close to the chest . . . trying to keep a few details from the public." He looked around the room soberly. "Forensics has determined that the intestines of one of the victims and the lungs of the other, both women in their early twenties, were consumed. The killer doesn't remove the organs all at once. Takes his time. Keeps the women alive while he does it."

"How could you tell the lungs and intestines had been eaten?" Detective Corsica asked. "And not just, well . . . discarded?"

"He cooked 'em on the victims' stoves. We found pieces on frying pans and on a fork, but no saliva. No DNA."

No one said a word.

Without bite marks on the bodies, I imagined it would be hard to determine with certainty that the offender had exhibited anthropophagic behavior, but now, with our case's connection to Dahmer—and the amputation of Colleen's hands—the proximal timing and removal of body parts spoke to more than just coincidence, which I didn't believe in anyway.

Before we could tell if the incidents were actually

linked, we would need to do a comparative case analysis, or CCA. By studying the physical evidence, eyewitness reports, crime scene locations and characteristics of the victims, we could judge the likelihood that the crimes were committed by the same offender.

"We found a small soil sample at the scene of the homicide in Champaign," Ellen explained. "The FBI Lab was able to use the NRCS's soil data surveys to—"

"NRCS?" Corsica asked.

"National Resources Conservation Service. Part of the Department of Agriculture. They have soil sample data from every county in the U.S. Anyway, they matched the sample to southeastern Wisconsin. Two counties— Milwaukee or Waukesha."

Nice. Maybe these guys were the real deal after all.

"That, however, *was* released to the media," Ralph grumbled. Then he echoed what I'd been thinking. "Obviously it's not one hundred percent certain, but now, with the timing, the severing of Ms. Hayes's hands, the links to cannibalism, to Dahmer, well, there's a good chance that what happened there and what's happening here are linked."

"You have case files from the other homicides?" I asked him.

A nod. "I'll get them as soon as we're done here. But for now, I want you to fill me in on what happened last night."

I did most of the talking, with Radar, Corsica, and Thorne offering a few details I hadn't heard yet:

(1) Colleen Hayes had been home from the time she talked to her husband at 6·35 p m until 9·15 p.m.

when a neighbor saw a car pull away from the street behind her house.

(2) According to Colleen, the blood in the kitchen came from a cut on her left hand when she was struggling with her attacker, who had a knife.

(3) There was no sign of forced entry at the home.

(4) A small square of tinfoil was found on the floor of the bar, but it contained no prints other than Vincent's.

When we finished, Ralph turned to Thorne. "Your department was responsible for bringing in Dahmer. What do you make of this wack job coercing the guy to leave a handcuffed man in that same alley?"

He reflected on that for a moment. "In 'ninety-one, it was a cuffed African-American man close to the same age as Lionel who eventually led us to Dahmer. The alley, of course, is where Konerak Sinthasomphone was found cuffed and naked. Maybe our guy's trying to say that Dahmer got caught; but that he's better than Dahmer, that he won't. What do you think, Corsica?"

She'd been lead on the Dahmer investigation. "I agree. Definitely." But then she saw the skepticism in my eyes. "What is it, Patrick?" My friends call me Pat, so I was cool with her calling me Patrick.

"I think it's premature to try guessing what this guy was trying to communicate by his actions or to conclude anything 'definite' about them."

"Well," Ralph said to me, "you were there last night. Any ideas on possible motive?"

"I'm not one to speculate on motives. The real issue

here isn't 'why it happened' but 'what happened.' On the surface there's a connection, but—"

"Hang on." Ellen adjusted her glasses. "You don't speculate on motives? What does that mean—you don't look for them?"

"No. I don't. I'd rather—"

"Patrick doesn't believe in motives." It was Corsica, a clear challenge in her tone.

"Actually," I countered, "that's not quite right. I do believe in motives, but more specifically in *reasons*. We all have reasons for the things we do. All behavior is, to some extent at least, undertaken to achieve a goal, but since trying to figure out specifically what that goal is— considering that the person doing it might not even know why he's doing it—ends up being fruitless, nothing more than a guessing game, I don't put much stock in the process. Besides, nowhere in our justice system does the law require showing motive."

"But what about first-degree murder or arson?" Corsica pressed me. "You need to prove intent in arson cases; premeditation to get a first-degree murder conviction."

"Premeditation and intent are different from motive." There was no way I should've had to be explaining this to her, especially not here in front of everyone. But she wasn't letting it drop and if she wanted a lesson, I could give her one. "Intent is what you're trying to accomplish, premeditation is how you're going to go about it, but motive is the reason why. The first two can be proven beyond reasonable doubt, the third cannot."

She gave me a dubious look, and I took it as a prompt to go on. "People act certain ways because of needs, desires, unconscious impulses, habits, goals, personality differences—all those things affect our choices and actions, and all of them intertwine with each other. It's impossible to untangle them and surmise their collective, or even their respective, influence in one word like 'greed' or 'lust' or 'hatred.' Besides, in the end, the why is always the same. Ultimately, all criminals commit their crimes for the same reason."

Ralph eyed me curiously. "And that is?"

"Because they believe it will make them happy."

"Really?"

"Yes."

"Everything they do?"

"Yes. Just like us."

"Come on, Patrick." Corsica sounded like she was mimicking a schoolteacher reprimanding a child. "Even *you* don't believe that everything everyone does is just because they're trying to be happy. You're just trying to be provocative and this isn't the time or place for those kinds of games."

Alrighty, then.

We could do this.

I took a breath and picked up the gauntlet that'd been tossed at my feet.

13

"Annise, no one ever chooses to do something that he thinks will make him miserable. Whether it's drugs, murder, workaholism, I don't care, it doesn't matter—even suicide—people act in ways they believe will bring relief, pleasure, or satisfaction. It all boils down to the desire for happiness. Happiness is the end to which we all aspire." I wasn't the first one to point this out; philosophers have noted it for centuries. For some reason, law enforcement has been slow to pick up on it.

But now I could tell it wasn't just Corsica. Ellen remained skeptical as well: "But people punish themselves all the time, Patrick. Mentally, emotionally, psychologically, physically. You're saying that they're doing it because they believe mental illness or social isolation makes them happy?"

"No. But why do people torture themselves emotionally?"

"Because of guilt or shame or low self-esteem," she answered, "or any number of reasons."

"But what is the goal? People don't dwell on their guilt or shame, beat themselves up emotionally, or isolate themselves socially in the hopes that they'll feel worse, but because they hope it'll eventually make them feel better—maybe about their penance, or as a way to quantify their guilt, or to quiet their consciences or to distract themselves or rationalize away their pain, or, as you just said, for any number of reasons. But ultimately, they want to be happy."

Ralph seemed to be right with me. "And you're saying it's the same for the guy who killed these women?"

"Yes. Criminals aren't essentially different from other people. They might commit crimes we can't imagine ourselves doing, but all of us are capable of the unthinkable, given the right circumstances, mental state, and precipitators."

A nod. He agreed. The nineties have been a violent decade. Milwaukee had 127 homicides last year, and I'd worked 29 of them, but considering how many cases the NCAVC assists with each year, I guessed that Ralph might've already been involved in more homicide investigations than I would be in my entire career.

"So," he said, "the secret to finding this psycho—if it's even the same guy in all three cases—is to find out what he thinks will make him happy."

"If we knew that," I admitted, "it would be helpful. Yes."

"Motive." Corsica looked triumphant.

I was ready to reply when Radar interjected, "But at this point that's not possible to determine."

"Once again," I reiterated, "I think that right now we should focus on what happened rather than spend time speculating on why it did."

It looked like everyone except Detective Corsica was satisfied, ready to move on.

Ralph aimed the tip of his pen at me, signaling that I was up. "I understand you and Radar spoke with Colleen Hayes this morning. What do we know?"

"The offender is Caucasian, large frame, approximately six feet tall. Brown eyes, unless he was wearing colored contact lenses. He only said four words when I spoke with him last night on Vincent's portable phone and I didn't note any distinctive accent. Colleen doesn't think she could recognize his voice again. I'm not sure I could either. She knew of only one offender, and he took her someplace near or just past the breweries and then to the pier where she was left. The car he used has a trunk. The space he took her to was cold, like an unheated garage or cellar."

In my mind I was following the possible travel routes a person might drive from the Hayes residence to the valley where the breweries are. "Based on the nature and sophistication of the crime, it's probable that the offender has a history of violence. He might already be in the system."

"Prints?" Ellen asked.

Thorne shook his head. "No incriminating ones. Not on the cuffs, not at the house. Nothing."

Detective Corsica turned to me. "You sent out a call last night that the suspect had gotten away when you actually had him in custody."

"Based on the information we had at the time, we thought a woman's life might be in imminent danger."

"Based on the information you had at the time." Her tone was condescending and I was getting tired of dealing with Detective Corsica's attitude.

"It seemed prudent to let officers search the neighborhood for a few minutes if it meant buying some time to protect Colleen Hayes. I made a judgment call."

"So," she said, "you initiated a waste of time and resources and—"

"With all due respect, Annise, I don't consider anything done in the line of protecting innocent life to be a—"

"What you did was—"

Thorne raised a hand, a stop sign to cut us off. "Alright, alright, you two. Easy."

Annise's eyes seared the air between us. I let her glower.

One more thing needed to be said. "There are still enough questions here that I think Vincent needs to remain a person of interest in this case."

"Agreed," Ralph acknowledged, then turned to Thorne. "But don't release that to the press. If he's innocent, the last thing we need is having them run him through their meat grinder."

Considering the cannibalistic behavior related to these crimes, Ralph hadn't perhaps chosen the best phrase there, but I figured it was a slip of the tongue. It didn't sound like he was a fan of the press. I wasn't one either and I agreed unreservedly with his suggestion.

We spoke for a few more minutes about which direction to take the investigation and then Thorne said, "So where does all this leave us?"

Ralph spoke up. "I'll bring Pat up to speed on the other cases from Illinois and Ohio. Beyond the obvious connection to Dahmer and dismemberment, we can try to see if we can identify any other ties to what happened last night."

Yes, the comparative case analysis I was thinking of earlier.

Thorne slid the papers on his desk into a single stack, straightened it punctiliously. "I assigned Thompson, Holdren, and Lyrie to this. I'll brief 'em on what we talked about here. They can start following up on the tip list— last I heard we've already had seventy-two names called in, plus four confessions. You know how these false confessions go, but we'll check 'em out. And we'll scan the DMV records for names of sedan-owning large-framed male Caucasians with brown eyes."

"I'll look at names of felons living in the area," Radar offered, "see what I can come up with for people with past convictions of assault, or, well, a history of maiming others. Amputating their limbs."

I had a feeling that last criterion would make it a short list. At least I hoped it would.

Detective Corsica motioned toward Ellen. "We can review open kidnapping and missing persons cases in the Midwest. Look for any connections. The FBI will have a lot more on those than we do here." Ellen nodded.

Ralph stood. "Good, let's see what we can get done on this thing, meet up again after lunch, say one thirty, unless any solid leads come in before then."

If we met again at one thirty, it might not give me the chance to catch Dr. Werjonic's three o'clock lecture and I began to prepare myself for the eventuality that I wouldn't make it today.

As important as my grad classes were, from the start I'd put my work here at the force first. Most of my professors were more than happy to provide me with printed copies of their lecture notes if I missed class. I hoped Dr. Werjonic wouldn't mind doing so as well.

The rest of the team went their separate ways while Ralph joined me at my desk to talk through the files he'd brought with him concerning the two unsolved homicides.

And as he outlined the cases, the uncomfortable thought scratched around in my head that a cannibal in the vein of Dahmer might be visiting, or possibly be operating out of, my city.

14

The training took place in the barn on the edge of their property at the base of the Rocky Mountains.

The lessons started when Joshua was eight years old. At the time, some of the things his father told him and did in front of him and taught him were frightening.

At the time.

And sometimes still.

He didn't know how old the barn was, but it'd looked old ever since they first moved to the property when he was five. That much he knew.

The rusted metal roof had probably been painted red at one time, but to him it looked like it might have been covered in dried blood. The tall wooden slats that made up the sides of the barn had mostly been bleached by the sun. The paint that was left was cracked and peeling or flaking away.

His father had been careful to keep the doors working, though their natural tendency was to tilt awkwardly and groan from their huge rusted hinges. Sometimes Joshua had helped with the important job of oiling them.

"Everything dies, Joshua," his father told him one day. They were walking through the field that ran alongside the barn. "You know that, don't you?"

"Yes, sir. Everything dies."

"It's the way of the world, the way things have been since the beginning. Trees, grass, animals, people. Even rivers can die. And mountains. Did you know that?"

Joshua stared long and hard at the mountains rising wild and rugged against the horizon. Of all the things he would have ever guessed could die, he never would have thought of mountains.

"Can mountains really die?"

"Yes."

"But how?"

"Sometimes they're killed by wind and rain, sometimes by people, sometimes by God."

"God kills mountains?"

Despite the recent oiling, the barn door gave a weary creak as his father leaned against it. "Over time he does. He wears them out with the years. He destroyed some and formed others in the Great Flood."

As the door opened, Joshua smelled the familiar scent of old hay and dried manure and a hint of leather from the saddles hanging on the boards near the horse stalls. The barn was mostly quiet, except for the tiny scuffling of mice beneath the hay. The air tasted dusty and dry.

"God kills mountains and rivers, animals and people," his father went on. "Even planets. In the Old Testament, the book of Deuteronomy, God says, 'I kill, and I make alive; I wound, and I heal.' Everything dies in the end, son, and since God is in control of life and death, he could stop it, but he doesn't. This universe started in the dark and it will end in the dark and until then, we breathe, we live, we do our best to love each other. We try to cherish what we can."

Joshua had never heard his father speak like this and it felt like he was becoming a part of something very special, a part of his father's grown-up world, almost as if he was being let in on a great secret, and he found it thrilling to know such big and hidden things.

His father led him toward the far side of the barn and Joshua thought he might have heard another sound in addition to the mice, but he wasn't sure. He was old enough to know that barns, even when they're empty, always seem to whisper, as if the animals that have lived and died inside them have never left. *Animal ghosts,* he thought to himself, *that never sleep.*

Sunlight crept through the narrow cracks between the boards on the sides of the barn. Shafts of light, cutting through the darkness. The streaks of sunlight were filled with dust motes and wandering flecks of hay disturbed by their movement as the two of them passed through the barn.

"Even the sun?" Joshua asked.

"The sun?"

"Will God kill the sun?"

"Yes. Someday far in the future. Even the sun. There will only be darkness at the end of all things."

Joshua thought about that. "But what matters then? I mean, if everything just dies? What we build or make or learn, if it's all just gone?"

His father didn't answer right away. "This moment matters."

"And I guess it's okay, though, if we go to heaven, right? To be with Mom?"

His father didn't reply and Joshua took it as some sort of rebuke, that mentioning his mom or heaven was some-how something bad and he did not bring them up again

He stood beside his father, half in the sunlight that would one day die, half in the shadows that would not.

"Son," his father said, "I've never shown you the place beneath the barn. The cellar. You can keep a secret, can't you?"

Another secret.

"Yes, sir."

His father paced across the stale, dry hay. Tiny slivers of straw dusted up in small clouds around his feet as he walked.

Joshua followed him to the corner of the barn.

It lay mostly in shadows. Joshua watched as his father swept his boot across the straw and, instead of simply hearing the crinkle of it brushing aside, he also heard the rough clatter of a wooden plank.

And then he heard something else. A muffled sound, somewhere beneath the boards.

"This is a very special place, Joshua. No one knows it's here."

Joshua wondered if his mother had known about it before she died three years ago. Wondered, but said nothing.

"But," his father went on, "I want you to know about it. You're the only one."

"Yes, sir."

"And you're big enough to keep a secret?"

"Yes, sir."

Joshua's father brushed some more of the straw away, revealing a wooden trapdoor about three feet wide and three feet long. He uncovered a latch that had been padlocked shut, then removed a key from his pocket and slipped it into the lock. "I'm bringing you here because it's time you learned about the special things. You're old enough now." His father clicked open the lock and set it aside. "Aren't you, Son?"

He looked at Joshua expectantly.

"Yes, sir."

His father slid the last bits of straw aside, revealing a large metal ring attached to one of the boards. Then he grasped it firmly, yanked open the trapdoor, and stepped to the side.

A black square gaped open in the ground before Joshua. Wooden steps descended and then disappeared into the cool darkness.

The sounds Joshua heard were coming from somewhere far below. They were louder now. At first Joshua thought they might be coming from some kind of hurt animal. He took a step back. "What's down there, Daddy?"

"I'm going to show you. This is where we're going to have the lessons."

"Is it an animal?"

"Death is natural," he replied, and Joshua knew that was not an answer, but he said nothing. "You understand this, right?"

"Yes, sir."

"Everything dies."

"Yes, sir. Everything dies."

"We have to kill to stay alive, Joshua. That's the way it is in the world. We kill cows and pigs and chickens to have meat, we kill plants to have fruits and vegetables. Just to stay alive. The life of one being depends on the death of another. This is natural. This is the way of the world."

Joshua had never thought of it like that before. It

seemed to make sense, but it also made him feel sad, almost guilty, as if he'd done something wrong just by being alive. Killing so many things.

His father drew a heavy flashlight out of his jacket pocket, clicked it on, and directed it into the darkness. "In the Bible God says, 'For the life of the flesh is in the blood: and I have given it to you upon the altar to make an atonement for your souls: for it is the blood that maketh an atonement for the soul.'"

Joshua didn't quite know what that meant, but it sounded important—it had to be important or else his father never would have mentioned it, or else it wouldn't be in the Bible. He didn't want to sound dumb, so he stayed quiet, acted like he knew what his father was talking about.

Atonement for the soul.

The blood.

They started down the steps.

His father held out his free hand to Joshua. The dark air of the barn seemed to wrap around them, surrounding them like a quiet blanket. And those shadows, that eternal darkness that would last as long as God, held Joshua for a moment. Then he took his father's hand as he walked beside him to the cellar.

The sounds continued.

Joshua was starting to get scared.

They reached the floor of the secret place.

Dirt. Packed down and trampled. In different places there were dark splotches on the ground. Wooden beams were propped against the walls to support the earth, kind of like in the mines his father had taken him

to once in the mountains west of Denver, not far from their home.

From behind them, sunlight slid down the steps and filtered through the air, but the darkness didn't seem to want to let any of it into the cellar itself.

Only after his father directed the flashlight beam across the cellar did Joshua see the man. He was standing with his back against the support beams about fifteen feet away. Some kind of metal chains had been attached to the wood and the man's wrists and ankles were locked in the chains. There was something in his mouth to keep him from making too much noise. He was fat and extra folds of skin rolled out from beneath his shirt.

"Who is he?" Joshua's voice caught.

"His name is Kenneth." His father drew a long hunting knife out of a sheaf on his belt, then held the knife's handle toward Joshua. "Take the knife, son."

But he didn't take it.

The man named Kenneth stared at them wide-eyed, shook his head frantically.

Joshua's father went over, removed a black hood from his jacket pocket, and tugged it over Kenneth's head. "This is your first time, Joshua. It'll be easier if you don't have to look at him."

Beneath the hood, the man was making sounds that Joshua did not like.

Joshua didn't move, didn't accept the knife, which his father brought back to him now.

His father spoke softly. "Take the knife, Joshua. is very important."

"But sir, it's . . . I'm scared."

Kenneth shook and rattled his chains, trying to pull himself free from the wall. But he couldn't do it. Joshua thought he wouldn't ever be able to do it.

"I know, Son. Don't be frightened. Just take the knife."

At last his father gently positioned the knife in Joshua's hand, as if it were a precious gift, and that's what Joshua thought of in that moment—a gift, and of course, his upcoming birthday.

A gift.

And Joshua thought of what he wanted. Instead of something like a shiny knife, it was something childish and embarrassing: a stuffed animal like he used to have when his mom was alive.

And he thought of going to sleep with it, holding it close, deep beneath the covers where his father wouldn't see and would not find it and be disappointed in him for turning to a stuffed animal for comfort.

The handle of the knife was well-worn and leather. Soft to the touch.

A gift from his father.

"Now, take the knife over to the man."

Joshua hesitated. He smelled bathroom smells and saw that the man's pants were stained wet in the front. Joshua wondered how long the man had been down here in the cellar, in the special place.

"Go on, Joshua. Go closer."

He took two steps.

"I want you to take the blade of the knife and push it into his belly."

The sounds coming from the man named Kenneth grew louder, more desperate.

"You need to learn how to do this, Joshua. You need to be able to do this yourself. Remember when I told you that everyone dies?"

Joshua didn't answer. He was too busy looking at the man.

"Son?"

"Yes, sir."

"Everything dies."

"Yes, sir."

"The life is in the blood. You remember that."

Joshua was silent.

"Say 'Yes, sir,'" his father told him.

"Yes, sir."

But Joshua didn't move any closer to the man and at last his father knelt beside him. "It'll feel kind of soft and springy. It might be a little difficult at first because the knife needs to push through his skin." He pointed to the end of the knife. "But, once the tip is inside, it'll get easier. See how it's curved here?"

"Yes, sir."

"That's so it'll poke in better and slide out easier when you're done."

His father walked to Kenneth, and then pulled up his shirt, revealing his round, white belly. Kenneth shook violently, and the fat in his stomach wobbled in a strange way.

"I want you to push the knife in and then move it back and forth. Like this." In the air in front of him, Joshua's father demonstrated the way he wanted him to wiggle the knife back and forth in the big man's belly. "See? You can slide it in and out too. It'll get easier each time."

Joshua said nothing. His heart squirmed in his chest.

"Go on, now."

Joshua stared at the man who was struggling so hard to get free.

Everything dies.

Yes, everything dies.

Joshua approached him.

"You can do it." His father reassured him, but when Joshua didn't raise the knife, his father wrapped his hand around Joshua's and bent over. "Here. This is your first time. I'll help you."

There was a lot of blood.

And nothing in the cellar smelled right when they were done.

It was hard, looking at the man hanging by his wrists and not moving. Not even a little bit. Not even breathing. Joshua kept expecting him to move. He couldn't believe that anyone could ever be that still. The hood was off now and the fat man was staring at Joshua, but he wasn't blinking at all, not once, and that was scary too.

Finally, his father noticed and reached down and closed the man's eyes. Then he put a hand on Joshua's shoulder. "You did well, Son, but I'm sorry. I shouldn't have pushed you, shouldn't have tried to make you do it all by yourself."

All Joshua could think was, *The life is in the blood.*

"From now on you can help me, okay? I'll show you how, and when you're ready you can do it by yourself. But only when you're ready. It'll get easier each time. There's no hurry. Don't worry. I'll teach you."

Then his father took the knife again and showed Joshua what to do when the person who'd been brought

to the special place beneath the barn wasn't moving anymore.

* * *

Now, nearly three decades later, Joshua sat in his basement and watched the CNN coverage of the story about
the ongoing homicide investigation in Champaign, Illinois, concerning the death of twenty-three-year-old
Juanita Worthy.

On the newscast they were interviewing an expert on
violent crimes against women, someone named Jake
Vanderveld, and he was speculating that the lungs of the
victim had not just been removed, but had also been consumed by the killer.

"Anthropophagy," he said soberly. "Cannibalistic behavior."

Joshua knew the term "anthropophagy" already. He'd
learned it long ago from his father, and now he was un-
derstandably intrigued by what the man had to say about
the crime. Joshua watched and listened and thought of
Dahmer.

Back before the city of Milwaukee had raised nearly
half a million dollars to buy Jeffrey's old apartment building just so that they could level it, Joshua had snuck in
with a video camera and walked through the place room
by room, taking careful footage of the living room where
Jeffrey cuffed and overpowered his victims, the bedroom
where he killed them and slept with their corpses, the
kitchen where he sat at the table and ate their skin and
meat and viscera and brains.

Visiting Jeffrey's apartment had made the connection
between them more real, more concrete, more intimate.

Joshua heard his wife, Sylvia, calling from upstairs, "What are you doing down there, honey?"

"Nothing. Just watching the news."

"Are you coming up? It's almost ten o'clock. I made you some brunch."

"I'll be there in a minute."

"I need to leave, remember? I have two houses to show before noon."

"I'll be right up." He turned the volume down a little so he could watch the last few minutes of the interview without Sylvia hearing it.

Joshua's job allowed him a somewhat flexible work schedule. He'd taken the rest of the day off because he had something to take care of in Plainfield, a couple hours northwest of his home on the outskirts of Milwaukee.

He figured that if he left in the next half hour there would be just enough time to make it there and back by dusk, or the gloaming, as it used to be called. That was the term he preferred, the one he'd first heard in the Celtic folk song "Loch Lomond," a song of death and the pining but ultimately futile hope of a soldier to return home to his sweetheart.

> 'Twas there that we parted in yon shady glen,
> On the steep, steep side o' Ben Lomon',
> Where in purple hue the Hieland hills we view,
> An' the moon comin' out in the gloamin'.

The moon coming out in the gloaming.
Tonight at dusk.
But until then, Plainfield.

He'd been to the small town numerous times and knew exactly where he was going. And, of course, since he was visiting Plainfield, he didn't just think of Jeffrey Dahmer, but also of Ed Gein, the cannibal and necrophile who'd made the small Wisconsin town famous in the 1950s.

Over the years most people had forgotten about Gein, but they hadn't forgotten about the novels and movies his life and crimes inspired: *Psycho*, *The Texas Chainsaw Massacre*, and even the Buffalo Bill character in *Silence of the Lambs*. One quiet Wisconsin handyman inspired the villains of three of the most iconoclastic horror movies of all time.

Ed had been in the habit of digging up graves and taking the bodies of the women back to his home where he would make lampshades and clothes out of their skin. He sewed together belts from their nipples.

At first Ed was just a grave robber, but eventually that wasn't enough for him. He killed Mary Hogan on December 8, 1954, managed to suppress his urges for a few years, and then murdered Bernice Worden almost exactly forty years ago on November 16, 1957, at the hardware store on Main Street.

Even though the original owners had sold the business long ago, amazingly, the place was still operating as a hardware store. Maybe the stories that surrounded it, the aura of death, actually attracted attention—and attention is almost always good for business.

In any case, Ed had taken Bernice's body to his home, hung it in his garage, and gutted her like a deer. That was how the police found her the next day when they paid Gein a visit. He'd also decapitated her.

Gein and Dahmer.

For some reason, Wisconsin had more than its share of anthropophagous psychopaths.

The Vanderveld interview ended and Joshua went to the basement's chest freezer, rooted around beneath the bags of frozen vegetables, the TV dinners and the venison steaks from the four-point buck he got bowhunting a few weeks ago, until he found the two packages wrapped in butcher paper.

He placed them in the small cooler he was taking with him on his trip, but he didn't add any ice. He wanted the contents of the packages to thaw on the way to Plainfield.

Even from the basement he could smell the sizzling sausage frying in the pan, just waiting for him in the kitchen, cooked up lovingly for him by his faithful wife, the woman he'd been married to for nearly five years.

He headed upstairs to join Sylvia for brunch.

15

Ralph and I worked all morning and even into the early afternoon, but we couldn't find any solid, incontrovertible connections between the cases in Ohio and Illinois and the one here in Wisconsin—all just circumstantial.

Though it was frustrating, admittedly, it wasn't all that unexpected. Investigations in real life aren't like the ones you see on TV. You don't find a clue every eight minutes and solve cases every forty-two. I've often thought of how great it would be if it worked that way, but it's just not the real world.

Now we were seated at the Skillet, a restaurant just down the street from HQ, looking over the menu. We needed to be back in forty-five minutes for the one-thirty briefing.

The national media outlets had already jumped on this case and with the reports of Hayes abandoning Lionel naked and cuffed in the same alley where Konerak Sinthasomphone had been found, and then the amputation of Colleen Hayes's hands, Dahmer and his cannibalistic crimes were already making their way through the news cycle.

An unholy resurrection of a man who—

"They have Hungarian beef goulash." Ralph jarred me out of my thoughts. He was pointing at the menu. "I've never been to a restaurant before that actually serves Hungarian beef goulash."

"Yeah." It took me a second to refocus, to be present here again. "I've heard it's good here."

"Really?"

"That's what they say."

"Huh." He set down the menu authoritatively. "Well, that's what I'm gonna get. Goulash. It just sounds like a man dish. I mean, can you imagine a one-hundred-five-pound supermodel ordering that? I'd say you gotta be at least two hundred pounds and have hair on your chest to truly enjoy a good bowl of Hungarian beef goulash."

Honestly, he was right; I couldn't picture a runway model working her way through a plate of goulash.

Ralph rapped his knuckle against the table. "Some things just sound tough. Like 'Bulgaria.' I'm a big boy, but I wouldn't want to mess with someone from Bulgaria. The word alone makes me think of meat cleavers and dark forests. Werewolves too."

"All that from 'Bulgaria'?"

"Yeah. Unlike 'France,' which makes me think of lattes and poetry about feet." He downed his coffee in one gulp. "Know what I mean?"

"Did you just say 'lattes and poetry about feet'?"

He shrugged. "It just came to me." He gestured toward my cup. "You sure you don't want any java?"

"Naw, I've never been able to get past the taste."

"Well, you gotta add sugar and cream."

"To kill the taste."

He considered that. "To calm it."

"Ah. Well, why would I want to develop a habit of drinking something that I need to . . . um . . . calm the taste of?"

"Because caffeine is a beautiful thing." He drew out the word "beautiful," turning it into its own paragraph, then snapped his fingers toward our server and ordered the goulash. I went for a medium-rare cheeseburger—one of my weaknesses—and while we waited for our food, we reviewed some of the details of the case.

Although documentation and collection of physical evidence are important, interpretation of that evidence in relationship to the nature of the crime is just as vital. All crimes occur in a specific place at a specific time by a specific individual and, though some people believe in "random acts of violence," I don't buy that. Crimes always have a context in time and space and in the life of that individual offender. The search for clues is essentially the search for context.

And that's what we were trying to do.

And failing at.

So far.

Ralph leaned across the table, his hefty forearms causing it to wobble. "So, seriously, Pat, what are you thinking here?"

"I'm not really one to venture hypotheses this early in an investigation."

"Motive and all that?"

"Well, like I said at the department, I try not to read too much into—"

He waved that off. "No, I get it: you don't trust your instincts. Motive. Whatever. Okay. But if you did?"

I was about to try staving off the topic again, but I changed my mind when I realized he was being persistent because he respected me and I wanted to show him just as much respect. I deliberated on his question carefully. "Ralph, do you ever read novels?"

"More of a movie guy myself." Then he added nonchalantly, "The two kinds of action movies."

"Two kinds?"

"Yeah, the Bruce Willis kind, and the chick flick kind."

"How are chick flicks action movies?"

He looked a little embarrassed. "Well, you watch one with your wife, and that night you get some . . ."

"Ah. Action."

A sly smile and a nod.

"Well, sometimes an author, or maybe a painter, will produce a piece of work to honor a previous artist, one who has passed away. Let's say, write a new Philip Marlowe crime novel, or a new Sherlock Holmes story or copy the strokes of Picasso. Or, I suppose, possibly film a movie in the style of Hitchcock. It's called a pastiche."

"A way to pay homage to 'em."

"Exactly."

He considered that. "And what—you think that's what our guy's doing here? A pastiche to Dahmer?"

"There's no way to know for sure, but it's something to think about, especially with the amputation and the location of . . ." I considered something that hadn't occurred to me before. "That pier where Colleen was found. It's just down the street from the chocolate factory where Dahmer worked. They might very well have shipped goods from there. I'd say it wasn't a mistake our guy left her at that pier. I don't believe in coincidences."

He eyed me. "Really?" To my surprise he sounded skeptical.

"Course not. Coincidences are just facts looked at out of context. You study a case from the right perspective and you'll see that they don't exist."

"But . . ." He tapped a thoughtful finger against the air. Obviously we were not on the same page here. "Coincidences happen all the time. You think of someone you haven't thought of in years, then ten minutes later you get a phone call from him. You dream of an event and then two days later it happens. What about déjà vu? Life is full of coincidences."

"I would say there has to be a scientific explanation for those things."

"Why?"

"Because . . . well . . ." As I debated how to answer, I found myself at a loss for words. His question really was a sweeping one, encompassing the breadth of a person's beliefs about the nature of reality, God, miracles, the supernatural—a lot more than I felt ready to delve into at the moment. "Well . . ."

The server returned. I prefer Cherry Coke, but the only cola on the menu here was Pepsi. She refilled Ralph's coffee and my soda, giving me a moment to consider my response.

"Pat, there's a limit to what science and reason can explain. For example, no philosopher yet has ever been able to prove that we're not all just brains in a jar."

I'd read about that famous philosophical dilemma before: "I think, therefore I am." But how do you know you're not just a mind thinking that you're a person with a body? It's the quintessential question of how we know we truly exist and I couldn't think of any good response.

He folded his hands. "I want to hear more about this deal with you and coincidences, but right now, finish up with what you were saying a minute ago. Pastiches. The alley. Dahmer."

"Right. The timing and nature of the previous homicides to what we have here certainly makes it appear that they're related."

"But we studied the case files all morning, didn't find anything solid. It's possible they're not."

"Correct. So let's just take the crimes last night for a sec. They go much deeper than just some teenager finding out that alley is next to where Dahmer used to live, and then spray-painting profane graffiti on a wall or leaving a chopped-up mannequin in the alley. We've had that before."

"I can only imagine."

"No, our guy was all in, playing for keeps: threatening a woman's life, forcing Vincent to drug and abduct another man, strip him, leave him out there in that specific alley."

"Not to mention cutting off Colleen's hands."

"Not to mention that."

He paused. "So, we hold back from assuming that the cases are connected, dial in as much as we can on the Dahmer angle, maybe explore any other possible Dahmer pastiches in the past, or things at the first two homicides that we might have missed that could be related to Dahmer's crimes. Maybe pastiches to other killers."

"Yes. Locations in particular. When he was a teenager,

Dahmer murdered his first victim in Bath Township, Ohio, just over an hour north of where the first body was found down near White Oak. There might be more there that we can look into."

"Interesting."

And that's when our food arrived.

16

Honestly, I was ready for a respite from thinking about cannibals, amputations, and dead bodies—especially now that I had a juicy cheeseburger in front of me. Ralph must have been thinking something along the same line because, as he went at his beef goulash, he asked me about my hobbies, my background, steering our conversation away from the case.

"I grew up not too far from here, in Horicon. I like to rock climb, get out west to Yosemite when I can. I was a wilderness guide for a while in college, got my criminal justice degree: UW–River Falls. Ended up attending the police academy two weeks after I graduated."

He eyed me. "And you're what? Twenty-seven? Twenty-eight?"

"Twenty-five."

Mentally, he did the calculations. "Then how are you a homicide detective already? A department as big as Milwaukee's, it must usually take what, at least six, seven years on the force for that?"

I wasn't really sure what to say. "I notice things. Thorne noticed that."

Ralph gazed across the restaurant and gestured toward

a man in a gray business suit four tables over, his empty dishes in front of him. "So, Armani over there; what do you notice about him?"

I glanced at him momentarily, then back at Ralph.

"He was expecting a petite woman whom he knows well, and whose company he enjoys, to meet him here more than twenty minutes ago. He's disappointed that she never showed and is still holding out hope that she will. He ordered the fish and chips and a large Pepsi, drives the black Ford Explorer parked outside, isn't a very big tipper, and is about to get a parking ticket."

"What the—?" Ralph stared at me. "How do you know all that?"

"There were two menus on his table when we first came in. Two waters, but no one else ever showed. He ordered her a cup of coffee. He checked his watch four times and finally ordered his meal."

"So he was expecting someone, okay, but how can you tell that it was a petite woman that he likes?"

I pointed to the main entrance on our left. "Whenever anyone comes in, he looks that way, but the door is backlit from the outside, so from where he's sitting it's not possible to see people's faces when they enter. You're left with—"

"Ah. Posture and frame." Ralph caught on. "So, when a group of people or a man, or maybe a tall or large-framed woman enters, you're saying he doesn't look as closely at them."

"But when a shorter, slimmer woman enters—"

"He watches her until she steps away from the door and isn't backlit," he concluded.

"Where he can see her face. Yes." The door opened as

we spoke, Armani looked that way as a six-foot-four guy lumbered in. Our man in the suit promptly glanced down at his watch.

"And you just happened to notice this while we were sitting here talking?"

"Yes."

A pause. I took a bite of my cheeseburger. It really was good.

"But you said he knows her well. What tells you that?"

I swallowed, wiped some ketchup from my chin. "Remember the coffee on the table?"

"Yeah, he ordered it for her. So what?"

"You typically wouldn't order coffee for someone you're meeting for the first time and he knew she took cream and added it. You wouldn't do that unless you're expecting someone momentarily."

"Cools it too quickly."

"From what I hear, yes. And you don't add cream to a woman's coffee unless you know her well—it's a bit of an intimate act. People are pretty protective about their coffee and what they put into it to . . . calm it. So he has—"

"A close relationship with her and he expected her right away."

"So it seems."

"And the Ford Explorer . . . Let me guess, his keys there next to the newspaper. You saw the vehicle parked out front when we came in. Guessed it was his?"

"Didn't have to guess. You can tell by the key fob that he's driving a rental. The Explorer out front has Maine plates and an Enterprise agreement form lying on the passenger seat."

He blinked. "You saw that when we passed by?"

"Yes. He's tanned; it's November in Wisconsin."

"And in Maine. So he's not from either state."

I shrugged. "Can't tell for sure, but it helps give context."

"And why's he about to get a ticket?"

"Parking is strictly enforced in the blocks surrounding police headquarters."

"Okay, I get that." We both ate for a moment, then he stopped and lowered his heaping spoonful of goulash. "You said he had fish and chips and a Pepsi. There's an empty tartar sauce packet on his plate, that's easy enough. And now that I think about it, the menu lists only Pepsi products and there's a little dark-colored pop left in his glass, so—"

"Soda."

"What?"

"We don't call it pop here; that's more of a Michigan deal. We call it soda. You should also know we call drinking fountains 'bubblers.'"

"You're kidding me."

"Nope. It's a Milwaukee thing. And yes, Pepsi is the only dark-colored soda being served today. Nowhere near as good as Cherry Coke."

"You still haven't explained how you know he isn't a big tipper."

"The cost of that meal, drink, and a coffee plus tax compared to the bills he set on the table. Only an eight percent tip."

Ralph examined the man's table once again, this time even more closely. "But there aren't any bills there."

"His server already picked them up."

He looked at me incredulously. "You're saying she came by before I even asked you to prove that you notice things?"

"Yes.

"And you calculated all that then—the tip, everything?"

"Yes."

"How did you know any of that would be pertinent to anything?"

"I didn't."

"Then how—"

I notice things.

I shrugged. "Luck, I guess."

He opened his mouth as if he were going to reply, then closed it again and chose to go for some beef goulash instead.

Moving past the topic of the guy at the table and following along with our discussion from earlier, I asked Ralph what he did before joining the FBI.

"I was in the Army for a while. Rangers. Bunch of missions in the Middle East." He was wolfing down his goulash in between words. "Man, I can't believe you counted up what bills he laid on the table."

Earlier, he'd referred to a guy watching a chick flick with his wife, and he wore a wedding ring. "So, married?"

"Yeah. Three years."

"Kids?"

"No. You?"

"No kids, no wife. I am seeing someone though. Actually, today is the one-year anniversary of when we first met."

He raised his coffee cup. "In that case, lunch is on me."

I thought again about how I would be having dinner with Taci tonight, discussing something that she wanted to talk about in private, but I didn't mention that, simply accepted Ralph's toast. "Thanks."

We were both well into our meals now and I brought up the topic I'd been curious about since we first met in the police headquarters lobby. "Ralph, I gotta ask you something."

"Shoot." He was in the middle of a bite of goulash.

I indicated toward his turtleneck. "No overstarched oxford. No tie." I figured maybe he didn't wear one because of the thickness of his neck and his broad chest— that any tie he wore would've ended up looking like a clown tie and his supervisors didn't want that. "Isn't it pretty much a uniform for guys who are Feds?"

"Got an exemption. I can't stand the idea of wearing a giant arrow pointing to my groin all day."

"Oh."

He looked at me slightly suspiciously. "I mean, can you?"

"Um, no. Of course not." Man, was I glad I didn't have a tie on today either. "And when you put it that way, I don't think I'll ever look at ties the same way again."

He took a giant mouthful of food. "It seems kind of desperate to me, a pretty blatant invitation to draw people's attention to . . . Well, it's kind of like—" He was talking with his mouth full of goulash again. "So, my wife, her best friend has this teenage daughter."

"Right."

"The kid is always wearing shorts with words written on the butt. What is that about? 'Syracuse'? Are you scri ous? I could never respect a college that's so desperate for students that it needs to advertise itself on the butts of teenage girls."

Hmm. That was actually a pretty good point.

"And then she wears these sweatpants with 'Cute' back there. Is that supposed to be referring to . . . ?"

"Um . . . Probably. Yeah." I thought of a time I'd seen a girl wearing shorts with ALL-STAR imprinted on the rump and I realized I didn't even want to know what she was trying to tell the world.

He shook his head. "I'll just say this: I'd be at a loss with a teenage daughter. They're a complete mystery to me. I'd be clueless."

"You and me both."

Ralph finished inhaling the goulash and I polished off my cheeseburger. We ate quickly so we could get back to the department, then headed out the door, past the Ford Explorer by the curb.

There was a parking ticket tucked beneath the windshield wiper.

17

Joshua parked the car in the pull-off at the end of the dirt road.

Barren, leafless trees ready for winter bordered him on both sides.

A sign on a leaning wooden pole beside a small clearing announced NO TRESPASSING.

The house that used to stand here was long gone.

Joshua wasn't sure exactly when it'd burned down, but he knew it was within a couple months of Ed Gein's arrest in November of 1957, and he was pretty sure the fire hadn't been accidental. Just like the people of Milwaukee who tried to purge the memory of Dahmer from their consciousness by razing his apartment building, the good people of Plainfield had undoubtedly hoped to sear the memory of their most infamous inhabitant by getting rid of the place he'd called home.

Joshua stepped out of the car and stretched his legs, then removed the cooler from the backseat.

It'd taken a fair amount of research, but eventually

he'd been able to locate the precise spot where the house had stood.

Ironically, or at least conveniently as far as Gein would have been concerned, it was less than five miles from the nearest graveyard—the same graveyard where things would happen this afternoon, during the next chapter of the saga Joshua had recently been putting into play.

Honestly, it'd never been his intention to kill Colleen Hayes. Cutting off her hands had been all he was planning to do to her, even from the start.

In fact, murdering her might actually have been counterproductive to what he was hoping to accomplish.

Well then, what about Petey Schwartz back on Friday?

No, nobody would connect the two crimes.

Besides, that wasn't planned. It was spontaneous and had nothing to do with the Hayes kidnapping or what he had in mind for Adele today.

Still, you remember what you did, remember how you—

Enough with those kinds of thoughts.

Joshua walked to the place where Ed Gein's kitchen used to be, set down the cooler, and took a seat beside it.

The view before him was the same one Ed Gein would have had if he were looking out his kitchen window.

Joshua pulled a bottle of cream soda out of the cooler, uncapped it, and took a long refreshing swallow.

Last night it hadn't been easy, doing to Colleen what he'd done. And, unquestionably, it would have been easier on her if he'd knocked her out beforehand, but somehow, though the deed itself was disturbing, her screams had brought him a degree of pleasure that'd surprised him.

It was a bit disconcerting.

That hadn't happened before, but then again, he'd never done something like that to someone and let the person live.

It'd led him to acknowledge a certain yearning rising to the surface, one that'd been birthed in him long ago in the cellar beneath the barn.

While he was listening to Colleen cry out, enjoying watching her suffer, he'd had a revelation of sorts, an epiphany about who he truly was, what he was becoming.

A voice of reason, of conscience: *Go to God for forgiveness, Joshua. Turn yourself in! Don't live in the den of the damned!*

More cream soda.

The den of the damned.

He shifted his thoughts back to Colleen. After cutting off her left hand, he'd faced a choice—drug her before doing the other one, or leave her awake during the process.

Of course he might have gagged her as well, but where he'd taken her, it wasn't as if they were going to be discovered. The screams hadn't posed much of a problem. And he kind of liked hearing the strangely muted, yet metallic sounds as they echoed all around him in that place and then disappeared into the thin night air.

While he'd tried to decide whether or not to leave her conscious before sawing off her right hand, he'd tightened the heavy-duty plastic tie around that wrist to stop the bleeding once he got started.

He thought she might pass out from the pain of losing that left hand, but she must have been a fighter because she didn't. In between her screams she'd struggled to pull free from the chair, begged him to stop, to let her go.

That ended up being distracting and with all of that going on, it took him a while to decide which direction to take things.

Finally, he chose to let her remain conscious while he laid the edge of the saw blade against her other wrist.

And then drew it firmly toward him.

Forward and back.

Forward and backward as the night became rich and thick with her screams and her blood.

His father had taught him all about that: "For the life of the flesh is in the blood: and I have given it to you upon the altar to make an atonement for your souls: for it is the blood that maketh an atonement for the soul." Third book of the Bible. Seventeenth chapter. Eleventh verse.

Atonement. And the blood.

He thought of Colleen now as he unwrapped the two packages and, sitting where Ed Gein might have sat, he did what Ed Gein might have done and ate the meat he had brought along with him from Milwaukee.

In a few minutes he would head to the house and pay a visit to Adele Westin. Joshua had researched more than just the location of Ed's house and the graveyard, and he knew that Adele, who was living with her fiancé, worked out of their home.

She was a woman who followed a very strict schedule, but a quick phone call could confirm that she was there this afternoon. Otherwise, if need be, he would wait as long as necessary until she returned.

Her fiancé wouldn't be arriving home from his shift until after two. Joshua figured that would give him plenty of time to get to Adele and then leave the token of his intentions toward her, as well as a note with his demands. All of this would, of course, initiate the next chapter in the story he was telling.

One that would be enough to attract the attention of the person he was hoping to meet.

And if not, what he had planned for Wednesday would most certainly do so, without a doubt.

On Wednesday, when the cop was dead, Joshua's point would be unmistakable and he would finally be able to get the one thing he wanted most—a partner.

18

Back at HQ, Ralph and I began reviewing the notes everyone else had left on my desk, sorting through what we would be discussing at the meeting that was scheduled to start in less than five minutes.

As far as sedan-owning, six-foot-tall, brown-eyed male Caucasians, we had thousands in the greater Milwaukee area. If you added an inch or two to either side of that and included men whose family members had sedans as well, the number rose exponentially. Gabriele Holdren, the officer who'd gotten the coffee for Vincent last night when I was with him in the interrogation room, was still comparing that list with the tip list—which hadn't produced anything so far either.

As expected, the four confessions had all been false. Ellen and Annise were still looking into missing persons cases, and Lyrie was on his way back from canvassing the Hayeses' neighborhood again to see if anyone could tell us the color of the sedan.

Radar had dug up the names of fourteen felons in the area who'd been convicted of violent crimes against women and he'd apparently left the department to follow up on one of them.

A lot of things were in play.

"I'm still curious about the handcuffs," I told Ralph. "Why didn't Colleen's abductor leave a pair for Vincent to use?"

"He had to know Vincent already had a pair."

"I can't really come up with any other compelling reason—unless Vincent's involved somehow." I evaluated the possibilities. "Vincent had planned to come home just after seven, but at the last minute he called Colleen to let her know he would be late, wouldn't be getting home until after ten. However, she was abducted just after nine. If the offender had known Vincent's schedule and been hoping to find Colleen alone—"

Ralph rubbed his chin roughly. "The guy would have taken her before seven, while Vincent was at work, before he was supposed to come home, not after nine."

I tried to steer myself away from making unfounded assumptions, but I found it hard to keep my thoughts from leaning in the direction of suspecting that Vincent was somehow involved in arranging his wife's abduction.

"I suppose her abductor could have been in the house already," Ralph mused. "Found the handcuffs, decided not to leave a pair, not to take the chance that the cuffs could lead us back to him."

"Yes," I said. "But that still doesn't explain how he would have known about Vincent's last-minute change of plans."

"After the briefing, let's have Thompson go back and see if any of the neighbors remember the sedan driving around earlier."

"And we should have someone interview Vincent again. Find out who might've known he owned that pair of handcuffs and who else knew he was going to be working late. Maybe Ellen could go."

"Or Corsica?" he said.

"Ellen. Not that I don't trust Corsica's competence in these sorts of things, but—"

"You don't trust Corsica's competence in these sorts of things."

"That's one way to put it."

"So, what is it between you two, anyway?"

"She has a tendency to jump to conclusions. More than once I've had to redirect an investigation before more innocent people got hurt."

"I'm sure she took well to that. The redirecting part."

"Oh, it was just peachy."

Ralph nodded. Jotted something on a notepad.

As we were finishing collecting our papers, I saw Lieutenant Thorne picking his way toward us through the labyrinth of desks, file cabinets, and business dividers that made up most of this floor of the department. He was carrying a magazine or catalog of some kind.

"We might have something," he announced. "A connection to the homicide in Illinois."

"What's that?"

He flopped the catalog onto the desk in front of me.

"Police tape."

19

"Your car down in the parking garage?" Thorne asked me.

"Yes." I picked up the catalog. "What do you mean 'police tape'?"

"Let's go. I'll walk with you. I want you two to look into this."

Okay, so either our second briefing of the day had been postponed or Thorne was giving us permission to miss it. In either case that was fine by me. I'd rather be out in the field any day investigating something than sitting in a meeting talking about it.

The three of us maneuvered past the desks and made our way to the hall that led to the elevators. I was flipping through the catalog. "What do we have?"

"A guy who sells souvenirs. Thompson managed to locate the most recent issue. He came across it while cross-checking tips from Illinois."

We filed into the elevator and he punched the button for the lower-level parking garage. "The guy who puts out this catalog has all his orders sent to a PO box, but we tracked down his name: Timothy Griffin. He lives in Fort Atkinson. Check out the back."

On the catalog's back cover, just below the return address, was a sticker advertising that a fifty-foot-long length of police tape was for sale:

"Just in! Maneater of The Midwest Police Tape! Soon to be A Collector's Item!! $350!"

It listed the date and location of the crime. The tape was purportedly from the Illinois homicide in which the woman's lungs had been removed and evidently consumed.

"Unbelievable," Ralph muttered.

As the elevator descended, I studied the catalog carefully.

The items were cross-referenced so you could search by killer, type of crime (pedophilia, homicide), postmortem activity (vampirism, cannibalism, rape), state, years, or price.

There were decks of trading cards of fifty-two of the most famous criminals in U.S. history, Christmas letters Dahmer had written to his mother, Gacy's clown makeup, Manson's Bible with his name scribbled on the inside front cover. Knickknacks, drill bits, pliers, saws, memorabilia, clothes and more. Hundreds of items. Even, supposedly, the original 1934 Albert Fish letter to Grace Budd's parents. It was one of the most infamous and disturbing writings of any sexual predator or serial killer of the last hundred years and the guy who'd sent out this catalog, Timothy Griffin, claimed to have the original copy.

Just thinking about the letter made my stomach turn.

Fish, who was put to death in New York back in 1936, was perhaps the most depraved sadomasochistic pedophile and cannibal ever captured in the U.S. The authorities never found out how many people he killed, but he claimed to "have had children in every state." Whether that meant molesting them or killing them was never established, but from what I'd read about the case, it wouldn't have surprised me if it were both. In 1928 he abducted a ten-year-old girl named Grace Budd, murdered her, cooked her, and then ate her. Six years later he wrote a letter to her parents about how much he'd enjoyed it.

That was the letter advertised in Griffin's catalog.

Sickening.

We reached the parking garage level. Exited the elevator.

"How would you ever verify that the stuff's legit?" Ralph, who'd been looking at the pages with me, asked Thorne. "I mean the signed letters, okay, I get that. Those might be available from relatives. But Gacy's clown makeup? Couldn't you buy makeup like that at dozens of stores here in Wisconsin alone? Just claim it was Gacy's?"

Gacy.

A man responsible for one of the biggest body counts of any serial killer in U.S. history.

Remembering what all these guys had done was somewhat overwhelming. It was hard not to find myself just getting numb to it all.

Gacy, of course, was the civic leader in the Chicago area who was convicted of killing thirty-three young men back in the 1970s. He dressed up as a clown and volunteered on weekends cheering up children in local hospitals. Three times he was named the local Jaycees chapter's Man of the Year and had been personally congratulated for his public service and contributions to the causes of the Democratic party by First Lady Rosalynn Carter. The police found a photo of her standing beside him when they were removing more than two dozen corpses buried in the crawl space beneath his house.

He claimed he'd been set up for the crimes.

Thorne shrugged. "You got me, but look at the price tags—people are shelling out big bucks for that garbage. Somebody believes it's authentic."

"And he knows about the lungs," I said. "Griffin does, that they were eaten. He calls the guy a 'maneater,' not just a killer. That information hasn't been released to the press."

Thorne nodded thoughtfully. "True."

Ralph let out a few choice words about what he thought of Griffin and his little business enterprise. Even though I was used to the rough language of cops, Ralph managed to phrase things in ways I'd never even heard before, but I found myself agreeing with the sentiment of everything he said.

I was glad to follow up on this, but Fort Atkinson was an hour away. I asked Thorne, "If Griffin lives in Fort Atkinson, will that be a jurisdictional problem?"

He deferred to Ralph who gave a knowing half grin. "That's one of the advantages of having me here, bro. If Griffin's selling crime scene tape from a homicide in Illinois, we have an interstate connection. And that means it's under my jurisdiction."

He might have been stretching things a bit, but it worked for me.

In the garage we found out that Radar had taken our

cruiser, but Thorne signed off for Ralph and me to use an undercover sedan that was typically used on drug busts. Ralph asked him, "Has this guy Griffin ever surfaced before? Any priors?"

"No. Thompson checked his record right off the bat. Apparently, he's a celebrity in his own right in certain circles, though. An author named Heather Isle—she writes those true crime books—anyway, she uses him as one of her 'expert' sources." Thorne turned to me. "You know her, right? The true crime writer?"

"No, Saundra Weathers. A novelist. Writes mysteries. She lived in my hometown, back when we were kids."

"It was . . ." I could see him struggling to find the right words. "The Weathers' tree house, right? Where you found—"

"Not theirs, exactly. No. But it was next to their property."

Thorne knew this was a touchy subject for me and he let it go at that. "Well, go have a talk with Griffin. See what he can tell us about the police tape and how he knows it was from the scene of a 'maneater.'"

We briefly discussed the observations Ralph and I had come up with while we were at the restaurant and at my desk a few minutes ago. Thorne promised to assign the projects to the task force and contact us if they came up with anything, then he left, and Ralph and I climbed into the UC car. I called in to check Griffin's DMV records and got his address.

"So I'm curious," Ralph said when I got off the radio. "What did you find in the tree house?"

"I'll tell you on the way."

+ + +

Plainfield, Wisconsin

Joshua caught hold of Adele Westin as she swayed, then supported her as she lost consciousness and drifted into his arms.

He lowered her gently to the kitchen's linoleum floor.

The drugs he'd used on her were powerful and she didn't wake up, not even when he brought out the pruning shears to get the item he'd decided to leave behind for her fiancé to show him how serious he was about his demands.

He left the note detailing what needed to happen before five o'clock, and after placing the proof in the refrigerator that he had Adele, Joshua carried her to the Ford Taurus and laid her in the trunk.

Then left for Milwaukee.

For the train yards.

Being mid-November in Wisconsin, it was starting to get dark early. Based on the drive time, he figured he'd be able to get started on her right when he needed to, just before the gloaming.

20

As I recount to Ralph the events surrounding the discovery in the tree house, it's as if I'm reliving them all over again, so I do my best to detach myself from the emotions, to view the memories from another person's point of view entirely . . .

You're a junior in high school.

Leaves, dead and brown, swirl on the ground, then skitter around you and across the mountain bike trail in front of you, caught up in little whirlwinds of air. Tiny tornadoes of late fall.

You pedal hard to try to outrun the impending storm.

The trail skirts along the edge of the vast marsh outside of town. You're on your way home after football practice and can't help but think of what happened yesterday afternoon.

You jump a root. Pick up speed.

Everyone has been talking about the girl all day. Nothing like this has ever happened in your hometown. No one knows what to do.

They haven't said much on the news, just that Mindy Wells had been last seen leaving her school at about three p.m. Her home was six blocks away. She never made it. The police were checking out a lead on a blue van that had been seen nearby. That was all.

At first, her mom thought that Mindy's father had picked her up. Then, when he came home alone, they thought maybe her grandmother had her. The family was new to the area and there weren't many other choices. But, no, when they checked, the grandmother didn't have Mindy either.

The police were called in and the rumors quickly spread that they were waiting for a ransom note, but from the beginning that hadn't seemed right to you. The family wasn't rich, and without a ransom demand, there aren't too many reasons to kidnap a child.

The water on the marsh becomes restless and choppy in anticipation of the coming storm. The angry wind scratches at your cheeks and gray steely clouds begin to drip rain onto your back.

You head for the old county road along the edge of the marsh where it'll be faster to get home.

She's an eleven-year-old girl. If you wanted to take her someplace where you could be alone with her, where would you go? A basement? An old barn? A shed? Somewhere that no one knew about, out here by the marsh?

You think these things.

You cannot help but think them.

The sky is crisscrossed by the stark Vs of Canada geese heading south, or in some cases, settling for a few hours to rest on the brackish waters of the marsh. Even with the rain picking up, even above the sound of your wheels whisking across the damp leaves on the trail, you hear the geese honking.

The police checked the neighborhood carefully but didn't find anything. They brought one of the neighbors in for questioning but nothing came of that and they let him go almost immediately.

Someone could have just driven up and forced the girl into a car and then taken off, that's what people said. It could have been that easy. It could have been anything.

But it wasn't just anything that happened, it was something very specific that happened at that time on that street to that girl. To Mindy Wells. Something that had never happened before, not in that place, not in that way.

The family is new to the area. She wouldn't have gotten into the car with just anyone.

She's an eleven-year-old girl.

You duck to avoid a branch. The tires of your mountain bike skid across a smear of mud, almost sending you off the trail. It rained yesterday afternoon, leaving the ground soggy. Most of the water has drained into the marsh, but it'll take a few days for the ground to dry out completely. Now, however, with the rain picking up, it didn't look like that was going to happen.

You picture the street that leads from the school to Mindy's house. You know it well, you've been on it any number of times, and as you think about it, you realize there's one spot where a thick row of hedges would have hidden the view of the street from all of the neighbors' homes.

One spot. Four blocks from the school.

A blind spot, and that term makes you think of football, of throwing downfield to your receivers. You have to know how to read the defense, how to pick your way past the cornerbacks, linebackers, and safeties, find their blind spots. It's all about location and timing. Getting the ball to the right place on the field at exactly the right time to catch the defense off guard.

The trail evens out, bending toward the dirt road you'll use to take the shortcut home. It's not far.

Is that where it happened? Where she was abducted? By those hedges four blocks from school?

If the person who took her had parked right there he could have forced her into his car and no one would have seen, overpowered her quickly, and no one would have known. There isn't anywhere else on that street that's hidden enough from view to do it without taking a big chance at being discovered. Nowhere else made sense.

But that would mean the kidnapper knew the area well, knew that street well, knew exactly where to do it.

A local.

Maybe.

Or someone who'd lived here.

And if he knew the area he would know where to take a girl. A place he could be alone with her.

You feel a chill.

The kids from your high school use the dirt road up ahead to get to an old tree house to party and hook up on the weekends. It overlooks the road as well as the marsh, so if you're up there, you're able to see anyone coming either by car or by jon boat.

It's a place where they know they can be alone. A place they know they won't be interrupted by adults, or if someone does show up, they can get away before getting caught. You've biked past it. You know where it is.

But unless a person knows where to look, it's not easy to find.

You arrive at the road. Pull your bike to a stop.

The storm has arrived and the wind drives cold pellets of rain against your face. If it were ten degrees colder out, the rain would be snow.

Besides the rutted older tracks, pressed into the mud of the road in front of you are two sets of fresher tire tracks from a vehicle with a wide wheelbase, a pickup or maybe an SUV. One set is shallower, and the orientation of the tread marks tells you that's from the return trip south, back to town. The other set is deeper, made when the mud was fresh.

You think about what you know, about the timing of the rain. It stopped in the middle of the afternoon yesterday, so that would mean someone drove out here during the rainstorm or shortly after it stopped, spent time here, and returned to town only after a substantial amount of the water had drained into the marsh.

That would have taken several hours.

Or maybe all night.

A chill ripples through you. You stare at those tracks, thinking about the time frame, and after a short moment of deliberation, rather than take the road south toward home, you aim your bike north, toward the trail that leads to the tree house.

It isn't anything, it's something—something specific that happened only once in only one way.

If the driver knew the area, he might know about the tree house.

Most people don't know where that trail is.

A local would, though.

Yes, or someone who'd lived nearby.

You pedal along the side of the road, paralleling the

tire tracks, but even from a distance, even in the dreary day, you can see where they stop.

Beside the trailhead to the tree house.

You feel your heart beating faster, not just from the exertion of pedaling, but from apprehension of what you fear might be waiting at the end of that trail.

You arrive, park your bike. Lean it against a tree.

After a moment you start walking along the path, into the woods.

A rush of adrenaline courses through you and your imagination plays out what might have happened.

One moment you're seeing things through the eyes of the kidnapper and the next through the eyes of the girl. It's startling how detailed you see everything. Not in bursts and blurs like some sort of psychic might, but in full color because you know the area and can imagine how things might have gone down.

Clarity.

Just like when you're on the football field, when everything slows down and you see it all without seeing, when you know where your receiver is going to be without consciously thinking about it. Time slows and you seem to slip through its seams, respond between the moments, pausing between the beats of your heart. Then you thread the needle. Move the ball down the field. Timing and location.

Clarity.

You're a girl, new to the area, walking home from school . . . There's a man grabbing you . . . forcing you into his blue van . . . driving you out here . . . where no one will disturb him . . .

No, you don't know if what you see in your mind really happened, but if it did, if—

You pass an old fire pit that's been here for years, one that's always littered with discarded beer cans and charred logs. Today glass shards from several broken Jack Daniel's bottles lie strewn across the leaves at the base of a log the kids sit on by the fire.

Nearby, you notice that the leaves are matted down from yesterday's rain, but the ones on the trail are kicked up. Maybe from someone walking through here—

Or from the girl, from being dragged through the woods, struggling, kicking, trying to get free . . .

Your heart somehow both tenses and races at the same time.

Through the bare forest you see the tree house ahead of you. It's perched on the muscular branches of an aging oak and you think of "The Monkey's Paw," the short story by W. W. Jacobs that you had to read for English lit. last year. The branches of the oak curl around the tree house like a gnarled hand clutching a talisman.

"Hello?" you call.

Silence.

The tree house is forty feet away.

"Mindy?"

Nothing. No reply.

You gaze around again at the empty, lonely forest, then use your hand to shield your eyes from the slanting rain, and walk to the base of the tree.

There's no ladder per se, just horizontal boards nailed to the trunk to form the rungs that lead to the platform that encircles the tree house. There's a narrow west-facing window that an occasional hunter will slide his shotgun barrel through when he uses this tree house as an impromptu blind to try to take down the geese settling onto the marsh.

Around to the other side is the opening you'll have to crawl through to access the tree house.

As you climb, you catch yourself wondering if it would be possible to carry a girl up these rungs.

If she were draped over your shoulders. If you were strong. If she were unconscious.

Getting her off your shoulders at the top and then sliding her onto the platform would certainly be difficult, but you decide that, yes, it would be possible.

You reach the top rung, ease onto the landing, then glance back. From this height you have a clear view of both the road and the marsh.

If someone came here last night he would've seen headlights coming this way long before they reached the trailhead. It would have given him plenty of time to slip away.

Your heart is hammering as you traverse the narrow platform, round the corner, and come to the opening that leads into the tree house itself.

It's a dark, square mouth two feet high and two feet wide. You'll need to get on your hands and knees to crawl inside.

But then you'll see. Then you'll know. Then you'll see that there's nothing here, and the police will do their job and find Mindy Wells at a friend's house or something, and then everything will get back to normal and you'll be able to focus on football again, on the state semifinals coming up this weekend. Everyone will be able to take a deep breath and forget that any of this misunderstanding ever happened.

You hear the rain splattering and tip-tapping on the roof of the tree house. Hollow. Indistinct. A rapid wet drumbeat.

And so.

You kneel.

And look into the room.

What little light has slipped in is shrouded by the cloudy, rainy day, but you immediately see that the tree house is not empty. Leaning with her back against the far wall, staring blankly at you, clothes missing, her legs tucked beneath her on the bare wooden planks, her hands on her lap, her wrists tightly bound with rough cord, is the girl.

Mindy Wells.

A terrible, terrible shiver runs through you. Your throat tightens. "Mindy?"

She doesn't move. Doesn't respond.

Only the sound of rain drumming above you.

You know how to check for a pulse—last spring your track coach had you monitor your heart rate when you did wind sprints. And even though you know it's too late, you know it is, it must be, you realize you have to find out. You can't leave without knowing for sure. You need to see if she is still alive.

As you crawl into the tree house, your heart seems to have knotted up solid inside your chest.

When you reach Mindy, it takes you a few seconds to work up the nerve, but then you press two fingers against her neck. Her skin has a damp, doughy feel.

There's no pulse and the coolness of the flesh makes the fact that she's dead seem all the more real.

You're careful not to disturb anything so it won't throw off the police when they investigate things, but for some reason covering her nakedness seems like the right thing to do, the least you can do for her, so before you leave, you take off your jacket and drape it gently over her chest and lap. She's not a large girl and your coat is big enough to at least offer her a small degree of modesty.

Her name was Mindy Wells.

She was eleven years old when she was raped and killed in your hometown and left in that tree house by the marsh.

They never found her killer.

But you're the one who found her body on that rainy day the week of the state football semifinals back when you were a junior in high school.

+ + +

I finished telling Ralph the story and he said nothing, just sat beside me in the car in stony silence.

Initially, I thought he might do what others had done over the years and jump to the conclusion that finding Mindy was what'd led me on the path to eventually enter law enforcement. But he didn't. Instead, he just leveled a hard gaze out the window and remained quiet.

It was another five miles before he spoke, his voice brusque and unyielding. "Kids are the worst."

"Yeah, they are."

"And you were only sixteen when you found her?"

"Yes."

He looked at me then. "That must have been terrible."

"It was."

It still is.

"And they never caught the scumbag who did it?"

I shook my head and then we were silent again. I didn't tell him that the guy had also killed at least one other young girl, Jenna Natara, the one whose death had invaded my dreams last night. It didn't seem like the right time to get into all that.

Once again he watched the bleak, brown countryside that was brushed with light snow pass by the window. Glancing toward him, I saw him brush a finger beneath his right eye and I wondered how many times he'd been called in on cases with children as the victims.

A few minutes later I parked beside the curb in front of Timothy Griffin's home, a ramshackle place in desperate need of paint and repair on the edge of town.

Ralph and I got out of the car.

"I saw you looking at me back there a minute ago," he said.

"I'm sorry, I was—"

"I just had something in my eye."

I paused. "Yeah, I know."

Catalog in hand, I followed him up the porch steps and stood by his side while he knocked on Griffin's door.

21

A waif of a woman answered, stared blankly at us. Out of high school, but not by much.

"Yes?" She had circles under her eyes and wore a tattered housecoat that drooped sadly over her stick-thin frame. It was as if she'd materialized out of thin air.

"Good afternoon, ma'am." I held up my badge. "I'm Detective Bowers, with the police department." I left out the fact that I was from Milwaukee and not Fort Atkinson. "This is Agent Hawkins with the FBI. Is Timothy Griffin here?"

"No." She offered nothing more. Her eyes remained vacuous.

"Do you know when he'll be back?"

"No."

Ralph indicated toward the living room. "Can we come in? Wait for him?"

"I'm not sure Timothy would want that." Even her voice sounded frail and tenuous, as if it might disintegrate if any other sounds invaded the air.

Though she didn't move, I got the sense that she might fade back into the house at any moment. "And how do you know Timothy?"

"I'm his girlfriend." She couldn't have been older than nineteen or twenty. From his DMV records, I knew that Timothy Griffin was forty-nine.

Ralph spoke up. "Ma'am, what's your name?"

"Mallory."

We waited, but she didn't give us a last name.

"Mallory, why wouldn't Timothy want us to come in and wait for him?"

"Timothy is a private person."

Ralph didn't give up. "This is concerning something quite important. If we find out later that you were hindering our investigation in any way, that would be an unfortunate thing. For you and for Timothy. And it could put innocent people at risk."

He was obviously banking on the fact that she wouldn't be clear about her right to refuse us entry. However, if she did let us in as we'd requested, evidence we found inside the home would be admissible in court. He was banking on her not knowing that too.

His bet paid off.

After a slight hesitation, Mallory stepped aside.

We joined her in the living room.

A drab, greenish carpet covered the floor. Two mismatched reclining chairs were positioned beside the heavily curtained windows. At the far end of the room, cheap Formica shelves held a cluttered array of knick-knacks. A variety of photos surrounded us on the walls. A TV faced the plaid couch; a VCR and twelve videos sat on top of it.

A nondescript, typical-looking living room, but immediately I noticed something that really disturbed me, I mean really disturbed me, but I thought it'd be better to bring it up when Ralph and I were alone, so for the moment I kept it to myself.

The air in the house was languid and stale, as if none of the windows or doors had been opened in months.

Mallory didn't seem like the hospitable type, so I was surprised when she offered us coffee, which Ralph accepted, even though he'd downed three cups at lunch—not to mention the two-liter bottle of Mountain Dew earlier in the morning. This man really did think caffeine was a beautiful thing. I declined, but thanked her.

"It might be cold," Mallory said to Ralph, referring to the coffee. She didn't sound apologetic, just explanatory. Everything she said was blank and devoid of emotion.

"No problem."

"Cream? Sugar?"

"Sure."

She stepped into the kitchen and when she was gone, Ralph spoke softly to me: "So, where do you think he keeps all the stuff he sells?"

"Everywhere."

He looked at me curiously. "What do you mean?"

I walked to one of the chairs and flipped forward the price tag that was attached to the top of it with a small piece of string.

"Oh, you gotta be kidding me."

I moved around the room, noting the price tags on the furniture, the novelty items and curios, the framed photos. Each tag included the date Griffin had acquired the item, the name of the celebrity killer or pedophile it was from, the catalog number, and his asking price. Nearly everything in the living room had a price tag.

At first I was a little confused by the photos on the walls, but then I recognized the father of a homicide victim from Madison last July and it hit me: the family photographs weren't pictures of Griffin and his relatives, but rather they were the family photos of victims of the killers and rapists he was profiteering from.

I tried to imagine what it would be like living in a house like this, sitting on that couch watching television as if nothing were any different about this living room from any other one on the block, but all the while you were surrounded by mementos and personal items and memorabilia of the country's vilest and most deranged murderers.

Being here troubled me as much as being at any of the crime scenes I've worked. And I've worked some bad ones. I had no idea what Mallory's personality had been like before she landed here with Timothy, but I couldn't imagine anyone remaining joyful and lighthearted living in a place like this.

A Bible was sitting next to a small ceramic bird without a price tag on a coffee table beside the couch and I recognized the Bible from the catalog: the one Charles Manson had owned. Checking the inside flap, I found that it did indeed contain his signature, but there was no telling if it was authentic or not.

I set it back down.

A framed letter hung on the wall in the hallway just off the living room.

"I'll be back in a sec," I told Ralph, then walked over to take a closer look.

It was the letter Albert Fish had sent to Grace Budd's

parents and, based on the wrinkled, aged appearance of the paper, it certainly did look like it might be the original.

In the living room behind me, Mallory returned with Ralph's coffee and while he inquired how long she'd known Griffin, I read the letter:

Dear Mrs. Budd.

In 1894 a friend of mine shipped as a deck hand on the Steamer Tacoma, *Capt. John Walker. They sailed from San Francisco for Hong Kong, China. On arriving there he and two others went ashore and got drunk. When they returned the boat was gone. At that time there was famine in China. Meat of any kind was from $1–3 per pound. So great was the suffering among the very poor that all children under 12 were sold for food in order to keep others from starving.*

A boy or girl under 14 was not safe in the street. You could go in any shop and ask for steak—chops—or stew meat. Part of the naked body of a boy or girl would be brought out and just what you wanted cut from it. A boy or girl's behind which is the sweetest part of the body and sold as veal cutlet brought the highest price. John staid there so long he acquired a taste for human flesh. On his return to N.Y. he stole two boys, one 7 and one 11. Took them to his home stripped them naked tied them in a closet. Then burned everything they had on.

Several times every day and night he spanked them—tortured them—to make their meat good and tender. First he killed the 11 year old boy, because he

*had the most meat. Every part of his body was cooked
and eaten except the head—bones and guts. He was
roasted in the oven, boiled, broiled, fried and stewed.
The little boy was next, went the same way. At that
time, I was living at 409 E 100 St. near—right side.
He told me so often how good human flesh was I made
up my mind to taste it.*

*On Sunday June the 3, 1928 I called on you at 406
W 15 St. Brought you pot cheese—strawberries. We
had lunch. Grace sat in my lap and kissed me. I made
up my mind to eat her. On the pretense of taking her
to a party. You said yes she could go. I took her to an
empty house in Westchester I had already picked out.*

*When we got there, I told her to remain outside.
She picked wildflowers. I went upstairs and stripped
all my clothes off. I knew if I did not I would get her
blood on them. When all was ready I went to the window and called her. Then I hid in a closet until she
was in the room. When she saw me all naked she began
to cry and tried to run down the stairs. I grabbed her
and she said she would tell her mamma.*

*First I stripped her naked. How she did kick—bite
and scratch. I choked her to death, then cut her in
small pieces so I could take my meat to my rooms. Cook
and eat it. It took me 9 days to eat her entire body.*

I couldn't read any further. I'd come across a copy of
this letter once while doing an assignment on the ethics
of the death penalty for a law class at Marquette, and I
knew that Fish went on to describe how he could've had
sex with Grace if he'd wished, but he had refrained, and
that she'd died a virgin.

I felt a palpable sweep of nausea.

A $1,250 price tag hung from the corner of the plaque. I seriously doubted that Griffin would set the price that high unless he thought he could actually get that much for it.

Supply and demand.

I turned away, closed my eyes.

Brutality.

Evil.

Man's inhumanity to man.

People actually spend their hard-earned cash on this stuff, actually surround themselves on purpose with these keepsakes of men who raped and killed innocent people.

A girl buried alive: Jenna Natara.

A body in a tree house: Mindy Wells.

A child slaughtered and eaten by a psychopath: Grace Budd.

I took a moment to collect myself, to try filtering out the disgust. Finally, I opened my eyes, but the disquieting residue of anger and nausea hadn't gone away.

Turning from the framed letter, I saw that a bedroom lay at the end of the hall.

I heard Ralph ask Mallory as politely as he could where Timothy had gone this afternoon as I walked to the master bedroom and slipped inside.

22

Crumpled, raggy blankets were sprawled across the bed; a small nightstand sat nearby, holding a lamp and a used condom that looked like it was still sticky wet. There was a tragically torn, stuffed dog placed beside one of the pillows. I recalled Mallory's young age again and felt a renewed surge of revulsion and anger.

A mound of dirty laundry lay between the two dressers, one of which had a jewelry box on it, the other, a photo of a man, a woman, and a curly-haired little girl at Disney World, a price tag hanging from the corner. A small, surprisingly ornate handheld mirror rested on the dresser next to the jewelry box. A musky, rangy scent permeated the room.

The closet was beside the window.

I left the catalog on the bed for the moment, glanced beneath it, peeked in the drawers, and then in the jewelry box, where I found nothing particularly unusual, except an enigmatic diamond ring that, based on the condition of the house, I could hardly believe they could afford to own.

Crossing the room, I opened the closet door and tugged the string hanging from the ceiling to turn on the overhead bulb.

On the right, eleven shirts hung from wire hangers. Griffin was into flannel. Based on the size of the shirts, I anticipated that he would be small-framed, shorter than I was, maybe five feet six to five feet eight. No dress shirts or slacks. Nothing stylish. A blaze orange jacket for rifle season, a camo one for bow season.

On the left side of the closet, Mallory's four dresses looked like hand-me-downs or thrift store ware. Just four dresses. That was it. No shirts. No skirts. No dress pants.

I had no idea what Griffin's profit margin was on his merchandise, but taking into account the price tags of some of the items, I couldn't help but wonder where all the money was going. Definitely not into his or Mallory's wardrobe or home improvements. Maybe that ring.

Six pairs of shoes on the floor—four of his, two of hers. I checked. He was size nine. She was size six and a half.

Next to the shoes was a stack of three shoeboxes. I opened the top one and found that it was filled with sales receipts. Hundreds of them. I checked the other two boxes and found more of the same, some of them dating back eighteen years.

As I shuffled through the receipts, I found that they were carefully categorized, not by the date of sale, but by the first letter of the last name of the person who'd purchased the merchandise.

To make it easier to keep track of repeat customers?
Possibly.

I processed what we knew, the gossamer threads of facts and clues, the disquieting questions before us.

Vincent Hayes. The timing of his wife's abduction.

The homicide in Illinois and the police tape.

Griffin's catalog.

The handcuffs.

The abductor knew they owned a pair.

Everything in this case was somehow woven together.

Griffin referred to the guy as a Maneater.

Someone had provided this guy with the police tape from the crime in Illinois.

Someone is—

There's no such thing as a coincidence.

I had a thought and flipped to the *H*'s.

And found what I was looking for.

The name on the receipt: Hayes.

The merchandise: a pair of handcuffs.

But it wasn't Vincent Hayes's name on the top of the receipt. It was his wife, Colleen's.

23

I stared at the receipt.

Colleen Hayes had bought the handcuffs two months ago and, according to the receipt, they were the ones used on Ted Oswald when he and his father were arrested back in April 1994.

Ted, who was eighteen at the time, and his father, James, were responsible for a string of bank robberies in southeastern Wisconsin. When they were confronted by James Lutz, a Waukesha police captain, they killed him, took a hostage, and after a shoot-out with authorities during which the hostage managed to escape, they tried to flee by motor vehicle but were pursued by the Waukesha County Sheriff Department deputies. After crashing into a tree, they were apprehended, tried, found guilty.

During the trial, details emerged about their conspiratorial plans to kill law enforcement officers and initiate some sort of private war against the authorities. Ever since Ted had been five years old, his mentally disturbed father, who called him his "spawn," had threatened to kill him if he didn't do exactly as he said. During the trial, Ted claimed he'd committed the crimes only because he was afraid for his life, but the jury didn't go for it. Currently both men were serving two life sentences plus more than four hundred fifty years.

Jeffrey Dahmer tried for the insanity defense, didn't convince the jury.

Ted Oswald pled coercion, didn't convince the jury.

I processed that. Even if it was only tangential, both of those killers had a connection to this case. Both had admitted to their crimes during their respective trials but had claimed mitigating circumstances—Dahmer, mental instability; Oswald, fear for his life.

Neither had been successful.

Insanity is a legal term, not a medical one, and I knew that if it can be determined that you could understand the difference between right and wrong at the time of your crime, legally, you can't be found to be insane.

This was actually why Dahmer lost his case—he took an action to cover up his crimes; namely, he lied to the police when they brought Konerak Sinthasomphone back to his apartment. The jury believed that this showed Dahmer knew he'd acted in ways that needed to be concealed.

Strange as it may seem, if he would've led the police right up to the body on his bed he might have been found insane and never gone to prison at all.

Still, I couldn't help but wonder what, if any, circumstances remove your responsibility for criminal behavior. At what point are you so mentally ill that you're no longer responsible for your actions? Are you ever justified in committing murder to avoid being murdered yourself, as Ted Oswald claimed he'd been? Are you vindicated of kidnapping someone in order to save your wife, as Vincent Hayes had evidently done?

All pertinent questions, but I didn't have a lot of time here to contemplate them.

Address them later.

On the receipt, I noticed that Griffin had acquired the cuffs from an unnamed source; however, if they were legit, only someone from the Waukesha County Sheriff Department would've had access to them.

Definitely worth checking out.

This was the only purchase made by Colleen or Vincent Hayes.

Down the hall, I heard the front door bang open and a high-pitched nasally voice calling out, "Whose car is that out—" He cut himself off in the middle. He must have seen Ralph. "Who are you? What are you doing in my house!"

I memorized the information on the receipt and replaced it in the shoebox.

"Ralph Hawkins. I'm with the FBI. Are you Timothy Griffin?"

Taking the catalog with me, I returned to the living room.

Griffin was just shy of five feet eight. Caucasian with some Latino heritage. He had slate gray eyes and a harsh scar on his neck that tightened the skin of his face, tugging the left side of his lip down into a rather imposing sneer. He was holding a handful of mail.

"FBI?" he said. "What's going on?"

"I'm Detective Bowers," I told Griffin, before he could ask. "We have a couple questions we'd like to ask you."

24

Griffin licked his lips, then said with fake gentility, "Well, are you here on business . . ." His gaze landed on the Manson Bible. Now I saw that after picking it up earlier I hadn't placed it in exactly the same position on the coffee table and he seemed to notice that as well. "Or pleasure? Here to make a few purchases? I get a lot of cops as customers."

I held up the catalog, back cover toward him, and pointed to the sticker. "We're here concerning this."

"Uh-huh."

"The crime scene tape. I'd like to see it," Ralph said.

Griffin looked like he might object to that, but then walked into the kitchen and returned with a roll of yellow caution tape. Without a word he handed it to Ralph. "Three hundred fifty dollars. Like it says in the catalog."

"'The Maneater of the Midwest,'" Ralph said. "That a description you came up with?"

"Uh-huh."

"Helps with sales, does it? Using a name like that?"

"Actually, yes, it does." He paused. "Even though it's only women so far. I'm using 'Maneater' in the general sense of the word. You understand." He gave us a contemptuous grin and I was tempted to smack it off his face.

Mallory left soundlessly to return Ralph's empty coffee cup to the kitchen, leaving the three of us alone. After a moment I heard the soft clink of dishes in the sink.

"What makes you think this killer eats human flesh?" I asked Griffin.

"The woman's lungs were gone."

"And?"

He scoffed lightly. "Let's just say I've been in this business long enough to make an educated guess. Certain types of killers have certain types of . . . well, tastes."

"The description says, 'soon to be a collector's item.' Why is that?"

"Oh, I don't think he's done. Not a guy like this. He's just getting started."

Ralph worked his jaw back and forth roughly. "Where did you get this police tape, Mr. Griffin?"

"Don't worry, it's authentic." He looked from Ralph to me. "I can cut you a deal if you want."

"That won't be necessary." Ralph pocketed the tape and it was clear he wasn't about to pay three hundred fifty dollars for it, wasn't about to cut a deal of any kind. "As I was saying, where did you get the crime scene tape?"

"I have a source."

"Who?"

"I think he would be averse to having me pass along his name." When he said the phrase "averse to," it seemed way too literary and refined to be coming from his mouth.

We waited.

He said nothing more.

From my experience, it's better not to hammer away at the person you're interviewing. That tends to make him defensive, but circling back around often catches him off guard.

"How do you know a woman named Colleen Hayes?" I asked Griffin.

He shook his head. "Hayes?" But then he appeared to piece things together. "You mean from the news? From last night?" Honestly, it didn't look like he realized this was the same Hayes family he'd done business with.

That was two months ago, Pat. Would he really remember? Unless—

"That's right," Ralph said. "From last night."

A shadow of unease was edging across Griffin's face. "What is this about, anyway? I haven't done anything wrong."

Ralph pressed him: "Where were you last night, Timothy? From, say, seven o'clock to midnight?"

"Here, watching movies."

"Were you alone?"

Griffin called to the kitchen, "Mallory!" His tone was brash and spiteful, and I got the sense that it was the typical way he addressed his live-in girlfriend, the one who was thirty years younger than he was.

She came around the corner, clutching a damp hand towel, eyes wide.

"Last night we were here watching movies, weren't we?" He paused. "Baby?"

"Yes." Her gaze never left him, never wandered our way, a sign that she was taking her cues from him.

Timothy gave us a satisfied smile. "See?"

"What movies did you watch?" Ralph directed the question at Mallory.

Griffin spoke up: "*The Fugitive* and—"

"I was asking the young lady," Ralph told him firmly.

"*The Fugitive*," she answered.

"And?"

She looked a bit lost. "And . . . *When Harry Met Sally.*" She stared at Griffin as if she was looking for approval from him.

"That's right, baby." Then he turned one hand palm up, as if to signify that she'd just cleared up everything, and when he spoke he addressed Ralph and me: "Well, then, there you go." He wavered the envelopes in the air with his other hand. "Now, if you gentlemen don't mind. Orders to fill. I'm sure you understand. Keep the tape. It's the least I can do. My civic duty."

I didn't think we were going to get much more out of him at the moment, but I didn't want to leave without the name of the person he'd gotten that crime scene tape from.

Ralph didn't move. Obviously he wasn't ready to leave yet either. "How do you do this, anyway?"

"This?"

"Sell this crap." He swept his hand through the air. "Make a living like this?"

With a slight dramatic flair, Griffin walked to the wall and put his palm against one of the photos, then slowly stroked the face and then the body of the woman in the picture. The hairstyle and clothes made me think it was taken in the late seventies. I didn't know who she was, but I memorized her face, and wondered what Mallory, who was still in the doorway, thought of the provocative way he let his fingers address the body of the photographed woman.

"Think about the news, Agent Hawkins. TV networks sell time to advertisers, then air footage of the most sensational crimes they can. You know it's true: If it bleeds, it leads. Like with Hayes last night. Advertisers buy that airtime, knowing full well what they're doing—playing off people's fixation with violence, evil, death. I just pass along my reminders to individuals rather than to the public at large."

People have a right to be informed about our world, and it is a brutal one, but it bothered me that Griffin actually had a point. News shows really are packaged to play to their viewers' morbid fascination with death.

Ralph said, "Mr. Griffin, what's the name of the person who sold you the crime scene tape?"

"I told you he—"

But Ralph strode toward him, invaded his personal space big-time. The air in the room seemed to tighten. "The name, Mr. Griffin." I thought Ralph might growl the words menacingly in order to be more intimidating, but he didn't. He just said them calmly, resolutely, and that seemed to be more effective because Griffin gulped almost imperceptibly, then tapped his tongue to the side of his lips.

"His name is Hendrich. Okay? Bruce Hendrich. I don't know if that's his real name or not. That's the one he gave me. In this business people aren't always as forthcoming and honest as they should be. I'm sure you know what I mean."

Ralph reached over and straightened Griffin's collar. "How do you reach him? This Mr. Hendrich?"

Having Ralph's huge hands so close to his throat seemed to make Griffin even more willing to share information, because he rather promptly told us a phone number and address from memory. The address was in Milwaukee, not Fort Atkinson.

"I just ship stuff there. I've never been there."

Ralph patted him on the shoulder. "Thank you, Timothy." Then he handed him one of his business cards. "If anyone tries to buy or sell any Dahmer items, let us know. And we're going to want the name of anyone who goes after that police tape."

"My records are confidential."

"Of course they are. But your address isn't. Wait till we notify the family members of victims about your little business venture here. I wonder how many of them might want to pay you a visit. Express how excited they are about you passing along your little 'reminders.'"

He turned to me. "We could give 'em some privacy, couldn't we, Detective? Make arrangements to make sure no officers interfere with the little block party?"

"That shouldn't be a problem." Since Griffin's business was run out of a post office box, releasing his residential address really might cause a bit of a stir with the neighbors and victims' family members.

When Griffin didn't reply, Ralph reflectively patted the top of one of the overstuffed chairs. "I may show up too. Bring the mini-weenies. I always like a good party."

"Okay," Timothy grumbled. "Alright. I'll call you if I hear anything."

"I appreciate that very much, Mr. Griffin."

Ralph nodded toward Mallory. "Good day, ma'am."

Once we were back in the car I said to Ralph, "Mini-weenies?"

"They're good with mustard and ranch dressing. What did you see in the hall?"

"The Albert Fish letter, but it's what I found in the bedroom that really caught my attention."

"And that was?"

I started the car. "Griffin sold Hayes the handcuffs. Colleen Hayes."

"Colleen?"

"Yes."

"Interesting. And how do we know that?"

I told him about the receipts. Ralph wasn't familiar with the Oswald case. I filled him in on what I knew.

Then, since there wasn't a car phone in this vehicle, I radioed the local dispatcher and asked her to put a call through to my adviser at Marquette and let him know I wouldn't be at the lecture this afternoon and to see if he could request that Dr. Werjonic leave a photocopy of his lecture notes in the Criminology and Law Studies graduate office. I could pick them up later this evening and hopefully carve out some time to review them before tomorrow's class. I gave her the number.

When I got off the radio I had an idea. "Ralph, the Waukesha County Sheriff Department is just a couple miles off the interstate. What do you say we swing by and see who the arresting officers were in the Oswald case?"

"Yeah, and maybe check the chain of custody for the evidence. Whoever had access to the Oswald evidence might have had access to the cuffs."

I aimed the car for the highway. "I like the way you think, Agent Hawkins. For a fed, that is."

"You're doing alright yourself, for a detective. At least so far."

"So far?"

"Yeah, but just don't get in my way."

It sounded like he was joking, I knew he was joking, but when I glanced at him, I realized I couldn't quite tell. Not for sure.

25

Plainfield, Wisconsin

It wasn't even a choice for Carl Kowalski. Not after finding that note in his kitchen. Not after seeing the horrible, horrible thing that Adele's kidnapper had left for him in the refrigerator.

At first when he walked through the front door and saw the note on the table, he'd thought it might be some kind of sick joke from one of his poker buddies.

But then he'd done what the note told him to do and looked in the refrigerator's meat/cheese drawer and found Adele's ring finger with the engagement ring he'd given her four months earlier still encircling the base of it. No. This was not a joke. Not by any stretch of the imagination.

Now he carefully positioned his van on the cemetery's access road to hide his activity from people who might happen to drive past on the nearby but infrequently used county highway. Then, shielded from view, he removed the shovel from the back of the vehicle.

It wasn't a large graveyard and wasn't visited often. He knew this since he was the one who mowed it on weekends. There was really very little chance that he would be interrupted, but if someone did happen to visit, he figured that since he worked the grounds, he'd at least be able to come up with an explanation for why he had the shovel.

But why he was digging up the grave of Miriam Flandry, that was another story entirely. No reasonable explanation for that came to mind.

Well, just get it over with quickly and you won't have to worry about it.

Carl walked to the fresh grave.

The note had been clear: Dig up Miriam's corpse. Skin it. Then leave it outside the hardware store where Gein had killed Bernice Worden back in 1957. Even though Carl hadn't been born at the time, he knew the story, knew what had happened there. Everyone in Plainfield knew the story.

According to the note, if he didn't do as requested, the person who'd taken Adele was going to skin *her* alive and leave her corpse on Carl's porch. Whoever was doing this—or why anyone would dream up something so gruesome—was a mystery to Carl. A dark, blank, terrible mystery.

But he could try to figure that out later. Right now he had to get to work.

He drove the shovel into the loose soil, dumped it to the side.

If only it didn't have to be Miriam. But that's what the note said—it had to be her.

She'd been eighty-one years old when she passed away two days ago. Carl, of course, had been at the funeral.

And yes, he knew that now he was desecrating her final resting place, but he told himself that the dead were dead, that you couldn't really desecrate them, not really. Their souls had gone on to another place. Bones and hair and decaying meat were all that was left.

It sounded crass and unsympathetic, but skinning a corpse was essentially no different than skinning a squirrel, gutting a deer, or carving a turkey. Embalmers and medical examiners did that kind of work on human cadavers all the time.

That's what Carl told himself.

But still, the thought of peeling the skin off a body that used to be a living, breathing human being with dreams and hopes and heartaches just like him was gut-wrenching. Especially considering who Miriam was, what she had meant to him over the years.

However, the thought of someone doing that to Adele while she was alive was even more horrifying and Carl vowed he was not going to let that happen.

The shoveling was going quickly, faster than he would've ever expected, which was good because according to the note, he had until five o'clock—exactly—to dig up the corpse, remove its skin, deliver it to the hardware store and call the kidnapper.

That didn't give him a lot of time, but the dirt wasn't packed down yet and, after working on a construction crew for the last ten years, he was used to hard physical labor. He would work as furiously as he had to in order to save Adele.

He threw another shovelful of dirt aside.

Then another.

It shouldn't be too long before he had her, and after he did, it wasn't far to the hardware store, so the only thing that might really slow him down was the skinning part. He needed to come up with a way to do that quickly.

So that's what he thought about as he dug up his recently deceased grandmother's body.

26

Ralph and I entered the Waukesha County Sheriff Department, which was located in an imposing, interconnected set of buildings that also housed the county courthouse and jail.

We were directed to a graying, portly detective in his early fifties who had a noticeable crescent-shaped birthmark on the right side of his neck. The photos on his desk showed him serving in several different police departments around Wisconsin over the years.

After taking a seat in front of his desk, we told him what we were looking for and why.

"So you think one of our deputies stole those cuffs and then sold them to Griffin?" Detective Browning said to me coolly.

"No, I don't. We're just trying to investigate how the cuffs, if they are legitimate, ended up in the hands of a man who sells memorabilia of serial killers."

"Uh-huh." But Browning still seemed antagonistic. It took Ralph's telling him that we would get the information one way or another, with his help or without it, before he grudgingly produced the paperwork showing who was involved in the Oswalds' arrest.

When I thanked him, he made it clear once again that he thought we were being out of line.

His hostile attitude surprised me. In the end I chalked it up to the fact that I had an FBI agent with me. To say there can be tension over interagency information requests is, unfortunately, a gross understatement.

Before Ralph and I left the building, we also picked up a copy of the chain of custody forms and evidence room visitation records for the Oswald case. There was so much evidence gathered against the father and son team—including parts of the van they were driving when they tried to flee, the cache of rifles they'd collected, thousands of rounds of ammunition, reams of paperwork and James's voluminous journals—that the number of items listed on the forms was substantial.

Material in hand, we cruised back to the interstate and headed for HQ.

+ + +

Milwaukee, Wisconsin

Joshua parked in the overgrown, empty lot just west of the deserted train yard.

Milwaukee used to be a major industrial railway shipping hub. To some extent it still was, but times change and trains weren't being used nearly as much as they had been twenty or thirty years ago.

A metal chain-link fence with wickedly sharp razor wire curling across the top of it ran along the entire perimeter of the train yard. However, there was a swinging gate here in the parking lot that was large enough for a car to pass through. Two sets of railroad tracks also entered beneath the fence, and then branched off in the yard into the nineteen dead-end tracks that held the abandoned cars.

Apart from a small crawl-hole in the fence that bordered the woods, this gate was the only way to access the yard.

Two days ago Joshua had cut through the chain that held the gate shut, then padlocked it closed again with his own lock and chain. His lock was still there, so obviously, no one had noticed, and that hadn't surprised him. This was not exactly a tourist hotspot.

The tracks that terminated in the yard were rusted and overgrown with scraggly weeds that broke through the thin, sporadic layer of snow. Dozens of boxcars, coal cars, tankers, and a few engines and cabooses that'd been retired from service sat languishing in the yard. With the rails in such disrepair, these cars weren't going anywhere any time soon.

Apparently, when a train car gets retired, there aren't a whole lot of places to leave it, and over the last twenty years, more and more cars from the Milwaukee Road, Wisconsin Central, and Soo Line railways had been abandoned here and left to the mercy of weather and time.

Wearing gloves so that he wouldn't leave any fingerprints, Joshua unlocked the gate, swung it open, drove toward the tracks containing the abandoned boxcars, then closed and padlocked the gate behind him.

He wouldn't be able to drive all the way to the boxcar that he would be using today, but he could get partway there, and then park out of sight behind a line of tankers.

Which was what he did.

Carrying Adele to the train car he'd prepared for this

afternoon wouldn't be a problem. A forest nudged up against the razor wire fence on the south end of the train yard and there was only a narrow channel between that fence and the line of boxcars stretching alongside it.

When he'd been scouting out locations, Joshua had driven around the neighborhood and confirmed that—even from the highway, the bridge just west of here, and the parking lot itself—a person walking along the edge of the fence would be hidden from view by the boxcars on one side and the woods on the other. Especially if they stayed in the drainage ditch that followed one section of the fence.

Of all the times Joshua had been in the yard, he'd seen only five people in here: two teen punks with spray cans, a wino, and a college-aged couple making out. But all of them had been on the other side of the yard near the coal cars.

Still, this was not the time to be careless, and before taking Adele to the boxcar, he wanted to make sure the coast was clear. So, leaving her locked in the trunk for the moment, he took his pistol, a 9mm Glock 19, from the glove box and walked along the edge of the ditch paralleling the razor wire fence.

Most of the cars in the yard had gang-related graffiti spray-painted on the sides and nearly all of them were ravaged with rust. The boxcars had large sliding doors, many of which were padlocked shut, a few were left open, some were missing entirely.

He went to a light gray Soo Line boxcar with a chained-shut door, slipped a key into the lock, which he'd made sure was the same kind he'd used on the front gate, and clicked it open.

Gloves still on, he cranked the door open, peered inside.

His materials were all there waiting for Adele. The rope and duct tape. The chair. The plastic bags, butcher paper, and heavy-duty plastic ties. The battery-operated light on the wall to the left. And the Civil War–era Gem-rig amputation saw that he had used to cut through Colleen Hayes's wrists last night.

He already had the necrotome with him in a sheath on his belt. The word meant "cutting instrument of the dead" and it was an Egyptian knife popular between 1500 and 1000 BC.

Necrotomes are, of course, extremely rare, but he'd managed to get this one at an auction in San Francisco five years ago. It was one of the actual knives used by the priests of ancient Egypt to slit open the abdomens of the people they were about to mummify in order to remove their inner organs. They did so by hand, pulling out all the organs except for the heart. Then they stored those organs in jars—all of them except for the brain, which they considered useless, and simply discarded.

Joshua kept the necrotome with him at all times.

He'd used it last Friday on Petey Schwartz when the homeless man followed him, then grabbed his jacket collar. Joshua had met Petey before, knew him in an informal way, and knew that he had violent tendencies. In an instant he'd whipped out the necrotome and buried it into Petey's stomach, just as his father had taught him to do with that hunting knife in the special place beneath the barn.

It'd all happened so fast that it was hard to differentiate one action from the next. It'd been impulse, pure and simple. Instinct. And now a man was dead.

He knew the verse, knew what killing would mean: "No murderer hath eternal life abiding in him." First John, chapter three, verse fifteen.

No eternal life.

But yet he desired eternal life. Believed in grace, in forgiveness, in atonement.

His life was a throbbing contradiction. Just like St. Paul, who wrote in Romans, chapter seven, "What I would, that do I not; but what I hate, that do I. For to will is present with me; but how to perform that which is good I find not. For the good that I would I do not: but the evil which I would not, that I do."

The evil which I would not.

That I do.

I do.

After making sure the coast was clear, Joshua returned to the car to retrieve the unconscious woman from the trunk.

27

The afternoon was stretching thin.

As I drove, Ralph scribbled notes on his pad and collected his thoughts. "So, Griffin could have known that the Hayes couple had their own cuffs. That puts him on our short list."

"Yes, but according to Colleen's description, her abductor was a large man; Griffin has a slight build."

He processed that. "True."

"Also, when I brought up Hayes's name, Griffin didn't seem familiar with it."

Ralph certainly knew, as I did, that killers are often accomplished liars, but even for them, first impressions are hard to fake. Often, our faces betray us before our minds can start coming up with ways to hide what our bodies have already subconsciously expressed.

"But, Pat, he has to be related to this somehow. He might not be at the center of it, but his connection with the crime scene tape and the cuffs is too much of a coincidence. They tie him to both the murder in Illinois and Colleen's abduction last night. Besides, he called Hendrich 'a source,' and mentioned he'd shipped 'stuff' to him. Is that how you'd phrase things if you'd only worked with the guy once?"

"I see what you mean," I admitted, "but both the cuffs and police tape could have come from a cop—there's no saying the police tape came from the killer."

"We need to find out more about Hendrich."

"Yes, we do," I said. "And cross-reference the names on the evidence room forms and the chain of custody list against the officers who worked the case in Illinois. An officer may have moved from—"

"Waukesha to Champaign."

"Yes."

While we'd been driving, Thorne had sent Lyrie to Hendrich's home address, but we hadn't heard from him yet whether he'd found out anything from him.

I said to Ralph, "It looks like we have a few things to follow up on." I ticked them off on my fingers as I exited the highway to get to HQ: "Check that police tape for prints, locate Bruce Hendrich, look into the people at the Waukesha sheriff's department who had access to the Oswald handcuffs, and find out how Colleen Hayes came to contact Timothy Griffin in the first place. Oh yeah, it'd be good to check the nearest video store to see if Timothy and Mallory rented *The Fugitive* and *When Harry Met Sally*."

"You think they made that up?"

"Those two videos weren't among the twelve in their living room, not by the TV or on the shelves. That points to renting them. People like to save time, money, and effort, so they most often shop, get gas, and rent videos from the grocery stores, service stations, and video stores closest to their homes. We should start there, see if they're customers."

"Good call."

"I think we have enough to get a warrant to look through Griffin's receipts, see what else Hendrich might have sold him."

"Or bought from him."

I nodded. "Also, we should get the warrant to cover Griffin's subscription list so we can cross-check the people who get his catalog against our suspect list and tip list."

"Nice." He jotted a few more notes.

I gave him an inventory of the items that were in the living room and included the photo that had a price tag on it in the bedroom. "Have them compare that list to the items on the receipts that he hasn't sold yet. And to the catalog."

"Did you write down that stuff when you were in the bedroom?"

"No."

"You just listed like four dozen different things. You're saying you remembered them?"

"Yes."

"All of them?"

"Yes. Why?"

He blinked. "Just checking."

I felt the juices flowing. Admittedly, we still had more questions than answers, but a slowly emerging web of interrelationships was beginning to form. I mentally unwound and then rewound them, exploring the possibilities, evaluating the implications. Even though I couldn't pin down anything solid yet, it felt good to have enough facts to be able to start sorting through them, searching for a pattern.

"How many do you think are women?" Ralph said, drawing me out of my thoughts.

"Who?"

"The people who buy that stuff from Griffin, you know, like Colleen. I mean, on the one hand you've got the revulsion most women feel toward violence, but on the other hand some ladies get off on that kind of stuff, on killers, you know, the lost boys—want to be their pen pals in prison, marry them when they get out, that sort of thing."

Since males are generally more interested in crime and, in fact, much more inclined to commit violent acts than women, I expected that most of Griffin's customers would be men. After all, ninety-five percent of the people in the prisons of the world are men—closer to ninety-eight percent if you look just at violent acts. Blame it on genetics, trace it back to upbringing, whatever it is, there's no arguing that men corner the market on crime, especially cruel and brutal ones. "It'll be interesting to see how it breaks down," I acknowledged.

"How far to the department?"

"A couple minutes."

Ralph turned to the dispatch radio. "I'll call this stuff in, get Ellen on the search warrant. If there's one thing the Bureau is good at, it's expediting search warrant requests."

At least that's one thing, I thought.

"I could make some sort of smart comment about that," I said, "but I'll refrain."

"I'm counting that as a smart comment, Tonto."

"Wasn't Tonto just the sidekick?"

"Yeah." A tiny smile. "He was."

28

Carl took Miriam's corpse to the maintenance building to skin it.

He laid it on the concrete floor and, as disturbing as this act was, started his work.

Almost immediately however, he discovered that it was too difficult to keep a firm grip on the body while he maneuvered his knife to strip off the flesh. In the 1950s, Gein had hung the corpse of his victim to do it, and that made a certain amount of macabre sense.

If he could use gravity to his advantage, it'd be a lot easier, go a lot quicker. He searched the shelves, found a chain, looped it over one of the rafters, and then under the arms and around the chest of the corpse, hoisted it into the air, and set to work.

+ + +

As Joshua stood beside the trunk of the sedan, he thought about last night and how it related to what was going to happen here in the train yards tonight.

Last evening he'd slipped in the back door of Vincent and Colleen's home even while Colleen was inside the house. He was in the kitchen closet, in fact, watching her through the slightly cracked-open door when she got the call from her husband telling her he was going to be late.

Joshua had heard her side of the conversation and that'd offered him both a problem and an opportunity.

"So, I'll see you about ten, then?" Colleen had said. Then, "Love you too. Bye."

Just knowing that he was there alone with Colleen was, admittedly, exhilarating. There was no longer any urgency to move on her.

Joshua had decided to wait and watch her and take her at nine.

His day job called for him to have a police scanner, so last night after he had Colleen, he'd used it to listen to the chatter regarding the chase for Vincent. Amidst the confusion, an officer had reported that he had the suspect in custody, but not long after that he announced that he was still at large.

So then, when Joshua's portable phone rang, he hadn't been sure if the person on the other end who was assuring him that he'd left a black man in the alley was Vincent or not. With all the sirens and all the chatter on the dispatch radio, he'd suspected it might be a cop.

Today he wasn't going to take any chances. He was going to get started on Adele before five, before Carl was scheduled to make the call.

He lifted her, still unconscious, from the trunk, then nudged the hatch closed with his elbow.

Last night, Colleen Hayes.

Tonight, Adele Westin.

And it was going to be even better than it had been with Colleen.

Trudging across the gravel, he carried his captive toward the boxcar.

29

We were almost to HQ when we heard from Corsica that Bruce Hendrich worked a couple days a week as a security guard in the abandoned train yards just off I-94 near the Domes.

I thought of the location of the yards. I'd driven past them dozens of times, but they were encircled with razor wire fence and I'd never entered them. The surrounding neighborhoods were infested with gangs, drug dealers, and junkies. You'd have to be either pretty bold or pretty stupid to work a part-time security job in that part of town.

Unless you just wanted a place where you could take people in the dark and not arouse suspicion.

I mentally reviewed the most likely travel routes from the Hayes residence to the yards. Unless the kidnapper took an unusually circuitous route, he would have had to pass by Miller Brewery to get there, which could explain the yeast smell that Colleen remembered.

My thoughts slipped back to the account of the tree house I'd given to Ralph earlier: *If someone knew the area, he would know where to take a girl. A place he could be alone with her.*

Different killers, same need: seclusion. The tree house made sense and so did the train yards.

There weren't any trains running through there these days, so it made sense that Colleen wouldn't have heard one pass by. The location was isolated enough so that, if her abductor had taken her to one of the freight cars or boxcars, no one would've heard her scream. Colleen had mentioned that it was cold, as though he might have taken her to a garage or something. A boxcar fit that too.

If he took her to the train yards, he would have plenty of privacy to do just about anything he wanted with her. And even if, by some chance, someone did happen to hear her scream, the yards weren't in a part of town where people were particularly inclined to call the authorities.

Before she ended the transmission, Corsica mentioned that Hendrich hadn't been home when Lyrie arrived to speak with him and it'd taken him a while to find out from a neighbor where Hendrich worked. Apparently, he was new to the area and wasn't that well-known by his neighbors. She mentioned that the team was looking more carefully into his background.

I resaddled the radio. "Ralph, let's stop by the train yards. Have a look around before it gets dark."

"Now you're talking my language."

To cover our bases, we called in to have Lyrie remain parked at Hendrich's house in case he returned home, then I turned our car around.

Sundown was almost here and I felt as if I were stepping into the zone again, the thing I live for, and I admit I didn't quite observe the speed limit as I drove toward the train yards.

+ + +

Joshua slid the unconscious woman into the boxcar, then promptly clicked on the battery-operated light, shut the door, and locked it from the inside.

He tied Adele to the chair.

Blond hair, a sea green sweater, black jeans. He decided to leave her clothes on while he worked on her. That way, when they found her without her hands or feet, the blood-drenched clothes would add to the dramatic effect. Increase the shock value.

Or maybe not. Maybe leaving her nude would shock them more.

Well, that was certainly something to consider.

Earlier he'd propped ten mattresses against the walls of the boxcar to absorb the sounds. Now, every time he took a step, there was only a tiny muffled echo from the wooden floorboards, an echo that was quickly devoured by the improvised baffling.

Adele was beginning to stir, but it would still take her a few minutes to wake up.

Next order of business, his clothes.

He knew it would be shockingly cold if he were to stand here naked himself, but he'd found out last night with Colleen Hayes that, even with the plastic ties around her wrists, there was still a lot of blood. Tonight he didn't want any of it getting on his clothes, so after one more moment of mental preparation, he removed his shoes, stripped off his clothes and placed them in one of the plastic bags, then tucked the bag in the corner of the boxcar.

Actually, he thought the chilled air might add to the

excitement of what he was doing. Sharpen his awareness. Heighten the experience.

Adele was blindfolded and that was important to Joshua. No woman other than his wife had ever seen him naked and he didn't want that to change tonight.

Barefoot now, and unclothed, he walked to the mattress he'd left the amputation saw on top of yesterday. Caught up in his thoughts, he absentmindedly stroked the blade for a moment. Yes, he was anxious to get started, but he wanted Adele to be fully awake and aware, like Colleen had been last night, before he cut off any of her extremities.

At last, leaving the saw there for the moment, he faced Adele, and naked, apart from the latex gloves he wore on his hands, he watched her as she slowly began to awaken.

30

I parked beside the train yard.

Somewhere nearby there was supposed to be an access road to the yard's parking lot, but I wasn't familiar with the labyrinthine roads in this neighborhood, nor was I in the mood to drive around trying to figure out where to go. I decided Ralph and I could find a quicker way past the fence.

Looking at the rusted condition of most of the train cars, I was struck by a thought: this wasn't just a train yard, it was a train graveyard.

I put that thought out of my mind: "graveyard" was not a term I wanted bouncing around inside my head at the moment.

The sun had dipped to the skyline, leaving the whole yard draped in one long sweeping shadow. Though the snow had stopped, the wind was picking up and scraped at my face as we exited the undercover car. I zipped up my leather jacket.

Ralph stood beside me, scrutinizing the area. The wind caught hold of his jacket and pressed it against his hulking chest, making it look like a dark, rippling second skin.

"How do you want to do this?" he asked me.

"How about I take the south side, you take the north?"

"So," he said, "besides Hendrich, what exactly are we looking for again?"

"Bad guys. Bodies. Clues."

"The usual."

"Right."

I dug through the contents of the sedan's trunk and came up with a hefty, heavy-duty Maglite flashlight. If I needed to take a closer look inside any of the train cars, this puppy would definitely do the trick.

Ralph eyed it. "You think that thing's big enough?"

I passed it from hand to hand, gauged the weight. "It can double as a club if I need it to."

"It could double as a baseball bat," he muttered, "if you cut a few inches off the end."

Actually, I kind of liked it. "It's not that bad."

He showed me his Mini Maglite, not much larger than a Magic Marker. "You gotta get one of these Bad Boys."

"That's not exactly what I would call a 'Bad Boy.'"

He grunted slightly, then studied the razor wire fence that enclosed the train yard. "So how do we get in?"

When I took a closer look at the formidable security fence, I realized that was actually a pretty good question.

We could walk along the fence that skirted a field on the side of the yard and eventually get to the parking area, but it was likely that the gate was locked and there wasn't any less razor wire there than there was on the rest of the fence. It wasn't going to be easy to climb over that no matter where we went.

It seemed that, with all the graffiti on the train cars,

there must be an easier way in, somewhere local gang members would use to access the yard to mark their territory.

Quickly, I evaluated what I knew of the neighborhood, then pointed. "The woods. It's relatively close to the Crips' territory." I was about to tell him who the Crips were but then realized he'd already be familiar with the gang from his NCAVC work. "Sections of it wouldn't be visible from the road."

"It'd help hide the access point."

"Right. If there's a hole in the fence, I'm guessing it would be over there somewhere. That's where they'd come through. The kids who spray-paint all the train cars."

He nodded and, flashlights in hand, we crossed the road to look for a way in.

+ + +

Carl arrived at Main Street.

Plainfield hadn't grown much since the 1950s when Ed Gein lived here—it still had fewer than a thousand residents, and the street still consisted of only a small family-owned diner, an antique shop, two taverns, a church, and, of course, the hardware store. It was like an idyllic little midwestern Mayberry with a nightmare hiding in its closet.

Carl parked his van just down the street from Magnus's Hardware Store.

Even though he wanted to get that body out of his van, he still had a little time before he needed to make the call to the kidnapper and he wanted to stick as close as he could to the time frame the note had laid out for him.

Down the block, a few people stepped out of Schroeder's Diner. He recognized them all and he wondered what they would think of him if they knew what he'd just done, what he had in the back of his van.

But in the end, truthfully, none of that really mattered. He would be linked to all of this anyway and his friends would think what they would think. He had no control over that. Maybe they'd understand, maybe not, but what mattered right now was making sure his fiancée was safe.

Go. Get this over with. Drop off Miriam's body, call the number, get Adele back home, deal with the consequences later.

After one more moment of consideration, he drove to the tiny parking lot behind the hardware store, exited the van, walked around back, and removed his grandmother's skinless remains.

31

Adele was almost awake.

Joshua adjusted the light he'd attached to the wall so that it shone directly at her face. Of course she was still blind-folded, but this way it would give him the light he needed.

The temperature was dropping, sending waves of shivers through his body. But the touch of the crisp air, along with his adrenaline and the tightening expectancy turned the shivers into rivers of secret, deep thrills. He'd never used drugs, but he felt like he was experiencing some sort of high right now.

It was still a little while before he expected the call from Carl that the skinned corpse had been left at the hardware store in Plainfield, but, just as with Colleen last night, Joshua had something in mind for the woman in front of him that had nothing to do with the message he'd written in the note he left behind.

No, with both Carl and Vincent, Joshua hadn't been entirely forthright and honest about his intentions regarding the women they loved. But he justified the slight misrepresentation, the deceit, if you will, as necessary. Yesterday his goal had been to get the police and the news media thinking about Dahmer.

Today, Gein.

Tomorrow he would let the news sink in, and then on Wednesday, build to the final climax with the Oswalds.

Within forty-eight hours he would have the attention of everyone who mattered, and once that happened, he would finally take his place alongside the man he'd grown to so ardently admire.

Griffin would be the key to all of this. He'd be able to get him in touch with the Maneater—when the time was right. After all, he got the police tape from the homicide in Illinois. He had a source close to the crime.

Adele moaned weakly and Joshua's heartbeat quickened. This was really what it was all about, wasn't it? This feeling, this urge, this anticipation of the moment before it all begins.

Before.

It all.

Begins.

He fingered the four plastic ties and waited anxiously, anxiously, anxiously for her to be aware enough for the evening's proceedings to get under way.

+ + +

I found what I was looking for beside one of the metal posts supporting the chain-link fence.

A small section of the flexible fence material had been pulled loose. A drainage ditch ran alongside the fence here, and Ralph and I needed to scramble down to get to the makeshift opening, but after we did, I bent the loose section of fencing back to provide enough room for him to squeeze through.

It was a tight fit, but after he made it, I knew I could

too. I lay on my back, he tugged the edge of the fence up from his side, and I squirmed through to join him.

Ralph motioned toward his radio. "I'll keep this on. Talk to me if you find anything."

"Ditto."

We split up. He lumbered north toward the coal cars, I headed in the direction of the parking lot.

Considering the location of Hendrich's residence, he wouldn't have walked here from home. And taking into account the sparse public transportation routes in this part of town, I figured that if Bruce were here, he would have driven.

I hadn't seen any vehicles in the parking lot, but there might be one hidden here in the yard, behind some train cars. Given the orientation of the tracks, the best place for someone to hide one was near a string of tanker cars not far from the parking lot.

Keeping an eye out for anyone else already in the yard, I made my way toward the tankers to see if Hendrich's car might just be here.

32

Other than the low hum of late-afternoon traffic on I-94 and the crunch of the gravel underfoot, the train yard was quiet.

I saw no tire tracks or sole impressions on the uneven scrubbing of snow, although some stretches of the yard had only enough snow to fill in the space between the gravel, so it wouldn't have been possible to track prints very far anyway.

I was nearly to the tankers. I still hadn't seen a vehicle.

When I looked beneath the train cars, hoping to catch sight of a car's tires somewhere beyond them, the view was too obscured by a stretch of tall leaning grass on the other side to see much of anything.

Just as I was starting to think that this search for a vehicle might be a waste of time, I glimpsed what I was looking for. Only the hood at first, but as I proceeded, the rest of the sedan came into view.

A Ford Taurus.

I hustled toward it, felt the hood.

Still warm.

In this weather, that meant that whoever had driven it here had to have arrived recently and the engine must have been running for quite a while to get the hood that warm.

I didn't know if it was Hendrich's car or not, but in either case, unless there was a way out of the yard that Ralph and I didn't know about, someone else was in here with us.

I radioed in the plates as I jogged over and inspected the gate. The keyed padlock and chain were shiny and new.

Scrutinizing the train yard, I still saw no movement.

Even though a dusting of snow was kicked up around the car, there wasn't enough for me to determine which direction the driver might have gone after exiting the vehicle.

Mainly it was the snow behind the car that was trampled.

Last night Colleen's abductor transported her in the trunk of a sedan.

My heartbeat quickened.

He has someone, Pat. He's here.

I radioed Ralph and told him what I'd found.

Anticipating that whoever had left the car wouldn't have walked back toward the parking lot, but would've likely headed toward a boxcar or freight car where he could work unseen, I followed the path toward the string of boxcars, then kept going past the place where Ralph and I had entered beneath the fence.

Just to my left were the hulking, abandoned freight and boxcars. To my right, the ditch sloped down toward the perimeter fence and the darkening woods that spread out of sight.

Glancing around, I could tell that I'd been correct

earlier when I guessed that this area was well hidden from view.

Yeah, this would definitely be the place to bring someone.

I knelt and scanned the tracks again, looking for movement, for signs of anyone walking on the other side of the rusted and long-abandoned boxcars beside me.

Still nothing.

If someone exchanged that lock at the main gate, he might have exchanged others as well. Especially the one to the train car he's using. Look for new locks, Pat. New chains.

There were a lot of cars to check and I needed to inspect the sliding doors on both sides, but new locks narrowed things down. It was a place to start.

Ralph's voice came through my radio again: "Anything?"

"No. You?"

"Not yet. Where are you?"

"Near the fence," I told him, "a hundred meters east of the parking lot. I'm checking the boxcars."

"Roger that. Keep me posted."

"Ten-four."

Then I went back to work looking for bad guys. Bodies. Clues. The usual.

Or in this case, anything that might be unusual.

Like new locks on old boxcar doors.

33

Carl entered his friend Rennie Stillwells's tavern just down the street from the hardware store. Rennie wouldn't officially open until five, but all the guys from the Wednesday-night poker crew knew he was always there by three.

"Hey, Rennie."

Rennie looked up from the bar. He was the only one in the room. "Carl. Hey, how ya doin'?"

"Good. How 'bout you?"

He shrugged. "Could be worse."

"Listen, do you mind if I use your phone, there?"

Without a word, Rennie set it on the bar. Slid it toward Carl.

"Um . . . you know . . . It's a bit personal . . . Has to do with Adele."

"Gotcha." Rennie winked as if he understood completely. "Help yourself. I gotta use the john anyway."

He stepped away and Carl turned the phone so the numbers faced him, then he pulled out the note that Adele's kidnapper had left for him, and spread it across the counter. The number: 888-359-5392.

He'd done as the note directed and the body was there

at the hardware store. In a sense, the ransom had been paid.

Call the number, Carl. So what if it's a few minutes early.

Thinking about Adele being with this man was just too terrifying for him to wait.

Sweating, his hand shaking noticeably as he tapped in the number, he held the receiver to his ear and waited while it rang.

No one picked up.

With each passing second he became more and more nervous, more afraid.

The note said to call this number, that she would be okay if you did!

But another voice: *No, you called early! You didn't wait!*

Still no one answered.

Then Carl heard police sirens and realized that someone must have already found Miriam Flandry's corpse and called the station, which was less than a mile away.

And all he could think of was why the man who'd taken Adele, who'd already severed off at least one of her fingers, wasn't answering.

And what he might be doing to her instead.

34

Joshua drew the heavy-duty zip tie taut around Adele's left wrist. She was awake now, still blindfolded, but she could obviously tell that she was restrained to the chair and that he was putting something around her wrist. She tried valiantly to pull free. "What are you doing?" Her voice was constricted and tight with concern, and Joshua had to admit to himself that he kind of liked that.

He thought that maybe it would be more frightening to her if he remained quiet. So instead of replying, he just cinched the second tie around her right wrist, tugging it tight enough to cut off the circulation to her hand.

"Ouch!" She winced. "Who are you! Stop it!"

When he still said nothing, she cried out louder, squirming to get free, and it reminded him of the way Colleen had acted the night before. It even reminded him of his first trip into the special place beneath the barn with his father, when that man named Kenneth who was shackled to the boards holding up the cellar's earthen walls, had tried so desperately but in the end, futilely, to escape.

"What do you want!" Adele screamed. The words thrummed for a moment inside the boxcar then the mat-

tresses swallowed the sounds, leaving a soft, hollow silence in their wake.

Joshua bent to do her right ankle but realized it might
be best to talk to her after all, to keep her preoccupied
until he got started with the Gemrig saw. "I just want you
to be still."

When he actually did reply to her this time, she was
quiet, and he wondered if maybe she'd become hopeful
that she could negotiate with him. He didn't like that his
words might be leading her on, might be making her
think he was going to have compassion on her. It just
didn't feel right to do that to her.

She stopped struggling for the moment, then shifted
her weight in the chair. "Please let me—oh my God!" She
was rubbing the fingers of her left hand together and it
was clear she'd just discovered that her ring finger was
missing. The first aid tape Joshua had wrapped around
the nub kept it from bleeding too much, and the adrenaline, fear, and the lingering effects of the drugs must have
distracted her from the pain. "What did you do to me!"

"I've asked Carl to do a job for me. That was to let
him know how important it is."

She took a handful of heavy breaths. "Okay. It's okay.
It doesn't matter, but can you let me go? I'll make sure
he does what you want."

It was clear that she was just trying to conciliate him.
Of course it mattered that someone had snipped off her
ring finger, and even though he could understand why
she was acting this way, saying these things, Joshua wasn't
sure he liked her downplaying the severity of what had
happened, all in a vain attempt to try to make him release
her.

"I won't tell," she gasped, and it sounded like she was trying to hold back tears. "I'll make Carl do what you want. He will. I promise."

Joshua enjoyed the screaming, but this begging made him uncomfortable. He finished with her right ankle. Turned to the left one, trying to tune out her pleading, but she kept on, kept promising that she would do whatever he wanted if he would just stop, just please, please, stop and let her go.

He retrieved the saw. That would change things. Once he actually got started.

The November air bristled across his bare skin, tiny needles that somehow brought him closer to the moment, more in tune with what he was doing. He closed his eyes, shivered deeply. Embraced the chill of the coming night.

Last evening he'd left Colleen conscious as he amputated her hands, and that'd been satisfying. Now, with Adele, since he was doing both her hands and feet, it would last that much longer.

Yes, getting started would make things better, would stop all her talking.

He decided to begin with her feet.

Joshua knelt and carefully positioned the blade of the amputation saw against the skin just above Adele's left foot, about half an inch below the plastic tie.

"Listen to me!" she cried, and started in again, wriggling frantically. "Whatever you're thinking about doing, you don't need to do this!" She'd obviously pieced two and two together, probably taking into account what had happened to her finger along with the fact that something was constricting her wrists and ankles. "Okay? Whatever you want, I'll make sure—"

"If you keep moving, this is going to hurt a lot worse and it'll take longer, and I'm guessing you wouldn't want either of those things to happen." He tugged on the end of the plastic tie again, cinching it deeper into her skin to make sure it was as snug as it needed to be, then he grasped her foot and held it firmly against the ground to keep it in position.

"No!"

He realigned the saw . . .

"Please stop!"

. . . Tightened his grip on the handle . . .

"No, I'll—"

And drove the blade forward, bringing a spray of hot blood and a bright, fresh scream from Adele.

The cut was just shy of half an inch deep. Joshua paused, took a moment to drink in the sound of this woman's cries. As he did, he felt—along with the excitement—a piercing stab of shame doing this, enjoying her suffering so much.

The reality that her pain brought him so much pleasure was unsettling. He'd done enough research on serial killers to know that the majority of them were sadists, relishing the act of making other people suffer.

You're a sadist, Joshua. You're a—

Never before throughout his life had he thought of himself in that way, not before this autumn when all this began. But now he was forced to admit that he really did enjoy causing pain, and the discovery of that dark part of his nature emerging so clearly, so distinctly, troubled him.

Adele was crying in between her shrieks of pain.

"The good that I would I do not: but the evil which I would not, that I do."

The evil which I would not.

That I do.

Joshua realized that he would never be the same again, not after giving free rein to this part of his nature. Acts like this undoubtedly changed a person in fundamental ways. Once you start down this road, with the type of crimes he was committing, there's no turning back. Yes, he might be able to find eventual forgiveness for his actions, but he would never be able to erase the impact they would have on his conscience, on his soul.

"Light is come into the world"—his father made him recite the verse from John, chapter three, so, so many times—"and men loved darkness rather than light, because their deeds were evil."

Their deeds were evil.

Are evil.

You are—

He shook the thought loose.

Adele's leg was quivering and it wasn't as easy as before to hold her foot in position against the floor.

He really should keep going.

As he angled the saw into the wound, Adele screeched again and tried to jerk her leg away from the blade. But then, when she gasped to get another breath, even with the mattresses inside the boxcar, even with the door closed, Joshua thought he heard a clang outside.

"Quiet," he told her firmly.

She directed her head toward him as if to look at him,

even though she was still blindfolded. Her leg quivered with pain.

Yes.

There it was.

He heard it again. Faint, but definitely the sound of something banging against the track near the boxcar.

Someone was outside, nearby, in the train yard.

Adele must have heard it too, because she yelled, her voice even louder than when the saw blade had bitten into her ankle. "I'm in here!"

Leaping to his feet, Joshua clamped his hand firmly over her mouth. "You don't want to upset me and I don't want to gag you. Be quiet now."

But almost immediately he decided the gag would be necessary.

He thought of the necrotome tucked in its sheath on his belt. Then his eyes flicked from the Gemrig saw, to the hypodermic needle containing the drugs he'd been planning on giving her later, to the Glock.

And Joshua decided what he needed to do.

35

Muffled sounds.

But it was impossible to tell which boxcar they were coming from.

I ran alongside the line of cars, trying to discern the origin of the sounds, but I couldn't. And then, just as suddenly as they began, they stopped.

Slowing so I could listen more carefully, I noticed a small area of snow was kicked up in front of the door of a car not too far down the track. I ran to it. The door was chained shut, but the chain allowed the door to remain open a crack, just a few centimeters wide. The chain ran through the metal handle to another handle bolted onto the side of the train car.

It had an old chain but a brand-new padlock, and even though it was a different brand than the one on the front gate, just the fact that it was new was enough for me.

The crack was just wide enough for a person to slip his hand through and lock the padlock from inside the car. A perfect hiding place—you're locked inside with the only access locked from the outside.

But then a realization: the wind that cut through the crack made a high-pitched shrieking sound.

Maybe that's what I'd heard.

Maybe that's all it was.

But I wasn't about to take any chances. I unholstered my weapon and called inside, "This is the police. Whoever's in the boxcar, lie down. Hands to the side!"

No sound, except for the impertinent wind.

I pounded on the wall of the boxcar with my fist. "Reply if you are in the boxcar!"

Silence.

The crack was certainly wide enough for someone to shoot through and I wasn't excited about putting my face in front of it. Finally, however, I clicked on the Maglite and, standing to the side, I tugged the door open as much as the chain would allow.

I aimed the beam of light into the car, waited to the count of three, then leaned over and peered through the crack.

The narrow width made it hard to see, and even with the flashlight I couldn't make out very much at all, but I could see what at first looked like a large sack or a slumped pile of clothes just on the edge of my vision. However, in an instant I realized it wasn't just a pile of clothes—it was a body with its back to me. I shouted again, but the person didn't move.

From this angle I couldn't tell whether I was looking at a man or a woman, although the frame looked small. A woman. Possibly a slightly built man or an adolescent boy. When I looked closer, I made out dark stains on the clothing near the person's rib cage.

Blood.

I shouted again to see if the victim would respond, but there was no reply. I tugged hard at the door again, but

I could only move it two or three centimeters before the chain caught. Without bolt cutters, there was no way I was getting into this boxcar.

The other side.

The sliding door on the other side.

I punched at my radio as I swept around the car to see if there was another way in. "Ralph, I've got someone down. Injured, maybe a fatality. I'm at the seventeenth boxcar from the east end, by the woods."

"On my way." By his tone I could tell he was already running.

The door on the other side of the car was welded shut, so I quickly returned to the side facing the forest. I studied the ground again, trying to see if there was any way to tell which direction the person who'd left this boxcar might have gone. But there simply wasn't enough snow.

I turned, searched for any movement, crouched and swept the Maglite's beam beneath the train car as I'd done earlier, but I still saw no evidence of anyone else nearby.

While I waited for Ralph to arrive, I called for backup, telling the dispatcher that there appeared to be at least one victim and that we needed an ambulance. "Make sure they have bolt cutters and the Jaws of Life. The front gate and the boxcar are both chained shut and I want to get into this car as fast as possible."

Ralph appeared, leaping over the coupler between two cars.

I pointed toward the boxcar's door. "Over here!"

He closed the distance between us. "So you can't tell, injury or fatality?"

"Not until we get inside."

He grabbed the metal handle and yanked at it, trying to get the door open, but the chain caught, held fast. "I tried that," I told him.

"Yeah," he said vaguely. "Let me see that flashlight."

I handed it to him and he attempted to slide it into the door handle, but the Maglite's casing was too wide. He slipped out his Mini Mag and wedged it in.

"That chain isn't going to break, Ralph."

"I'm not trying to break the chain."

I could've kicked myself for not thinking of it earlier— of course, the handle. Torque it loose from the boxcar and the chain is useless.

He took a deep breath and pulled down fiercely on the flashlight. I thought it might break but it didn't. However, it didn't do the trick either. The door handle didn't pull free.

"I need more leverage," he mumbled, then turned and inspected the area surrounding the car.

Wondering if there might be a loose fence post he could use, I studied the fence line but didn't see anything promising. When I turned around to look for him, I saw that he'd gone to a flat car on a neighboring track and now hoisted a three-foot-long pipe into the air. He jogged back to me, augured the pipe into position, clenched his teeth with the effort, and cranked down. Hard.

With a tight, high-pitched squeal, the handle on the door bent, but only slightly.

He repositioned the pipe.

Yeah, he was going to be able to pry that loose.

The ladder on the car was rusted but looked climbable. "I'm going to have a look around."

Holstering my gun and jamming my flashlight beneath my belt, I scrambled up and stood on top of the boxcar.

The day was languishing around us, night crawling quickly over the city, the visibility fading fast.

I turned in a circle, studying first the area north of us, then the parking lot, then the fence line.

And that's when I saw him.

He was about forty meters away, moving stealthily through the drainage ditch on his way to the loose section of fence that Ralph and I had used earlier to access the train yard. Details were hard to make out in this light, but I could tell he was a dark-haired male Caucasian, large frame, wearing blue jeans and a maroon or brown-colored down coat.

Knowing that he'd very likely been the one to attack the person in the boxcar beneath me, I wasn't going to take any chances. I unholstered my SIG. "Milwaukee Police! You by the fence, do not move!"

He paused, still facing the other direction. Before I could give him any more instructions, there was a mighty cry as Ralph hefted on the pipe. A harsh metallic *snap* ripped through the air. I heard the door slide open and then the sound of Ralph jumping into the train car.

I kept the gun aimed at the suspect. "Hands up!" But the wind caught hold of the words, throwing them back at me, and he didn't move. I shouted louder, "Hands up! Now!"

Slowly, the man raised his hands.

"Turn around!"

He didn't move.

"Dead!" Ralph yelled to me. "Male! Late thirties!"

The suspect didn't move.

"Turn around!" I repeated. "Face me—and keep your hands in the air!" A beat of silence from Ralph, and he must have been checking the victim for an ID because a second later he called, "It's Hendrich."

What?

Then who's the guy by the culvert?

"Turn toward my voice! Slowly!"

The suspect began to turn slowly, just as I'd commanded, but then all at once he slung his right arm out in front of him and leveled it at me.

Time seemed to pause in midbreath.

In the wide swath of shadows, his hand was shielded enough that I couldn't tell whether or not he held a weapon. In that instant I had to decide what to do— assume he had a gun and drop him, or assume he didn't and let him live.

Instinct took over and I made my choice.

36

I didn't fire.

I couldn't, not if I wasn't able to tell for certain that he had a weapon. Instead of firing, I dropped to one knee so that if he did have a gun he wouldn't have a clear shot, then hollered, "Hands up!" I sighted down the barrel of my SIG. "Now!"

But he did have a weapon and before I'd even finished shouting, he'd squeezed the trigger.

The bullet clanged off the side of the boxcar and I returned fire, but in the fraction of a second it'd taken me to respond, he'd dropped down into the gully.

Go, Pat!

Now!

I rolled to the edge of the boxcar, half slid, half leapt down the ladder, and found Ralph with his back to the car, gun out, aimed in the direction of the shooter. "Where?"

"The fence. Eleven o'clock. Forty meters."

He signaled to me that he was going first, and before I could out-alpha-male him for the honor, he bolted toward the fence yelling, "Cover me."

I rounded the corner of the train car and leveled my weapon at the place where I'd last seen the shooter, but only seconds after Ralph left for the opening in the fence, I realized that the suspect had already made it through the hole. He appeared only as a dark blur of movement in the forest.

"Ralph! The woods!"

I had no shot. Not from here. Not with these trees, not at this distance.

Sirens told me that backup was on its way, but they weren't close enough to do any good right now.

The forest stretched about the length of a football field and ended at an empty parking lot in a low-income neighborhood full of crack houses, dark alleys, and abandoned buildings. If the shooter made it that far, there'd be a hundred places to hide. The guy was really moving and I could tell that if I took the time to run to the opening in the fence, he'd make it to the neighborhood and be gone for good.

Only one other option.

"West Reagan Street," I yelled to Ralph as I sprinted toward the fence. "Call it in!"

I holstered my gun and tugged off my jacket.

Don't do this, Pat. You're going to regret it.

Yeah, maybe, but I was gonna do it anyway.

As soon as I reached the fence, I flipped the coat up across the razor wire above me and, without giving myself time for second guesses, I climbed. At the top, using the jacket to pad my hands from the curling, bladed wire, I pulled myself up, but even through the fabric, the metal barbs slivered into my hands. My palms screamed at me and, hastily, trying to keep from toppling backward, I scrunched up the leather beneath my hands and managed—barely—to hold on.

I scrambled my legs up, collected myself for what was to come, then brought them to the top, doing my best to keep my balance and not let the razor wire catch on my pants legs. But as I was bridging the fence, the fabric by my heel caught on the wire, and when I tugged to get it free, I lost my balance and the momentum pitched me forward, over to the other side. I hit the frozen ground hard and off balance, rolled, came up with my gun in my hand. The Maglite had dropped out of my belt, though, on the far side of the fence.

You really do need a smaller flash—
Go!

Leaving the jacket behind, I raced after the suspect through the shadow-riddled forest.

37

Branches flicked past my face. There was hardly enough light to see where the suspect was going, but I was just able to make out his outline moving swiftly through the woods on the fringe of the night.

I leapt over a fallen log, rushed past a pile of garbage and a rusted shopping cart that'd somehow found its way in here.

Just past the tree line, streetlights had blinked on. The shooter emerged from the trees, dashed through the circle of light cast down by one of them, and disappeared somewhere beyond it.

A sprawling, boarded-up building squatted on the other side of the street and blocked a direct path through the neighborhood. I couldn't tell which direction the runner had gone to avoid it—right or left.

I bolted forward, ducked to miss another branch, and, a handful of seconds later, burst through the edge of the trees and stood by the curb.

No sign of the man I was chasing.

Right or left?

No idea.

He held his gun in his right hand.

Hurry!

I made a choice.

Right.

All things being equal, if he fired with his right hand, he'd be right-handed. I recalled Dr. Werjonic's research, his writings on cognitive maps and fleeing suspects: "Right-handed people typically turn right upon entering a novel environment."

I dashed toward a row of cramped low-income apartments.

When I came to the intersection, I saw no sign of the shooter.

I ran forward, checked an alley, then gazed down the block.

Nothing.

No cars were moving. No pedestrians. Admittedly, this wasn't the kind of neighborhood where people typically take casual strolls in the twilight, but tonight the streets seemed uncharacteristically deserted.

Another hurried search through another alley and I came up empty again. In frustration I let my foot find a nearby trash can. If it hadn't been chained to a telephone pole, it would have cleared the street. As it was, I left a sizable dent in the side that I might have been proud of any other time.

Immediately, curtains in the nearest apartment building fluttered open and in the porch light I saw a young African-American boy, maybe four or five years old, peering out at me. I was already hurrying back toward the streetlight where the suspect had disappeared, but I didn't want to frighten the boy, so I hid my gun, continued on casually, and then the curtain closed, and he slipped from view and was gone once again.

When I got to the spot where the suspect had exited the woods, I heard Ralph hurtling through the darkness toward me, the light from his flashlight marking his path. "Anything?" he called as he burst through the edge of the forest.

"No."

He cursed loudly.

Just as we started scouring the street in the other direction, a patrol car came peeling around the corner.

"Let 'em sweep the area," I told Ralph. "I want to get back to the train yard and make sure there aren't any more victims."

He pulled out his radio. "Or suspects."

"Yeah." I was already heading into the forest. "Or suspects."

38

Joshua made it to his car, which he'd parked four blocks from the train yard. The Ford Taurus he'd left behind wasn't his, of course. He'd stolen it a few days ago so there wouldn't be any chance that his own vehicle would be identified at the scene of any of the crimes. It seemed like a slim possibility anyway, but it wasn't a chance he was willing to take.

He'd planned on torching the Taurus when all of this was done, but now it looked like that wasn't going to happen.

How did they find you?

Joshua had no idea.

Once inside the car, he snapped on the scanner and listened to the chatter back and forth between the squads.

And thought of last night.

The squads.

The sirens.

The abduction of Colleen Hayes.

Joshua was a fan of true crime books and three weeks ago he'd finished Heather Isle's newest book about David Spanbauer, a rapist and child murderer in Wisconsin earlier in the decade. The story had intrigued him so much that he'd looked up the true crime expert the author had cited numerous times—a "collector of memorabilia," as Isle put it, Timothy Griffin.

Eventually, that led Joshua to find out about the products Griffin offered through his direct-sales business.

Which had naturally intrigued him.

It took a little work, but Joshua tracked down the guy's home address.

He waited until one evening when both Griffin and his young girlfriend were out, and then, just as he'd done with Dahmer's apartment before it was destroyed, he took his camera into Griffin's home and captured footage of the place's interior. He even got footage of the basement and the cache of items beneath the stairwell, the collectibles without price tags on them. The ones that, apparently, were not for sale.

The special items, Joshua. You know all about those.

Checking the boxes of receipts in the bedroom closet, Joshua had found one for a pair of handcuffs from the Oswald case, which ended up being perfect for what he had in mind.

The Oswald case.

The one that mirrored, in so many dark ways, his own.

Because of his special connection with their story, he'd wanted to save their crimes for the climax. And this discovery, in a way, would help him do just that.

According to the receipt, a woman named Colleen Hayes had purchased the specific cuffs. So, rather than leave a pair of his own that might be able to be traced, he decided to let her husband use their own pair when he was forced to abduct the African-American man.

That way, it helped Joshua by turning the spotlight of the investigation onto the husband.

As Joshua's father had taught him years ago, you always give the police what they want. And they want fingerprints, DNA, hair, semen; they want sole impressions from shoes; they want any hard physical evidence that they can hang a name onto: cuffs, Vincent. Done.

They'll keep looking until they find what they want, but when they have it in hand, they'll be content to formulate their theories based on their cursory findings and then work diligently to prove themselves right. More often than not, that's a lot easier, a lot more convenient, than ruthlessly ferreting out the truth.

Because of that, Joshua was careful not to leave trace evidence that could be tied to him at the scenes, and, when possible, he tried to leave evidence that pointed to someone else.

But tonight he'd been forced to leave a veritable stockpile of evidence behind in that boxcar. From the start he'd been careful about prints, but DNA was nearly impossible *not* to leave. However, he'd never been arrested, so even if law enforcement did somehow manage to get his DNA, they wouldn't have anything to compare their samples to.

Now, he checked his watch and saw that it was almost five, almost time for Carl to call with his update on what he'd done to Miriam Flandry.

Joshua clicked on his portable phone, the one that he'd made sure was untraceable.

So, things this evening had not gone as planned, but

everything could still move forward as long as Carl had been obedient and done his job.

If he had, Gein's name would rise to the forefront of the news cycle once again, the national media would start playing and replaying Carl's and Adele's story, and everyone would take notice.

And right now that was what mattered most.

39

Ralph and I found a woman, unconscious, bound to a chair, plastic ties tightly cinched around her wrists and ankles. The door to this boxcar had been chained shut and Ralph had used the pipe for the second time today to wrench off the handle.

Her pulse was weak and thready, and she didn't respond when we called to her or slapped her cheek, but she was breathing. She was alive.

Thank God she was alive.

Ralph slipped out an automatic knife from his pocket, an Ox Forge Black Knife, and cut her free from the ropes and tape binding her to the chair. He quickly slit the plastic ties as well, then we eased her to the floor.

Blood seeped from a deep cut in her ankle, most likely from the bloody, discarded amputation saw on the floor next to the chair. I applied pressure to her bleeding ankle while Ralph supported her neck to keep her airway open.

It looked like we'd interrupted the guy just as he was getting started on her.

During our trip back here through the woods, the dispatcher had assured me that four paramedics were on their way, and now the echoing sirens told me they were close.

Actually, it sounded like the emergency vehicles were probably stuck behind the locked gate. Hopefully they'd brought the bolt cutters and Jaws of Life as I'd ordered.

My attention went back to the woman.

Caucasian. Mid-twenties. Medium build. Shoulder-length, blond hair. Aquamarine eyes, no contact lenses. Smeared mascara—she'd been crying—no other makeup. Fair skin, attractive features. No visible piercings, scars, tattoos or identifying marks. When we checked for an ID, we found none. The ring finger of her left hand had been cut off, the hand carefully bandaged to stop the bleeding.

Her abductor had removed her shoes and I could see that her feet, which had been bluish from the lack of oxygenated blood when we arrived, were regaining their color now that the plastic ties were gone. Her hands were doing better as well. All good signs.

Both Ralph and I were quiet as we waited for the EMTs to get here. I didn't know what he was thinking, but I was trying to decompress, to process what had happened this afternoon.

I couldn't stop images of the day from whipping like cyclone winds through my mind: the visit to Griffin's nightmarish home, the inexplicably terse conversation with Detective Browning in Waukesha, arriving at the train yards.

Wriggling under the fence.

Locating the sedan.

Finding Hendrich's body.

Getting shot at.

Scaling the fence and chasing the shooter through the forest.

Losing him.

Ending up here, with this unidentified woman who was evidently our guy's next intended victim.

And with the memories came a swirl of emotions: rage, confusion, grief over Hendrich's death, hope that this woman would be able to identify her attacker.

None of this whiplash of tumultuous emotions was unusual for my job, but this afternoon had been unusually intense and I suspected it would take some time to work through all the feelings.

"What are you thinking?" Ralph asked me, drawing me back to the present.

"A lot of things, I guess." I indicated toward the woman. "Mostly, that I'm thankful we got here when we did for her, but I'm angry we didn't get here—"

"Soon enough to save Hendrich."

"Yeah."

"His body was still warm," Ralph said. "I'm not sure how long he might have been dead. Hopefully the forensics guys can figure all that out, but we didn't see anyone else leave the train yard, so I have to think he was killed right before we got here, right before the suspect fled."

"Unless the killer didn't escape at all."

"You think he's still here? A second guy?"

"It's possible." Thankfully, the sirens had drawn closer, and I could tell by the sound that they'd made it past the parking lot gate. I was anxious to scour the train yards more carefully, but we would need a team of people to do that thoroughly, and they were going to be here any moment. "I'll get some more officers out there searching in a sec."

Considering the number of train cars and tracks, the

EMTs probably wouldn't be able to drive all the way to this boxcar, but I imagined they should at least be able to make it as far as the Ford Taurus. Rolling a gurney from there might pose a bit of a problem, but carrying a stretcher would be manageable.

We radioed in our exact position and a bevy of officers beat the paramedics to our car. I had one of them take my place beside the woman and then directed the others where to look in the train yard and woods for other victims, suspects, accomplices or witnesses.

While I was giving instructions, the paramedics came jogging up carrying a stretcher.

No drugs were visible in the boxcar, but I told the EMTs to start with the working assumption that the woman had been given Propotol, the same pharmaceutical that'd been left at the Hayes house last night for Vincent to knock out the African-American man he'd been directed to abduct.

Three more officers showed up and I sent them to help the others.

With impressive speed and proficiency the paramedics got the woman ready, and I helped them carry the stretcher to one of the two waiting ambulances.

As they loaded her, one of the EMTs saw the cuts on my hands from grabbing the razor wire through the inadequate protection of my jacket. She offered to treat them, but I decided that bandaging my hands in gauze would slow me down too much; however, in the end, I let her clean the wounds and wrap some first aid tape around them so I could work without leaving my blood everywhere.

The night wind was biting and cold, so on my way

back to the train car where we'd found the woman, I retrieved the flashlight, and then my jacket, which was still snagged on the top of the fence. It was sliced up some, but overall it was in reasonably good shape.

I didn't even want to think about how my hands would have looked if the jacket hadn't been there to protect them.

When the officer who'd brought the bolt cutters arrived, Ralph took them from him and the three of us left to search the other boxcars for more victims. Ralph made short work of the rusted chains on the remaining cars, but we didn't find anyone else in the yard. Neither did any of the other officers.

No victims.

No suspects.

No witnesses.

Except that little boy you saw through the window, out past the woods.

No, he'd only looked out when I kicked the garbage can.

It's possible he might have seen something before you got there and that's why he was at the window in the first place.

I sent an officer to go and talk with him. Other officers were already canvassing the neighborhood. Before sending them out, I'd noted that our guy was Caucasian and knew where to go to disappear in this nearly one hundred percent African-American neighborhood. "See if anyone saw a white guy running through here, someone who didn't belong."

By the time Ralph and I returned to the boxcar where we'd found the woman, Officer Gabriele Holdren had arrived and now informed us that the crime scene investigative unit, or CSIU, was on its way.

"ETA?" I asked her.

"Should be here in the next four or five minutes."

I'm not the biggest fan of our force's CSIU. Captain Domyslawski didn't budget nearly enough money to purchase the kind of resources or attract the kind of personnel he should've, and it showed through all too often in the form of lost or mislabeled evidence, contaminated crime scenes, and inadequate case documentation.

Four or five minutes, huh?

Well, at least that gave me a little time to look around before they started in.

I'll take what I can get.

I asked Gabriele to wait outside, then climbed into the boxcar. "Ralph, I want your eyes in here."

He heaved himself up and stood beside me.

Both of us had our flashlights on and they illuminated, in a somewhat eerie fashion, the macabre contents of the boxcar.

"Alright, Mr. I-Notice-Things," Ralph said bluntly, but softly enough for only me to hear, "you're on."

I snapped on a pair of latex gloves over my taped-up hands. "Yes, I am."

Carefully, I began to study the contents of the boxcar.

40

A private little torture chamber.

That's what our guy had constructed.

Ten mattresses lined the walls, evidently to serve as makeshift baffles to absorb the sound of his victims' screams.

I recalled that the kidnapper hadn't gagged Colleen last night when he maimed her, so he must have trusted that the mattresses really did do their job.

There was a half-used roll of duct tape on the floor next to a length of leftover rope. Beside them lay the antique-looking amputation saw I'd noticed when we first came in. Blood stained the floor beneath the sturdy chair in the middle of the boxcar, probably from Colleen last night, as well as from the injuries of the woman we'd found here just a few minutes ago.

Maybe from others too.

True. Considering the brutality of these crimes and the setup the guy had in here, there was no compelling reason to think that the two women were the only ones he had ever brought to this boxcar.

The only other things I noticed were a light—now turned off—on the wall, the shredded ropes, tape, the plastic ties left from when Ralph had cut the woman free, some sheets of butcher paper, and two plastic garbage bags in the northeast corner, one neatly folded up, the other crumpled on top of it.

When you process a crime scene, you follow a pretty well-established set of five procedures: orientation, observation, examination, analysis, and evaluation. I quickly, almost instinctively, ran through what needed to be done:

1. Orientation: look at the big picture, including the place and timing of the crime, whether it's indoors or outdoors, what the location might tell you about the offender's familiarity with the area, if the crime appeared to be related to other crimes, and so on.

2. Observation: note both the unusual and the obvious, remembering that the obvious is often the easiest thing to miss.

3. Examination: collect and scrutinize physical evidence, such as fingerprints, DNA, hair samples, and so on—the things that come to mind for most people when they hear about police officers processing a crime scene.

4. Analysis: take into account everything you know and probe deeper into the pertinence each fact or clue might have to the case. This should happen at the scene while everything is fresh in your mind, as well as later during a briefing when you recap the investigation.

5. Evaluation: form a working hypothesis that you don't try to prove, but rather try to disprove. Too many times initial hypotheses aren't correct and trying to find ways to make the facts fit them only throws a

monkey wrench into the works. This was the main problem I see with too many of the officers I work with, including, perhaps especially, Detective Corsica.

Five steps.

So, right now, number one—orientation.

The big picture.

I spoke my thoughts aloud to Ralph. "Track with me here. Last night Colleen is abducted and an unusual and disturbing ransom demand is left behind for her husband. Then, even though Vincent does as he was told, the kidnapper saws off her hands."

"And it looks like he was about to do that again here tonight, but this time to cut off both her hands and her feet."

I nodded. "Escalation."

"So," he said, tracking with me, "we have another 'ransom' demand tonight?"

"Very likely. Yes."

Another pastiche?

"Ralph, we need to get a car over to the alley where Radar and I found Lionel last night—and one to the pier where the guy left Colleen." I thought about it, then added, "And let's get someone to the bar too, where Vincent abducted Lionel."

He called it in while I studied the inside of the boxcar and compared it to what Colleen had told me this morning about the place her abductor had taken her.

When Ralph got off the radio I said, "This boxcar fits the description Colleen gave us. I think we should proceed with the theory that she was brought here too."

"Agreed."

I took a minute to mentally review the Dahmer connection, the locations, the information we had about the previous homicides, then noted the obvious: "The Taurus was inside the gate, so whoever drove it in there— whether that was Hendrich or someone else—must have had access to a key to that gate."

And keys to the two boxcars.

It struck me that we still hadn't heard back from the station about the sedan's plates and whether the car was registered to Hendrich. When I mentioned that, Gabriele, who was lingering near the entrance to the boxcar and had apparently been listening in on our conversation, offered to follow up on it.

"Good," I told her. She left to make the call, I turned to Ralph. "Chaining the gate shut, parking in that particular place, choosing this line of boxcars, once again speaks to our guy's familiarity with the area. With the forest paralleling the tracks, he would have been hidden from view from every nearby road, and from where the car is parked, he would have had to carry the victim, or lead her, more than sixty meters to the boxcar . . ."

"By the way, what's with you and the metric system? You never heard of yards before?"

"Science, medicine, forensics, they all use the metric system," I defended myself. "That's why they measure things in milliliters, millimeters, and so on. Metric is the measuring system of the world. Even track and field events use the metric system."

"Yeah, well football doesn't. It's a game of inches, not centimeters. It doesn't even sound American to talk like that. From now on, convert so I know what you're talking about."

"Um . . . a meter is just a little longer than a—"

"Yard. Yeah, I know that one. Everyone knows that one. But everything else—how many millimeters are in a foot? How many kilometers are in a mile? I don't know that stuff. No more of this metric nonsense. It's too European—reminds me of France."

"You really don't like France."

"No, I do not."

"What happened in France, Ralph?"

"I'll tell you someday." He eyed the ten old and mismatched mattresses, then left the topic of the metric system behind. "It'd be tough for one person to carry those in by himself, don't you think? A lot easier with two people."

And a lot of trips driving in—unless you have a U-Haul.

Hmm . . . a moving truck . . .

"And he obviously got 'em from somewhere," I muttered. "I mean, who would have ten used mattresses just lying around? A hotel? A used furniture store? A Goodwill store?"

"We should have some officers follow up on that."

"There's a Salvation Army thrift store about half a mile from here." It was Gabriele again. She'd returned and was lingering by the door.

"Try them," I told her. "See if they're still open, if they might've sold some guy ten used mattresses."

A nod. She left.

"Okay, step two," I told Ralph. "We try to notice the obvious."

41

"Notice the obvious?"

"Yeah, it's often the hardest thing to see. It's like Pascal wrote in *Les Pensées*, 'For we always find the thing obscure which we wish to prove and that clear which we use for the proof; for, when a thing is put forward to be proved, we first fill ourselves with the imagination that it is, therefore, obscure and, on the contrary, that what is to prove it is clear, and so we understand it easily.' "

"I'm not sure I quite followed that."

"We start with the preconception that what we want to find out is obscure, but it might not be. It might be clear, but our preconceptions blind us."

"Oh. Why didn't he just say that?"

"He was a philosopher."

"And you memorized that?"

"Seemed like a good idea at the time." I inspected the chair. It was bolted to the floor to keep the struggling victims from tipping it over. "We have three new locks . . ." I said softly. "The boxcar with Hendrich, the one with the woman, the front gate. They're the only new locks in the yard. But they're not all the same type of padlock. The brand of the one on the front gate and this boxcar match;

the other doesn't and it was on a rusty chain while the other two had new chains."

"Maybe he had to come in here a bunch of times to deliver those mattresses and that chair, brought different locks on each trip."

"Yeah." I mulled that over. "Maybe."

A swarm of questions buzzed through my mind.

How many people did he bring here? Just these two victims, or have there been more? If this is the same guy who was committing the cannibalistic homicides elsewhere in the Midwest, is this his base of operation? If so, why is it so far from the other two locations?

And why are there two different styles of locks?

Two different offenders?

I heard someone outside mention that the CSIU had arrived in the parking lot.

Just a couple more minutes.

I knew that the crime scene unit would search for DNA and prints and would compare the blood samples to find out whatever they could about the offender. They had the instruments and materials for all that, Ralph and I didn't. But DNA and prints help you only if you have something to compare them to. If the guy wasn't in the system, his name wasn't going to pop up.

Tonight the CSIU had a lot of evidence to process: the Taurus, two boxcars and their contents, the locks and chains, the fence material around that opening, the gate . . . and I had a sense that this guy was smart. Careful. That he wasn't going to leave behind anything that he didn't want to.

I'm no expert on blood spatter analysis, but when I scrutinized the stains on the wooden floor, I could tell that some were darker, had seeped in more. The fresh blood from the woman tonight had sprayed across the floor when her left ankle was cut. The other stains were just below where Colleen's wrists would have been if she'd been sitting in the chair.

I bent beside it. "Ralph, look at the blood spatter on the floor here: the pattern of the darker stains."

He studied them with me. "Dried. Soaked in more. From Colleen."

"So it would seem."

He could tell I was looking at something else. "What is it?"

"Well, at first it sprayed a little, you can see that, but then it stops abruptly." I pointed. "Almost in a straight line."

"So, the blood hit him. His arm maybe. Or his leg."

"Yeah, I'm not sure, but . . ."

Ralph saw me glance toward the plastic bags. "Ah. He learned his lesson. Bagged up a set of clothes tonight."

"He didn't have a bag of clothes with him when he fled, so he might have stashed one somewhere or slipped a pair of clothes back on." I pointed to the bags. "If he did stick some clothes in there, even momentarily, he might have inadvertently left us a little present."

"His DNA. From his clothes."

"Yes." The CSIU would have undoubtedly checked the outside of the bags for prints; the inside was another story, something they might easily have missed.

"Nice."

I finished looking at the blood spatter while Ralph examined the amputation saw. "There's a date engraved on the handle—1864."

Often, killers will choose a very specific and unique weapon that holds some sort of special meaning to them. But that's not smart. The more unique your weapon, the easier it is to trace. An amputation saw that old had to be rare. There are experts in just about every obscure field, and I expected we could find someone who specialized in Civil War–era surgical instruments. He or she would be able to tell us more about the saw, maybe where our guy might have purchased it, or even who he might be.

"That's good," I said. "That'll help."

"You think our guy got it from Griffin?"

"It's worth checking out. Did you hear if the search warrant went through?"

"No, actually. Let me go call Ellen." He stepped away to radio Agent Parker.

As I moved on to analysis, I played out in my mind the way I would put things in my report later tonight:

We searched the train yards, saw no one. I discovered the Ford Taurus inside the gate near the parking lot on the west side. After I found Hendrich's body in one of the boxcars, I located a man fleeing along the fence line. The suspect engaged me with his firearm, I returned fire but did not hit him. He fled. A chase ensued. He was able to avoid apprehension.

Okay, yes. But how did he know when to leave?

That really was the question.

If the shooter was in the boxcar with the woman, why did he leave when he did, right as he was getting started with her?

He had to have known that you and Ralph were in the train yard.

So did he have the door open? Possibly, but that didn't

really make sense, not if he was torturing a woman inside the car and not if he trusted the mattresses to absorb her screams. Did he hear us? Maybe, but how? We weren't making any noise except speaking quietly into our radios. So, if he were—

I heard someone climbing into the boxcar behind me. I figured it would be one of the CSIU members, but when I turned around, I saw it was Radar instead.

42

"Hey," he exclaimed, "I just heard—the doctors are saying they're hopeful about saving her hands and feet. The circulation had been cut off for a while, but you two did good. The cut on her ankle is pretty deep, but they expect she'll walk again too. Oh, and it's not Hendrich's car."

"It's not?"

"No. It's stolen. Reported a couple days ago by a guy named Norman Darr. Lives in Pewaukee. The VIN number led us to him, but the plates on the Taurus are from a second car that was in the same parking lot. That's why it took a while to figure out what we were looking at. Our guy switched the plates with it before driving off."

"To avoid being tracked down by an APB. Clever."

This was the first time I'd seen Radar since our morning briefing. Thorne had mentioned earlier that he'd gone to look into the names of one of the felons he'd been investigating and I asked him if he'd found anything.

He shook his head.

Back on topic: "The car is one thing," I said, "but we really need to find out who this woman is."

"Well, based on what I heard, either she's married or engaged. That's something to start with."

I looked at him quizzically. "Where'd you hear that?"

"I mean, I didn't hear it *exactly*, but—the missing finger. Think about it—why would he remove her ring finger? That specific one?" This was classic Radar—inferences, hunches, intuition, gut instincts.

Yeah, but they almost always end up being right on the money.

"Could be symbolic." I didn't really believe that, but for some reason I felt obliged to play devil's advocate. "He sees himself as marrying her? Having some sort of relationship with her?"

Radar shook his head. "I doubt it. Think about it— escalation, Pat. He left it behind to prove to her husband or fiancé that he had her and that he was serious about carrying out whatever threat he'd made in his note. He didn't leave Colleen's finger for Vincent last night. He might have thought he needed something a little more persuasive this time around to make sure his demands were carried out."

"But they were carried out last night."

Yeah, except you caught Vincent.

I tried to work all this through in my head, see where it might be leading.

Even though it wasn't verifiable yet, what Radar was saying made sense. I accepted it for now, and moved on. "So . . . if you're right, he made a demand of the woman's lover. And that would be persuasive. I mean, finding my fiancée's or wife's finger would certainly be enough to convince me that a kidnapper was deadly serious."

Over the past few months, Taci and I had discussed

getting married and when I mentioned wives and fian-
cées, my thoughts naturally jumped to her. I glanced at
my watch and saw that it was nearly six. Undoubtedly I'd
need to stick around here for at least a couple hours. I
was never going to make it back home in time to cook
dinner for her by seven.

Earlier, she'd mentioned that she had something she
wanted to talk with me about privately and I hadn't gotten the best vibe from her when she said that. I knew
something was up, and I had the sense that canceling
might not be the best idea.

Meet her later for dessert. That should work.

Radar eyed me. "You okay?"

"Yeah. Sorry." *Wrap this up in here, then find a phone
and call her.*

"Anyway," he said, "I'm thinking the guy might not
have gone to the police. As you said, he knew the kidnapper was deadly serious."

"Right."

Just thinking about what sort of demand the suspect
might have made of the woman's lover was disturbing—
especially if he was escalating as it appeared he was.

"Alright," I said, "we need to get word out about this
woman. I want to make sure we stop her husband or fiancé or whoever from doing whatever her abductor demanded. We can release word about her condition to the
media, about the severed finger, emphasizing that she's
okay, safe, and under police protection."

Calculating when Colleen had been found at the pier
this morning and the time of a round-trip drive during
the day, I said, "The warm hood on the Taurus . . . There
might be more than one missing woman within a six-

hour drive of here, but I doubt there'd be more than one whose left ring finger was left behind."

"I thought you don't like working with the media?"

"Well, right now time is what matters most. Stopping the woman's spouse or lover from carrying out the kidnapper's demands, whatever those might be, and maybe getting us something we can use to actually find this woman's attacker trumps everything. Get a physical description of her out now and as soon as she regains consciousness, release her photo to the press."

"I'll call it in."

He left and I quickly moved on in my mind to step five: evaluation.

Everyone is tempted to prove what he believes, and that affects not only conscious decision-making but the way our minds subconsciously process information. There's even a name for it: confirmation bias. Most of the time we're not even aware of it happening. Naturally, no one likes to be wrong, but the best investigators step back and actually try to find holes in their own theories. This moves you toward objectivity, and that always brings you closer to the truth.

However, the CSIU arrived just as I was beginning to form a working hypothesis that I could try to disprove.

"I want the different spots of blood spatter on the floor checked separately," I told them. "I don't care how many favors we have to pull in to get the DNA results back fast. We have no idea how many people this guy may have brought to this train yard. Until further notice, this whole area—everything inside this fence—is a crime scene."

"That's a big crime scene," one of them objected.

A thought: "Let's make it even bigger. We also need to include the woods."

"The woods?"

"He knew where the fence was pulled loose, which path to take through the forest. That makes the fence part of the scene."

"And the woods."

"Yeah," I replied, "and the woods. Because he might have tossed evidence—his phone, a knife, his gun. Possibly a set of clothes."

They looked at me wearily, no doubt thinking about how long all this might take, but they said nothing more.

Then, even if they weren't as skilled at their jobs as I might've liked, I needed to respect them enough to let them do what Thorne had sent them here to do.

Two things were on my immediate agenda: (1) call Taci; (2) get back to the boxcar I'd been standing on when the suspect fired at me and take a look at Bruce Hendrich's body.

43

Joshua didn't know exactly why he hadn't killed Adele Westin.

He could have stabbed her with the necrotome, shot her with the Glock, taken the amputation saw to her neck—any of a number of things.

No murderer hath eternal life abiding in him.

He protested against the thought, turned away from it.

However, in this case, killing Adele would probably have been the best idea. Not to take any chances. After all, he'd already let Colleen live, and look where that'd led.

Was that how law enforcement had found him at the train yard? He'd been careful with her, careful to make sure there was no way for her to tell where they were, but theoretically it was still possible.

The deadline had come and long since gone, and Carl had not called.

That bothered Joshua. It wasn't going to make any difference anymore in the way he treated Adele, but still, the man's fiancée had been abducted, her finger amputated and left behind, and he wasn't even committed to her enough to call at the appointed time?

If anyone ever took Sylvia away from him, Joshua wouldn't have taken any chance whatsoever that she would be killed. He would have called the number no matter what. He would have gone to the ends of the earth to save his wife and he couldn't imagine how Carl had not made a simple phone call to save his fiancée.

Joshua needed to sort out a few things before going home, before returning to his normal life.

So that's what he thought about as the search for him went on in the train yard and the neighboring woods.

+ + +

One of the squads in the parking lot had a car phone, so I tapped in Taci's number.

I caught her just as she was about to leave her apartment to run some errands before coming over for dinner. Though I felt bad about having to cancel, the homicide investigation obviously took precedence over our supper plans and I trusted that she would understand.

It wasn't my place to tell her details about the case, but I was able to notify her that there'd been a homicide. "I'm not sure when I'll be done here, but maybe we could grab a late supper, or dessert, whatever you feel up to."

"No. That's okay. That's where you need to be. We can connect at breakfast tomorrow. I have some reading to do tonight anyway."

"There was something important you wanted to discuss," I said. "Maybe I should call you? When I get home?"

She reiterated that it was something she wanted to discuss in person, so we agreed to meet at seven thirty tomorrow morning for breakfast at Anthony's Café, then we said our "I love yous" and hung up. It was only when I was walking back to the boxcar to have a look at Hendrich's body that I realized I'd hung up without wishing her a happy anniversary.

And she had done the same with me.

44

As I approached the car, Ralph caught up with me and told me that the search warrant had gone through and that Ellen and Corsica were on their way to Fort Atkinson to pick up Griffin's sales receipts and a copy of his subscription list.

"Perfect."

He went on: "We'll have the team look over the receipts in the morning." Then he informed me that Lyrie had radioed in that he was still in Hendrich's neighborhood. Apparently, Thompson was checking the names of officers in Champaign to see if any had ever lived in Waukesha. Lieutenant Thorne was at some sort of meeting with the captain. "The lieutenant scheduled a briefing tomorrow morning at ten in order to give the CSIU a little time to process some of the evidence first."

Ten o'clock should give me enough time to have breakfast with Taci, and then a chance to review the team's findings before the briefing.

"Sounds good."

My attention shifted to the homicide scene.

Three CSIU members were already working the boxcar where Hendrich's body had been found. One was dusting for prints, another was photographing the body, the third was searching for trace evidence on the east end of the car. They'd set up floodlights and the inside of the boxcar was such a bright contrast to the darkness outside that it was almost jarring.

The photographer mumbled something about how this guy had not died in a very desirable way. The words floated toward me and then disappeared into a narrow, shy spot in the air above the corpse, but I wasn't really listening to her. I was looking at Hendrich's body.

He was in his late thirties, Caucasian, slight build, with salt-and-pepper hair and a goatee. A frenzy of blood was spread across his abdomen.

And he was now and forever dead.

At the scene of a homicide, evil isn't airbrushed or sanitized as it is on the evening news. Out here it gets right in your face and you can't turn the channel or look away. Newscasters must know that if they dwell too long on the realities of death it'll be too depressing and people will flip the channel to watch *Seinfeld*. Evil is either sensationalized or muted. On the air it's almost never shown to be honestly, fully, what it is.

If you believe in eternity, Bruce's soul was either in paradise or the inferno. If you don't believe in eternity, you'd have to accept that he had entered oblivion and all that he had been was now and would forever be no more.

I couldn't help but think about how paper-thin the fabric of life is. I once worked a case in which a man slipped in the shower and the broken glass from the stall gouged into his throat and he bled to death in less than a minute—just that quick.

It might be a screech of tires as someone swerves into

your lane. Or a heart attack or stroke. Or something as harmless as dropping a bar of soap in the shower. And that's it. Most people live their whole lives without ever realizing that every moment is a near-death experience.

Truthfully, when I think about it, it's baffling and astonishing to me that I'm here, in this place at this time, breathing, thinking, dreaming, believing. Aware of being aware of being alive.

And it's mind-boggling that we die, every one of us, that all of humanity's hopes and dreams come to an end, one person, one tragic death at a time.

Without heaven to spend eternity in, or another go-around here on earth to try to make things right, what could possibly, ultimately matter?

No wonder so many people believe in reincarnation.

And in heaven.

I wasn't exactly sure what I believed about those things, but doing this job I've learned three things for certain, three things I do know for sure: life is a mystery, death is a tragedy, and hope—when it exists—is always a gift.

Hendrich was wearing civilian clothes, no security guard uniform. There was blood on the floor of the boxcar, but none leading to it, which told me he was killed in here.

I wondered how long he might have been kept in this train car before he was killed.

Evidence and evident both come from the same root word meaning "obvious," but all too often the two concepts—what is evident and what is evidence—don't mesh very well in an investigation. Evidence isn't always evident and what's evident doesn't always end up being evidence.

I wanted the walls and the wounds and the clues to speak to me; wanted everything in the boxcar to bring a collective voice together and whisper to me the name of the killer, but for the moment I noticed nothing else that seemed in any way pertinent. All the evidence was silent.

As I looked around the boxcar, I ran through the five investigative steps but came up with nothing revelatory.

"Did you go through his pockets?" I asked the head of the CSIU team.

"Not yet."

"Now would be good."

After a small pause, he did, and produced $14.73, a well-used, much-stained handkerchief, a set of keys, a wallet, and a pocketknife. I knew that the CSIU team would follow up on all these things later. I wanted to follow up on one of them now.

The keys.

45

I still had on the same pair of latex gloves from earlier, and now, so that I wouldn't cross-contaminate the two scenes, I donned a new pair. My hands were sore and tender and, to say the least, it didn't exactly feel good tugging gloves off and on.

First, I took the keys to the lock on this boxcar, then to the gate, then jogged back to the boxcar where we'd found the woman.

None of the keys opened any of the locks. Hendrich didn't have a Ford Taurus key on the ring.

All of which intrigued me.

I returned the keys to be logged in as evidence, and Ralph and Radar ran into me outside the boxcar. "Nothing from the neighborhood," Ralph announced. "No one saw anything, not even that little kid."

"Okay . . ." The wind still hadn't let up and I caught myself muttering, "I wonder if he heard me . . ."

"Heard you?" Radar said.

"I shouted into the boxcar when I first saw Hendrich's body," I explained, "but considering the distance to the car where we found the woman, also the mattresses and the wind . . ." I started for the boxcar door. "I'll yell at you two."

Ralph looked confused. "What do you mean, you'll yell at us?"

I indicated toward the car where we'd found the woman. "Go down there. I'll stay here and yell like I did when I was trying to see if there was anyone in this boxcar. We'll try it a couple times, door open, closed. You get the idea."

He caught on. "See if it was possible for the guy who attacked her to hear you shouting."

"Right."

It only took a few minutes to do the reenactment and when we reconvened, Radar shook his head. "Nothing."

But you heard the muted cries, Pat . . .

How?

Well, if it was the woman, she would have been scream-ing as loudly as she could.

I'm not sure that explained what I'd heard, but the reenactment did tell us one thing. "So," I said, "it's un-likely the shooter heard us; and if his door was closed, he didn't see us either, unless someone else—"

"Warned him," Radar said, concluding what I'd been finding myself inclining toward. "A sentry? A scout? Is that what you're thinking?"

"We need to stay open to the possibility."

"But where did he go?"

"It's possible to get over the fence." I held up my gloved, bandaged hands. "I improvised, but someone could have certainly planned better than I did. When our attention was focused on the shooter, the other person— if there really was another person—could've fled in an-other direction."

This line of reasoning opened up a whole range of interesting possibilities.

If there were two offenders, were they working together?
If not, how do you explain the timing?

Ralph must have been thinking the same thing. "Isn't it too much of a coincidence that there were two separate crimes right here, at the same time?"

I tried to process what we had going on here. Two victims. One shooter. Even though the proximity of the crimes favored the possibility that the victims were attacked by the same offender, the MO really was completely different: the woman had been restrained in a chair just as Colleen Hayes had been last night, the man had not. He had no ligature marks and had been stabbed numerous times in his stomach, unlike any of the other victims, not even from the homicides in Illinois and Ohio. No lungs removed here. No intestines eaten. No limbs sawed off. All the other victims had been women, this guy wasn't.

"It's true," I admitted. "There are a lot of things that don't measure up here."

"Unless we really are talking about two different offenders," Radar offered.

"Or three."

They looked at me curiously. "Three?" Ralph said.

"The out-of-state homicides, the kidnappings, and Hendrich's murder."

He shook his head. "But they're not entirely unrelated. Griffin's merchandise sales to Colleen Hayes, the police tape from the murder in Illinois, tie them all together."

I said, "The two homicides in Ohio and Illinois bear no semblance to the pattern of abduction, coercion, and mutilation that we saw with the Hayes family and now, evidently, with this woman tonight. There was no ransom note in the previous deaths and the victims of the last two days were left alive, even though they could have easily been killed."

"And here, there's no cannibali—" Ralph caught himself short. "The hands."

We were quiet. We didn't know what Colleen's abductor had done with her hands, but we could imagine, and by the looks on Ralph's and Radar's faces, I think we all were.

Backpedaling a little, I stated the obvious: "Hendrich was a part-time security guard here. Maybe he just came upon our guy and got taken out."

Don't assume too much in any direction.

Radar offered to dig up a list of Caucasians fitting our suspect's description who might visit this neighborhood regularly enough to become familiar with the woods, invisible to the neighbors. "You were right, Pat. We've got a white guy who knows how to evaporate into a neighborhood of gangbangers of another race. I'll look at social workers, youth coaches, parole officers, pizza delivery guys. Everyone. I don't care. Including cops."

Even though I didn't like to even consider the idea that a cop could be involved, I agreed that it was worth pursuing.

Ralph said to me, "I'll stick with you. Coordinate the searches. I'll stay as late as I need to."

My eyes were on the flashlight beams from the officers who were working their way through the forest. "Good to hear, Tonto."

46

Joshua's wife had supper waiting for him when he came through the door, but she looked at him with concern as he dropped his keys onto the counter. "What is it, hon?"

"What?"

"You look pale. Like you just saw a ghost."

"No, it's just . . . traffic. It's nothing." He kissed her. "I'll be back in a sec. Let me kick off my shoes."

As he crossed the hallway to the bedroom, he tried to piece together what had happened out there tonight.

Just before coming into the house, he'd heard through the police scanner that law enforcement had made the connection to Carl Kowalski, which explained why he hadn't called at five—he was in custody. But at least he'd done as asked and Miriam Flandry's skinned corpse had been found. The media would undoubtedly be jumping all over the story tonight.

Joshua put his gun away.

And of course, when law enforcement made the connection to Carl, they'd also discovered that the woman who'd been found in the train yards, the woman who was missing a finger, was Carl's fiancée, Adele Westin.

But.

They'd also found Bruce Hendrich. He was the part-time security guard whose hours Joshua had researched so thoroughly, been so careful to avoid whenever he entered the train yard. And now he was found dead there. Stabbed. Locked in another boxcar.

Why then? Why there?

From Hendrich's schedule, Joshua knew he hadn't been on the docket to work today.

Questions chasing him, Joshua returned to the kitchen and helped Sylvia set the table.

"Did you have a good afternoon?" she asked him.

"Yes." He tried to concentrate on her, to not let the events of the day come between them. "How did the house showings go?"

"Didn't sell any, but you know what they say . . ." She smiled, but Joshua could see that it was a bit forced, that she wasn't exactly optimistic but was trying hard to be. "Just live it through."

"That's right," he said. "Just live it through. It'll all work out. You're good at what you do."

A welcome smile. "Thank you, dear."

He looked over the meat loaf, baked potatoes, and carrots she'd prepared. "Supper looks great."

A pause. "Where were you all day?" she asked. "I tried calling."

"Running errands. Taking care of a few things."

After they'd said grace and started eating, his thoughts wandered back to the train yard.

Was it possible that it was all a coincidence?

Possible, perhaps, but how likely was that?

There was only one other explanation.

Someone knew. Someone knew he was going to be in the yard, knew he was going to have a woman there tonight.

It was unfathomable to think that, but Joshua let himself think it anyway. Because he had to.

And if that was the case, if someone knew, that might explain why law enforcement showed up when they did—the person could have contacted them, called in a tip.

But then why leave Hendrich dead? And locked in a train car?

Someone out there is trying to set you up, trying to frame you for Hendrich's murder.

But why?

As Sylvia ate, she told Joshua all about her day and he listened, not just because it was something a good husband should do, but because he was genuinely interested in her life. But despite that, admittedly, his attention did drift at times to what had happened tonight, to what was going to happen in the next two days.

Tonight he would watch the news, find out what he could about how it might have been that Hendrich happened to show up dead when he did at the train yard. It was important to make sure everything was set for Wednesday, for what was going to happen with the cop, so tomorrow, he would return briefly to look over the best places to park near the bank on Highway 83 in Wales—the same bank the Oswalds held up the day they were arrested.

The scripture verse was not just true for him, it would

be true for the cop as well: "The good that I would I do not: but the evil which I would not, that I do."

That.

I.

Do.

Yes, the officer he had in mind would find out the true meaning of those words.

47

Two years ago the Maneater of the Midwest began to call himself, in his own mind, what he truly was.

A ghoul.

Of course he'd heard of ghouls before that. He knew what they were, that they liked to consume human corpses, often those dug up from graveyards, but the day when he finally began to think of himself in terms of being one, of placing himself in that category, was freeing and, in a way, like coming home.

When you're this way, you can't help but want to find someone else like you. It's inevitable. So, over the years he'd always hoped to meet another actual ghoul. Curiosity mostly—though he hadn't been sure how he would respond if he truly found one. He had not always worked alone, but he had not yet found anyone else who shared his particular interests.

However, there were a few times when he *had* met people who gave off hints that perhaps, yes, just perhaps, they would understand, so those were the times when he'd tested the waters, put out feelers, so to speak, to see if he'd found a kindred spirit.

After a few beers, or on a long car ride, or during a

period of marijuana-induced honesty, he would say something like, "Did you ever wonder about those soccer players back in the seventies? Up in the Andes Mountains? Remember hearing about that?" And maybe his friend would say yes she had, or maybe she would give him a blank look and shake her head no.

"Yeah," he would say, "when their plane crashed. Twenty-nine out of the forty-five survived. The mountain was isolated, snow-covered. The survivors had nothing to eat and when some of them started dying, they knew they needed to find something fast. They were all starving."

And at that point he would pause and study the face of the person he was talking to, study it to see if she was able to jump ahead to the inevitable conclusion.

Finally, it would come. "You don't mean they . . . that they ate each other?"

"Well, only the dead ones," he might joke, depending on the situation. In either case, it was a critical point, the telling moment. "Yes, they had to," he would say. "If they were going to survive."

And here came the reaction that would either end the conversation for good, or give him hope that perhaps he'd finally found someone who could understand.

Usually, the reaction was the same: "Ew. That's horrible!" or "That's disgusting" or "I'd rather die myself! I would never do that!" or the like, and what could he do? The Maneater wasn't the type of person to argue. So he would agree with her about how unthinkable such a thing was. "You're right. It's disgusting. I can't imagine how civilized people could ever do that."

He would say things like that, and then take a long

draft of beer or a drag of his joint and never bring up the subject to that person again.

However, there was one woman he'd met who seemed to contemplate the situation a little more clearheadedly. They'd gone out for supper and were walking through downtown Milwaukee when he'd brought up the question. She'd thought about it and said, "The thing is, those guys had to survive, right? I mean, why should all of them die when some of them could live? Why, when there was fresh meat lying there preserved for them in the snow? Should they starve to death, just because of a social stigma, the cultural conventions of Western society?"

"Good point." He decided to step out on a limb. "In some cultures it's perfectly acceptable to eat other people. Cannibalism isn't frowned on in other places as much as it is in America, or, say, Britain. There was a group of Indians who ate their parents' dead bodies."

"As a show of respect," she said. "Yes, I've heard of that."

He stopped walking. Took her hand. "You have?"

"We studied it in this anthropology class I had last year. Herodotus, right? He wrote about it?"

"I guess. I don't know; I'm not sure." But it wasn't a guess and he did know. For sure.

He was nervous to ask the next question, but he had to find out the answer. "And what did you think of that? When you heard about it?"

"What's wrong in one country might not be wrong in another. That's the way the world is. I think a person's morality, her set of values, is determined by what culture she grows up in. We shouldn't judge other people's values."

The politically correct answer, but an obviously untenable moral position.

After all, in the 1940s it was culturally acceptable in Germany to kill Jews by the millions. In some tribes in Africa, raping women is considered normal and acceptable—at least by the men. But nobody who's being raped or tortured to death just shrugs it off and accepts that the person doing it to him is simply following his or her cultural values, so, oh well, what's right for him is right for him, no big deal.

No. Nobody who's on the short end of justice wants to be treated subjectively. Relativism and equity just don't go hand in hand.

The Maneater had an extraordinary memory. He didn't like to call attention to it to others and he didn't take any pride in it himself, but it was there and he couldn't help but make use of it. And that night he'd thought of the passage this woman had just referred to: Godley's 1921 translation of *The Histories* by Herodotus, Book 3:38, an excerpt he'd read twice and remembered word for word:

> When Darius was king, he summoned the Greeks who were with him and asked them for what price they would eat their fathers' dead bodies. They answered that there was no price for which they would do it. Then Darius summoned those Indians who are called Callatiae, who eat their parents, and asked them (the Greeks being present and understanding through interpreters what was said) what would make them willing to burn their fathers at death. The Indians

cried aloud, that he should not speak of so hor-
rid an act. So firmly rooted are these beliefs;
and it is, I think, rightly said in Pindar's poem
that custom is lord of all.

Custom is lord of all.

Morality is not etched in stone but written, as it were,
on a rubber band.

Simply the result of cultural mores.

What an attractive, attractive idea for those wielding
power.

But this wasn't the time to debate the determinants
of ethical action with his date, it was actually his chance
to agree with her. "You're right about that," he said,
"and, well, those dead people up on the slopes of that
mountain in the Andes weren't really people anymore
actually. They were only meat that was going to rot
eventually or just freeze and lie there indefinitely. I
mean, right? And in a situation like that, what choice did
the survivors really have? I mean what else could they be
expected to do?"

He watched her carefully, searched her eyes to gauge
her reaction, to look for hints of what she might say, what
she might be thinking. "So, what do you think? Could
you have done it?"

"Done it?"

"Yes."

"You mean eaten someone?"

"To survive. Yes."

"Well, I suppose, if I was on the brink of death, I guess
I might have."

But really, that begged the question. How close to the

brink of death does a person have to be, really, before it would be okay? How much desperation would justify cannibalism? Do you really need to be starving to death? What about famished? What about simply hungry? Or just sitting down for supper? How many hours away from death by starvation do you need to be to justify chewing off the skin or sucking the marrow out of another primate's bones?

Cultures disagree.

So, really, it was a matter of societal preference.

Pindar's poem is right: custom is lord of all.

Perhaps morally untenable, but still, a philosophical position that suited the Maneater.

The one wielding power.

He liked this woman and decided on the spot that he would cut out and eat her intestines.

She was the first one, the one he still remembered the most fondly to this day.

Now, tonight he was at a club. Trance music. Psychedelic cycling lights. Sweaty, pumping bodies. He was seated at the bar next to a woman who'd been flirting with him for the last twenty minutes. Even though it was just after ten o'clock, she'd made it clear what she wanted to do, but he hadn't even gotten her name yet.

He decided to just go ahead, see where that might lead. "I don't sleep with women I don't know."

"Well, then"—there was a breezy, alcohol-induced smile in her voice—"my name is Celeste."

"Hello, Celeste."

"And you are?"

He made up a name. "Ashton."

"Well, Ashton"—she really was too tipsy for her own good, already, at this time of night—"do you need a last name, or is Celeste enough for you?"

"Celeste is plenty." He smiled and with one hand he took hold of her barstool and pulled it closer to him.

"Mmm," she cooed. "I like a man who's got some strength. Do you have endurance too?"

"Oh yes," he said. "I can make things last for a long, long time."

"Ooh. I like the sound of that."

She finished her shot, turned the glass upside down and, somewhat unevenly, set it on the bar. "I also like a man who's not all talk. Are you all talk?"

"I'm not all talk, no."

She stood and swayed a bit. He rose as well and she put her arm in his.

He led her out of the club.

They went to her apartment. He enjoyed himself with her for a while, and as he did, the Maneater thought back to the events of the night, to the train yards, to killing Hendrich, a man whose identity he and Griffin had decided to use if there was ever a need.

And he thought of why he'd led Hendrich to that car and then killed him there, because of what he'd found in that other train car. Because of the man he'd followed and then identified and because of the phone call from Griffin warning him that the police were following up on Hendrich.

Why was Joshua doing this? Setting up these elaborate schemes? Dahmer? Now Gein?

To get your attention?

Well, if that was the reason, it had worked.

The Maneater thought about what to do about that as he spent time with Celeste who, as it turned out, wasn't so thankful that he could make things last for a long, long time.

Not thankful about that at all.

48

I stayed at the train yards until almost eleven. We had a dozen officers comb the woods. I even helped them, but we found nothing.

Everyone was focused, sharp. This was no longer just the case of a kidnapper's twisted demands; with Hendrich's murder, it was a full-fledged homicide investigation.

But then at last, just as in all investigations, it was time to go home.

But I had two stops to make first.

Many of the criminology students in my grad program at Marquette have other jobs—some work in law enforcement, others are city officials. I've even had two people from the District Attorney's Office in some of my classes. Because of the diverse schedules of the students, the graduate office has a work area that's open late, and it's not unusual to find people studying at all hours of the night hunched over a computer or a criminology textbook.

On the way to my apartment I swung by to pick up a copy of Dr. Werjonic's lecture notes, then snagged an extra-large fried potato and steak burrito from Henry's Burrito Heaven, and headed to my apartment.

I spread out the paperwork on the kitchen table and as I dug into my late supper, I reviewed five pieces of information we'd come up with over the last few hours.

1. Adele Westin was the name of the woman we'd found in the boxcar. I hated to admit that the media had helped us out, but this time around the press had done an admirable job of getting the word out quickly. A man from Plainfield named Carl Kowalski, a man who'd been arrested for grave robbery while we were at the train yards, told the police about the finger. One of the officers in Plainfield had heard about it on the news and made the connection. A little serendipitous, but often that's just the way things work in cases. Which led to #2:

2. Kowalski had not only desecrated his grandmother's grave, he had also skinned the corpse and left it at the same hardware store where Gein had committed one of his murders four decades ago.

3. During the day, Ellen and Corsica had come up with sixteen unsolved missing persons cases in Ohio, Illinois, and Wisconsin spanning the last two years involving women who fit the general description (race, age, build, hair color, socioeconomic status) of the women killed in Illinois and Ohio.

4. Thompson reported that no Champaign officers had ever worked in the Waukesha area and the chain of custody forms didn't raise any red flags.

5. When Ellen and Corsica had delivered the search warrant and picked up Griffin's receipts and subscrip-

tion list, Corsica had asked him for a physical description of Hendrich, hoping to find out if he really was
the guy who'd dealt with him, or if someone else had
impersonated him, but Griffin said they'd only com-
municated by mail or by phone. She'd also asked
about amputation saws, but he claimed he'd never
sold one—though he would like to get his hands on
one if she had a contact.

I reviewed: Dahmer and Gein.

Two cannibals.

Two days.

And bad things come in threes.

Wonderful.

As both Radar and I had observed earlier, most killers
escalate. I couldn't imagine what our guy had in mind for
later this week, not if he was moving up the ladder from
Dahmer and Gein.

After going through the case files and filling out my
police report concerning the events of the evening, I
came to the place where I needed to tip my thoughts in
a less visceral, less disturbing direction, take a break from
all the grisly images—both the ones on the pages before
me and the ones in my head.

It was late, but I tried calling Taci.

She didn't pick up.

*You'll just have to sort things out in the morning during
breakfast.*

Maybe I could get some emotional distance from all of
this by looking not at the specifics of the cases, but at the
theories concerning how to investigate them instead.

I opened up the manila folder Dr. Werjonic had left for me and slid the papers out.

There was a note on top of the stack of papers:

Ring me in the morning, Detective Bowers, between 11:00 and 11:05. I'm at the downtown Sheraton. I think I may be able to help you with this case.

Cheers.
—C.W.

I slowly set down the papers.

Dr. Calvin Werjonic PhD, JD, eminent professor, world-renowned criminologist, was offering to help me with this case? Sure, the news media had released information regarding it, but how did he know I was the one working it?

Curious to see if any of his lecture notes might be applicable to what we were looking at here, I spread the photocopied pages across the table.

To my disappointment, his notes weren't typed or organized in any clearly discernible manner, but they were handwritten scribbles that were, in most cases, almost indecipherable.

He'd probably been teaching the material for so long that he didn't need many prompts to get him started on each topic. That might have been good if I were sitting in a lecture hall listening to him, but it wasn't good for me sitting here in my apartment tonight.

However, he did include photocopied pages from one of his articles that appeared last year in the *Journal of the*

International Association of Crime Analysts, a succinct summary of his two-pronged approach:

> Geospatial investigation involves the evaluation of locations related to a crime to deduce the most statistically probable region out of which the offender bases his criminal activity. The complementary field of environmental criminology focuses on understanding the way offenders cognitively map their environments and rationally choose to act within their awareness space while committing their crimes.
>
> The two approaches work in conjunction with each other to provide a vigorous and robust new paradigm for analyzing linked serial offenses and tracking those who commit them.
>
> Unlike profilers, who deal with the psychological reasons that might have motivated a crime, environmental criminologists look for the significance of the location of the crime to both the offender and the victim. Instead of asking what the offender might have been thinking while he committed the crime, we ask why he was there at that specific place at that specific time:
>
> (1) What do the choice of the crime's location and the timing of the crime tell us about the offender and the victim?
> (2) What purpose do these locations serve for him? Expediency? Opportunity? Isolation?

(3) What do the locations of the crimes tell us about how he's choosing his victims?

(4) What led him to this specific victim and location? How and when did his life intersect with the victim's to create the encounter that precipitated this crime?

These were four lines of inquiry worth thinking about, in depth, in regard to this case.

The article went on to discuss victimology, that is, the study of the victim and inferences that could be drawn from his or her cognitive maps. Fascinated, I read the rest of it carefully with a highlighter in hand.

When I was done, I shuffled through the rest of the notes and realized that I wasn't going to be able to decode them all tonight, not when I was so tired, but that I might be able to make my way through them better in the morning when I was fresh.

Today had become one of those days when it seemed like the morning couldn't possibly have occurred within the same twenty-four-hour span of time. Too much had happened, too much had filled in the spaces between the moments.

Tomorrow never looked so good.

At last, I crawled into bed with thoughts of the case and of Taci and of the nightmares I'd had last evening all vying for my attention, all wrestling to be the thing that followed me into my dreams.

And when I closed my eyes, I had no idea which of them would win.

DAY 3

Tuesday, November 18

The Landfill

49

6:02 a.m.

The nightmares left me alone.

I dreamt of Taci instead, and woke up thinking about our weekend getaway to Tennessee the first weekend of October. We'd been close as a couple when we headed down there and when we returned, we were even closer, with shared memories of day hikes in the Smoky Mountains and evenings in front of the fireplace at a bed-and-breakfast nestled up in the hills.

It was a nice note to start the day on and when I got out of bed I felt much more rested than I had yesterday morning, which was a relief because I had the feeling this might shape up to be another long day.

I wasn't scheduled to meet Taci until seven thirty, nearly an hour and a half from now. Anthony's Café was downtown, which gave me an idea.

When you're working cases like this, the odd hours, the long hours, it's easy to eat poorly—admittedly one of my weaknesses. And, for me at least, it's easy to miss workouts. Getting motivated to exercise wasn't usually the issue for me because I loved to trail run, climb, hike, anything outdoors. But finding the time to get out and play when you're in the middle of a case can be tricky.

My climbing buddy, Reinhold Draeger, operated the South Wall Climbing Gym, which wasn't too far from Anthony's Café. The morning's agenda seemed to lay itself out neatly for me: slip in a workout at the gym, grab breakfast with Taci, review Werjonic's notes and the case files, meet with the task force at HQ, then call Dr. Werjonic at eleven.

Even though I climb with ropes when I'm at the crags, working out close to the ground without them is a great way to develop finger strength, leg work, and breathing. It's called bouldering and an hour of that would be more than enough of a workout for this morning.

Before leaving my apartment, I taped up my hands to protect the sores from being torn open by the holds, some of which were pretty sketchy. Then I took off.

Because of my unusual work hours, Reinhold had given me a key to the gym and now I parked, went in the back entrance, and had the place to myself. Climbers have their own jargon and, while most people might talk about pulling themselves up a climb when they're making moves, we talk about pulling them down. So, after warming up and working past the pain in my hands, that's what I did on some of the stoutest climbs in the bouldering cave.

Counterintuitively, it often seems that stepping away from a case and letting that curious, secret part of my brain work on it is the best way to get a fresh perspective.

Often it's in the moments of quiet that the tiny threads of a case imperceptibly intertwine. I guess it's human nature, though. We gather facts, try to process them, but don't often tie them together until we're in the shower or on the golf course or waking up in the middle of the night. Just ask any novelist, any artist, any scientist.

And sometimes we think of them when we're upside down in a bouldering cave.

Sometimes.

Like today.

Halfway through one of the hardest climbs in the cave, a V9 problem that I'd never been able to send, it struck me.

Indiana.

He passed through Indiana.

All sixteen missing persons, as well as the homicide victims we knew about, came from Ohio, Illinois, and Wisconsin. Why did the offender—or offenders—skip over the state of Indiana?

The questions from the article that I'd read last night from Dr. Werjonic flashed through my mind:

(1) What does the choice of the crime's location tell us about the offender and the victim?

(2) What purpose do these locations serve for him? Expediency? Opportunity? Isolation?

(3) What do the locations of the crimes tell us about how he's choosing his victims?

(4) What led him to this specific victim, and location? How and when did his life intersect with the victim's to create the encounter that precipitated this crime?

The conclusion about why he skipped over Indiana: he wasn't familiar with the state.

His awareness space didn't include it.

We needed to find people who'd lived, worked, or attended college in the three states in question—but not in Indiana. Specifically, the metro areas of Milwaukee, Champaign, and Cincinnati. Looking more closely at the tip list and suspect list would be the place to start.

I dropped from the climb and landed on my feet on the bouldering pads beneath the route. I wanted to get right at it, start looking into that, but Taci and I had apparently hit some sort of snag in our relationship, and I needed to iron that out first.

Hopefully it wouldn't take too long.

In truth, I was somewhat anxious about what we might be discussing, but I assured myself that whatever was on her mind was something we'd be able to settle without too much hassle.

As soon as I'd showered and changed, I gathered my things and walked down the street to Anthony's Café.

50

The café was cheery and busy this morning, with people chatting, sipping lattes, or in some cases, working their way through a muffin or croissant while perusing today's edition of the *Milwaukee Journal*—which, I noticed, had a front-page article about the crimes last night. Photos of Gein and Dahmer appeared in the right-hand column.

Great.

Well, you're the one who suggested going to the media.

Obviously, this was not the kind of private setting Taci had been intimating she wanted to meet in. However, there was a corner by the fireplace with a few empty tables. I stowed my things at one of them and when I went back to the counter, I saw Taci striding through the front door.

She smiled. "Hey."

"Morning."

Her eyes went immediately to my hands, which I'd retaped since my shower, then to the rips in my leather jacket. "Pat, what happened?"

"Fencing."

"Fencing? You were fencing?"

"In a sense." Somewhat awkwardly, I slipped my hands into my pocket. "It's not a big deal."

"Uh-huh."

"I'm fine."

"That's what you always say."

"Always, when?"

"You get hurt."

"I don't get hurt. That much."

A half smile, hands on her hips, but it wasn't a real reprimand. "How many times have you gotten injured while doing something on the city's payroll?"

"That's not even a fair—"

"How many times?"

"A couple. Maybe. Over the years."

"Mm-hm." She took my arm. "Let's get some breakfast."

So. Good signs so far. She was in a pleasant mood. I was in a pleasant mood. I began to relax.

She ordered a feta cheese and spinach bagel sandwich; I grabbed two chocolate muffins and two bananas so the health factor would even itself out.

She had coffee. I had tea.

Honestly, neither of us was good at chitchat, but we made our way through the obligatory small talk you're supposed to have when you're a couple catching up—she told me about her rounds at the hospital, I told her about driving to Fort Atkinson and back yesterday afternoon.

"So you were the one who found her in the boxcar? You and the FBI agent?"

I guessed where she'd heard it. "The news?"

She nodded toward someone nearby who was reading the paper. "I glanced at the headlines on the rack outside."

"Yeah, that was me."

"The public relations officers said you guys arrived just in time to save her. They're praising you."

"You learned that from glancing at the headlines?"

"Okay, maybe it was a little more than a glance."

"At a little more than the headlines?"

I saw the flicker of a smile. "Possibly."

"I'm just glad we got there when we did." But as I said the words, I couldn't help but think of the conversation I'd had with Ralph last night in which I'd said almost the same thing, and of course the second part of that conversation too: *"But angry we didn't get there soon enough to save Hendrich."*

Taci sighed softly, then gave a small head-shake of exasperation. "Do you ever wonder, Pat, how these people, how they come to do these things?"

"Sometimes, yes, I do."

"What he was going to do is just unthinkable," she said. "How could you get someone to even consider maiming someone like that?"

Actually, the answer wasn't all that mysterious or elusive. "Make it seem natural, reasonable. Unavoidable. The only conceivable choice at that particular time."

She had a curious look in her eyes. It might have been concern.

"Radar once told me," I explained, "that no one does the unthinkable, because to them, in that moment, it seems like the most natural and logical thing to do—the inevitable thing. I think he's right."

"But how could you make something like that inevitable?"

"When people kill, when rapists rape, when people

torture each other, they're doing what seems perfectly reasonable to them in that moment. Nobody ever does something that, in his own mind, as he's doing it, is unthinkable."

"So, they rationalize it?"

That seemed like too mild a way to put it.

I thought for a moment. "I'd just say that behind every unspeakable act is a person who is, in his own mind, completely justified in carrying it out."

She sipped at her coffee and let my words settle in.

"So, how are you doing through all this, Pat?"

"I'm okay."

"They said he was going to cut off her hands, her feet."

"Taci, I can't really talk about the case. You know that."

"Pat, it was on CNN."

"I get that, but—"

"No one's saying much at the medical center. Is she going to be okay? You can tell me that much."

I didn't even know she'd been in to work already this morning. "It looks like it. Yes."

"Good."

Silence, then: "Are you any closer to catching the guy who's doing this?"

"Really, I can't . . ." I caught myself. Even after being together for a year and going through this type of thing before, I knew it was natural for her to ask these sorts of questions. I had the sense that I should avoid addressing them entirely, but I decided I could answer this one without necessarily divulging too much.

"Honestly, I don't know how close we are. There was

some evidence there at the train yard that I think is going to help us; some things to follow up on, so that's good. But right now we don't have a name, a face, anything specific. Now, really—"

"You can't talk about it."

"Right. I'm sorry. I can't."

For a few minutes we both ate our breakfast in a sort of strange, quiet limbo. The light mood that'd been present when we first met seemed to have been smothered by our discussion about doing the unthinkable.

Finally, I decided to just go ahead and get to the point. "So, you mentioned . . . There was something else, something you wanted to talk about?"

"Yes." But instead of telling me what it was, she was quiet once again.

She looked toward the counter and scoffed lightly, but it wasn't derision I heard. When she went on, I sensed it was her way of, perhaps subconsciously, avoiding addressing what she'd come here to say. "See her? Over there? The tag sticking out of the back of her shirt? I'll never understand that. A woman will spend an hour putting on makeup and getting her hair right and won't bother to take three seconds to make sure that the tag isn't sticking out the back of her shirt. It's . . ." Her voice trailed off.

"What is it, Taci, really? What's wrong?"

She set down her coffee, looked at me with a thread of sadness in her eyes, and said eight words, "I do love you, Pat. You know that."

Oh, that was not good.

"Why did you put it that way?"

"What way?"

"Why did you say 'I do love you' and not just 'I love you'?"

She took a deep breath and it seemed as if she was about to say something, but then she must have changed her mind, because she closed her mouth and just sat there, quietly staring past me at a spot on the wall that didn't exist.

The longer the moment stretched out without her replying, the less I wanted her to. Instead, I wanted to take back my question. I had the strange sense that finding out the truth was going to be far more painful than just pretending everything was okay.

But in the end I had to ask. I had to find out. "What's going on, Taci?"

"I do."

"Love me?"

"Yes."

"Then stop putting it that way."

She brushed her hand across the table, slowly sweeping a few bagel crumbs to the floor.

"What is it you're trying to say?" I watched her. Didn't lean any closer to her; didn't edge any farther away.

She strung the next words together, as if they were something she needed to say in one breath or she wouldn't be able to say at all: "I love you, but being with you is only going to hurt you."

I felt the bottom drop out of the moment.

"How is it going to hurt me? Your being with me?"

Silence.

"Taci, I have no idea where all this is coming from. We love each other. We've been in a relationship for nearly a year. We've talked about getting—"

"Don't say it."

"About getting—"

"Patrick—"

"About getting married, Taci. C'mon, don't pretend we haven't. Don't try to rewrite our past. Things are good, they've been—"

"I'm not pretending anything. And I'm not talking about how things have been or how they are. I'm saying . . . it's about who we are."

Despite myself, I could sense my words becoming sharper each time I spoke. "What does that mean—'who we are'?"

"Who I am."

I'd seen so many of my friends in the department struggle in their relationships, in their marriages, so many who've ended up apart, separated, divorced, alone. It's the tired cliché of crime novels—the cop who struggles in a relationship because of—wait, here comes the big shocker—*the pressures and obligations of his job!*

Wow. What an unexpected plot twist that was.

Taci and I had talked about all that early on and I'd told her that if we ever came to the place where we were thinking about taking things to the next level, if it looked like I'd have to choose between her and the force, I would either leave her before we got serious, or I'd leave the force so I could be with her. And we had gotten serious. And she'd never asked me to choose.

And it didn't even sound like she was asking me to do that now.

"Taci, if you're saying my job is doing this, hurting us, I'll quit."

She shook her head.

"No. I mean it."

"I know. But that's not the thing."

"Listen to me. I will. I love you more than—"

"It's not you, Pat. It's me. That's what I'm trying to . . . It's . . . me."

Her words seemed like solid objects that were wedging their way between us, pushing us apart.

"How is it you?"

She touched away a stray tear and I wasn't sure at all how to respond to that.

I asked the question I had to ask. "Is there someone else?"

She shook her head firmly. "No. It's not that. There isn't anyone. There's never been. Not since we got together."

"Then what are you saying?"

Then, like the proverbial floodgates opening, she finally told me what she'd come here for: "I was in the hospital yesterday, on rounds with my attending physician. I hadn't gotten any sleep the night before and I was on my fourth or fifth cup of coffee, I don't know. Well, the doctor, he asked how everything was going and I said good, that things were good, and they were . . . They are. But he could tell how both tired and wired I was. 'Get used to it,' he told me. 'It doesn't get any easier.'"

And with that, a weight lifted from my shoulders.

So that was what this was all about. Work had gotten to her. The long hours of residency and the stress of putting in twenty-four-hour shifts, hundred-hour weeks, that's what'd brought all this up.

"But it *will* get easier, Taci. You know it will. When your residency is over."

"Pat, that's the thing. I don't want it to get easier. I

want it to stay the way it is. With the adrenaline and the hours, the stress, and the trauma of life and death right there in front of me every day. The rush. Living on that sharp edge. That's what I realized when the doctor said that. I'm not made for having kids and going to soccer games and chaperoning field trips. I don't want the weekends off to go antique shopping. I don't want to come home to a safe little life every day after work."

I stared at her. "And you think that's how it would be with me? A quiet, safe little suburban life? Are you kidding me?"

"I'm saying I don't have what it would take to make our relationship work. It wouldn't be right to treat you that way." She paused as if to gain the courage to go on. "You'd always be in second place. There. I don't know how else to say it. I don't want to hurt you. I'm sorry. It took me a long time to figure this out, I know it did. Too long. I'm really sorry. I am."

I could feel the moment splintering apart like a piece of china that'd just been tipped off a table and shattered on the floor.

"I can't change who I am," she said, "and I don't want to—and I couldn't live like that, with the knowledge that I was holding you back from being loved like you deserve."

"I'm a big boy, Taci. I can—"

"Don't say you can handle it. Love isn't supposed to be something that needs to be handled; it's supposed to be the thing that helps you handle everything else."

I had the sense that I was falling, that I'd just stepped off an escarpment and was now plummeting through a thin stretch of air toward the bottom of a cliff.

"I love you." It was all I could think to say, words that I knew, even as I said them, weren't going to change anything.

"Yes," she said simply.

The whole conversation seemed surreal. Two people who love each other, two single, available adults who respect each other, who're committed to each other and care deeply about each other and have been together for this long being torn apart by nothing more than uncertainties, priorities that might change over time.

At that moment I realized it: hope has the potential to dissolve right before your eyes. You can be looking at it, something golden and precious, like the way I felt when she was joking around with me when she first walked in here, and then suddenly it's folding back into the air, leaving a dark trail behind—the dissipating smoke of the very things you used to gain strength from.

"Taci, listen, things have been crazy for us both lately. I understand that. But there's no reason to—"

She clutched her purse in front of her now as if she was using it as an emotional shield. "I can't." And before I could stop her, before I could come up with anything to say that might salvage things, she rose. "I'm sorry. I just care about you too much to . . . to . . . Second place isn't right. Not for you, Pat, not for anyone who's in love."

I stood up as well, tried to think of a way to talk her out of this, but no words came to me.

She made her way toward the door and slipped outside.

My feet seemed like they'd been rooted there forever. *Go! If you just let her walk away, you'll always regret it!*

I hurried outside and made it to her car just as she was climbing in.

"Taci, please. Let's talk about—"

"No, Pat. It'll only end up hurting worse. Please." These were the words she said as she closed the door. Then she pulled onto the road and drove down the street.

Those were the final words she said.

Of course every relationship suffers fractures. I get that. Of course they do, but people work through them, especially when they're in love.

How is this happening? This cannot be happening!

But it was happening.

It had happened.

She turned the corner.

And then the woman I loved, Taci Vardis, disappeared out of sight.

51

As I returned to my car and drove to HQ, the questions hit me hard: How could she just let things end like that? Just abandon everything that'd been, the us we'd become, and say it was over? How can someone that important to your life, that central to all of your dreams and plans, so suddenly and unexpectedly walk away?

It happens every day, Pat. People break up. They divorce. Just like that. It's over. All the time.

I thought it might've actually been easier if she were leaving me for someone else, but then it hit me that, ironically, she was leaving me so that *I* could find someone else.

And she was doing it because she loved me.

A tumble of clouds hung in the sky, lavender gray and still marred with the remnants of night. I left them, and the day they were ushering in, behind and rolled into the dark mouth of the police headquarters' underground parking garage.

Ten minutes later, at my desk, I was trying to focus on the case, but it didn't feel like I'd ever be able to concentrate on anything again, only that I would feel numb and distracted and full of unanswered questions from now on.

Ralph's low voice rumbled through the room. "Just think . . ." I looked up. He was walking my way, holding up a manila folder. "As computers take over, there's gonna come a day when these things disappear. Completely obsolete. Can't wait for that."

To me it seemed like the more we used computers, the more things we printed out. Manila folders weren't disappearing at all from the department; they were multiplying like rabbits.

"Yes," I acknowledged distractedly.

He joined me at my desk. "So, how did it go last night?"

"How did what go?"

"Dinner. On your anniversary."

"Actually, it turned out to be breakfast."

A sly grin. "You dog, you."

"No, no. Not like that. I mean : . ."

"Did you guys check out any . . . action movies?" He gave me a wink.

Oh man.

How to do this.

I debated about whether or not to tell him what'd just happened at Anthony's. In the end, perhaps naively, I decided it probably couldn't hurt anything. "This morning, just now at breakfast, Taci broke up with me."

"What? The day after your anniversary?"

"She wanted to tell me last night."

"Oh man, that's cold." It looked like he was about to say more, maybe express in his own distinctively colorful way what he thought of a woman who would do that, but he held back—likely because he wasn't sure if I was bitter, or if maybe I hoped there was some way we could get back together again.

"Apparently," I said, "it was a choice between me and her career."

We were both quiet, then he rested a giant paw on my shoulder. "If there's anything, seriously, anything I can do. Anything you need, let me know. I've been there. If you can't go to your friends when you need 'em, what good are they anyway?"

I barely knew this man and he already considered himself my friend, one close enough to help me when I was really hurting. And in that moment, I realized the feeling was mutual.

"I'll let you know, Ralph. Thanks."

He removed his hand. "Maybe we grab a beer tonight, you know? After work? Get your mind off things?"

"Yeah. We'll see."

Then he smacked me on the arm in what I took to be a friendly gesture, but one that just might leave a bruise. "Hang in there, bro."

"Thanks." I held back from rubbing my arm. "I will."

He stepped away and I tried to dial in to the case again, but thoughts of Taci just wouldn't leave me alone. I shut my eyes and concentrated, concentrated, concentrated, promised myself I wasn't going to cry. That I wouldn't let it hurt that bad.

And in the end I succeeded.

I took the pain and shock and dismay and buried them as deeply as I could, telling myself that if I stuffed them down far enough, they wouldn't be able to bother me any-more.

I didn't want the tape on my hands all day and the bleeding had stopped, so I peeled it off. Tossed it in the trash. Then I went back to work, reviewing what we knew about yesterday's homicide and the attack on Adele Westin, a woman who was engaged to a man who was willing to do the unthinkable to save her from a madman.

But I hadn't succeeded in burying my feelings. Not really. When you stuff your pain like that, it can never be called a success.

52

Watching the news last night had been informative to Joshua.

He'd learned more about Hendrich's murder. The Channel 11 News team was reporting that he'd been, "brutally attacked in a neighborhood known for its aggressive gangs and uncontrolled street violence."

By the end of the night, the anchorwoman was stating that unnamed sources in the police department were confirming "that law enforcement personnel are looking closely at outsiders who frequent that neighborhood" and "that if you have any information regarding the crimes, you should call the police."

They gave a hotline number.

As Joshua had thought, Hendrich had been off duty yesterday and no one was sure why he'd been in the train yard in the first place.

The coverage was extensive enough for Joshua to realize that it was all possibly a coincidence after all.

But then how did he get in after you locked the gate? You really think he crawled in under the fence? Or was he in there already?

Yes, there were still questions. A lot of questions. But

Joshua had enough information right now to move forward with his plans, right after a visit to the bookshelf to remind himself why he did what he did.

Yesterday he'd thought about the cache he'd found stashed under the basement steps at Timothy Griffin's house in Fort Atkinson.

Now, he went to look at the cache of his own.

Over the years he'd kept a memento from each victim, all the way back to that first time in the barn when his father gave him one of Kenneth's teeth.

Coincidently, his collection was in the basement, just like Griffin's was, but Joshua's wasn't in a fake cabinet under the steps, but rather in a small enclosed space behind a bookcase that he'd built when he first moved into the house, before he and Sylvia got married.

Nomads in the Sahara value their freedom and their ability to pitch their tents wherever they please so much that they call houses "graves of the living."

In the United States we call a nice big home the Great American Dream.

A grave or a dream. Depending on your perspective.

Two truths piercing each other: freedom and security. And you end up with the great irony of American life—living in the grave you have always dreamt of owning.

He slid the bookcase aside and looked at the crate that bristled with bones. He didn't know how many there were, the statistics of it all were, perhaps surprisingly, one of the things he hadn't kept track of. It was as if a part of his mind needed to shut that out in order for him to live as normal a life as he could.

But even though he couldn't remember the name of each victim, just seeing the bones brought the flood of images and memories back again, merging across each other, faces pulled from time in an order that didn't make sense but that played out in his mind as real, just the same.

They were mostly images of things that'd happened beneath the barn, in that secret place his father took him to. Images of the victims, and the most striking memories of all—of the last day Joshua ever went down there.

He reached into the box and picked up the tractor keys.

Curled his hand around them.

And remembered.

It all.

The day he'd left, the day he'd locked that trapdoor shut, leaving those two people behind him—one, a corpse; the other, soon to become one.

You saw what your father was doing, Joshua. You had to do something. You were finally old enough to take action. Fourteen years old. You had to do it. You know you did.

Yes—running up the steps that day, out of the secret place, into the barn.

You were scared. You had to stop him.

Yes—hearing his father pound up the stairs after him, knowing he was going to make him do things that he didn't want to do, that he would always hate himself for doing.

Yes—closing the trapdoor and locking it quickly, then standing beside it for a long time, listening to his father bang on it from the bottom and yell. Yell so many things. Bargaining. Threatening. Cursing. And then screaming.

And then the banging started all over again.

His father had handed him the knife before he ran up

the stairs, so he knew his father wouldn't be able to use it to chip away at the thick wood of the trapdoor to escape.

But still, to make sure there was no way for him to get out, Joshua had positioned a long piece of sheet metal over the opening and then drove the tractor over the two ends, positioning the tires, just so, to hold the metal firmly in place. No one else knew about the place beneath the barn. No one else came to their ranch. No one would be moving that tractor.

Now he uncurled his fingers and looked at the keys.

He'd gone out there every day for three weeks, spent long hours sitting in the barn on the seat of the tractor listening to the muted sounds coming from beneath him. The screaming, the pounding. Eventually the crying. His father had a lot of meat down there and it took him a while to die. But eventually, with time, the sounds stopped.

Joshua went out there for another week after that, listening to the enduring stretches of silence, then he left the house for good and never went back.

You were brave to stop him. You were right to leave.

But another voice inside his head convicted him of his sins and would not stop recounting them, naming them, would not let him rest, never rest, for sealing his father in that earthen tomb with the man he'd just killed.

Thinking of what it would have been like for his father down there made Joshua remember an article he'd read so many times.

He replaced the keys in the crate, closed up the bookcase, and then removed from the shelf his well-worn copy of *Wisconsin Death Trip,* Michael Lesy's cult classic first published in 1973.

The entire book was a collection of reproduced newspa-

per clippings from the 1890s and obscure, somewhat troubling turn-of-the-century black-and-white photographs.

Nearly all of the articles were reports of pestilence,
suicide, murder, arson, and announcements of people being declared insane and committed to a nearby asylum. It
seemed there'd been an inexplicable outbreak of madness
in that area of the state around the turn of the century.

No one knew why, but it was well documented.

Black River Falls, Wisconsin.

The 1890s.

The photographs showed life in Wisconsin at the time.
Some photos were the typical tired-looking nineteenth-
century women in somber dresses, scowling ministers, and
stern, thickly mustached men in work clothes. But most
of the photos skewed toward the bizarre—a woman with
a malicious grin holding two snakes with a third draped
around her neck, lithographs of dwarfs and deer heads and
a one-legged man, and young children who'd died and
were lying in small tragic caskets laid out in a neat row on
the wooden floor of a funeral home.

The book had no page numbers, but Joshua had dog-
eared the page that contained a copy of the newspaper
article from the *Badger State Banner* on April 14, 1898:

> A horrifying discovery was made at the Rose-
> dale Cemetery in Pardeeville. The grave of Mrs.
> Sarah Smith was unearthed for the purpose of
> removing the remains and, on opening the cof-
> fin, it was discovered that she had been buried
> while in a trance.
>
> The body was partly turned over and the
> right hand was drawn up to the face. The fin-

gers indicated that they had been bitten by the
woman on finding herself buried alive.

The fingers had been bitten—not the fingernails.

That was the line Joshua had always found the most
intriguing.

How much of her fingers did Sarah Smith chew off
after she woke up in that coffin?

How much meat did she swallow?

*You are a lost and evil man, Joshua. A man beyond re-
demption!*

Beyond atonement!

You did that to your own father!

That thought jarred him back to the present. He
closed the book. Put it back on the shelf.

And went to pray.

Perhaps he would find a way not to go scout out the
bank today. Perhaps he would find a way not to go rent
the moving truck he would need when he took the children tomorrow. Perhaps he would find a way to stop all
this before it went too far.

*It's already gone too far, Joshua. There's no turning
back. You're going to finish this. It's who you've become.*

Yes. He had to pray first, see if he could find the
strength to change.

Then he had to go to work.

In the normal world, where no one knew what he
really was.

53

Indiana.

Why had he skipped over Indiana?

If Dr. Werjonic's theories were right, it would most likely be because the killer lacked familiarity with the area.

But when I reviewed the tip list and suspect list as I'd decided to do while I was at the climbing gym, I found that in most cases there simply wasn't enough information about the people's backgrounds to make any real headway in that direction.

Slightly frustrated, I reviewed the other case files that the task force members had left on my desk. Based on Ellen's interviews with Vincent, it was looking more and more like he couldn't possibly be complicit in his wife's abduction. Additionally, only the guys at work knew he would be staying late.

Ellen had cross-referenced the names on the evidence room forms from the Waukesha County Sheriff Department but found no clues as to who might have gotten the cuffs to Griffin.

After I had a good grasp on where we were with the case, I figured I should probably prepare as much as possible for my call to Dr. Werjonic following our briefing. I wouldn't have much time to look over his notes later, so I turned my attention to the photocopied pages he'd left for me.

It took a few minutes, but eventually I started to get used to his cryptic scribbles and was able to make out most of his writing.

As I did so, I was struck by how his theories meshed with what I'd already learned hands-on doing my job, the information that was hardly ever emphasized at all to new cops and often seemed so inscrutable to my peers: the primacy of the timing and location of a crime, the understanding that people are motivated to commit crimes for reasons they themselves might not even understand and that spending time speculating about what those reasons might be stalls out an investigation.

But Dr. Werjonic took things even further.

He scrapped the whole notion of looking for means, motive, and opportunity in lieu of searching for context, patterns, and cues.

Three interrelated concepts wove through all that he taught: activity nodes, distance decay, and victimology: "When investigating serial crimes, the key lies not in asking what the victims have in common, but *where* they have in common."

An activity node is simply a place where we spend time. So, when identifying activity nodes, you look for the eight "nodes" of a person's life activities: the places he would normally eat, sleep, work, shop, study, worship, exercise, and relax.

Each activity node has specific attraction factors that lead people to spend time there—that might be saving time, money, or effort, a balance of risk versus rewards, or participating in pleasurable or necessary activities.

Then you can map out the person's travel routes in terms of those activity nodes (circles) and the routes or roads between them (lines). Those circles and lines cover only a fraction of the geographic area of a city and help shape the person's cognitive map of his surroundings. Almost all crimes occur within this awareness space—both with respect to victims and to offenders.

In an investigation, you establish someone's awareness space by pulling up his club memberships and frequent-buyer club cards, going through his credit card receipts, and analyzing where he typically purchases his gasoline and groceries and at what time of day, and so on. Also, by interviewing family and friends about his routines. Basically, doing all you can to examine the eight nodes of his life.

Distance decay is simply the decrease in likelihood of a crime occurring as the distance from a person's awareness space increases. That's it.

I thought again of Indiana.

He skipped over it because it wasn't part of his cognitive map.

All of this made sense to me. People are creatures of habit. Basically, costs in terms of time, energy, and effort increase as the distance from their awareness spaces increases. So we avoid that. And killers are just as influenced by this "least amount of effort" principle as the rest of us are. Taking that into account, you get one of the primary reasons why eighty percent of murders occur within one mile of the killer's home.

As Dr. Werjonic wrote:

> In crime sprees, the distribution, timing, and progression of the crimes show us how the

criminal understands his environment and in-
teracts with the locations. The offender makes
a choice to act at that time and in that place.
It's a rational decision that's affected by cues
from his environment and his social interac-
tions.

In homicide investigations, it's possible, of course, for
the initial encounter between the victim and the offender,
the abduction, the murder, and the body disposal to all
occur in the same general area, even in the same room,
but often, especially in cases of serial homicide, several of
those acts occur in different places.

Dr. Werjonic postulated that the site of the initial encounter was perhaps the most important one in the analysis of serial offenses, something I'd never heard before.

Contrariwise, law enforcement officers usually consider the site of the murder or the place where the body
is disposed of as the most important location, but Werjonic was theorizing that in the specific cases of tracking
serial offenders, by locating the place where the life of
the offender and the life of the victims first intersected,
you can begin to look for connections between them.
That'll help you more accurately zero in on the travel
routes, the nodes, the awareness space of the killer, and
then you can work backward to find his anchor point, or
home base.

Interesting.

I pulled out a map of Milwaukee and one of Wisconsin
so I could analyze what happened both here and in Plainfield. I tacked them to a corkboard easel, which I rolled
to my desk. Since it looked like there might be two of-

fenders, for now I focused on the crimes this week rather than on the previous homicides.

It felt a little old-school to be doing this, to be sticking pins on a map, but I didn't care. Anything that would help move this case forward.

I used different-colored tacks—blue for the sites where we'd found Colleen, Adele, and Hendrich (the pier and the train yards), red for their homes, green for the site where Vincent had left Lionel and where Carl had left his grandmother's corpse.

Actually, since we knew two of the abduction sites (the Hayes and Kowalski homes), and we had the site where their abductor had taken the women to mutilate them (the boxcar), I was optimistic. We didn't know if Hendrich's murder was actually connected, however, so for now, I set him mentally in a different category and focused on the women.

Unfortunately, we didn't know where or how the initial encounter between either of them and their abductor occurred. How did he choose those two families who, at least on the surface, seemed to have nothing in common and lived in different parts of the state?

This was shaping up to be one of the central questions in this case.

Because of the pastiches we were looking at, or whatever you called them, I thought we should perhaps analyze the sites of Dahmer's and Gein's crimes as well—the graveyard, the bars Dahmer frequented, the hardware store, their residences . . .

With these sites added to the mix, the number of data points would grow exponentially—even before I added in the victims' travel patterns.

No wonder Dr. Werjonic used computers to analyze his data. Looking for and prioritizing the importance of each of these locations in my head, or even on paper, would be terrifically difficult, especially since I wasn't very familiar with the algorithms he used to account for distance decay.

As I was thinking about all that, Thompson came in, smiling, carrying a Daily Donuts box. He was a burly, fun-loving guy in his late thirties. Happily married. Volunteered as a youth group leader at his church. He was also the most diehard Packers fan I knew—and around here, that was saying something. I'd never seen him without some kind of Packers paraphernalia on—a hat, shirt, belt buckle. Today, it was a lapel pin.

He set down the box.

A cop bringing in doughnuts. I felt like I was in the lead-up to a punch line. "Doughnuts?" I said. "Really?"

"Not quite." He reached into the box and brought out his prize. "Cherry turnovers."

Oh. Well, in that case.

He took a substantial bite. "Want one?" As he spoke, he didn't seem too concerned with closing his mouth to hide the half-chewed cherry turnover he was eating, and despite myself, the images of cannibalism from this case flashed through my mind and all I could think of was that he was chewing . . .

Well.

I didn't even want to go there.

I turned away.

"Um, no thanks."

"Suit yourself. But they're good." He finished the turnover, then fished around in the box again and produced another one. He leaned closer and stared over my shoulder at the board as he bit into it. "Trying to map it out, huh?"

"Something like that."

Crumbs from the turnover inadvertently dropped onto my desk. "Oops," he mumbled. "Sorry about that."

I tipped the papers to the side over the garbage can to get rid of the crumbs. "No big deal." Down the hall, Ellen, Corsica, and Lieutenant Thorne were heading toward the conference room and I invited Thompson to follow me.

"Don't worry." He picked up his box of cherry turnovers. "I brought enough for everyone."

Not at the rate you're eating them, I thought.

"Good thinking," I said.

+ + +

The praying hadn't helped.

Even swinging by the hospital fifteen minutes ago on his way to work to walk past Adele's and Colleen's rooms hadn't helped. Whispering prayers for them as he strode past their doorways, past the officers assigned to guard their rooms, had been good but hadn't been enough to change Joshua's mind about tomorrow.

"Men loved darkness rather than light, because their deeds were evil."

Your deeds.

Are.

Evil.

Joshua felt compelled to act, drawn, as it were, toward the darkness by a force more powerful than his will.

During his lunch break he planned to drive to the

bank under the pretense of making a withdrawal, but he would really be estimating where SWAT would set up their barricades, deciding where he would be able to park to still see the bank entrance. Then he would rent the moving truck.

Despite his misgivings and conflicted feelings, he was beginning to understand who he truly was.

He was going ahead with everything.

Yes, he would see this through to the end.

It would end tomorrow afternoon at four twenty-five.

Sundown.

The gloaming.

54

The briefing went surprisingly quickly, with everyone summarizing what he or she had been working on: Radar had dug up a list of Caucasian public health workers, social workers, coaches, paramedics, and cops who worked in the West Reagan Street neighborhood. So far no leads. He was still working on getting in touch with an expert on Civil War–era medical instruments to see if we might be able to trace that amputation saw we'd found in the boxcar. It turned out it was harder to find an expert than we'd thought it would be.

Corsica was looking over Griffin's receipts. Nothing yet to report.

Thompson found out that Movie Flicks Video Store, which was only six blocks from the Griffin house, had a record of Griffin renting both *The Fugitive* and *When Harry Met Sally* on Sunday evening. While it wasn't possible to know if, or when, Griffin and Mallory actually watched the movies, at least, so far, their story was checking out. Thompson was also evaluating U-Haul and moving truck rentals to see if he could find something that might lead us to someone using one to transport ten mattresses.

Lyrie had come up dry yesterday trying to find a neighbor or work associate who'd seen a sedan that they didn't recognize in the area preceding Vincent's call home at around seven o'clock. He'd spoken with Adele Westin and she wasn't able to give a physical description of her abductor.

After the search warrant was issued for Timothy Griffin's receipts, Ralph had done a background check on Griffin and now distributed his findings. "Nothing striking," he noted. "You can read it over when we're done in here."

Gabriele had spoken with the people at the Salvation Army thrift store and found out the director was out of town at a fundraising dinner and wouldn't be back until tomorrow. However, she was going to continue to follow up on hotels, used-furniture stores, and thrift stores in that part of town to see if we could track down where the offender got the mattresses from, in the hopes that someone at the store would be able to identify him.

Thorne told us he'd looked up the other true crime books Heather Isle had written and one was about Ted and James Oswald. "No address for Ms. Isle that I can find. No photo on the book. I'm working at tracking her down to have a chat. Ask her a few questions about her sources."

The Oswalds again. They just kept popping up on the periphery of this case.

Looking for a connection between this week's victims, Ellen reported that she'd spoken with Adele, Colleen, Vincent and, on the phone, with Carl, who was still in custody in Plainfield. The couples had never met, never lived near each other. There were no areas of their lives that appeared to overlap. "I'm going to follow up on that more. There's got to be something there."

The CSIU didn't come up with much either. Based on the temperature of Hendrich's body and the temperature in the boxcar, they estimated time of death to be between two and four p.m., which didn't really narrow things down too much for us. No incriminating prints were found in the stolen Ford Taurus, the locks, the fence, the items in the boxcars, or the police tape. Initial tests showed that only two people's blood was present on the floor of the boxcar, so I was at least thankful there wasn't evidence of additional crimes. The CSIU did find some DNA inside the plastic bag—apparently our guy put something in there after all. No DNA results yet, though. Two weeks at the earliest.

The guy who was abducting these women and (if he was the same person) who'd killed Hendrich was good. Apart from the DNA in the bag, so far pretty much everything we'd put into play was coming up empty. It was almost like he knew exactly what we would be looking for and how to keep us from finding it.

I summarized the information from Dr. Werjonic that I'd been reading regarding nodes, distance decay, and victimology. "One of the points that Dr. Werjonic kept bringing out really grabbed me," I told them. "Sometimes the killer chooses the locations for expedience, sometimes the locations choose the crimes."

"What does that mean?" Thorne asked.

"Well, the killer didn't choose the bar, the alley, the pier or the hardware store, or that specific graveyard for expedience, or to save time, money, or effort; he was evidently choosing them because of their significance to the lives of Dahmer and Gein. In a sense, the locations chose the crimes, which means that something more important than saving time, money, or effort is guiding our guy's crime spree."

"Telling a story?" Corsica said.

"Paying homage?" Ralph suggested.

"Maybe. I don't know. But it wasn't just Dahmer's apartment—it was the alley that was significant in his eventual arrest. It wasn't Gein's house, but the same hardware store where Gein shot and killed his final victim—the scene that led the police to his home. So we're looking at the locations that eventually led to these two guys' apprehension, not just at their crimes."

Thorne nodded. "Good."

"So here's what I'm thinking. If we could postulate other killers that our guy might want to draw attention to—or pay homage to, or whatever—we could stake out the locations that were significant to their arrest. Try to get one step ahead of this guy."

Nods around the table.

"But," Ellen said, "we'd be looking for someone on the same level of depravity as Dahmer or Gein? From Wisconsin? That should be a short list. There can't be too many other killers from the state with that kind of grisly reputation."

"I'll see what I can find," Radar offered.

I gave assignments to everyone else.

Thompson would delve deeper into the pastiche idea, see what other connections the victims and missing persons in this crime spree—or this set of crime sprees— might have that paralleled Dahmer's or Gein's life or their crimes. This included looking into the possibility that

Ralph and I had talked about yesterday, that the homicide near Cincinnati might have some sort of connection to Dahmer's first murder in Bath, Ohio.

Ellen and Ralph would keep pursuing the victimology research.

Corsica announced that she would continue focusing on the receipts and compare Griffin's catalog subscription list to our suspect list. Also, she'd see if there was anything else Hendrich might have bought from or sold to Griffin to try to establish if someone had been setting him up from the start.

Gabriele and Lyrie would visit the hospital, interview Colleen, and try to find out who else besides Griffin might have known about the cuffs. Earlier interviews with Vincent hadn't produced any names.

Thorne was going to keep looking for a way to reach Heather Isle and focus on leads related to Hendrich's homicide.

I decided to examine the Oswald case. Ted and James weren't cannibals, weren't as infamous as Dahmer or Gein, but their case was certainly bizarre, and had been highly publicized when they were arrested back in 1994. Certainly, with the cuffs, the Heather Isle book, and the unsuccessful pleas of Dahmer and Ted regarding diminished responsibility for their crimes because of extenuating circumstances, it seemed that the Oswalds were at least tangentially connected to this investigation.

We ended the briefing at 10:54 a.m., with everyone heading off to work on their respective projects. I'd seen the chaplain visiting Colleen at the hospital yesterday and now, on my way to my desk, I asked him how she was. "Okay," he told me. "I think she's more concerned about what's going to happen to her husband than she is about being attacked . . . in the manner she was." It was selfless and courageous of her, but I'd gotten a similar feeling when Radar and I visited her room on Monday.

I rolled out my chair and took a seat at my desk.

On the note that Dr. Werjonic had left for me, he'd requested that I call him between 11:00 and 11:05, which seemed quirkily specific, but it just might have been that he liked things to be prompt and precise.

First, I put a call through to Detective Browning, the man whom Ralph and I had spoken with at the Waukesha Sheriff's Department, to get the Oswald case files delivered here to HQ. I had the sense he wouldn't be too happy about it, but right now worrying about hurting the guy's feelings was not at the top of my priority list.

No answer.

I left a message explaining what we needed.

As I was hanging up, I saw the receptionist directing someone toward my desk.

I recognized him immediately from the grad office brochure about the current lecture series.

Dr. Calvin Werjonic.

The visiting professor had decided not to wait for my call but had come to see me in person.

55

Tall. Slim. Distinguished. Dressed in a conservative dun-colored suit, he carried a tan London Fog trench coat draped over one arm and greeted me with a genteel smile and an outstretched hand. "Calvin Werjonic. And you must be Detective Bowers." His English accent was rich and sonorous. His eyes, studious and precise, taking everything in.

"It's a pleasure to meet you."

After a firm handshake, he gestured toward the papers on my desk. "I admit my handwriting isn't . . . well, I'd say what it used to be, but it's always been rather . . . tried." He pulled out an actual, real-life pocket watch and checked the time. "Well, shall we chat here, or is there a better place to discuss your case?"

"Um, honestly, I'm thrilled you would offer to help, but—"

He flagged a finger in the air to stop me. "Most assuredly, I don't expect you to tell me anything about the case that's not already public knowledge. Taking that into account, I'll offer what help I can. And you have no obligation to accept any of my observations or implement anything I might suggest. So, then, here? Or is there another, more suitable place?"

"Let's step into the conference room."

His eyes were on the maps on which I'd stuck the thumbtacks for the scenes of the crimes. "Interesting . . ." he mumbled. "And can we take this with us?"

"Sure."

I wheeled the board with the maps as I led Dr. Werjonic to the room with the empty Daily Donuts box on the table. "Doughnuts," he mused when we arrived. "Isn't that a bit of a cliché? Here in America?"

"Actually," I said, defending my country, albeit lamely, "they were cherry turnovers."

"I see."

"Officer Thompson's favorite."

"Of course."

Not really sure if that helped.

He took a seat. "Well then, let's get started."

"Just so we're clear, you're offering to help me with the case I'm currently working on, and—"

"To be sure: the one involving the mutilation of Colleen Hayes, the abduction of Adele Westin, and the murder of Bruce Hendrich. And possibly the connection to two homicides in two other states."

I blinked. "How did you . . . ?"

"Come, come. The soil samples from the murder in Champaign that matched only two counties of southeast Wisconsin—there was a report on the news. That, and the anthropophagic behavior."

"That wasn't made public."

"True." He smiled. "But thank you for confirming it."

Okay, now that was just plain sneaky. "But how did you know last night that I was the one on this case anyway? That information wasn't released until the newspapers came out this morning."

"Based on your grades and your request for the photo-copied notes—which, I must say, is quite admirable—I can tell this program is a priority for you. The graduate assistant who requested I leave the notes for you mentioned the request came via a dispatcher, so I realized you were calling it in from the field. After a quick review of your attendance records, I noted that there has been a high correlation between your absences and high-profile homicide investigations in the city over the last six months."

"You teach in Vancouver. How do you possibly know about our homicide investigations here in Milwaukee?"

"I stay current."

I wasn't sure what to say. "So"—I tracked with his train of thought—"from there it was simple enough to infer my involvement in this current case, the most high-profile one in months."

He smiled. "Timing and location, Detective. It always cracks down to timing and location."

"Alright, so just to reiterate: I can't divulge anything confidential about the case. It's an ongoing investigation."

"How about if I just tell you what I can, based on what I already know. From television, the newspapers, that sort of thing. Start there. See if that helps at all."

"Fair enough."

He steepled his fingers. "The Dahmer and Gein locations relate to the story he's telling more than to the travel routes he's taking. For instance, we don't know that he himself has ever visited the New Territories Bar or the alley in Milwaukee, or the graveyard or the hardware store in Plainfield for that matter. Remember, he sent other people to those sites."

"True. Good point."

He gestured toward the map. "Which does not help us in our efforts to use geographic profiling to discern the most likely location of the kidnapper's anchor point, but that's not the issue anymore, is it? Since we already know where it is."

"We do?"

"The boxcar." He stood and, with his finger, he traced, on the map, one after the other, the roads that branched out from the train yard's parking lot. "The location of the train yards determined his travel routes more than his home address did, which will not help us in finding his home. He knows these neighborhoods. He was familiar enough with the woods to flee through them in nearly dark conditions, and then to make it through the neighborhood—yet being a Caucasian, he would likely be highly noticeable to the people living along those streets."

"We were thinking the same thing."

"Yes. The news accounts last night implied as much. Which reminds me, you've forgotten one key location."

"Which one is that?"

"The parking lot in Pewaukee from which the Ford Taurus was stolen."

I was embarrassed I'd missed that. "I'll add it."

"So, knowing the anchor point—the boxcar—I would suggest you begin to analyze the possible travel routes to and from the train yard to the other sites you've already noted."

At least that thought had already crossed my mind. "The algorithms in your notes."

"The last three pages, yes. And you'll want to closely

examine the victimology here. Find out how the two couples targeted in these crimes are connected to each other."

"We're working on it."

"Of course."

Time to pick his brain. "I've been thinking, Dr. Werjonic—"

"Calvin, please."

"Calvin—I've been thinking . . . The guy who killed the women in Ohio and Illinois passed by Indiana." I shared one little piece of information that wasn't exactly public knowledge yet, but I kept it vague enough to feel comfortable telling him. "Of the other missing persons cases in Wisconsin, Ohio, Illinois, and Indiana we're looking at—"

"Let me guess—you don't have any in Indiana that fit the MO or victim demographic from those cases or the two out-of-state victims."

"Correct. I'm wondering why he would skip that geographic region."

"That, my boy, is a very good question." He stared into space for a moment, then consulted his pocket watch again. "I'm terribly sorry, but I'm afraid I must be going. I have a lunch appointment and a short drive ahead of me. It seems a writer is working on a book and wanted to interview me while I was in town. Investigating some cold cases, as it were."

I thought back to my conversation with Thorne yesterday afternoon when he mentioned that a true crime writer used Griffin as one of her sources. He'd brought her up again at our briefing a few minutes ago. "It's not a true crime book, is it?"

"It is."

"The writer's name wouldn't, by any chance, be Heather Isle?"

"No, a gent named Slate Seagirt . . ." Calvin nodded, then smiled faintly. "Ah. Clever. A nom de plume."

A pseudonym . . . ?

I processed that aloud: "Both 'heather' and 'slate' can mean gray . . . An 'isle' is an island . . ." I hadn't heard the word "seagirt" before, but its meaning was easy enough to decipher: "Seagirt—girted by the sea."

"Yes." Calvin looked pleased that I'd ventured a cursory guess at the word's etymology. "Surrounded by water."

"What's the cold case about?"

"Something concerning the tragic unsolved murder of a young girl whose body was found in a tree house."

56

I stared at him. "Mindy Wells?"

"I wasn't told her name. Are you familiar with the case?"

I wondered if I should tell him what happened to Mindy back when I was in high school, and after a brief deliberation I decided it would be fine as long as I stuck to the facts in the public record.

When I was done, he carefully deliberated on what I'd said. "Perhaps what intrigues me the most is not *that* this chap contacted me but that he contacted me *now*. With your connection to the case, it's too convenient. I don't believe in coincidences."

"As a matter of fact, neither do I."

"A man after my own heart." His voice was softer now; he was deep in thought.

Someone knuckle-rapped on the door, then pressed it open before I could invite him in. It was Radar and he looked anxious. Obviously he had something he wanted to share because he jumped right in: "Pat, we might have some—" Only then did he notice Calvin. "I'm sorry, I didn't mean to—"

"No, no. It's quite alright." Calvin stood. "I was just

on my way out." He extended his hand to me. "I look forward to speaking with you again soon, Detective. So I can share with you a description of this gray island."

"Call me." We shook hands again. "As soon as your meal is over."

"Yes, of course." He drew on his overcoat, then doffed an imaginary cap to Radar before exiting, but only after letting his eyes linger one more time on the maps on the corkboard.

"Who was that?" Radar asked.

"That was Dr. Calvin Werjonic."

"The guy you mentioned at the briefing?"

"Yes."

For a moment Radar seemed distracted, then caught himself, returned abruptly to the conversation: "Sorry, as I was saying, we might have something."

"What is it?"

"The receipts. We found a discrepancy."

Oh yeah, I liked discrepancies. Discrepancies are always a good thing.

"What discrepancy?

"Well, it might be just an accounting error, but—"

"What discrepancy?"

"It seems there was one item that, well . . ." He said nothing more, just handed me a receipt. Ralph, who'd been walking past the open door, saw us and joined us in the conference room.

"It seems there was one item that what?" I asked Radar.

"There was one item that Griffin sold that he didn't buy."

57

A chill.

I gazed unbelievingly at the receipt.

The item Griffin had sold but didn't buy was a book of nursery rhymes with one specific page missing.

Oh.

No.

I snatched my things off my desk. "Ralph, we're going to need another search warrant. There's more in Griffin's house."

"How do you know?"

"'Hush, little baby, don't say a word.' The nursery rhyme. There was a copy of the song under Jenna's pillow—she's the seven-year-old we found dead three years ago. She'd been raped, then buried alive in a shallow grave. The song had been ripped out of a book. We identified which nursery rhyme book it was from but we never found the book itself." I slapped the receipt down on the table. "Griffin sold it. But he never bought it."

I expected an expletive but got only shocked silence instead.

"I'm going to Fort Atkinson." I pulled out my car

keys. "Have the local authorities get to his house now and hold him on something, I don't care what, and get me a search warrant for the rest of the house by the time I get up there. Fax it to the Fort Atkinson Police Department."

"Got it."

"I'm coming with you, Pat," Radar said.

"We'll take my car."

We hurried to the parking garage, my thoughts running through everything once again, tying threads together into one dark, terrible fabric.

You matched the semen found at the scene of Jenna's murder to that found on Mindy Wells's body. Dr. Werjonic is meeting the true crime author, the guy who's writing a book about her . . .

I recalled the items in Griffin and Mallory's bedroom that weren't for sale.

A handheld mirror on Mallory's dresser. A nice mirror. Ornate.

A diamond ring in her jewelry box.

A stuffed dog on the bed.

There's more. Something else . . .

In my head, I ran through the complete lyrics to the song:

Hush, little baby, don't say a word,
  Daddy's gonna buy you a mockingbird.
And if that mockingbird don't sing,
  Daddy's gonna buy you a diamond ring.
And if that diamond ring turns brass,
  Daddy's gonna buy you a looking glass.

And if that looking glass gets broke,
    Daddy's gonna buy you a billy goat.
And if that billy goat don't pull,
    Daddy's gonna buy you a cart and bull.
And if that cart and bull turn over,
    Daddy's gonna buy you a dog named Rover.
And if that dog named Rover won't bark.
    Daddy's gonna buy you a horse and cart.
And if that horse and cart fall down,
    Well, you'll still be the sweetest little baby in town.

We had the diamond ring, the looking glass (the mirror), and, if I was right about the stuffed dog, we had "the dog named Rover."

What else?

Oh. Yes.

There'd been a ceramic bird resting next to the Manson Bible in the living room. No price tag on it. I'm no expert on birds, but I had a distinct feeling I knew what kind of bird that was.

A mockingbird.

Which meant that if Griffin really was collecting the items from the song, we needed a billy goat, a cart and bull, a horse and cart. I doubted that he would have live animals sequestered somewhere, but if that dog really did signify "the dog named Rover," then it was likely he had other ways of representing the other animals too—perhaps more stuffed animals, toys, or maybe photographs or pictures of some type. Who knows.

Daddy's gonna buy you a diamond ring.

A looking glass.

A mockingbird.

I wondered what the items represented to him.

Victims? Could each relate to another victim?

Hush, little baby . . .

He'd called Mallory "baby" twice while we were at the house. A harmless term of endearment, yes, unless it meant something a lot deeper to him.

Radar and I jumped into my car and took off.

58

As I drove, Radar read me the file that Ralph had put together last night on Griffin.

"Okay, so Timothy went to high school in Deerfield, dropped out when he was a sophomore, eventually got his GED and worked for a decade in a series of odd jobs in Milwaukee—three years delivering garbage, McDonald's burger flipper, construction. Then a plumber's apprentice in Beaver Dam. Looks like none of them was a good fit for him. Attended one year of tech school, dropped out. Evidently, he started collecting and selling this paraphernalia soon after that."

"Beaver Dam's just twelve miles from Horicon. He could easily have known the area." I remembered the coats in his closet. "He's a hunter."

"The tree house. Goose hunting?"

"Possibly."

Radar was quiet.

"Never anything to do with law enforcement, though?" I asked. "Did he enter and drop out of any police academies?"

"Nothing's listed. Nope."

"Man, we gotta find out how he's trafficking stuff that ought to be in police evidence rooms."

"No kidding."

"What else?"

"He's lived in Fort Atkinson since June 1996. Mallory moved in with him about a month later on the day she turned eighteen."

"Which means—"

"He had a relationship with her before that, when she was still a minor."

I felt my hands tighten around the steering wheel. "How do we know when she moved in?"

"She changed the address on her driver's license."

After Radar finished reading the files, we were silent and I was thinking about the case of Jenna Natara, the investigation that wouldn't leave me alone, even when I slept.

"Pat, I know you're angry."

"Don't tell me not to be, don't—"

"No, I get it. It's okay. It's a good thing."

"It's good that I'm angry?"

"It shows you care. As my dad used to say, anger is the cousin of love."

I looked at him quizzically. "What does that mean?"

"The more you love something, the more angry you'll be when that thing is threatened or attacked. If you love children, you'll be incensed at pedophiles; if you love your wife, you'll get angry when someone insults her; if you love endangered species, you'll be furious when they're hunted to the point of extinction; if you love unborn children, you'll be outraged about abortion. Anger always, and only, runs as deep as love."

I'd never thought of it like that. "Your dad was a smart man."

"Yes, he was."

A thought: *To find out what you truly love the most, look for what makes you the most angry.*

Anger is the cousin of love . . .

I said, "You know how psychologists will tell you that no one can make you angry, that you only choose to become angry?"

"Sure."

"I can't remember a time ever in my life when I've chosen to be angry. And I've never met anyone who's said to me, 'This guy cut me off on the interstate and I decided to get angry.'"

"Anger's a response"—Radar was right with me—"not a choice."

"Right. Nobody ever chooses to become angry, we can only choose not to respond with anger. If we want to."

"Okay." He could tell there was more. "And?"

"And I'm not going to do that with Griffin."

"You're going to remain angry."

"Yeah, and respond that way."

"So am I."

"I guess we'll see where that leads."

He was quiet. "Yes, we will."

The trip went by fast and before I knew it I was pulling up to the side of the road in front of Timothy Griffin's dilapidated house on the outskirts of Fort Atkinson.

59

Two cars from the Fort Atkinson Police Department were already at the house when we arrived.

A sergeant whose name tag read J. CARVER met us at the porch.

"Do you have him?" I asked.

He shook his head. "House was empty when we got here, but since we had the search warrant . . . well . . ." He pointed to the door. "We accessed the property."

There was a shattered lock on the door and I liked this guy already.

"What else?"

"We found a false cabinet under the basement stairs. There's a box. A bunch of toys and some children's clothing."

"Show me."

While we were descending the steps, I could feel my heart twisting in my chest. Radar and I pulled on latex gloves.

"They haven't disturbed anything," I asked Carver, "have they? The other officers?"

"No. I made sure they didn't touch anything until you got here." Carver seemed like a pro and I was glad he was the one calling the shots for his team.

We reached the basement and he led us around the back of the stairs to the place where the officers had dismantled the cabinet. The basement itself was cluttered with unfinished woodworking projects, stacks of cardboard boxes, a shotgun on the workbench where Griffin may have been working on it, an old, warped pool table.

The square cardboard box they'd found was about half a meter tall, deep, and wide. It held a clutch of toys, some children's clothes beneath them, and, apparently, something bulky that I couldn't make out beneath the toys and clothing.

The toys in the box that caught my attention right off the bat were a plastic horse about the right size for a Barbie doll to ride on and a stuffed goat. As well as two small plastic pushcarts.

Beside them, tucked into the side of the box, was a carefully folded-up page torn from a coloring book with a sketchily colored-in bull.

Fire rose inside me.

I wondered if Griffin had colored in the picture himself or if an abducted child had done so.

Despite myself, I felt something inside of me slipping, something that'd been rooted firmly for a long time in what I believed about right and wrong, about justice and mercy: I wanted Timothy Griffin out of the way for good and I wanted to be the one to take him out. And if things played out like that, I knew that afterward I wouldn't regret it at all.

But honestly, thinking those things frightened me.

Keep the demons at bay.

Keep them at bay.

Yeah, well maybe not this time.

As I removed the toys and then the children's clothes—outfits that looked like they would've fit someone Jenna's size—I saw what was bunched up beneath them.

A jacket.

Even though the arms of the coat weren't visible, I said quietly, "There's a small rip on the left sleeve, about halfway down."

Radar was on one knee beside me, looking into the box as well. "How do you know that?"

"Because it used to be mine."

60

I took the jacket out of the box.

The rip was right where I remembered it.

In a voice that I couldn't help from being hushed, I explained to Radar and the other officers how I'd left this jacket in the tree house to cover Mindy Wells's naked corpse. "I don't know what happened to it after the investigation. I never saw it again."

How did Griffin get this? From the evidence room? But he was never a cop . . .

I laid the jacket down softly, gentleness at this moment seemed to be a way of honoring the memory of Mindy Wells, then I stood and faced the four officers who'd been here when Radar and I arrived. "We need to find Griffin and Mallory. Now. Do any of you have any idea where they might be?"

They all shook their heads.

"He wasn't here when he fled," I said. "Yet somehow he knew we were coming to his house."

"Why do you say that?" Carver asked.

Radar answered for me, pointing at the box. "If he was taking off for good, he wouldn't have left that behind, especially if he knew you were coming with a search warrant."

So, where was he?

The obvious: he and Mallory were just out running errands.

Maybe.

But we couldn't afford to assume that right now.

"Did you put out an APB on his car yet?" I asked Carver.

"Yeah. So far no word."

The only people who knew we were going to be here were Ralph, Radar, me, the judge whom Ralph contacted . . .

And the Fort Atkinson police.

Did someone warn Griffin that the police were on their way?

I asked Carver, "Who received the fax of the search warrant?"

"I did."

"Who else besides the people in this room knew about it? Knew you were coming here?"

He gestured toward the three other men. "I grabbed these guys while we were at the station, but when we got here we radioed dispatch our location. So it could have been anyone."

"No, not if you radioed in your position after you arrived. Griffin was already gone when you got here."

There was always the possibility that Griffin had been at a neighbor's house or something, saw the squads arrive, and just didn't come home.

No, his car is missing from the driveway.

Okay. How to do this and not end up accusing one of them of warning Griffin . . .

"Do any of you know Griffin?"

All four men shook their heads.

I glanced at Radar, who was eyeing them, one after another. "Officer Webb," he said to a stout young officer with short bristly hair and pale blue eyes. "You knew him, didn't you?"

"No."

"But you've seen him, right? It's a small town. You see people around."

"I don't know, I—"

He looked rattled and Radar didn't let up. "Officer Webb, did you call him? Tell him you were on the way over here?"

"No, of course not!" But he didn't look Radar in the eye, and when he said the words he was tapping the forefinger and thumb of his right hand rapidly together.

I was about to push the issue, but Radar spoke up first. "You know something and you're holding out. Right now you need to tell us what it is. We have—"

Surprisingly, that's all it took. Webb held up a hand in quick surrender. "Listen, listen, all I did was call my sister. That's it. That's all. I just told her Griffin might be involved in something."

"Your sister?" I said. "Why your sister?"

"She's friends with Mallory. Cuts her hair. I was, you know, worried Griffin might . . . well, do something to her if he got scared. Desperate."

Carver was glaring at his man, obviously ticked, but if Webb was telling the truth, I could at least understand where he was coming from. "How did she warn Mallory?" I asked him. "Where were they when your sister called her?"

"I don't even know if she called her. I just—"

"Listen to me," Radar interrupted him. "Do you have any idea where they might have gone?"

"I'm sorry, I didn't know they might—"

"Can you think of anywhere at all Griffin might have taken her?" Radar repeated, even more emphatically.

Webb was visibly shaken, but I could tell he was really thinking about it. "Okay, there's this place, a couple miles outside of town. I don't know, maybe . . . My sister went there with them a couple times to party. It's near the dump. This abandoned farmhouse. No one lives out there, but it's—"

I cut him off. "You say it's near the landfill?"

"Yeah."

An unsettling set of dark possibilities wound its way, like a snake slithering from a forgotten hole, into my thoughts. In 1996, Dahmer's belongings had been taken to an undisclosed landfill. According to what Radar had read me earlier, Griffin worked for three years as a garbage collector in Milwaukee. The timing didn't fit for him to have been one of the people who drove the dump truck to dispose of Dahmer's possessions, but he might easily know the person who did.

But the Fort Atkinson landfill?

Yeah, just far enough from Milwaukee to discourage souvenir hounds.

Griffin moved to Fort Atkinson in June 1996—the same month the city of Milwaukee disposed of Dahmer's things.

I don't believe in coincidences.

I started for the stairs, gestured toward Radar, and said to Webb, "You're riding with us. We're going to that farmhouse."

61

On the way to the house we radioed the dispatcher here in
Fort Atkinson and told him to call Lieutenant Thorne to
find out the name of the two city workers who'd delivered
Dahmer's possessions to the landfill. "And we need to know
if the landfill they used was the one here in Fort Atkinson."

We also called for backup to be sent to the farmhouse—an ambulance too. I didn't say so, but I wanted
it there because I knew if I was left alone with Griffin, he
would be needing it.

The town of Fort Atkinson didn't have a SWAT team,
but Webb told us they'd call in the one for Jefferson
County.

We were only two or three minutes from the landfill.
"How long till they get here?"

"Twenty minutes. Fifteen maybe—but I'd say that's
pushing it."

Not what I wanted to hear.

Standing around waiting for people to show up to do
what I was prepared to do right now wasn't what I had
in mind for this afternoon. I wanted to go and get Griffin
the minute we arrived.

If he's even there.

That was true. It was also true that I wasn't in my jurisdiction. Admittedly, that did put a few wrinkles in things.

I could work through a few wrinkles.

When we were about half a mile from the farmhouse, the dispatcher radioed back, relaying the message from Thorne: yes, the landfill was the one in Fort Atkinson; the names of the two city workers were Roger Kennedy and Dane Strickland. I hadn't heard of either of the two men before, but I knew we were going to have a talk with them before everything involving this case was said and done.

Just as we were finishing up the transmission, we arrived at the farmhouse.

It was a small, ranch-style home, half burned down. The roof on the east side was caved in, the walls were blackened, the windows broken.

Griffin's car was parked out front.

But why would he come here to flee?

Officer Webb, Radar, and I exited the car and unholstered our weapons. Radar immediately took position behind a nearby tree that gave him a clear line on the front door. Webb crouched behind the car, using the hood to steady his shooting arm.

I kept my door open, eased behind it, and eyed the farmhouse for movement. Saw none.

The sky was pregnant with snow. Clouds hung down like heavy, dark scabs.

The wind was dead. The day, still.

I really wanted to go into that house right now, but it wasn't smart for any number of reasons—not the least of which: we had a possible hostage situation and storming the place without finding out where Mallory was could put her life in danger.

The air reeked of damp rot and dank smoke from the landfill that lay only a hundred meters beyond the house, surrounded by an eight-foot-tall wooden fence.

With the air smelling like this and the house in the shape it was, I couldn't imagine anyone coming out here to party, as Webb had mentioned, but then I remembered we were talking about two people who lived in a home filled with memorabilia of serial killers and pedophiles. Who on earth knew why they did what they did.

Carver pulled up, parked, got out and we consulted for a moment. I was anxious to use the mic on his cruiser's PA system to try to call Griffin out of the house, Carver was bent on waiting for the Jefferson County SWAT team.

"With all due respect, Detective," he said at last, "this is our jurisdiction; this is our case. Since it was a federal search warrant at the house and you're working with the Feds, I had no problem with your involvement there, but out here, this is our turf. He's our guy to bring in."

He had a point and if I were in his place I might've been saying the same things. "Sergeant, I couldn't care less about who gets the credit for bringing this guy in. And I want that girl, Mallory, safe, just like you do, but . . ." I thought of what to say next, changed my tune a bit, and gestured toward Radar. "How about Sergeant Walker and I take the back of the house. Cover it until the tactical unit gets here."

"Good. Thanks." He nodded, and Radar and I circled around in case Griffin tried to leave the house and flee through the landfill.

I wasn't sure exactly how everything was going to play out, but I did know that if I found out Mallory was in danger, from back here it'd be a lot easier to move on the house without any of Carver's guys getting in the way.

62

Over the next few minutes more officers arrived and took position around the farmhouse.

SWAT was still five minutes out.

Carver called through his car's mic numerous times, trying to get anyone who might be in the house to acknowledge that they were there, but no one answered.

From the radio transmissions among the team members, I knew that no one had seen any movement and I was getting more and more antsy to find out if Griffin was actually in the house, or if we were wasting our time out here.

His car is out front.

Yes, but if Griffin really was guilty, he'd been shrewd enough to avoid suspicion in at least two homicides stretching back almost a decade, even while he marketed in the kind of merchandise he did. The car could easily be a ploy to distract us while he fled in another vehicle.

"Radar, I can't just sit around here doing nothing. I want to have a look around that landfill. You with me?"

"You bet."

I radioed Carver; he agreed it would be good to cover the landfill and sent two other officers to take our place behind the house. They were more than happy to man our positions rather than accept the job of trekking across a reeking dump.

"Okay," I said to Radar. "Get ready for the smell."

"It's been too late for that since we got here."

We started for the fence. Wooden. Eight feet tall. No razor wire on top.

No problem.

Moments later we were inside.

I paused. Studied the mounds of garbage around me.

We were in an area filled with discarded appliances—dishwashers, refrigerators, dryers, washing machines, ovens. Based on the number of units here compared to the population of Fort Atkinson, it was clear that this place had been the town's landfill for a long time.

The rusted appliances jutted up at odd angles from the piles of trash all around us, some half buried in garbage, some jumbled awkwardly on top of each other in precarious stacks. The area looked like an alien, garbage-strewn, metal-encrusted planet.

Simply put, if Griffin was here, he could be almost anywhere.

"What are you thinking, Pat?"

"I'm thinking I hear a bulldozer." I pointed across a mound of garbage to our right.

A man was driving a dated bulldozer into the landfill, aiming it toward a giant mountain of garbage bags. I couldn't make out the face of the driver, but from here his build looked too big for him to be Griffin.

"You think that's him?"

I shook my head. "No. But go see if he's noticed anyone. Then, get him out of here. I don't want any civilians in the area. I'm going to have a look around here."

"Be careful."

"You too."

Gun out, Radar took off, picking his way over the garbage and carefully surveying the rotting landscape as he went.

Occasional telephone poles rose at random intervals along the fence that Radar and I had just scaled. The poles had vapor lights, now off, and I imagined that they served to illuminate the perimeter of the dump at night to keep out scavengers that would undoubtedly be drawn here from the nearby forest looking for food—rats, skunks, raccoons, wild dogs that might dig under the fence, maybe even bears, rooting through the garbage.

Around me, deep tread marks furrowed the ground from the bulldozers and earth movers that had pushed the remnants of people's daily lives into the hills of refuse. Throughout the landfill were sporadic fires, and plumes of nascent gases were escaping through gaps in the mountains of trash.

"Griffin!" I called. The word sounded thick, almost liquid. It was a strange effect and I wasn't sure what caused it, but it was eerie and unsettling. "We've got this area surrounded."

It was partly true.

That farmhouse was definitely surrounded.

I proceeded through the cemetery of hulking appliances. Saw no movement. "We found that box under your steps. Thanks for selling the nursery rhyme book. That was helpful."

Does he know? Does he know it was you who found Mindy's body?

It was possible he might've found out I'd worked Jenna's disappearance—he could have easily researched things after I'd visited him yesterday with Ralph, but I doubted he would have known that I was the one who'd found Mindy.

The cuffs. The Oswald connection . . .

"Did you consult with Isle—Seagirt—on the Oswald true crime book?"

No answer.

"Why do you call Mallory 'baby,' Timothy?" It took a little work to make sure my voice carried, but I made sure it did. "Is she the one you did all this for?"

No reply. Just the faint sounds of garbage settling, the rumble of the bulldozer's engine shutting down as Radar spoke with the operator.

I came to a refrigerator. Held my gun steady. "How'd you get the jacket, Griffin?" I stepped quickly around it, leveling my weapon as I did. No one. "Did you know someone at the station? In the evidence room?"

Snow started to fall. Lonely, rogue flakes wandering aimlessly through the stagnant air.

As I was about to call out again, I heard a mound of garbage shift behind me and I spun to see what it was, but I was a fraction of a second too slow.

Griffin had appeared from behind a chest freezer that was tilted on end. With his unmistakably scarred neck, his twisted grin, and a primal fire in his eyes, he looked like a rabid animal.

He had a tire iron in his hands, had just cocked it back, and was swinging it violently toward my head.

63

I threw up my arm to take the brunt of the blow.

He was strong for someone his size and the force of the impact against my forearm threw me off balance. I tumbled backward, tripped over an overstuffed garbage bag that lay behind me, and landed on the ground, but I was able to keep my gun directed at Griffin's chest. "Drop the tire iron!"

To my surprise, he did, then stood still, leering at me.

"Hands up!"

Again he obeyed, and I was kind of wishing he hadn't, that he would have rushed me instead. I could have ended this whole thing on the spot.

"The jacket," he said. "I knew it was you."

"It was me, what?" Without taking the gun off him, I stood up.

"With Mindy. You found her." He grinned, and as he spoke, every word seemed to drip with venom. "Did you like seeing her like that? The way I left her? She was special to me. She was my first."

Hot anger coursed through me, tightening everything. "How did you know?"

"Your name was in the papers. You think I didn't keep

clippings of the girls? And just a kid yourself, huh? Sixteen? How's that been for you over the years? Detective?"

I felt my finger pressing against the cool steel of the trigger. Just a little more pressure, just one twitch and he would be dead.

Keep the demons at bay.

"On your knees." He was less than three meters away and didn't move.

"On your knees." He didn't comply.

I was about to order him again, but I suddenly realized that I kind of hoped he would go for a weapon and give me an excuse to squeeze the trigger.

"Were there others?" I kept my finger on the trigger. "Besides Jenna and Mindy?"

"There are always others. You should know that, Detective."

"Who?"

"I'm afraid that's my little secret."

"Who is Slate Seagirt?"

He smiled, but on him it wasn't really a smile. "Oh, you're gonna have a load of fun when you find that out."

"Who's the Maneater of the Midwest?"

"Now there's a man who knows how to acquire what he wants. Does it for a living."

"Who is he?"

He glanced to his left and then lowered his hands.

"Hands up!"

But he didn't raise them. Instead, he flicked his right hand toward his jacket pocket and simultaneously his chest blossomed open like a grisly, bloody flower as the sound of three gunshots ricocheted through the air. He swayed limply forward and dropped face-first onto the garbage-strewn ground.

Heart hammering, I looked over and saw Radar standing twenty-five meters away, his weapon still level, his eyes still drawing a bead on where Griffin had stood only a moment earlier. We were virtually aiming our guns at each other. He'd managed to fire even before I could. We simultaneously lowered our weapons.

"You okay, Pat?"

"Yeah."

He'd hit Griffin center mass, just like we were taught at the academy. Textbook. And the shots did what they were supposed to do. They took the subject down.

I didn't think there was any way Griffin was alive, but I held my gun on him even as I bent, cuffed his hands behind him, felt for a pulse.

"I had to fire." Radar was on his way toward me. "He was reaching for a weapon."

"Yeah." I wished Griffin had been able to tell me the Maneater's identity—if he even knew it—but I doubted that he would have told us, even if Radar hadn't fired.

No pulse. Griffin was gone. I searched the pocket he'd been reaching for, but I found only his car keys. No weapon.

I hesitated.

"What is it?" Radar knelt beside me.

"Hang on."

I checked his other jacket pockets, found nothing. Felt for a holster; he wasn't wearing one.

"Oh." Radar caught on. "You're not telling me . . ."

"Wait." At last, on the back of his belt, I found a

sheath. Gloves on, I snapped it open and it yielded a serious-looking hunting knife.

"He might have been going for this," I said.

But even as I spoke, a question rose inside me: from where Radar had been standing, could he have seen Griffin reaching for his pocket?

Radar was quiet for a moment. "I got two kids, Pat. I can't . . . I can't, you know . . ."

"Yeah."

The decision was easy. I wrapped Griffin's fingers around the knife's handle, then dropped it beside his body. "It's a good thing you fired when you did, Radar."

He watched me silently.

"He could have killed me if he got to me with that blade," I said honestly.

"Yeah, he could have."

It's hard to say what justice really is. If it's balancing the scales, then it's a lot rarer than we like to think. Sometimes they can't be balanced. Even by killing a person who deserves to die.

I stood.

Part of me wished that Griffin hadn't died so quickly, that he would have been injured instead and lain there suffering and begging and sputtering for breath. It wouldn't have made up for what he did to those girls, but it would have at least been a step in the right direction.

Radar was quiet. "Thank you."

"No. Thank you."

My nightmare from Sunday night came to mind again, but now there was an added moment in the dream where the man who was shoveling dirt into the shallow grave on top of the crying girl sealed in the sleeping bag looked at me. I saw his face, and it was Griffin. That grin, that un-even, self-satisfied grin.

I could only imagine what special place in hell was reserved for guys like him.

And actually, I have to admit, that thought did bring me a degree of satisfaction.

Griffin lay dead in a pool of his own blood, facedown in the trash, the knife by his side, a small price tag dangling from the handle. And we left him like that, Radar and I did, as we walked back toward the house.

64

Mallory was okay.

Griffin had hit her on the side of the head with the tire iron. I only had a bruised arm from where he'd smacked me, but the blow he'd delivered to her had knocked the girl out. Apparently, he'd left her unconscious in the house to make his escape. He must have assaulted her just before we arrived at the farmhouse, maybe when he saw our cars approaching.

A Grade III concussion, but she would be alright.

An ambulance had arrived at the scene while Radar and I were busy in the landfill looking for Griffin. The EMTs had already placed Mallory on a gurney and now they were wheeling her toward the ambulance. She was crying tiny childlike tears, and I didn't know if it was because of grief over Timothy's death or relief that he was finally out of her life for good.

I said to the paramedics, "I need to speak with her for a moment."

At first they were resistant, but then Carver saw what was going on and waved for them to let me through. I would've gone anyway, but I appreciated his support.

I leaned over Mallory, spoke as gently as I could. "Do

you remember me? I was at your house yesterday, I'm Detective Bowers."

She nodded.

"Did they tell you what happened to Timothy out here today?"

She nodded again and this time sniffed back a tear, but I still couldn't tell what emotion or state of mind was causing her to cry.

"Mallory, do you know who Timothy got the police tape from? The tape from the murder in Illinois?"

"The Maneater. He said the Maneater got it for him."

So Griffin did have information about his identity after all.

"Do you know who that is? The Maneater?"

She shook her head.

I wasn't sure how to put this, but finally just said it plainly: "Do you know what Timothy did to the girls?" She looked at me with a curious expression that was somehow also devoid of emotion. "He killed some little girls, Mallory."

She nodded slowly. Didn't seem surprised.

"Did you know that? Did you know anything about that?"

She shook her head and I believed she was telling the truth.

The EMTs looked at me impatiently. I held up a hand: *just a few more seconds.*

Griffin had said there were more. That there are always more.

"Mallory, can I ask you, when Agent Hawkins and I were at your house, Timothy touched a photograph on the wall. A picture of a woman. Do you remember that?"

She gazed at me for a moment, then looked away as she nodded.

"Who is that woman? Do you know her?"

Mallory stopped crying. There was a long pause and it came to the point where I thought she might not answer at all. Finally, she said softly, "She was my mother. She was his wife."

And then she brushed off the last remaining tear and stared into space as they wheeled her into the ambulance.

Mallory was not just Griffin's lover.

She was also his daughter.

It was very possible that he had called her "baby" for more than one reason after all.

I took a look in the farmhouse.

Though the walls were charred and half of the roof was missing, there was still furniture inside. I'd seen photos of the interior of Dahmer's apartment and I could tell where the furniture in this house had come from: these were the very things that were supposed to have been destroyed and dumped in an undisclosed landfill.

Come to think of it, they may very well have been delivered as scheduled, only to be retrieved by Griffin and brought to this farmhouse down the road.

It wasn't just furniture. Griffin had set up the entire place to look as much as possible like the inside of Dahmer's apartment, even down to the detail of having an altar with a skull and candles around it in the closet, just like the one Dahmer had built.

And in the kitchen was the refrigerator where Jeffrey Dahmer had kept his meals.

The coup de grâce for any demented collector of serial killer memorabilia.

It was dusk before Radar and I were finally able to take off.

He'd been involved in a lethal shooting in another jurisdiction, and it took several hours for us to fill out the paperwork and finish our debriefing with the chief of police and district attorney. However, honestly, no one was giving Radar a hard time. On the contrary, by the pats on the back and nods of encouragement from the other officers, it was clear they were glad he'd taken Griffin out.

"Sergeant Walker fired just before you could?" the DA asked me in our interview.

"Yes."

"And he had that knife with him, Griffin did?"

"Yes. If Walker hadn't taken the shot . . ." I let my voice trail off.

"Griffin might have come at you with that knife."

"Yes."

"And your firearm? You had it unholstered? You were covering the suspect?"

"That's right, but Sergeant Walker responded before I was able to."

"It's a good thing he was here, then."

"Yes. It is."

I showed him where I was standing when Griffin died, he noted it on his form and that was that.

When I gazed again at the place Radar had been when he fired, I still couldn't tell if the angle would have been right for him to see Griffin reaching for his pocket. Truthfully, I just couldn't tell.

At first, I thought I might ask him about it.

But then, after a moment, I decided I would not.

Finally, we left and jumped onto I-94 toward Milwaukee.

There were still a number of things on my mind to take care of tonight: (1) find out if the other task force members had made any progress on the case of the man who'd fled the boxcar; (2) send someone to interview the city workers, Roger Kennedy and Dane Strickland, and find out if they were connected in any way to Griffin; (3) get an update from Dr. Werjonic on Slate Seagirt and what the true crime writer might know about the murder of Mindy Wells.

65

I drove.

Radar sat beside me. Quiet. Reflective. I wondered what it was like for him right now. Lethal shootings by cops are much rarer than people think and I knew he'd never been involved with one before. I wondered if dropping that knife by the body should've bothered me more than it did.

It was a hard question to answer.

Since we'd rushed out of the department this morning right after my meeting with Dr. Werjonic, and then driven straight to Griffin's place—and from there to the farmhouse by the landfill—Radar and I had both missed lunch. In fact, the only thing I'd eaten all day were the muffins and bananas I'd had at breakfast when Taci broke up with me.

Not a memory I wanted to be carrying with me right now.

I hadn't even had any of Thompson's cherry turnovers.

My stomach could definitely tell.

We stopped at a gas station that had a Subway. I filled up the car while Radar grabbed us some foot-longs.

We'd gone about another five miles before it occurred to me that I'd once again missed Dr. Werjonic's afternoon seminar. This time, though, I figured I could get copies of the notes easily enough when I connected with him about Slate Seagirt.

"So, how are you doing, Radar?"

"Good."

I was no counselor by any stretch of the imagination, but it seemed like I should at least offer whatever help I could. "If you want to talk about . . ."

"I'm good."

I drove for a bit. "You remember when Lyrie was involved in that shooting last year? The gang kid? He—"

"I don't need to talk to Padilla, Pat. I'm good."

I didn't have to mention a name. Radar knew right away I'd been talking about our police chaplain.

A pause. "Right."

We continued down the highway as darkness spread across the countryside. It was almost ten minutes before Radar spoke again. "Do you believe in hell, Pat?"

"Hell?"

"Yeah. For people like Griffin."

"You know, when we were back there, I was thinking to myself that there's gotta be a place set aside down there for guys like him. I'm not sure if I believe in a literal fire and brimstone hell, but for people like Griffin I sure hope one exists. What about you?"

"I believe there'll be a reckoning."

"A reckoning? You mean like Judgment Day?"

"I guess so." He didn't go on right away. "I guess because I believe that both love is real, and so is justice."

I thought I could see where he was going with this.

"You're saying justice doesn't always happen in this life. People get away with rape, murder, whatever, so—"

"Yeah. So if there's no hell, there's no final justice in the universe, not really. It'd mean those people just commit their crimes and then die like everyone else. If justice exists, if it's more than just wishful thinking—"

"There must be a hell."

"Yeah, or a reckoning, or whatever, and if there's no heaven, there's no hope, no victory; we would all just die and be gone. Love wouldn't win in the end."

I'd never thought of it quite like that, but what he said rang true to me. "So you think, Griffin, he went there? To hell?"

"I think he deserved to." It wasn't quite a direct answer. I thought maybe he would go on, but he left it at that and, though his words made me curious, so did I.

Then he was silent and I was silent and we drove toward police headquarters so he could pick up his car and go home to his wife and kids. And I could get back to work.

66

The only other person Joshua had ever heard speak of the Vaniad, the blood oath of the Teutonic Warrior, was James Oswald, a man who reminded him so much of his own father.

Joshua didn't know what the oath was exactly, his father had mentioned it but never shared it with him. Perhaps he would have gotten around to it if Joshua had not buried him alive.

However, Joshua did know that breaking the oath was tantamount to treason to those who'd taken it. His father had made that much clear to him. And in a press conference after his arrest, James Oswald vilified his son, Ted, for supposedly breaking the oath.

The mention of the Vaniad by James Oswald back in 1994 was what had first interested Joshua in his case. Heather Isle's book about Ted and James had been helpful in his research too. The more he found out about the relationship of the father and son, the more his interest was piqued. That was why he'd chosen to end this week's saga at the bank in Wales where they'd committed their final robbery.

Earlier today when he'd gone by the bank, he'd almost

been able to picture where SWAT would set up their command center, where the media vans would position themselves to do their remotes.

After leaving the bank, he'd rented the moving truck and had it delivered to the department store parking lot, where it was waiting for him.

Now, Joshua thought about tomorrow.

He had the funeral to attend at noon and then he could swing by the department store for the item he would be delivering to police headquarters. Then he would go to the school to pick up the children.

After he'd gotten them out of the school, he would deliver the package—something that would certainly be enough to convince the officer he had in mind to do as he was told.

And finally, at dusk, everything would culminate with Joshua's final ransom demand being met, live on national TV.

+ + +

With traffic, the trip to headquarters was slower than it should have been and it was 5:42 p.m. before I finally pulled into my parking spot in the underground garage.

"Hey, listen," I said to Radar, "I think I'm going to meet up with Ralph later tonight, have a couple beers, process things. You're welcome to join us."

"Yeah, I think I'll pass. I just need to get home."

"Right, well, listen, you did good out there."

He opened his door to leave, but then stopped short and looked at me, his eyes intense, searching. "Would you have done it?"

"Done it?"

"Fired. If you were standing where I was. If you saw what I did."

I didn't know what to say to that; I didn't know what he'd seen. "Of course."

"Thanks."

"For?"

"Finding that knife on his belt."

Again I wasn't sure how to respond. "Yeah."

Then he exited the car and walked silently across the parking garage toward his Jeep.

When I reached my desk, I found a voice message from Dr. Werjonic that he was hoping we might be able to meet for dinner. Ralph had also left me a note asking me to call him so he could take me out for that beer he'd promised me this morning.

I was still digesting the sub, but my hunger wasn't completely satiated and I figured I could manage eating again in an hour or so. Make up for that missed lunch.

Ralph left a number. I called it and found out it was the Overnite Motel, one of the cheapest motels on this side of the city. A federal employee who was actually saving taxpayers' money. Imagine that.

He wasn't there, but I left a message with the front desk for him to call me. Then I dialed Dr. Werjonic, who picked up immediately. Before we could get to discussing any dinner plans, I asked him about his meeting with Slate.

"Oh, it was quite interesting as a matter of fact. I'm anxious to tell you about it. But over dinner. Yes?"

"Yes."

"I'm afraid, however, that I'm not too familiar with

your city. Everywhere I turn, I see another bar serving beer, burgers, and bratwurst. Unfortunately, that's not exactly my cuisine of choice."

"I know just the place to go—Tanner's Pub. It has one of the largest selections of single malt whiskey outside of Britain."

"You don't say?"

"And fish and chips like you wouldn't believe. It used to be a speakeasy."

"Hmm . . . like the Safe House?"

The Safe House is a famous restaurant in downtown Milwaukee, situated halfway down a dingy alley across the street from the Pabst Theater. You have to know where it is because there's a secret entrance and you need to tell them the password to get in. The place is themed around spy memorabilia. If it has anything to do with espionage, it'll be on the walls of the Safe House.

"Atmosphere is completely different," I told Calvin. "Instead of a 007 motif, Tanner's is more like . . . well, I guess, more like a corner pub in London."

"Brilliant."

I was telling him the location when Ralph returned my call on the other line. "Hang on a second, Calvin."

A little phone shuffling and it was all set up—the three of us would meet at Tanner's. They'd get together in thirty minutes and, since I'd been gone most of the day and needed to catch up a little here at my desk, I'd join them as soon as I could, hopefully within the hour.

When we spoke, Ralph told me to check his work-space, that there was a pile of manila folders there. "The Oswald case files you wanted from Detective Browning over at the Waukesha county sheriff's department. And you're not gonna believe this: they were hand delivered by Browning himself."

Well, that was unexpected.

"There's a video too," he went on, "of footage from archived news coverage of the case. Some interesting stuff in there. We'll talk."

On my desk, Thorne had left me a copy of Heather Isle's (or Slate Seagirt's, as the case might've been) true crime book about the Oswalds, entitled *The Spawn*.

I hung up the phone, and, after calling Ellen to ask her to find the sanitation workers Dane Strickland and Roger Kennedy and ask them about their relationship with Timothy Griffin, I found the files Ralph had told me about, flipped open the top folder, and began to read.

67

During the day the Maneater had been busy with other obligations at work and hadn't been able to spend time with Celeste, but now at last he returned to her.

She was still alive.

That pleased him.

Last night, before any of this, as they walked through the door to her apartment, she'd offered to give him, as she put it, "Perfumed whispers and sweet laughter, a night wrapped in melodies and dreams and fantasies finally coming true."

"It's from a poem," she explained with a half-inebriated smile. "I learned it for this one class in college and never forgot it. Not even *once*."

"That's impressive," he'd told her.

As it turned out, fantasies really had come true last night. And now, as he took her to the pen where the cattle used to be slaughtered back when Brantner Meats was still in business, he was confident they were about to come true all over again.

But not with perfumed whispers and sweet laughter.

No. Other sounds altogether.

68

Bizarre.

That was the best way to describe the Oswalds' crimes. From an early age James had indoctrinated Ted to kill. During the trial, Ted's defense attorney pointed out that James Oswald would often threaten to shoot his son, sometimes aiming a rifle at his head. When Ted was five years old, his father apparently killed puppies in front of him and mocked him if he showed any form of emotional response.

The files contained transcripts of the trial proceedings between Ted and the prosecuting attorney:

OSWALD: I thought the only way I could say no to him was to prepare to fight to the end. He didn't say "I will kill you." It was the implication.

BENEDICT: What made you actually believe it?

OSWALD: His details, the expression on his face. He'd show papers with lists of people he was going to kill. I can give you an example.

BENEDICT: Please do.

OSWALD: My physics teacher. I had gotten an A first semester, a B+ second semester. He [James Oswald] was irate. He described how he was going to

have me get this guy. He was going to have me
build a silencer in front of him and then shoot him
in the belly and watch him barf . . . He [James Os-
wald] would as easily do it to me as to anyone else.

I scanned the next few lines of testimony and came to
Ted's account of the one time he'd actually attempted to
leave: "The dark side became a reality in the barn. Once
you entered, there was no going back. The only way out
was death. I couldn't go to the refrigerator and get a glass
of milk, go to the bathroom, go outside, pick up a pencil,
watch TV without asking permission. I packed my clothes
in a bag, attempted to go through the glass door. He
caught me and stripped me down to my underwear. He
had me kneel down, basically recite that he was the commander of the barn, the only way out was through him."

One piece of information I already knew: Eventually
the father and son were tied to a string of bank robberies
spread throughout southeastern Wisconsin. Each time
they would arrive heavily armed, wearing clear plastic
masks, and threaten the lives of bank employees if they
called the police.

After they were caught, it took the officers all day to go
through the Oswalds' Dodge County farm. Law enforcement had been told the barn was rigged to explode, and the
bomb squad spent hours searching the area around the barn
and the house with metal detectors looking for traps, before
they actually entered and found the Oswalds' extensive ar-
senal of ammunition and weapons, including .50 caliber rifles. In the end, no bombs or booby traps were found.

In one news conference, it was brought out that the
FBI had obtained a photograph of James standing next

to Timothy McVeigh, the Oklahoma City Bomber. When the reporters asked James what he thought of the Oklahoma City bombing, he said simply, "I think it was the wrong target."

The case files Browning had dropped off were comprehensive and, in some cases, inexplicably so. Not only did they include Ted Oswald's Waukesha County criminal court records (case #1994CF000227), the records of the civil suit filed by Diane Lutz, the widow of the officer they'd killed (#1995CV001632), but also strangely enough, Ted's Watertown Public Library card (number WT 50934), his USA wrestling competitor's membership card from 1990 to 1991, and the freshman picture from his high school yearbook (page 116).

It's sometimes baffling what people consider evidence.

Perhaps most troubling were the pages from Ted's journal.

The diary contained drawings of swastikas, swords, assault rifles, and an often-repeated saying, "freedom for the strong." He detailed his father's and his plan to carry out raids in Indiana and Michigan, to kill the "pigs" and to start "Jajauna," the code word they used to describe the crime spree they were precipitating. According to Ted's journal, he was planning to "conquer world by 39 instead of 38."

He had disturbing, chilling, but remarkably puerile plans for more crimes:

Day 1
    Do one pig in morning and one in afternoon.
    Make sure all heros are killed.
    Get birth certificate of real dead person.

Day 2
    8am—wake up
    10am—hit 1st taget
    —Get away
    1pm—look for new target
    4pm—hit 2nd target
    —Get away
    10 pm—Bed in AC at big Hotel

Day 3
    Same as Day 2

March 4, 1995, an article in the *Milwaukee Journal* reported that in his testimony, Ted claimed that his father "believed he [James] was a different species born out of humanity, a mutant. His goal of humanity was to become a superman . . . that's what I was supposed to become. I was nothing but his spawn . . . his property."

The Spawn, the title of the true crime book.

In the end, the jury didn't believe that Ted was afraid for his life when he committed the crimes, and convicted him to two life sentences plus more than four hundred fifty years.

Ted had recently turned eighteen when he and his father killed Captain Lutz. The sentencing of minors is almost never as severe as adults and I couldn't imagine he would have gotten as harsh of a sentence like he did if he'd been seventeen.

Quite an eye-opening birthday present.

I lost myself in reviewing the files and when I looked up, I saw that more than an hour had passed and I was already late for meeting up with Ralph and Calvin at Tanner's Pub.

69

Dr. Werjonic flagged me from a booth against the back wall.

Ralph had a pint of beer in front of him, Calvin a shot glass of whiskey. Both of their plates had already been cleared away.

On the way over I took in the place.

Hundreds of bottles of liquor rested on shelves above the bar and a variety of British memorabilia decorated the walls—pictures, postcards, photos of soccer matches. The bathroom doors halfway down a short hallway were labeled LADIES and GENTS. Darts to the right, bagpipe music overhead, the smell of fish and chips all around. Just like I remembered from the time Taci and I came here a couple months ago. Right now that was not an easy memory to contend with.

"Sorry I'm late," I told them as I took a seat. "I was reading over the Oswald files. Kind of lost track of time."

"It's a crazy case, isn't it?" Ralph said.

"Sure is."

He pounded the table with his fist. "Well, let me get you something to drink. You want some food too?"

"I could eat something."

I ordered a pint of lager from a local microbrewery that had just opened, and a platter of fish and chips.

Second supper.

"Good choice of a restaurant, my boy," Calvin exclaimed. "I feel like I'm back home."

"Glad to hear that."

He slid me a manila folder—they were everywhere today. "Notes from today's lecture. I thought you might be interested."

"You read my mind."

The two of them had heard about what'd happened with Griffin and they peppered me with questions, so even though I was anxious to hear about Slate, I took some time to fill them in on Griffin's death.

Considering that Dr. Werjonic had consulted with law enforcement agencies all over the world, on the way here I'd decided that tomorrow morning I would ask Thorne if we could bring him in on the case as a consultant. In the meantime, considering Calvin wasn't yet working with the department, I shared as much as I could.

"And Mallory?" Ralph asked concernedly. "How's she doing?"

"Hard to say. I couldn't really tell if she was sad or relieved that Griffin was dead." My food arrived. I waited until the server had walked away. "Just before they wheeled her onto the ambulance, she told me something pretty unnerving: the woman in the photo—you remember, Ralph, the one Griffin was—"

"Stroking a little too fondly."

"Yeah. Well, Mallory told me that was her mother, Griffin's wife."

A stony kind of silence followed my words, then Ralph

gave a long, low whistle. "That's one"—he glanced at Dr. Werjonic and perhaps thought he was too distinguished to appreciate a little cussing, and appeared to alter course right in the middle of his thought—"screwed-up family."

"Indeed," Calvin agreed.

"So . . ." I was ready to move past Griffin and his crimes. "Slate," I said to Calvin. "Let's hear about him."

"Caucasian. Mid-fifties. Slightly graying hair. Brown eyes. Attached earlobes. Approximately eighty-five kilos."

At the mention of kilos Ralph glanced at me grumpily.

"Um, about a hundred eighty-five pounds," I whispered to him.

"Based on his height and approximate body mass index, that would put him"—Calvin did a quick calculation in his head—"I would say about forty-five pounds overweight. Married. Right-handed. Bites his fingernails rather than clipping them. He was dressed casually in khakis and an inexpensive oxford that he hadn't taken the care to tuck in all the way. On the right side of his neck he had a distinctive birthmark in the shape of a crescent."

Ralph glanced at me and it was clear he was thinking the same thing I was. He said, "Sounds like Detective Browning from the Waukesha Sheriff's Department."

Yup, he was thinking the same thing.

The birthmark was the clincher.

Calvin eyed us curiously. "A detective, you say?"

"He wasn't too happy about having us look into the Oswald records," Ralph answered. "And this could explain why."

I thought things through. "Well, if he really is the author and used Griffin as his source, then their association could explain how Griffin got his hands on the Oswald cuffs. And it could explain why Browning hand-delivered the Oswald files today. He was coming to town anyway."

"To meet with me," Calvin said.

"To meet with you."

"A tit for a tat," he mused. "Browning obtains the information he needs for his books, then in exchange, he gives Griffin access to evidence. Criminal symbiosis."

It was becoming clearer to me that even though all the threads weren't ostensibly visible, everything in this investigation was linked, inextricably, beneath the surface. My kind of case.

I recalled the photos Browning had on his desk of him serving at different police departments in the state throughout the years. "Browning's been around a long time. He could probably get access to other evidence rooms without too much trouble."

I wondered if he knew anything about Griffin's involvement in Mindy's and Jenna's murders. It seemed like a stretch that he would've known and not done anything to apprehend him, but if he was relying on Griffin for information for his books, he had a dog in the hunt and it was possible.

Motives.

You just can't untangle people's motives.

"He only gave me the name Slate," Calvin noted. "I didn't actually ask to see his driver's license, so I can't confirm if he really is this detective."

I asked, "What exactly did he say?"

Calvin filled us in about their meal. Slate—or Browning, if it really was him—was researching Mindy's case and wanted to apply some of Calvin's geographic-profiling theories to try to postulate where the killer might live.

"I told him that he would need more locations for the calculations to be effective. He had certainly done his research—his knowledge of the intricacies of the case was impressive. Patrick, you mentioned the jacket just now in your account of what happened at the Griffin home. Slate mentioned it too."

"What did he say?"

"Just that it was found with the child, but he had a crime scene photo of the inside of the tree house." Calvin evaluated that for a moment, then tapped the table lightly. "I've been thinking, the timing of his contacting me might not have been because of your connection to the case, but because of my visit to Milwaukee for the lecture series. It would make sense that he would try to speak to me while I'm here."

"Well," I said, "if Browning really is Slate, we need to have a little talk with him."

"I'll take care of that first thing in the morning." Ralph's words were iron and I knew I would not want to be in Browning's shoes during that little exchange.

Ralph finished off his pint. "By the way, Pat, Griffin's subscription list didn't yield anything. So it looks like that's another dead end."

"Well," Calvin remarked. "That's helpful."

We both looked at him. "It's helpful that we ran into a dead end?" I asked.

"Every dead end shows you more clearly the pattern of the labyrinth. You now have one more piece of information that will help you fail your way to success."

That was an interesting way to put it.

But actually, I kind of liked it.

"I've been thinking about Indiana," Calvin added. "I

have some ideas, but I'd like to check on a few things first. Perhaps I can share them with you in the morning?"

"Great."

"Ring me at eight."

"Will do."

It was only after Calvin had left and Ralph and I were on our way to the door ourselves that he brought up the topic of Taci. "How are you doing, man? You okay?"

Truthfully, I'd been so consumed with this case and what'd happened with Griffin that I hadn't been thinking much about the breakup—at least not as much as I would've expected. "Better than I thought," I told him.

"Yeah, well, you'll be tempted to do it, but don't."

"Don't do what?"

"Dwell on it. Let pain become your home."

I hesitated. "Okay. Thanks."

"I'm saying this because you brood. I can tell."

"I brood?"

"Yeah. You brood. You're a brooder."

"I'm not a brooder."

"Oh, I'll bet you are." We came to the door and he paused, eyed me up. "I'll bet you're Mr. Brooder when no one else is around."

"Really?" I opened the door, led him outside. "And who are you, Captain Sunshine?"

"That the best you can come up with?" He stopped beside me, folded his Herculean arms. "I'll wait. Go on. Try again. I'm in no hurry."

I thought hard, but no clever comebacks came to mind and that just annoyed me worse.

"Thought so." He turned his collar to the wind. "Go get some sleep, man. You and Radar nailed Griffin. That's a good thing. Tomorrow we go at this again. Be ready. Things are starting to heat up."

"Right."

"I'll see you in the morning."

"See you tomorrow, Ralph."

Then I went home to watch the video footage that Browning had left us, and to read the notes Calvin had given me at the pub, and to page through Heather Isle's—or Detective Browning's—book: anything to keep me distracted, to keep me from thinking about Taci.

No, I told myself. I wasn't going to brood.

I was going to solve this case.

DAY 4

The Hospital Room

70

4:42 a.m.

Joshua's bedside phone rang.

Sylvia was asleep beside him, her arm draped lovingly across his chest, and she jerked involuntarily when the phone jangled. He was already awake, however, thinking about what would happen at First Capital Bank in just under twelve hours.

Surprised by getting a call at this time of night, he slid out from under Sylvia's arm to answer the phone. She rolled in the other direction with a soft, sleep-infused sigh.

Joshua spoke into the receiver. "Yes?"

"Someone has not been playing well with others."

"What?"

"I know what you were doing in that train car, Joshua."

An initial, almost debilitating chill swept over him, but it dissolved quickly with the revelation that this did not sound like something a cop would say. "Train car?"

"You'll learn it's not smart to leave that much evidence behind. Remember, everything you touch is an arrow leading back to you. You have to leave arrows that point somewhere else."

Words that might have come from the mouth of Joshua's own father, if he were not dead.

This is the man! This is the one you've been trying to get the attention of! The one from Illinois and Ohio!

Joshua stepped as far from the bed as the phone cord would allow, then whispered so Sylvia wouldn't hear, "You're the one who killed Hendrich."

"Yes."

"Why?"

"To leave an arrow pointing somewhere else."

Joshua processed that. "The gate was locked, how'd you get him in there?"

"The hole in the fence. It's amazing how compliant someone will be when he believes his life is in danger and that it might be spared."

"And you banged on the track to alert me? Why?"

"You were cutting it too close. One of the detectives was on his way to your boxcar."

"But how did you find me? How did you—"

"Colleen."

"Colleen?"

"Let's just call it luck."

Joshua's heart was racing almost as much as it had when he'd listened to Colleen scream in the boxcar. "When can I meet you?"

"Is that what you want? Is that why you're doing all this?"

"Yes."

"Auditioning?"

He hadn't thought of it exactly that way before. "Yes."

"What you've been doing is child's play—having someone leave a man in an alley? Coercing someone to drop off a corpse at a hardware store? I'm not sure you're taking this seriously."

How does he know? How did he find you!

"I can assure you that I am."

"Why the hands?"

"Colleen's?"

"Yes, why did you cut off her hands?"

"My father taught me that, except he did it after they were dead."

"They?"

"The people he brought to the place beneath the barn. He first took me down there when I was eight. He showed me what to do."

Joshua expected the man to ask him what'd happened there under the barn, or what exactly his father had taught him to do, or maybe, if he'd eaten Colleen's hands. But the man did not ask any of those things. Instead he said, "What do you have planned next?"

"Something special. It involves a police officer."

"Go on."

Joshua was beginning to get the sense that he'd already shared too much with this man. He didn't recognize the voice, but he wondered if it might possibly be a law enforcement officer after all. "That's all I can tell you."

"I need to know you're serious."

"I am. Quite serious."

"When will it happen? With the officer?"

"Today at twilight."

Sundown

Dusk.

The gloaming.

"Four twenty-five. To be exact."

"Four twenty-five."

"Yes."

"If I'm impressed, I'll contact you and we'll meet. If I'm not impressed, you'll never hear from me again."

"We're the same," Joshua said, sensing that the man was about to hang up. "You know that. You and I."

"If I thought you were the same as me, I'd never agree to meet with you."

"Why not?"

"Because I'd be afraid you were going to kill and eat me. But not necessarily in that order."

And then the line went dead.

71

Life is paradox.

That's what I was thinking when I woke up, sat up in bed, and stared at the phone, trying to decide if I should call Taci.

Paradox.

We want joy, but we read novels that make us cry. We're desperate to be truly known by others; yet we go to incredible lengths to hide who we really are. We say we want truth, then rationalize it away when it gets too personal.

We want the paradoxical extremes of security and adventure, of independence and intimacy, and if we have neither, or only one or the other, we're in psychological trouble: anyone who wants only intimacy is clingy and dependent; anyone who wants only independence is self-centered and dangerous.

We want to be free, but not too free; loved but not too tied down.

Paradox.

In essence, to be emotionally healthy, to be well-rounded, somehow we need to find a way to live in the constant tension of our desires; only people in perpetual conflict with themselves come the closest to finding peace.

Or love.

So.

Taci.

I knew her schedule for today, knew she would be leaving for the hospital at eight to work a twenty-four-hour rotation. So, she would still be home right now.

But then gone for twenty-four hours.

Call her.

No, no, no. Don't call her.

I was caught in the middle of human nature's greatest paradox of all: only when you love someone enough to let her walk away and not hold it against her have you finally found the truest form of love.

But then, it's too late.

With that thought hovering around me, I didn't call her, but left for the bathroom to shower and get dressed.

A quick recap.

I ran it through in my mind.

Griffin was dead, Mallory recovering. We hadn't learned yet if Browning knew about Griffin's crimes, but this morning Ralph was going to find out.

I was waiting to hear back from Ellen whether Roger Kennedy and Dane Strickland, the men responsible for dumping Dahmer's possessions in the Fort Atkinson landfill, had known Griffin.

The person who'd killed Bruce Hendrich was still at large. We didn't know yet if he was also the man who'd abducted Adele Westin and Colleen Hayes. Additionally, the man who'd killed the women in Ohio and Illinois was still at large. We didn't know whether he was the same man either. One man, or two, or three, we still didn't know.

After reviewing the notes Calvin had given me last night, as well as the last three pages of the stack he'd provided earlier, I realized I didn't have the mathematical background to do the geographic-profiling calculations in any reasonable amount of time. I would definitely need a computer and his software to analyze this data properly.

At the pub he'd said to call him at eight, just ten minutes from now. We could set up a time to go over the numbers then.

Last night I'd stayed up late, going through the Oswald video footage and case files, and there were papers strewn all across my living room floor.

But Radar was on my mind and, instead of picking up the papers, I phoned Reverend Padilla, the police chaplain. "I think maybe you should talk with Radar."

"About the shooting?"

"Yes. He seemed, well . . . I'm a little worried about how it might be affecting him."

"I'll give him a call."

Then I got in touch with Thorne. He had no problem with us consulting with Calvin about the case.

"Just fill out the paperwork when you get to the department," he told me.

"Great."

At last I scooped up the papers and popped the video out of the VCR.

By a fluke, WISN Channel 12 News had a cameraman

stationed in the area during the Oswalds' apprehension. The station had gotten the dispatch call and sent out a camera crew since they thought it was going to be a hostage situation.

As it turned out, the cameraman had gotten live footage of the Oswalds driving through a police barricade, trying to escape, and then crashing into a tree. I remembered seeing a minute or two of the footage back in 1994 after their arrest—it was played repeatedly for the next few weeks as the daily news reports followed the story.

But last night I'd watched the complete footage, as well as parts of the news shows, and now I gathered together the notes I'd jotted down:

- Van: Blue. Stolen from 46-year-old Judy Opat. They made her drive it when they abducted her. After she jumped out, they tried to escape but within thirty seconds crashed into a tree.
- SWAT surrounded them, but they refused to throw their guns out of the van. The standoff lasted three hours (thankfully the footage didn't).
- Earlier that morning, the Oswalds had robbed a bank in Wales at 9:30. At 9:36 a.m., the officers received a call and dispatched vehicles to apprehend the suspects.
- The chase ensued from the corner of 18 and 83.
- As they fled, they were approached by Captain James Lutz on Meadowbrook Road. They shot him six times, fatally wounding him.
- After Lutz's murder, the chase re-ensued at the intersection of SS and G near the Rocky Point subdivision on the west side of Pewaukee Lake. The

shoot-out occurred when the suspects were hemmed
in by a roadblock on the corner of SS and Oak Street.

• Other injuries from the shoot-out—Judy was hit by
a bullet that entered her right shoulder and exited
her armpit, two other officers were shot and treated,
one suffered minor abrasions. The officers, hostage,
and subsequently, the suspects, were all treated at
Waukesha Memorial Hospital.

After cleaning up the living room, I called Calvin and
told him he was in as a consultant.

"Splendid. Then I think there are some things we
should discuss this morning."

We agreed to meet at eight forty-five at Marquette in
the Criminology and Law Studies grad office where he
was heading to prepare his lecture for this afternoon's
seminar. "I'll bring my computer," he offered. "Then we
can plug in the data, try to find out where our offender
might actually live."

That gave me just under half an hour before I needed
to leave.

Figuring I'd make the best of it, I set about reviewing
Werjonic's algorithms so I could at least try to understand what we would be discussing at eight forty-five.

72

8:25 a.m.
8 hours until the gloaming

An infected and barbarous heart.

The words seemed almost audible to Joshua, who tried to tune them out, tried to bury them beneath the memory of killing Petey Schwartz last Friday, the man whose funeral he was going to attend today at noon.

You have an infected and barbarous heart.

He chose a tie and slung it around his neck.

Attending the funeral of a man you've killed contains a sad and tragic irony. Perhaps even a touch of sadism. But killing Petey had not been something Joshua had been planning to do at all. They both just happened to be in the wrong place at the wrong time.

Still, when the moment came, when the homeless man came at him, Joshua had, without hesitation, plunged the necrotome into his belly just the way his father had taught him to do in the barn when he was a boy.

And he had moved it back and forth.

Just like his father had taught him.

Petey had looked at him strangely as Joshua hugged

"He was flying over it," I said reflectively.

"The missing persons cases you mentioned yesterday. Were they spread out or clustered?"

"Clustered." I picked up one of his markers. "May I?"

"Of course."

Using the marker, I placed dots on the map where the sixteen women lived or were last seen.

He studied the distribution.

The clusters were grouped vaguely around Milwaukee, Madison, and Green Bay, Wisconsin; Rockford and Champaign, Illinois; and Cincinnati, Ohio.

He pointed to the cities. "We'll want to see if General Mitchell International Airport has direct flights from Milwaukee to these cities."

It took us only a few minutes on the phone to find out that you could get to all the cities, but not all of the flights were direct, not all were daily. However, Rockford, Madison, and Green Bay would all be within a couple hours' drive. The killer could've easily taken the roads you can see to get to them.

"Maybe we shouldn't look at shipping centers or distribution centers per se," Calvin said, "but at businesses that do business with other businesses."

"Consulting firms?"

"Along those lines, yes. A firm that might be flying people throughout this tri-state region. Have your task force check the flight manifests from perhaps a week before and a week after the crimes in those locations. See if the same name shows up." He paused. "That will, admittedly, take some time, however."

I was ready to get started on it right away. "Did you come up with anything on your computer?"

him closer, held him until the man had no more strength to stand on his own. Then he helped him to the ground so he could finish bleeding to death on the sidewalk.

After he had, Joshua stared at the body.

No one will even miss him.

No one will ever know.

This is the perfect time to do it.

But eating Petey Schwartz's diseased, unbathed flesh was not something Joshua was ready to do. He'd learned long ago, when his father was still alive, that you have to use discernment. You have to exhibit self-control.

He finished with the tie.

The city paid to bury vagrants, but the West Reagan Street Mission was the one to arrange memorial services for the homeless people in the neighborhood who died.

There was no way they could afford a service at an actual funeral home and there was no practical way for the homeless people who would be attending to get there anyway, so the service would be held right there at the mission, just three blocks from the train yards.

As Joshua headed out the door, he ran through his plan for the day one last time. He would head to work for a few hours, attend Petey Schwartz's funeral at noon, then stop by Kohl's department store to get the box he would be sending the police officer.

Then he could pick up the children, deliver the package, and wait for the cop to die.

Finally, this evening when it was all said and done, he would meet the man who'd called him earlier this morning. The man who was going to become his partner.

73

I parked on Wells Street, walked from there, and found Calvin in the graduate office, bent over the highest-end laptop computer I'd ever seen, meticulously entering data.

He didn't look up. "Good morning, Detective."

I knew he was expecting me, but it could have been someone else walking in—yet there was certainty in his voice when he identified who I was.

"Everyone's gait is distinctive," I surmised. "You remembered mine."

"Quite right." He pointed at his computer screen. "I've taken the liberty of entering the information that you mapped out yesterday on the corkboard. First, we'll treat the homicides from Ohio and Illinois as if they're separate from the abduction/demand crimes here this week, and then recalculate the data as if the crimes were all linked. Agreed?"

I liked that he was diving right in. "Agreed."

"So . . ." But instead of turning his attention to the computer screen, he directed me to an AAA map of the Midwest. With red Magic Marker he'd identified Milwaukee, Wisconsin, and the sites of the homicides in Champaign, Illinois, and White Oak, Ohio. "Entrance

and exit routes . . . drive times. What do you think they would be?"

The sites formed a lopsided triangle. "I don't know. Let's see, from Milwaukee to White Oak . . . I'd say almost seven hours. From there to Champaign, four or so. From Champaign back to Milwaukee, another four hours."

"Very good." He traced the highways with his finger as he told me the mileage: "Three hundred seventy-seven miles. Two hundred twenty-seven. Two twenty-five. Who would drive that far to commit his crimes?"

I didn't want to assume too much. "Ralph and Agent Parker, she's another FBI agent on the case, they already looked into traveling salesmen, that sort of thing, before getting up here. Distribution centers for food service, trucking routes, all that—didn't come up with anything. No companies that have routes or shipping centers i[n] those cities or the surrounding small towns."

He looked thoughtful for a moment. "I was not awa[re] of that." He eyed the map more carefully, then mutter[ed] something about awareness space and distance decay, b[ut] it was hard to hear what he was saying.

Then all at once his eyes lit up. "My boy, I think [per]haps we've been looking at the wrong roads."

"Which ones should we be looking at?"

"The ones you can't see."

"The ones you can't see?"

He grinned and pointed at the ceiling.

"Um . . ." Then it hit me. "What? You mean [by] air? Flying?"

"That could explain why he skipped over India[na,] wasn't driving through it."

"Yes, yes, of course." He positioned himself in front of the keyboard. "So let's look at the specific abduction/demand cases." A few keystrokes later, a map of Milwaukee with a myriad of lines and circles of different colors appeared.

Lines and nodes.

The awareness spaces of the victims.

"You've been busy," I said.

"Indeed." He tapped the screen. "Here. The boxcar as the anchor point. Then the sites you noted on your corkboard map yesterday. Plus, I've taken the liberty of adding the victimology information your team came up with—the typical travel routes and activity nodes for Colleen Hayes and Adele Westin."

"How did you get those?"

"After you rang me at eight, I contacted Agent Hawkins, told him that Lieutenant Thorne had agreed to let me consult on the case, and he shared with me what Agent Parker and he had come up with yesterday in their research into the lives of the victims. Incidentally, the two women's lives did intersect at one point, only not at the same time."

"Where is that?"

"The Milwaukee Regional Medical Center. It seems Adele was in a small fender bender last summer and spent the night there. Colleen, of course, was taken there this week."

But Colleen was taken there after the crime, so the link wouldn't involve the initial encounters with their abductor. "That's stretching it a bit. Do you think it matters?"

"Everything matters."

Hmm. I kind of liked that line.

I might just add it to my repertoire.

"Of course," he acknowledged, "it's also possible that the abductor chose Adele simply because of the availability of the recently buried corpse of her fiancé's grandmother."

"Or he might have killed Miriam Flandry himself to provide the necessary corpse for his plan."

"The timing would favor that," he said quietly.

"I'll have the team look into the circumstances surrounding her death."

He typed, the map morphed. "As you can see, the centroid spatial distribution helps us identify the most likely location for the abductor's residential address . . . Here." He paused, then gestured toward the screen. "Near Franklin Heights. On the north side of the city. You'll want to have your task force focus on people on the tip list and suspect list who live in this sixteen-block radius."

Amazing.

If it really was accurate, that is.

Even though there was a clock on the wall, he consulted his pocket watch just as he had yesterday. "I'm sorry, this afternoon's lecture is a new one and, with the time I spent on this research this morning, well, let's just say I have some long hours of preparation in front of me."

He slid me a packet of photocopied pages. "I took the liberty. You never know what the day might bring."

"Notes for today's lecture."

"What I have so far."

"Thanks."

"Ring me if your team finds out anything."

"I will."

"And we'll reconnect again, perhaps after lunch. If I can, I'll swing by police headquarters before the seminar."

"Great."

Notes in hand, and feeling like we might have an avenue of inquiry that could take us someplace productive, I left for police headquarters.

74

9:25 a.m.
7 hours until the gloaming

I found Corsica, Lyrie, and Gabriele in the conference room.

The other task force members were either out following up on leads or hadn't made it to the office yet. Thompson had called in asking what kind of doughnuts people wanted—he was going to "pick up a few for the crew on the way in."

I told the three people who were here what Calvin and I had been thinking. "We'll need to make some calls to airports, check flight manifests, and I want someone to go through the suspect list and tip list looking for people who live in that area near Franklin Heights. Also, let's find out what we can about Miriam Flandry's death—if there were any indications of foul play. Oh, and consulting firms in the cities under question, businesses that do business with businesses."

We split up the assignments and set to work.

+ + +

The more attached you get to people before they die, the more you'll ache after they're gone.

So, really, the Maneater could think of no good reason to put yourself through any of that, to form any sort of emotional attachments with the people around you. After all, since you'll be leaving them eventually, or they'll be leaving you, why cause more grief in the world by extending or receiving love in the first place?

Now, this morning, he didn't find it difficult at all to get the person he'd decided to abduct into his car. She was a petite woman and he was strong for his size.

He carried her into the slaughterhouse and set her in one of the walk-in freezers that was now without power, but quite soundproof and secure. She was still unconscious when he locked the freezer door.

He would come back and visit her later, then take her to the place in the building where he'd taken Celeste last night.

A test? Maybe. You could call it that. But the Maneater wanted to know how serious Joshua really was about all of this.

If he did carry out something memorable at dusk, as he claimed he was going to do, they would meet up tonight and the Maneater would reward him with this woman.

And they would share their first meal together.

75

In light of our current projects, the ten o'clock meeting had been cancelled. It seemed more prudent to pursue our leads than to sit around a table talking about them.

While we were working, Ellen showed up and told us she'd interviewed the two waste management workers who drove the truck of Dahmer's things. Both claimed they didn't know Griffin or anything about him, but Strickland did know Detective Browning and went deer hunting with him.

It was a link.

Links form a chain.

Chains form a case.

She went on. "When I asked him if he might have mentioned to Browning where Dahmer's possessions had been deposited, his memory seemed to become a bit fuzzy."

Yes, so information could've easily been passed from Strickland to Browning to Griffin, if the links were connected.

As she was finishing up, Radar walked in and informed

us that he'd just spoken with Colleen Hayes downstairs. "She was brought over here to see Vincent—he's still in custody. Anyway, I thought we could finally get some answers from her about those cuffs. I pressed her about why she'd purchased a pair that had been used in the Oswalds' arrest. It took some prodding, but she told me that a guy at work had thrown out a catalog. She saw it in the trash, flipped through it, saw the cuffs. She thought it would be . . . well, discreet to order them through there."

That was a little disappointing. "So she didn't ask specifically for the ones involved in the Oswalds' arrest?" I said.

"It didn't sound like it, no."

So, the killer could have found out about the cuffs from Griffin's records and chosen Colleen that way. The connection between Adele and Colleen might not be the breakthrough clue we were hoping it would be after all.

"Does she know who threw out the catalog?"

He shook his head. "No, and she said she didn't know who the guy was she ordered them from either, that it was all done through a post office box. The cuffs were shipped to her house."

Another corner of the labyrinth closed off, moving us inexorably in another direction.

As far as the rest of our progress, Miriam Flandry's stroke hadn't seemed in any way suspicious and no autopsy had been done. The search for consulting firms had come up dry, but Lyrie had found that four people on the suspect list and tip list did live in the Franklin Heights area.

I turned to Thompson who'd arrived during our recap

and had, as promised, brought plenty of chocolate cream-filled and glazed doughnuts for everyone. "Don't you go to church in that area?" I asked him. "Over near Franklin Heights?"

"Yeah."

"Why don't you follow up on those names. See what you can dig up."

"Right." He grabbed three doughnuts and left again. Didn't even get a chance to sit down.

The rest of us went back to work.

It took a little while, but all three airlines that flew out of General Mitchell Airport and serviced the cities we were looking at faxed us the flight manifests we'd requested and we took our time inspecting them. In the end, however, we didn't come up with any names that matched.

It was possible this whole airline idea was off base.

Come on, Pat, you're missing something here!

I rubbed my head, then studied the maps on the corkboard again, thought about what Calvin had said about consulting firms, businesses that do businesses with other businesses.

Roads you can't see . . .

Notice the obvious, Pat . . . The truth isn't as obscure as it appears . . . Our preconceptions blind us to—

"Hang on," I said. "Chartered flights. Private jets. And let's take a closer look not just at consulting firms but at any businesses that have satellite offices in those cities."

Agreement from the team.

We pulled out phone books and began to make some calls.

76

Ellen struck gold.

She found one company, High Profile Charter Service, based out of Milwaukee, that made regular chartered stops in Cincinnati and Champaign and had even done so two days before their respective murders, then returned to Milwaukee the day after them. They'd also sent a flight to Green Bay two days prior to the disappearance of a woman from nearby Appleton.

There weren't any flights to Rockford or Madison, but again, those cities weren't too far from Milwaukee and it made sense that the killer could have driven to them easily enough.

When we checked which company had chartered the flights in question, we found that they were all hired by Hathaway & Erikson, LLC, one of the biggest acquisition firms in the Greater Milwaukee area.

A business that did business with other businesses.

I remembered what Griffin had said right before he was killed, when I asked him about the Maneater: "Now there's a man who knows how to acquire what he wants. Does it for a living."

A man who knows how to acquire what he wants.

Does it for a living.

A guy who works at an acquisitions firm? A double entendre from the man who called Mallory "baby"?

I wouldn't put it past him.

Oh yeah, things were popping.

High Profile Charter Service didn't have flight manifests, but they did have a record that nine people had been on the flight to Cincinnati, seven to Champaign, and five to Green Bay.

"If we get those names from the acquisition firm," Corsica said, "and the same name appears on all the lists—"

"We have our guy," Radar exclaimed.

I didn't think we could go quite that far, but I had the sense that it would certainly be one circumstantial link to the crimes that would be hard to discount.

As it turned out, only Corsica was able to leave the department with me at the moment, but I didn't care. I was willing to work with just about anyone if it meant moving things forward.

We grabbed our things and left to pay a visit to Hathaway & Erikson, LLC.

77

A crowd of fifteen people had gathered in the West
Reagan Street Mission's cafeteria to remember Petey
Schwartz.

The small congregation sat behind folding tables with
Styrofoam cups of coffee in front of them.

All of the people, besides Joshua, worked for the mission or were transients who'd known Petey. And yet, because of his past involvement with the center, Joshua did
not stand out.

The question that seemed so hard to answer gnawed
at him: "What kind of a God could ever forgive someone
who's done the things you've done?"

And the answer he tried to cling to: "What kind of a
God would he be if he couldn't?"

The Reverend Hezekiah Tate, the African-American
preacher who'd started this shelter for the homeless more
than thirty years ago, walked slowly to the front of the
cafeteria, greeted those who'd come, unfolded his weath-
ered Bible and laid it on the antique lectern he always
preached from.

After a few brief opening remarks, he started in with
his "word from the Lord." He spoke with the honest

intensity, the intonation, the cadence of a veteran black preacher. "We all have choices that we face in this life. Petey had choices. I have choices. You have choices."

Yes, and you have chosen evil, Joshua. You will have to answer for that, you will—

"Scripture is clear that we are each responsible for our own choices. No one can take credit for the godly works of another; no one will bear the blame for another's ungodly acts. And this has been true, this is true, this will always be true. Amen?"

The small group of homeless people knew Tate, knew the way he preached, and chimed in, "Amen."

"In Ezekiel eighteen, and verse four, we read that the word of the Lord came to Ezekiel and said unto him, 'The soul that sinneth, it shall die.'"

It shall die, Joshua.

You shall—

"'If a father shall beget a son that is a robber, a shedder of blood, and that doeth the like to any one of these things . . .'"

A shedder of blood.

Like you, Joshua.

A son.

Who is.

A shedder of blood.

"'Shall he then live? He shall not live: he hath done all these abominations; he shall surely die; his blood shall be upon him . . . The soul that sinneth, it shall die.'"

Tate emphasized that last word, let it ring and echo through the room, then went on. "'The son shall not bear the iniquity of the father, neither shall the father bear the iniquity of the son: the righteousness of the righteous shall be upon him, and the wickedness of the wicked shall be upon him. Therefore repent, and turn yourselves from all your transgressions; so iniquity shall not be your ruin. Cast away from you all your transgressions, whereby ye have transgressed; and make you a new heart and a new spirit.' "

Repent, Joshua, it's not too late. You have to—

"And where does this new heart and this new spirit come from?" Reverend Tate asked rhetorically. "Only through faith *in the grace of God*, only through mercy *at the hand of God*, only through hope *in the Son of God*. Amen?"

"Amens" from the ragtag congregation.

"As the Lord told Ezekiel in the thirty-sixth chapter, the twenty-sixth verse: 'A new heart also will I give you, and a new spirit will I put within you: and I will take away the stony heart out of your flesh, and I will give you an heart of flesh.' "

Tate's voice took on a flavor of fire born of love. "This new spirit comes to us only *from* God and is a gift *of* God and draws us closer *to* God. Amen?"

More amens. Two disabled vets, one of whom was missing a leg, and both of whom lived under an I-94 overpass, lifted their foam cups in an impromptu toast to the preacher.

Tate wrapped up his brief but passionate homily: "This new heart, this new spirit, this new hope, come to all who will turn to the Lord to find forgiveness and atonement for their sins. This, Petey did right here in this very cafeteria, one month ago. And this you can do today, if you have never done so before. Right here, in the same place where Petey was saved, you can be too." He took an expectant breath. "Let us pray. And let us take responsibility for our sins, let us bring our hearts to God, let us trust in the Lord Jesus Christ, the one whose blood—"

—*Blood. Always blood*—

"—cleanseth us from all sin."

Tate began his prayer by referencing St. Paul's conclusion about the struggle against his sinful nature: "Who shall deliver me from the body of this death? I thank God through Jesus Christ our Lord . . ."

As Reverend Tate went on, Joshua felt the crushing weight of his past, of his choices, nearly smothering him.

He had to leave.

So, while everyone else's eyes were closed and heads were bowed, Joshua slipped out of the cafeteria. He made it to his car before he started to cry. And there he prayed and prayed, begging the God who had spoken those words to Ezekiel so long ago to speak to him today.

"A shedder of blood shall not live. He hath done all these abominations; he shall surely die; his blood shall be upon him."

He tried to grab hold of hope, but the promise of a new heart, a new spirit, a gift offered, was overwhelmed by a palpable darkness, one that felt almost visceral and alive, a consuming presence sliding into his heart, rising above the moment and muscling its way into his soul.

Joshua ended his prayer.

Wiped away his tears.

It was too late for redemption.

He left to pick up the shoebox.

78

Corsica and I were almost to the offices of Hathaway & Erikson, LLC.

Everything was cycling around inside my head: the abductions, the murders, the unsolved missing persons cases. All seemingly intertwined, yet separate. Depending on how you looked at it, they were all one case, or more than a dozen.

How all that worked, I wasn't quite sure.

Corsica spoke up, interrupting my thoughts. "I heard about you and Taci."

"What?"

"You and Taci. I heard what happened."

"Oh."

"People talk. You know. You two have been together for a while. I . . . Well, we heard it from one of the doctors who works over there at the medical center."

"I see."

I pulled onto the road that would take us to the acquisitions firm. As far as I was concerned, we couldn't get there quickly enough.

"It's hard," Annise said. "Going through something like that."

I could hardly believe she was talking to me like this. We'd never before spoken about anything remotely personal and I really had no idea how to respond.

She went on. "Just wanted you to know, I feel for you. I know you cared about her."

I pulled into the parking lot.

"Thanks."

"You don't have to hate someone for loving something else more than you. You know?"

I was about to say that I didn't hate Taci, that I would never hate her, but I stopped myself short. I figured Annise must certainly know that. "Thanks," I said again.

"Okay." And then the conversation I never would have expected was over.

Though I might not have liked Annise very much, might never like her very much, as we left the car, I realized I was ashamed that I'd never tried to understand her. But she had just now, in her own way, tried to understand me.

Inside the building, we showed the receptionist our IDs and when we requested to speak to someone about their corporate flights to out-of-state accounts, she directed us to the senior vice president, a woman named Faye Palmer.

Palmer's corner office was stylish and yet simple. The window peeked out over a parklike employee break area outside. Everything about Palmer seemed to say "high-level corporate VP": designer pants suit, stylish hair, a pleasant yet brisk and professional demeanor.

She got right down to business. "So, how exactly can I help you, Detectives?"

I told her forthrightly about the flights, asked her for the names of the people who'd been aboard them.

She tapped a finger against her desk but gave no indication that she was going to grant the request. "And you're certain that someone on these flights is involved in some way in these crimes?"

"By no means." Corsica's voice was unequivocal. "We're simply pursuing every possible lead."

After evaluating that, Palmer nodded and went to her file cabinet. It took her a little while, but at last she produced a manila folder—I just couldn't seem to get away from those things this week. She shuffled through the sheets, then pulled out three.

I could tell she was about to glance them over, but then without doing so, handed the pages to me.

She must have noticed my surprise that she didn't look at them. "I don't want my perception of any of my employees to be shaded," she explained, "even marginally, with unfounded suspicion. I'm sure you'll let me know if you find anything regarding any of them."

"I'm sure we will," Corsica answered.

We thanked Palmer for her help and excused ourselves from her office.

I could barely contain my curiosity as we returned to the reception area.

Finally, when we were alone and in a corner of the room, I held up the papers, and Corsica and I examined the names.

79

Three names appeared on all three lists: Janelle Warner, Andre Demell, and Richard Basque.

Just three names.

The violent nature of the crimes made it highly unlikely that a woman would be the killer. Yes, we would speak with Janelle, but I wanted to start with the two men on our list.

"Which one first?" I asked Corsica. "Demell or Basque?"

"Let's go with Mr. Demell."

We asked the receptionist to try his office number, but when she consulted her appointment book, she informed us that he would be out most of today meeting with some of their clients.

"But he is here in town?" I said.

"Yes."

We set up an appointment for four thirty.

Janelle Warner would meet with us at one fifteen.

"What about Richard Basque? Is he in?"

The receptionist sighed and I got the impression she was growing tired of helping us, which didn't bother me one bit as long as she got us the meetings we needed.

She rang Basque's office, spoke for a moment on the

phone, and then announced that he would be out in a minute. Somewhat impolitely she flicked her hand toward the chairs in the reception area. "You can have a seat if you like."

"That won't be necessary," Corsica told her with a slight touch of attitude. "If it's only going to be a minute."

I folded up the flight manifests and slid them into my pocket.

And thought of the best way to frame the questions I was going to ask Mr. Basque.

80

Basque stepped through the doorway.

Caucasian. Late twenties or early thirties. Perceptive, turquoise eyes. Handsome. Dressed *GQ*-esque in a charcoal suit and tie. Six-two, athletic build, dark hair. A confident, endearing smile.

If he really was the "Maneater of the Midwest," he was not all what you might envision when you pictured a cannibalistic murderer.

Or, well, maybe he was.

Even though it wasn't by any means fair to make the comparison, with his good looks and charming smile, Basque reminded me of the quintessential psychopath Ted Bundy—the clean-cut, all-American, articulate, smiling, serial killing, homicidal maniac.

We greeted Basque and he led us to his office on the second floor.

After we'd all taken a seat, he let his gaze pass from me to Corsica and then back to me. He smiled. "Can I have my secretary bring you anything? Coffee? A glass of water?"

"No, thank you." I still wasn't really sure how to address the issue that this guy just happened to keep showing up in cities scattered throughout the Midwest right around the time women were disappearing or showing up dead.

But I didn't have to try to figure out how to be polite because Corsica cut to the chase for me: "We're investigating a series of homicides."

"Homicides."

"Yes."

He waited for us to elaborate.

I said, "Do you know a woman named Juanita Worthy?"

He thought about it, shook his head. "I'm afraid not. Who is she?"

"A woman who was killed in Illinois."

"I'm sorry to hear that."

Corsica spoke up, "What about Marianne Lojeski?"

He shook his head again.

"Bruce Hendrich?"

He looked at us quizzically. "Honestly, I don't know any of these people and I'm not entirely sure why you're asking me if I do."

I thought about bringing up the flight manifests, but as long as he was denying knowing any of the victims there might be a better approach. "Mr. Basque, would you be willing to share a copy of your schedule with us? Your days off? Your personal calendar?"

It would have been easy to miss.

It happened for only an instant, but it did happen.

His gaze flickered cold and an icy intensity fell across his eyes, one so stark and soulless that it actually sent a shiver through me, but then, in the time it takes to blink, he collected himself and offered us a smile that looked remarkably genuine. "Certainly. Now, tell me, why are you asking me this?" He raised an eyebrow, asked light-heartedly, "I'm not a suspect, am I?"

I let Corsica answer. She folded her hands, laid them gently on her lap, repeated the same words she'd told his boss earlier, "By no means. We're simply pursuing every possible lead."

"I see."

I took a few minutes to ask about his business trips to Ohio and Illinois and if he knew anything about the Hayes or Westin kidnappings here in Milwaukee this week. He shook his head and told me that, no, he did not—other than what he'd heard on the news—but that he genuinely wished there was some way he could help.

He sounded like he meant it and he wasn't in any hurry to get rid of us. He didn't seem nervous or in-timidated, was pleasant and cordial the whole time. And for some reason, even though I hated the idea of going with my gut or letting unfounded assumptions guide me around, the more personable and patient he was, the more I found myself thinking he was guilty.

Finally, when we had no more questions, he brought me a copy of his personal schedule and wished us well in our investigation, then gave me his card. "If there's any-thing I can do for you, feel free to call. I'll do whatever I can to help make sure you get this monster before he commits any more crimes."

As soon as we were outside the building, Corsica said, "It's him."

I agree, I thought.

"I think we need a little more evidence before we can arrest him," I said.

"Alright, then." She opened up the car door. "Let's go get it."

+ + +

Since leaving for the store, Joshua had decided to take only one of the children.

It would be easier to handle that way. And besides, the more he thought about the logistics of it, the more he realized there really was no compelling reason to take them both.

So.

The boy.

He would take the boy and leave the girl at the school to be picked up by her mother.

He paused as he walked down the children's shoe aisle at Kohl's.

He needed something to hold the proof he was sending the sergeant.

A shoebox would be just the right size.

He chose one and carried it to the checkout counter.

"Will this be all, sir?"

"Yes. Just that one pair."

He paid for the shoes and went to the school to get the boy.

+ + +

Corsica read me Basque's work records as I drove back to HQ.

According to his personal schedule, the time he took

off corresponded with twelve of the disappearances and both of the homicides.

I don't like to jump to conclusions, but I'm not stupid. This guy was looking really good for these crimes. Almost too good.

Prove it wrong; don't assume.

We radioed ahead to the team to have them dig up everything they could on Richard Devin Basque.

"I want it waiting for me when we arrive," I said.

81

Inside the department again, the task force reconvened.

Before we launched into examining the background information on Basque, Ralph, who'd just returned from Fort Atkinson, filled us in on Browning.

"I'll make this quick," he said, "'cause I know we gotta get to Basque: Browning denied knowing anything about Griffin's involvement. Might have been telling the truth, but when I took a careful look at his employment record, I saw—well, guess where he used to work?" He didn't wait for a reply. "Horicon. At the time of Mindy Wells's death. He was the officer assigned to signing items into and out of the evidence room."

Just thinking about Mindy's death cut into me, and the fact that a police officer might have known something about her killer and done nothing about it, leaving him free to kill again, cut into me even more.

"He's being questioned about it by the DA as we speak. Oh, and this might be a bit of good news. Sergeant Carver and his team over in Fort Atkinson found a journal hidden beneath a loose board in the kitchen of that farmhouse near the landfill." Ralph held up two fingers.

"Jenna and Mindy, that's it, the only two homicides written about in the journal."

"Griffin told me there were others," I said. "That there are always others."

"Bragging?" Ellen suggested. "Narcissism? According to what you told us, it fits right in with his personality."

I hoped she was right. It sounded strange to say in reference to the death of anyone, but if those were the only two girls whom he'd killed, that would at least be one thing to be thankful for.

In either case I was confident that the Fort Atkinson PD wouldn't let this thing rest until they'd found out the true extent of Griffin's crimes.

We turned our attention to Basque.

"Alright," I said to the team. "Tell me everything we know about him."

We went through the peripheral stuff first—where he'd lived, worked, gone to school, all in the Greater Milwaukee area. He had an off-the-charts IQ. He was single, never married, no known children. He had a gym membership downtown, paid his taxes on time, donated regularly to three different charities.

Thorne shook his head. "This guy's something else. A perfect record, not even a parking ticket."

"And he's never lived in the Franklin Heights area?" I said, trying to tie all the investigative threads together.

Lyric answered. "No."

Ellen looked anxious to share what she'd found. "When I was calling around checking on his work, I learned who his temp had been for a couple weeks in September. Filled in for his secretary." Whether she intended to or not, she gave a dramatic pause. "Colleen Hayes."

Okay, now that was interesting.

I recalled what we'd learned earlier. "She said she found Griffin's catalog in a trash can at work," I looked around. "Who has that copy of Griffin's subscription list?"

Gabriele jogged to the other room and returned with it, scanned it, and said, "Yeah, Basque's on the list. He's a subscriber."

That was it. "We need to have another chat with this guy."

But when we tried his office we found out he'd left for the day. The receptionist didn't know where he'd gone.

"Let's get a car to his house," I told Thorne. "I'm not sure if we have enough to bring him in for questioning, but we can give it a shot. Maybe find out something before he lawyers up. We might have rattled him when we visited his office. He could have taken off."

"I'll put out an APB," Thorne said. That could create a legal mess to mop up later if this ended up being a dead end, but I trusted Thorne to handle it and I was glad he was ready to make the call.

Earlier, Corsica and I had set up a one-fifteen appointment to have a talk with Janelle Warner, the other Hathaway & Erikson employee who'd flown with Basque and Demell. However, right now I didn't want to leave headquarters. Ellen offered to go over there with Corsica and talk with Ms. Warner, hoping she might be able to tell us something about Basque's behavior on their trips.

As they were getting ready to go, we received word that Calvin had arrived and was in the lobby. "Call him in," I said. "I want to get his take on this too."

82

1:25 p.m.
3 hours until the gloaming

Joshua entered the school.

"Yes?" The secretary at the front desk was a stern-looking woman with a single eyebrow that bridged across both of her dark, scolding eyes. "May I help you?" Somehow she made it sound like a reprimand rather than a question.

He showed her his credentials, then told her the children's last name. "I'm afraid I have to deliver some bad news regarding their father. He's been in an accident."

"An accident?" Her voice had softened only slightly.

"He's at the Milwaukee Regional Medical Center."

"What happened?"

"A car accident. It's quite serious, I'm afraid. Their mother is there with him now. She asked me to come by and speak with the children."

"We can't release students to anyone who's not family or who's not on their emergency contact form," she replied.

"No, I'm not here to take them home. Their grandmother will be by shortly. But their mother wanted to make sure it would be me rather than their grandmother who told them. I'm sure you understand."

Before she could reply, the principal poked her head out of the office door behind the reception desk and asked her to pick up some payroll forms from the central office.

After the principal had closed the door again, the secretary hesitated for a moment, but at last reached across her desk, picked up a visitor's tag, and handed it to Joshua.

She told him which rooms the boy and the girl were in. He thanked her, and as he pinned the tag to his shirt, he headed down the hall toward room 118, Tod's second grade classroom.

He would take the boy, exit through another door, and leave the girl here.

+ + +

We filled Calvin in as comprehensively and yet as quickly as we could on the different aspects of the case.

He reflected on what we'd said. "And the mattresses? Nothing in that part of the city?"

Gabriele shook her head.

"Maybe you don't need to look at places that sell mattresses, but places that use them, that use mismatched ones. From what I've heard, the West Reagan Street neighborhood is low income, has a high population of vagrants. Are there any homeless shelters in the area?"

"I'll find out." I grabbed a phone book and it took only a moment to look it up. "West Reagan Street Mission is only three blocks from the train yards. The ad here says they have beds available, free job training, medical care and meals."

"Try them," Calvin said. "See if they might've perhaps received a recent donation to purchase new mattresses and, if so, who donated the money or picked up the old ones. Even if we don't get a name, that'll give us a date to work with."

I tracked with him. "Then we can check moving truck rentals that week."

"It's always about timing and location," he noted contemplatively.

I nodded for Gabriele to make the call even as Radar, who'd been working down the hall, came hurrying toward us. "I came up with someone who might be the next pastiche. David Spanbauer. He was a serial rapist, killed three people. Very disturbed, and Isle did one of her true crime books on him."

Yes, that was a good thought. "He was caught up in Appleton, wasn't he?" I said.

"Yeah. I'm not sure about the exact address."

"Find out. Call the Appleton PD. Have them send a car over to stake out the location."

Two cases.

The homicides. The abductions.

Related? Unrelated?

I still couldn't tell.

Somehow, unimaginably, they seemed to be both.

"Let's not forget the Oswalds." I was thinking this through, processing it aloud. "We need to get a car to . . ." I ran through the pertinent locations in my mind: *The intersection of Highways 18 and 83 where they first encountered the police . . . Meadowbrook Road where they shot*

Captain Lutz . . . the residence where they abducted Judy Opat . . . the bank they robbed in Wales . . . the corner of SS and Oak Street where they ran the roadblock.

Which one?

Which one?

Screw it.

All of 'em.

I gave the word, the squads were dispatched.

Gabriele, who'd been on the line with someone from the West Reagan Street Mission, hung up. "They got a donation to purchase new mattresses a week ago."

"Who was it from?" Calvin asked.

"Anonymous."

Of course.

"Who picked up the old mattresses?"

"The guy I spoke with didn't know."

Thompson used to patrol that neighborhood and would have been the guy to send, but he was out checking on leads in the Franklin Heights area. I said to Lyrie, "Get to the mission. Talk to the other staff, the homeless guys. Somebody knows who took those old mattresses."

He nodded, then left.

Gabriele offered to contact moving companies and see if she could get names of people who'd rented out a truck one week ago.

"Perfect."

Calvin was busy at his computer, plugging in information. I sat down beside him and told him all the sites the team had pulled up regarding Basque's known activity nodes.

I wanted to see if his geographic profiling approach could come up with an anchor point for the Maneater, and if it did, if Basque's home would be anywhere near it.

83

Sergeant Brandon Walker, or Radar as he preferred to be called by his friends, was at his desk making calls to Basque's work associates at Hathaway & Erikson, trying to find out if anyone knew where he'd gone this afternoon, when one of the officers who worked the front lobby walked up to his desk carrying a package the size of a shoebox.

"This came for you. It was left in the lobby. No idea who it's from." He shook the box a little and there was a soft, dull thud as whatever was inside it bumped against the sides of the box. "You want me to trash it?"

"No. I'll take it."

Radar accepted the package and the other officer returned downstairs.

Radar studied it.

The box was wrapped in what appeared to be the same type of butcher paper that was left in the boxcar where Adele Westin was found. Words on the top: "Attn. Sergeant Walker. Open at once." No return address.

He flipped it over.

Another note, written neatly in black Magic Marker: "This is from the person on the phone."

Radar blinked, looked around the room.

A moment later his desk phone rang. He stared at it unbelievingly, then at the words on the package.

The phone rang again.

He picked up. "Yes?"

"Did it arrive yet?"

"Did what arrive?"

"The evidence."

"Evidence of what?"

"How serious I am." The voice was muffled but somehow familiar. Radar tried his hardest but couldn't identify it.

"Who is this?"

"I'm the one who sent you the box. Open it up."

"First tell me who I'm speaking to."

"Open the box, Radar."

Radar?

He called you Radar.

He knows you!

Radar waved for Ralph Hawkins, who was seated at a nearby desk, to trace the call. He knew it'd take him a little while to get down to the tech room and put that into play, and he wasn't at all sure he'd be able to keep this guy on the line long enough, but it was worth a try.

"Open the box," the man repeated.

Ralph left, walking briskly down the hallway.

"What's in it?"

"Something from your son."

Radar felt a deep tremor ripple through him.

Thoughts, too many thoughts, raced through his mind. Thoughts of the case and what the abductor of the two women had done—*he kidnaps family members, makes a demand of a loved one, amputates extremities of his captives.*

A finger.

Hands.

He was about to cut off both Adele's hands and feet when Pat and Ralph arrived at the train yard.

Radar stared at the box, then felt the edges of it for a clue as to what might be inside.

Yeah, he could tell. It was a shoebox alright.

He felt himself go weak as he positioned himself in his chair and placed the phone receiver between his shoulder and his ear. He flicked out the blade of the pocketknife from his drawer, then slipped it through the butcher paper, careful not to push it in too far.

This can't be happening. This cannot be what it seems.

He slid the blade along the edge of the box's lid.

Heart hammering, mind spinning.

A moment later he finished. The lid was free.

He stared at the box. All he had to do was open it up.

He set down the knife. Cradled the box gently on his lap. The man on the other end of the line was quiet, waiting for his reaction.

Radar felt a small sweep of nausea as he reached for the lid.

And opened the shoebox.

84

Inside was one of his son's shoes. One of Tod's shoes.

Just the shoe.

Only the shoe. That was all.

Oh, thank God, thank God, thank God.

But then, immediately, the stark and terrifying truth hit him hard. *He has Tod. He took him.*

"If you do as I say," the man declared, "I promise I won't harm him."

"I don't believe you."

"You'll have to believe me. Or you won't like what's going to happen to your son."

Radar steeled his voice and tried not to sound shaken. "Let me talk to him."

The line went silent for a moment; then Tod's voice came on. "Daddy?"

"Tod, are you okay? Did he—"

"I'm okay."

"Did he touch you? Did he hurt you?"

"No. But I wanna go home."

The more you love someone, the angrier you'll be when he's threatened or attacked.

Well, Radar couldn't think of a time when he'd been angrier than this.

Before he could ask his son any more questions, there was a shuffling sound as the man took the phone back from Tod.

All Radar could think of was the rest of his family—his wife, Gayle, his daughter, Angie. "What about my wife and daughter?"

"I don't have them."

He wanted to lash out at this man, curse him, threaten him, but from investigating the previous crimes, he knew how brutal and ruthless the guy was and he couldn't bear to think of what might happen to Tod if he ticked him off. He managed to hold back for his son's sake.

The man went on. "I don't like the idea of hurting a child and I have no intention of doing so. You can either trust me or not, but if you choose not to do as I ask, I swear I will slice him apart one finger, one toe, one limb, at a time." Radar realized he was saying this with Tod right there by his side and he felt a fresh gust of anger. "You know I'm serious," the man said. "Do not test me."

Rage. Yes. It was there, but there was also a shroud of fear.

Radar reminded himself that none of the other demands had been anything that put anyone in real danger—not digging up the corpse, not even abducting Lionel. The goal hadn't been to hurt anyone, just to draw attention to another criminal's previous crimes.

It'll be alright.

Just do it. Do what he says. For Tod's sake.

"What is it? What do you want me to do?"

Then the man told Radar his demands.

85

Radar's heart seemed to freeze in midbeat inside his chest.

Stall—you don't have to really carry it out. Just stall. Go to the bank, deal with things when you get there.

"And if this is not done on time," the man told him, "I will kill Tod. I hope you're taking me as seriously as you need to."

"I hear you."

Stay on the line, stay on the line. Maybe the trace will go through—

"I'm going to give you four phone numbers. Write them down."

Radar got out a pen. "Whose numbers are they?"

"Cable news networks. Once you're in the bank, I want you to call them and tell them where you are and that they need to be there, filming by four twenty-five. I want them recording it live when it happens. I'll call you again when you're at the bank."

The man hung up.

+ + +

Calvin cancelled his lecture for this afternoon so he could help us, a gesture that, as much as I appreciated it, definitely took me by surprise. I'd left him alone a few minutes ago so he could focus on his algorithms and now, as I headed to my desk, I saw Radar lowering his phone's receiver. He was breathing heavily, staring at a shoebox on his lap. He looked shaken.

"Hey, you alright?"

He looked my way. "Sure."

But he didn't look sure. "Something up?"

He shook his head, then covered the box carefully with the lid. Stood. "Just Gayle. I need to step out for a bit. If I get any calls, take a message and have the dispatcher pass it along to me."

"So everything's okay?"

He nodded. "Yeah, it's just, something came up with one of the kids. Tod."

"Get sick at school?"

Radar looked distracted.

"I mean school's not out yet. Did he get sick? I just didn't know if—"

"Yeah, no. He's at home. He's safe."

He picked up his keys. "I'll be on the radio, okay? Call me if anything comes up."

"Okay."

He started for the hall.

"Hey, Radar."

He turned and looked at me.

"Why did you put it that way?"

"What way?"

"You said, 'He's safe.' Why didn't you just say, 'He's okay'?"

"He is," he assured me. "He's okay. I'll talk to you in a minute."

And then, with the box tucked under his arm, he left for the stairs.

86

Ralph came tromping up to my desk. "Where's Radar?"

"He stepped out a minute ago." I could already feel a rising tide of sharp concern. "What's up?"

"He stepped out?"

"Yeah. What's going on?"

"He wanted me to trace a call he just got, but we couldn't get a line on it. Where did he go?"

I stood. "He said his wife called, that something was going on with his son."

Ralph looked confused. "Why would he ask me to trace a call if it was his wife on the other end of the line?"

I was already on my way to the elevator bay. "I don't know, but I'm going to find out."

+ + +

Radar had flown down the stairs, made it to the parking garage, and left the building as quickly as he could.

He could tell that Pat knew something was up, that much was obvious. Even though he'd wanted to wait until he heard from Ralph about the trace, he'd thought that if he hung around the station, there would've been all sorts of questions and it would have eaten up time—

and that would have gotten in the way of what needed to happen right now: protecting Tod by following his abductor's instructions.

Still, once Radar was on the road, he radioed dispatch to relay the message to Ralph to get a car out if he'd been able to trace the call.

Then he turned off his radio and headed toward Wales.

+ + +

I didn't catch Radar.

I tried radioing him.

He didn't answer.

A dark thought plagued me, something I didn't want to admit could possibly be true.

But then I had to admit it very well might be.

He'd told me that his son was home, that he was "safe," not that he was "okay."

That was easy enough to check on.

Back at my desk, I called Radar's house. No one picked up. I tried radioing him again, but he didn't answer.

Okay, so call the school where his kids attend.

The principal answered and told me the secretary had gone to the central office. "Before she left she mentioned that a man had come to speak with the Walker children regarding a car accident their father had been in."

"Who was he? The man who came by?"

"If he was the fellow I saw at the reception desk, I've never seen him before. Hang on." A moment passed, then she said, "Mrs. Unger didn't write down his name."

"So, he left through the front doors again?"

"I haven't seen anyone walk past my office."

"When? When did he come in?"

"About one thirty, I think."

That was too long ago, way too long. "Page Tod Walker and have someone check his classroom for him. Also, see if you can reach Mrs. Unger. We need to know who that man was."

I handed the phone to Ralph. "Find out what you can. See if you can get a description of the guy. Something's happened to Radar's son. I think someone took him."

"What are you going to do?"

"I'm going to find Radar."

+ + +

Joshua wanted to see if his wife could record the news for him this afternoon. He tried the home number, but she wasn't there. He gave her a ring at the real estate office. They told him she'd stepped out earlier, but that they were expecting her back any time and would give her the message.

Okay, if she didn't get back to him, watching it live would have to be enough.

He drove the boy, who was safely tucked in the back of the moving truck, toward the bank in Wales.

87

3:25 p.m.
1 hour until the gloaming

I went to grab my things. Ralph called over to me and told me that neither Tod's teacher nor the principal could give us anything on the man except that he was "big and white." No one had been able to locate Mrs. Unger.

I tried Radar on the radio one last time.

Still nothing.

Tod was missing and all I could think of was that box Radar had been holding, and of the finger the kidnapper had left behind in Carl Kowalski's refrigerator and what he'd done to Colleen and Adele.

He abducts. He makes demands. He mutilates his captives. And he's escalating.

What? What would he have asked Radar to do?

Honestly, I had no clue.

When Radar left, he'd implied that he was going to his house, so I decided to try there first. From here I could get there just as quickly as if we dispatched a car. And he was my partner. I wanted to be the one there if something bad really was going down. I asked Ralph to stay on top of things here and to call me if we heard from Radar.

Calvin saw me getting ready to go and when I mentioned vaguely that I was following up on a lead, he surprised me and offered to come with me.

"I can't do that."

"Actually, my boy, you can, as long as I'm not in the front seat."

I wished he didn't know so much about law enforcement.

"I'm sorry, I—"

"You drive," he said, as if that were a choice. "I'll bring my computer. With the information your team pulled up on Basque's activity nodes, I'm close to formulating a crude model of his cognitive map."

"You can work on that here."

"But you can't get my results in real time."

"Can you find him? Can you predict where he might've gone?"

"No. But I might be able to find his anchor point."

I rubbed my head and tried to think things through.

It was possible that Basque had something to do with what was going on with Radar and Tod. I wasn't sure how, but I was willing to do whatever it took to find them, especially if, as I feared, something bad had happened to Tod.

This was way unorthodox, but Calvin would be safe in the back of the car and I could pick his brain as we drove.

"Don't tell anyone I'm doing this."

He closed up his laptop and headed with me for the elevators. "Mum's the word."

88

No one was at Radar's house.

Ralph radioed me that he'd spoken with the principal again and, providentially, she'd been able to stop Gayle Walker and Angie just as they were leaving car line. "A squad's on the way to pick them up."

"But Tod's not with them?"

"No."

I was parked beside the curb in front of Radar's home, trying to figure out what the next step should be. Calvin had been quietly working through Euclidean distance and linear decay models, and now he said, "I might have something, my boy. The west side of the city. Industrial district."

"His anchor point?"

"It's the best I can do with the data we have."

"You sure about this?"

"Not at all."

If Radar and Tod weren't here and Gayle and Angie were safe, then sitting around waiting for something to happen wasn't doing anyone any good.

You still don't know if there's one offender or two. Basque might have Tod. The timing from when he left the acquisitions firm works.

If anything came up here with Radar, I could always come back, but if Basque was our guy and he'd gone to the anchor point for his crimes, we might have a chance at tracking him down. And even if he wasn't there, if we could somehow locate it, there might be something there that could lead us to him.

I radioed Ralph, who said he'd station another car at the house, then I pulled onto the street.

The industrial district Calvin was speaking of wasn't far.

"Alright," I said to Calvin. "Which street?"

"Head toward Bracken Street. We'll see what we can find out from there."

I called in to have squads focus the APB search for Basque's car in that area of the city.

As we drove, Calvin tried to explain his calculations, but most of it was beyond me. As far as I could see, the labyrinth was just becoming more and more complex.

We were failing, yes.

But it didn't seem like we were doing so on our way to success.

Five minutes later as we were about to turn onto Bracken Street, we got word that the more directed, focused search had produced results.

Two officers had spotted Basque's car about a half mile from us in the parking lot of a textile factory. A squad was there now and the officers were checking inside the factory.

I said to Calvin, "I doubt he'd park right in front of the building where he takes his victims."

"I concur. I believe he would want seclusion. And taking potential victims to a working factory would provide very little isolation."

"He could take them to someplace private, restrain them, drive the car to another location."

"And then return on foot."

I got on the radio again, gave dispatch our location, and asked if they could identify any abandoned buildings or closed businesses nearby.

"How nearby?"

"Half a mile." I figured we could start with that, move out from there.

After a moment of checking, the dispatcher told me there was an abandoned slaughterhouse less than a quarter mile away.

That worked for me as a place to start.

I whipped the car around the corner and found the side street we were looking for.

89

3:56 p.m.
29 minutes until the gloaming

The slaughterhouse loomed in front of me, a giant black corpse of a building.

I parked, then called dispatch and requested backup and an ambulance. They asked if there was a victim. "Not that I know of." *It's possible Tod is here.* "But I want to be prepared if there is." They told me one would be here in four to five minutes.

Yesterday at the farmhouse in Fort Atkinson I'd needed to wait for backup because I feared that Mallory might be in danger. There, we rolled in with sirens blaring. Here, I'd come in quietly. As far as I could tell, I had the element of surprise on my side.

And I was going to use it.

"Calvin, you're staying here."

"On your toes in there," he cautioned me.

"Right."

I left him by the car and went to find a way into the slaughterhouse.

+ + +

Radar rolled to a stop in the bank's parking lot.

He took a deep breath, paused for a moment to try to calm his nerves, then went inside to meet the kidnapper's demands.

+ + +

I ended up having to crawl through a broken window on the second floor. Fortunately, the climb hadn't been hard at all, nothing compared to the bouldering problems at the gym.

Gun out, I descended the stairs.

The slaughterhouse looked as though it hadn't been used in years, but still somehow, the air was filled with the damp smell of decay and rot, as if death had never left this place.

My thoughts raced. I couldn't keep them still and they flipped through all that we knew about the crimes this week, the earlier homicides, the missing persons.

Locations and travel routes.

Trying to thread everything together.

The mattresses . . . the mission on West Reagan Street . . . the location of Basque's car . . .

I reached ground level. Abandoned offices on my left. Dull patches of light fighting their way through the grimy windows.

No sign of anyone. No sounds except for water dripping somewhere out of sight. As I moved forward, half a dozen rats scurried across the concrete floor in front of me.

I passed through a long narrow corridor that led to a winding chute that cows would've evidently been led along on their way to the slaughter.

There was an opening up ahead on my left that appeared to lead to the pens where Brantner Meats used to keep their cattle.

As I was approaching it, I heard the sounds.

Maybe someone gasping; I couldn't be sure. Whatever it was, someone was hurt and the wet, strangled cough that followed sent an unsettling chill dipping into my stomach.

I leveled my gun and edged forward, peering around the corner.

And saw him.

Basque.

He was holding a scalpel, standing over a woman. Blood all over her, spread across her neck and chest and abdomen.

I whipped around the corner. "Drop the knife! Back away from her!"

He was only four, maybe five meters away.

He did not comply, just stood as still as death and looked at me thoughtfully.

"Hands up! Back away from the woman, Richard!" But he didn't move, he just eyed me, the blade dripping red at his feet. His gaze was fastened on my gun, as if he were curious about it, as if it were something he'd never seen before and he was wondering what exactly it was for.

I stepped closer to him, reminding myself that backup was on its way. "Richard, drop that knife and put your hands in the air."

Above us, on long tracks, hung rusted meat hooks, somber and still—which only served to make the scene more macabre.

Another step.

Careful, Pat.

All at once Basque spun and started for the far door. Barring an immediate and direct threat to someone's life, I wasn't about to shoot him in the back, but I could catch him and I could take him down. I yelled for him to stop even as I dashed toward him.

But after we'd both gone only a few steps, he spun and fired a handgun at me, but he was off balance and missed. I squeezed the trigger, but my SIG refused to fire. Odds were ten thousand to one against it, but it jammed now when I needed it most and before I could process that, he shot at me again. This time he hit my left shoulder, sending me spiraling sideways, off balance. I landed hard on the ground, and hot pain exploded from my shoulder and seared through my whole body.

Judging from the pain coming from both the anterior and the posterior of my shoulder, it was probably a through and through, entering just below the bone of my shoulder and exiting near my armpit. I still had mobility of my arm, but it was sure going to hurt to move it.

Too bad.

I jumped to my feet and rushed him, snagging one of the meat hooks hanging above us as I did. I swung it fiercely toward him and it traveled down the track even faster than I thought it would. Basque managed to dodge it, but while he was distracted it gave me just enough time I needed to close the space between us, and then I was on him, tackling him just like I'd taken down Vincent

Hayes on Sunday night. My shoulder screamed at me as we collided with the concrete.

Behind me I could hear the woman coughing, struggling to breathe.

At impact, Basque's gun spun across the ground, but he still had the scalpel and made use of it, driving it into my right thigh. A fresh burst of pain sprayed through me, but I was able to wrench his arm back to control him. The scalpel was still sticking out of my leg when I cuffed him. Looking toward the woman, I knew I needed to clear her airway if she was going to make it.

His gun wasn't jammed, so I picked it up and aimed it at him. "You move, you try to run, you're going down."

He didn't acknowledge that, just lay there, cuffed, watching me silently, not trying to escape. Reserved and calm. He still hadn't spoken a word.

I ran to the woman. As gently as I could, I tilted her head to the side to help drain blood from her mouth.

Now that I was this close to her, I was able to see the extent of her injuries. There were ghastly wounds in her abdomen, her chest, her throat. I'd never seen anything like it. Maybe Basque had heard me coming and cut her in ways to make sure she wouldn't survive in case he was caught or killed.

I couldn't imagine that there was any way to save her. Not with injuries like this.

Come on, Pat! You have to help her!

She spit out a mouthful of blood and grabbed a breath.

As I tried to stop the bleeding from her throat, I heard Basque from behind me: "I think we may need an ambulance, don't you, Detective?"

He sounded cool and relaxed, and that just served to make his mockery all the more infuriating.

I could feel myself slipping into the furious darkness, the abyss that lies within each of us.

The demons.

Keep the demons at bay.

I refused to acknowledge Basque and focused on the woman.

But she'd almost bled out.

I wanted to reassure her, tell her that everything was going to be alright, that help was on its way, that she just needed to relax, but I knew those words would be lies. This woman was dying. Sirens were approaching—from the sound of it, a couple squads and at least one ambulance, but the paramedics were never going to make it in here soon enough to save her.

There are times when a lie can be a gift, if even a small one, and now I told her, "Shh. It's going to be okay. You're alright."

She nodded and instead of terror in her eyes, there was a sweep of peace. She knew I was lying. And she forgave me.

She closed her eyes, maybe so I wouldn't have to be looking into them when she died. Then the gurgling stopped, her hands went limp, and though I tried to stem the bleeding and revive her, it was impossible.

At last I rose, hands bloody from trying to save her. Pain raged through my shoulder and my leg, but it was nothing like the pain ripping through my heart.

I faced Basque.

A tight fist of anger balled up inside me.

Going to him, I yanked him to his feet to read him his

rights, but he was still focused on the woman. "I guess we won't be needing that ambulance after all."

That did it.

Brutality.

Evil.

Man's inhumanity to man.

I punched him. Hard. Connected solidly with his jaw and he flew backward, still cuffed, and slammed to the ground.

And then I was on him. I hit him again, heard the bones in his jaw crack. The back of his skull smacked solidly against the concrete.

I raised my fist a third time, thought of that scalpel still in my leg, what I could do with it, thought of yesterday when I'd left Griffin's knife beside him, thought of justice and what it means and how it fails and what to do when it does.

A life for a life, isn't that what they say? Justice the way it was meant to be?

Radar told me he believed in a reckoning. Well, we could have reckoning right here and now.

The sound of sirens in the parking lot rang through the slaughterhouse. The officers, the EMTs would probably be here in less than a minute.

"Why do you do this, Pat?" Taci had asked me.

"To keep the demons at bay."

Basque was looking directly into my eyes and I was looking into his, as if we were poring through each other's souls, seeing if, perhaps there was no difference there after all.

His lip was split open from when I'd punched him. Blood smeared across his teeth. His tongue tapped at the blood, then retreated into his mouth. Then he spoke, even through the pain of his broken jaw. It must have taken great effort, hurt terribly, but he managed to keep his tone calm. However, even he couldn't stop his words from sounding juicy and uneven from the shattered bones. "It feels good, doesn't it, Detective? If feels really good."

I felt a final tug toward the darkness, toward the part of my heart I've tried to tell myself isn't there, toward the things that lead us over the edge.

Dark things.

I squeezed my fist tighter. Cocked it back.

I could hear officers calling, entering the slaughter-house.

The scalpel.

The gun.

End this.

No! You're not like him, Pat. You're not capable of the unthinkable.

Yes, you are.

We all are.

Anger is a response, not a choice. We can only choose what to do with it. Let it lead us around on a leash, or—

"Do you know where Tod Walker is?" I asked Basque.

"No."

"This week, these abductions, was that you?"

"No."

"Do not lie to me."

"It was not me."

Two officers flared into the room, weapons raised. "Down!" one of them yelled. "Step away from—"

"No, that's Bowers," the other one cut in.

I saw the ice in Basque's eyes again, just as I had at the acquisitions firm, and the realization of what he was capable of, what all of us are capable of, struck me, chilled me, repulsed me.

I stood, then stepped back and let one of the other officers lean over Basque.

A scalpel is a good slicing weapon but not a good stabbing one and even though the blade had gone into my thigh a couple centimeters, it wasn't nearly as severe a puncture wound as it could have been. It might bleed a little, but I was tired of having that thing sticking out of me. I reached down, braced myself, pried it out.

One of the officers was watching, his mouth agape. I tossed the scalpel to the ground. "Evidence doesn't leave the scene of a crime." Jammed or not, I retrieved my SIG.

More officers flared into the room and it was over. We had Basque, we were taking him in. He would spend the rest of his life in a cell. Justice? Maybe not, but at least it was a step in the right direction.

I was splashing the blood off my hands in a pool of dank water near a cattle stall when Ellen came jogging around the corner. "Pat!" She was out of breath. "We found Radar."

"What? Where?"

"At a bank. He's at a bank."

"A bank?"

"Holding up a bank."

"What?"

"First Capital." She paused long enough to catch her breath. "In Wales."

Wales? That's where the bank was that the Oswalds held

up, the one that led to them being chased and appre-hended . . . It should have been staked out!

"He has hostages," she said. "He's asking for you."

My thoughts buzzed: *The kidnapper took Tod. He's forcing Radar to do this just like he forced Vincent to ab-duct Lionel, like he forced Carl to skin that corpse . . .*

Basque spit out a mouthful of blood as the officers hoisted him to his feet. "Read him his rights," I called, then turned back to Ellen. "He has hostages?"

"Yes, and he said you have to be there by four twenty-five."

"Or what?"

She shook her head. "We don't know."

I looked at my watch. I had twenty-four minutes.

A half-hour drive? I'd never make it in time.

Oh yes, I would.

"Call it in." I was hurrying toward the door, trying hard not to limp. "And get word to Radar that I'm on my way."

90

The paramedics were unloading a gurney when I got out-side.

I didn't want them to hassle me. So I was thankful I was still wearing my leather jacket and that the blood from my shoulder hadn't seeped through too much. "There's a woman inside," I told them. "She didn't make it. The suspect's jaw is broken. Don't give him anything for pain."

Calvin was standing beside my car. He gasped when he saw me, and gestured toward my leg. "My dear boy, you've been shot!"

I looked where he was pointing. "Stabbed, actually." I didn't mention my shoulder.

"That must hurt, terribly."

Yes, it does.

"I'm okay." On my way to the car I was able to grab a pressure bandage from a paramedic and tighten it around my thigh. At the last minute I went ahead and threw one around my shoulder too, then opened the driver's door.

"You can't be serious, my boy," Calvin said. "I'll drive."

For just a moment I actually thought about letting

him. It would've given me a chance to put pressure on the gunshot wound and quiet the bleeding. Besides, using my injured leg to work the gas and the brake was not something I was looking forward to, but letting him drive was too far outside of protocol even for me. "I'm good."

I thanked him for helping me find the slaughterhouse, got directions from dispatch, and took off for First Capital Bank in Wales.

+ + +

Radar had done as Tod's kidnapper had demanded.

Once he was inside the bank, once he had the three bank employees and two customers restrained, he'd called the cable news stations and instructed them to send their news crews immediately, to have their cameras ready, because they would need to catch what was going to happen at 4:25.

And now, already, the news crews and law enforcement were starting to arrive. SWAT was setting up a perimeter around the parking lot.

The phone rang. Earlier Tod's kidnapper had told him to expect a call and Radar picked up.

The man let him speak to his son, who was terrified, crying, then he warned Radar again not to let him down. "You would not want to see what Tod's going to look like if you don't do what I said. I'll be watching."

Then before hanging up, he told Radar what had happened beneath the barn.

Convinced the man was telling the truth, Radar lowered the receiver and tried to steel himself to actually do what would be necessary to save his son's life.

+ + +

Ralph stepped out of his car.

Sheriff's deputies, local police, and a SWAT team had taken position around the bank. News crews from four different cable stations were setting up remotes just beyond the police tape. More news vans were on their way.

He looked around, then asked a lieutenant who appeared to be calling the shots, "Who was in charge here?"

"I'm in charge," the man answered sharply. "Who are you?"

"Were."

"Were?"

"You were in charge." Ralph flipped out his creds. "Hand me that megaphone."

91

Radar heard Ralph calling to him through a megaphone, commanding him to exit the bank, but he ignored the agent's orders.

Out the window, Radar could see more emergency vehicles pulling in. SWAT and local police were there in full force. He recognized the Flight for Life helicopter from the Milwaukee Regional Medical Center hovering overhead.

He turned and looked at the five hostages who were lying facedown on the floor, their hands and feet secured with the plastic cuffs he'd brought with him.

The phone rang. Radar stared at it, wondering if it was Tod's kidnapper again.

He picked up.

"What are you doing, Radar?" It was Ralph.

"He's got my son. The guy from this week. He's got Tod."

"He was the one on the phone, wasn't he? The call you wanted me to trace?"

"Yes. Did you get it?"

"No. Just so you know, Gayle and Angie, they're fine. They're at the station. They're safe."

"Thank God."

"Is Tod . . . I mean, do you know if . . . ?"

"I talked to him. He wasn't hurt, but he was crying. Scared."

A pause. "What did he ask you to do, Radar? Just take the bank? If that's it, then it's done. Let those people go."

"He said they need to stay here."

"Until when?"

"Just get Pat over here."

"He's on his way."

"And don't have SWAT move in, Ralph. This is my kid we're talking about."

Another pause. "I won't. But just be easy, bro. Do you know anything at all about the guy who took Tod?"

"He called me Radar."

"What?"

"He knows me somehow, but I couldn't recognize his voice. I've been thinking about it, I have no idea who he could be."

"Someone from the department?"

"I don't know. But he didn't attract attention when he dropped off that package for me in the lobby."

"I'll do some checking on guys who fit our suspect's description. Pat will be here in a couple minutes. In the meantime, don't do anything stupid."

92

4:21 p.m.
4 minutes until the gloaming

I screeched to a stop alongside the police barricade. I didn't want the bloody dressings caught on camera, so I tugged them off and left them on the seat.

Fortunately, my jacket covered most of the blood, but as I stepped out of the car, I zipped it up anyway. Two officers met me and, as television cameras followed us, hustled me to a SWAT van the size of a small mobile home.

Inside, I found Ralph, the SWAT commander, as well as Lieutenant Thorne, Lyric, and a female officer from internal affairs. What she was doing here right now was anyone's guess.

"Heard you were shot," Thorne said concernedly. "You alright?" Everyone else was asking the same question with their eyes.

"Yeah." I indicated toward the bank. "What do we know?"

"Are you sure you're—?"

"I'm fine." I waited for the update. Ralph spoke up:

"As far as we can tell, he's got three bank employees, two or three customers."

"Do we have a video feed of the surveillance cameras?"

"Not yet. SWAT's working on it."

I saw two phones and headsets. "Who's talking with him?"

"For now, me. Radar mentioned that the guy who took his son, he called him by his nickname. Called him Radar."

"What? He knows him?"

Ralph shook his head. "We don't know. But right now we need to move. He told me you have to be in there by 4:25. I don't know why, but he's really sketchy right now and I don't want to push things."

My gun had jammed earlier, but Radar didn't know that and I guessed he wouldn't want me coming in armed. I unholstered my weapon, handed it to Ralph. "Let's go."

"You need a vest."

"He's my partner. He's not going to shoot me."

"You go in there," Ralph said firmly, "you're going in wearing a vest."

This wasn't the time to argue and I didn't want to waste what few precious minutes we had.

I couldn't help but cringe as I slumped off the jacket.

Everyone in the van stared at the blood covering half of my chest and most of my sleeve. "It's not as bad as it looks," I assured them, even though it hurt like it was. I picked up a vest and began to put it on, trying not to move my left arm at all, but it wasn't possible and pain chugged through me again, this time, actually making me dizzy.

I had to stop, close my eyes, and try to funnel the pain into another place.

Ralph carefully helped me into the vest. When he was done, I pointed to his voluminous FBI jacket tossed on a chair in the corner. "I don't want to walk past those cameras with my shirt covered with blood and I don't want to alarm the hostages. My jacket's gonna be too hard to get into. Let me use that thing." There was still a dark stain on my pant leg where I'd been stabbed with the scalpel, but I could deal with that.

He grabbed the jacket and helped me ease it on. "Congratulations," he said, trying to keep things light. "You've been promoted."

"Thanks." I zipped up. "Tonto."

Using one of the portable phones in the SWAT van, Ralph put a call through to the bank and then nodded for me. "We're a go. He's waiting for you. Be careful in there."

"I will."

Leaving the van, I held out my hands to show that I wasn't armed. With the gunshot wound, it hurt terribly to move that left arm, let alone hold it to the side, but I did the best I could. Trying to conceal my limp, I crossed the parking lot.

The walk seemed to take forever.

I made it to the door.

Paused.

Then laid my hand against the glass and pressed it open.

93

Five hostages on the floor, all restrained. Radar stood beside the counter, his weapon out, a wild, flighty look in his eyes.

"Get away from the door, Pat."

I edged in, let the door close behind me. "I heard about Tod. I'm sorry."

He eyed me. "You're limping."

"I got him. The killer. The guy from Ohio and Illinois."

"Basque?"

"Yeah."

His eyes were on my leg. "Did he shoot you?"

"Yes," I told him honestly. I didn't clarify that it was in the shoulder. "Listen, Radar, I'm unarmed. You can lower your weapon."

He didn't. But he didn't pat me down either. He believed me.

He waved the gun toward the bank's office. It had a glass wall that offered a view of the lobby, and I imagined he wanted to go in there so we could talk privately, but also so he could keep an eye on the hostages.

We entered, he closed the door and told me to stand on the other side of the desk. As I angled across the room, he kept the gun trained on me, then ran a hand through his hair. "He's gonna kill Tod, Pat."

"As far as we know, he hasn't killed anyone. Basque was the one who—"

"No." Radar shook his head. "You don't get it. I talked to him a few minutes ago. This time he's serious. He's gonna do it. He told me what his father made him do to people he brought to their barn when he was a kid. He wasn't making it up, Pat. I could tell." He smiled oddly and I could see that Ralph had been right: Radar was losing it. "Gut instincts. Intuition. Remember? That's me."

"Calm down for a sec. Think this through. How did he get that package to you at HQ?"

"Dropped it off in the lobby. No one noticed him."

"Ralph said he called you Radar, and we know he entered the department without being questioned about why he was there. Do you have any idea who he could be?"

He shook his head. "I couldn't recognize his voice. It's gotta be someone on the force. He said he's gonna be watching."

I tried to think of who in the department fit Colleen's description of her abductor. A few people came to mind, but then I realized I needed to be mentally here, in this moment, helping talk Radar down. I could figure out who the kidnapper was once I didn't have a gun aimed at me.

However, as hard as I tried, thoughts of the kidnapper's demands, his crimes, his acts, his choice of locations, refused to leave me alone.

The alley . . . the hardware store . . . the bank . . .

No, no, no. It wasn't just the locations we were talking about.

It was the victims too.

Konerak Sinthasomphone for Dahmer.

Bernice Worden for Gein.

And now Captain James Lutz for the Oswalds . . .

I looked through the glass window at the hostages lying on the floor in the bank lobby. "It wasn't just the bank, was it? That's not what he wants?"

"No." Radar's voice cracked.

"Tie the stories together. His and the Oswalds'. That's the way it ends, isn't it? That's why he wanted the media here. He wants you to kill a cop, just like they killed Lutz."

He had tears in his eyes. He nodded.

It was hard to get the next question out, but the answer might help us narrow things down. "Did he ask for me by name?"

Radar shook his head. "I chose you. Because you're my partner, because I knew you'd understand."

I thought of what the kidnapper had done to Colleen Hayes, what he'd been in the process of doing to Adele Westin when Ralph and I arrived in the train yard. He was escalating and I didn't even want to think about what he might have in mind for Radar's son.

I didn't doubt for a second that he would do terrible, terrible things to the boy if his demands were not met.

Using my good arm, I reached for the zipper.

Radar leveled the gun at me. "Don't move, Pat!"

"I'm unarmed, Radar. And if you're going to kill me, you don't need to worry about me taking off this jacket."

He was breathing rapidly, his hand shaking. Logic wasn't in play here, emotion was. And that's what was going to determine everything.

"I have body armor on," I told him. "I'm going to take it off, okay? That's all."

"Why?" He was obviously scared, desperate, and not thinking clearly. And he had a gun—a very bad combination.

"Just relax, Radar." I was able to keep my voice reasonably steady, but my heart was jackhammering in my chest, my thoughts whipping and twisting around each other. It had happened to me just a handful of times in my life, in those moments when death seemed to be on my heels and I actually had enough time to think about it—contrary to what people tell you, the "fight-or-flight instinct" doesn't always kick in; instead, you become unnaturally calm. It's almost frightening how rational you can be. It doesn't make sense, but a sweep of clarity, of perspective, comes over you.

"I believe you that he's serious . . ." I'd lost a lot of blood and I was starting to feel dizzy. I wasn't sure how long I could stand here. "That he'll kill Tod unless you do it."

As awkward and painful as it was, I managed to slide out of the oversized Windbreaker. The vest covered my chest, but Radar could obviously see my blood-soaked sleeve. He stared at me, shocked. "It's just the shoulder," I told him. "I'm okay. Do you really believe he'll let Tod live? If you do what he said?"

"I don't know. Your shoulder, man, your leg, it's . . .

I don't know—but I can't take the chance." He was definitely in a bad, bad, place. Confused, terrified, and I wanted so badly to help him, but I also didn't want to die here today.

I unsnapped the bulletproof vest. Getting it off was not going to be easy or feel very good at all, but—

"Stop, Pat. When I said you'd understand, I meant it."

I paused with the vest. "I know."

He didn't go on right away. "I'm not going to shoot you." His voice held a deep, unsettling resolve. "I need you."

"You need me?"

"To be there for Tod and Angie. To help Gayle with—"

"What are you—no, Radar."

"Yes." He nodded. "If I shoot you, we're both gone. I'd be in prison and you'd be—"

"Radar, stop. We'll find Tod, okay? We just need to—"

"Quiet."

I wanted to rush him, disarm him, but he was on the other side of the desk and I'd never be able to move quickly enough to get there before he could do it, not with my injured leg.

"You need to show 'em," he said. "Prove it. That's what he told me. Take my body outside. Hold it up for the cameras. That's how it ends. All caught on tape. Just like the Oswalds—"

"Don't even talk like that, Radar."

"It's all gotta be on TV. It's gotta be live."

I made a move toward him, but froze when he raised the gun and pointed it at his own chest. "Don't come any closer, Pat."

Stop him, Pat. Come on, you have to—

"You tell them I love them," he said. "That's why I did it, okay? My kids, Gayle, because—"

An idea came to me. I blurted it out, hoping, praying he would listen and wouldn't fire.

But he closed his eyes, angled the gun toward his heart.

"Radar, no—!"

94

Ralph was inside the SWAT van when the phone rang. He picked up the receiver, listened, then announced through the radio to the team, "Do not fire! I repeat, do not fire! Whatever happens, hold your fire! He's coming out."

Nods of acknowledgment, but everyone kept their guns trained on the bank's entrance just the same.

But it didn't open.

Stillness.

A moment passed.

Then another.

Time stretched thin.

And then the sharp sound of a gunshot rang from inside the building and cracked through the wire-tight surface of the day.

"Hold your fire!" Ralph yelled again.

Just one shot. That was it. Then all was still.

The line had gone dead. Ralph punched in the bank's number. Pat answered, his voice soft, grim. "Radar's dead. The hostages are okay. Tell SWAT to lower their weapons. I'm coming out."

95

Joshua had left the boy securely in the back of the moving truck where he'd parked it just across the street from the bank before any of this began.

He'd stepped out of the cab to watch what was going on, and now stood just outside of the police perimeter, news crews all around him.

Just a few moments ago he'd heard the gunshot.

Now, along with everyone else, he stared anxiously at the door to see what would happen next.

Earlier, when he first saw the man wearing the FBI jacket enter the bank, he'd been upset that they weren't using a cop like he'd demanded, but then he recognized the face of the guy entering: Bowers. Why he was wearing an FBI jacket was beyond him, unless he was doing it for some jurisdictional reason. Joshua didn't know, but it didn't matter as long as he went in.

Part of his demands included Radar carrying out the body, emerging from the front door for all the news cameras to catch the climax on film, just like the cameraman from WISN Channel 12 News had caught the chase and apprehension of the Oswalds back in 1994.

And so, from just across the street, Joshua watched and waited for the story to come full circle at last.

+ + +

With my shoulder I couldn't do it, couldn't carry him. One of the hostages was a big guy, bigger even than me. After I freed him from the plastic cuffs, I had him pick up Radar's body.

Even though I had the FBI jacket on again, I knew that the SWAT team would be tweaked, looking for any movement, ready to fire, so as I nudged the front door open, I did so slowly, carefully, my arms to the side, hands out. "It's over!" I yelled. "The hostages are okay." I hesitated. I couldn't help it. "Sergeant Walker is gone."

At least a dozen news cameras were aimed at me from across the street.

I stepped aside and held the door open. The man who'd been a hostage and was now carrying Radar's limp body, joined me outside. As I'd instructed him, he stayed stationary long enough to make sure the cameras caught the image of him standing there, just as the kidnapper had demanded.

Then, he lowered Radar to the ground and held up his hands as he edged away from me. Four SWAT members rushed forward, I slowed them down, told them what'd gone down inside, then three of them bent over Radar's bloody body while the fourth walked toward the EMTs to lead them over here. They would roll Radar away, a blanket drawn up over his head as they passed the media, all those news cameras. Then transport him. Lights off.

The shock hit me all at once.

I began to crash.

The adrenaline that'd been chugging through me since I first entered the slaughterhouse seemed to dissipate in one fell swoop. That, along with the impact of what had happened to Tod and Radar, were all working to drain my strength and I felt weak, disoriented.

You still have to find Tod. You still need to get the guy who took him.

As the EMTs approached, I found myself unable to stand on my own and I leaned against the side of the building to keep from dropping to the ground. Ralph came sprinting up to me, then supported me while two EMTs hurried toward us with a gurney.

I was vaguely aware of the Flight for Life helicopter landing in a vacant parking lot down the block. If it was for me, I wasn't so sure I needed it, but it would definitely make the trip to the medical center go a lot faster.

I blinked to keep focused, but was overwhelmed by the melee of law enforcement personnel suddenly swarming around us. As always with these things, there were too many people here: cops, lawyers, a hostage negotiator, counselors, the police chaplain, SWAT, Lyrie and Thompson from the task force, support personnel. As I collapsed onto the gurney, I saw some of the officers were helping hostages out of the bank.

Then I was lying on my back, staring at the darkening sky and the paramedics were wheeling me toward the helicopter and the world was spinning in a slow, delirious circle and all I could think of was Radar and what had happened to him and his family.

96

Joshua watched it all.

Bowers emerged from the bank entrance, then the guy carrying Sergeant Walker's bloody corpse appeared behind him. Somehow Bowers had overpowered Walker and taken him out.

Or did Radar take his own life?

Was it possible?

Either way, a cop had died. It'd been filmed. It was over. Joshua was certain that the man who'd called him earlier in the day, before sunrise, would be impressed.

And they would finally meet.

He made his way through the crowd inside the cordoned-off area, then went back to the moving truck to take care of the boy.

+ + +

Ralph crouched beside me as the paramedics worked to cut off his jacket so they could get to the bullet's entrance and exit wounds. As they did, he said to me softly, in a voice meant only for me, "People see what they expect to see."

When I looked at him, I realized he knew. "How did—?"

"You're not the only one who notices things. The

bloody shirt Radar had on—that's the one you were wearing when you got here."

So, he'd figured it out: when I was standing outside the door and the SWAT members first rushed forward, I'd told them the truth, and one of them had quickly informed the paramedics—*pretend he's dead, buy us some time*.

I kept my voice low. "I didn't know if anyone else was on the line when I called from the bank. That's why I said what I did, when I told you he was dead."

"It was smart."

"He almost didn't go for it."

"Thank God he did."

Hopefully, it would provide us the window we needed to save his son.

The helicopter rotors started gearing up and I had to yell in order for Ralph to hear me. "We need to find Tod!"

He shouted that he was on it, that he would find the boy. I asked him one last question: "Do we know who the woman was, the one in the slaughterhouse?" But before he could answer, my attention was drawn to something else.

A moving truck at the end of the street, turning the corner.

"No," Ralph replied, "but we're gonna find out!"

I grabbed his sleeve and pointed to the moving truck. It was too far away to make out the plates, but when he saw it, he realized what I was thinking, spun, and bolted back toward the squads parked beside the bank.

97

Ralph cussed.

He hadn't been able to get to a car in time or maneuver past the news vans fast enough, and the moving truck had disappeared before he could catch it. He hadn't even been able to identify which company it was from.

He had local law enforcement send some cars out looking for it, then returned to the SWAT van.

A call was waiting for him from Gabriele at the department. She asked about Radar and Pat, he told her what she needed to know, then asked her to get some officers to start calling moving companies that had trucks out today. She informed him that Richard Basque had been transported to the Milwaukee Regional Medical Center for surgery on his broken jaw.

"Do we know the name of the victim yet?"

"Not yet. But she has a tattoo on her left ankle. A custom job. We're calling parlors now to try to find out who did the artwork."

Ralph thought about Tod, about the victim, about what he could do right now. He told Gabriele, "I'm gonna go talk to Basque."

Then he hung up and took off.

+ + +

Joshua left the boy in the moving truck in the parking lot of the Kohl's department store where he'd purchased the shoes earlier in the day and where his car was waiting for him.

An anonymous phone call to the police would lead them to the truck, which he'd rented under a false name. They would find Tod Walker in the back, safe and sound.

Once in his own vehicle, Joshua turned on the police scanner and heard that a man named Richard Basque had been arrested at a slaughterhouse in Milwaukee. By the sound of it, by the description of what he'd done to the woman, Joshua realized it was almost certainly the man who'd killed the women in Ohio and Illinois, the Maneater.

The suspect had been transported to the medical center to be treated for "injuries sustained during his apprehension."

Joshua had a decision to make: stay clear of Basque or go and meet him.

If he's transferred to jail, you might not get another chance.

Perhaps the safer choice would be to lie low, see how things played out, but the desire that'd been lurking inside him for so long, the one that'd led him to orchestrate all of this—that overriding longing to meet someone like himself, a partner, someone who would understand him— was so overpowering that in the end Joshua couldn't hold himself back.

Once he was on the road, he called in Tod's location from his portable phone, then directed his car toward the Milwaukee Regional Medical Center.

+ + +

While we flew to the hospital, I tried to piece the case together.

Who was capable of doing something like this? Committing these crimes this week?

Everyone is capable of the unthinkable, Pat. All of us are, you told Taci that yourself.

Motives.

You can never untangle people's motives.

But who? Who was he?

He knows the city, knows that neighborhood near the train yards . . . He went to Pewaukee to steal the Taurus . . . He got the mattresses from the mission . . .

According to Calvin, our guy used that boxcar as his anchor point and most likely lives or has an activity node in the Franklin Heights area.

Everything matters.

Yes, and he knows drugs, had access to Propotol, could've met Adele when she was in Milwaukee after that fender bender.

After she was taken to the hospital.

Wait.

The kidnapper got his hands on an amputation saw, had a connection to the homeless mission—they offer free medical care.

A doctor could've gotten into the school, convinced that secretary that he needed to talk to the Walker children.

Oh, there was definitely something I needed to check on.

We were close to the medical center. I could call it in as soon as we landed.

98

The helicopter nestled onto the landing pad.

The paramedics had bandaged my shoulder and my leg and given me some saline solution in an IV, and I was much less dizzy now than I'd been outside the bank.

As soon as we were in the building, I told them un-equivocally that I needed a phone. They tried to hold me back and get me a hospital gown since I had no shirt on, but I hobbled to the nurses' station, and, despite the objections of the woman behind the desk, I picked up the receiver.

I reached Officer Gabriele Holdren at HQ. Apparently, she'd already spoken with Ralph and he hadn't been able to get to the moving truck before it got away.

"Gabriele, pull up the accident report of when Adele Westin had the traffic incident last summer and had to spend the night at the medical center. See if you can find out who the doctor was who treated her—we might not have it, but the hospital will if you can find the date."

But even as I said the words, other thoughts about the case caught me, carried me in another direction entirely.

Tod's kidnapper had referred to Radar by his nick-name, but only people at the department did that. He hadn't drawn undue attention when he dropped off the shoebox. It had to be—

Someone who knows Radar . . . who knew to switch the plates on the stolen car to bypass an APB, someone who's been to crime scenes and knows how to avoid leaving prints, DNA.

I thought again of big guys on the force. Caucasians approximately six feet tall.

Wait.

Thompson was the one who first dug up the copy of Griffin's catalog, he goes to church in the Franklin Heights area . . .

I could hardly believe what I was considering.

He used to patrol over by the train yards. He was there at the bank just now . . . He was the one standing sentry by Colleen's door on Monday . . .

Thompson had left this morning to check on the Franklin Heights addresses. The next time I saw him was at the bank. He would've had time to get Tod and drive over there. The timing worked.

Timing and location. It's always about timing and location.

We were looking for a person who could get access to the children in the school . . .

Who could do that? A social worker? A doctor? A counselor?

Or a police officer.

I told Gabriele, "And find out who the responding officer was at the accident."

A pause. "The responding officer? You think our guy is a cop?"

"Just do it. And locate Thompson. I'll stay on the

phone. Is there any word on the victim from the slaughterhouse? Who she is?"

"Not yet. But we're looking into it."

"Where's Basque?"

"Should be there at the hospital by now. Ellen and Lyrie are guarding him. Ralph is on his way."

"Okay, radio Thompson and pull those accident reports ASAP."

I asked the nurse at the desk where Basque's room was and she looked it up while I waited for Gabriele to get back on the line.

+ + +

Joshua arrived at the hospital.

It wasn't hard for a man with his credentials to find out where they were treating the suspect from the homicide in the slaughterhouse, and after swinging by the admissions desk, he learned Basque was one building over in the trauma center next to the Flight for Life landing pad.

He started across the parking lot, then had a second thought, retrieved one of the needles with the tranquilizer from his car, and continued on to the building.

+ + +

The nurse informed me that Basque was only two hallways over.

Good. I could head there in a minute, after I heard from Gabriele.

Someone from the station must have called ahead to tell Taci that I was being brought here, because, as I was waiting for Gabriele to give me an update, she came hurrying down the hall, flanked by two doctors.

"Pat!" She rushed to me. "Lieutenant Thorne called me, told me what happened. Are you okay? How's your shoulder? Your leg?" There was deep concern in her voice, no trace of the awkwardness from yesterday morning when she'd told me she loved her job more than she loved me.

"I'm okay. Thanks for being here."

"Of course."

Seeing her in her element here, I knew it really would have torn her up to be with me, that it wouldn't have been fair for me to ask her to stay in a relationship if she wasn't able to give it what she felt she needed to.

Truly loving her, Pat, it's going to mean letting her go.

It was hard to process all that with everything else going on.

Come on, Gabriele, hurry!

"We need to get you to an exam room," Taci said emphatically.

"Yes, Detective," one of the doctors told me. "We need to have a look at that shoulder."

"And that leg," the other added.

Taci took my hand and it felt both awkward and familiar at the same time, but I didn't pull away.

Gabriele was still on another line.

"Just a sec," I told them.

+ + +

Hospitals don't have metal detectors, don't pat people down as they come through the door, so Joshua knew that getting his necrotome into the building wouldn't be a problem. He went in a side door, showed his identification to the receptionist stationed behind a small window.

"I was called in. They want me to talk with the man they brought in from the slaughterhouse. Richard Basque."

"I think they're getting ready to take him into surgery now. There are some officers with him."

"Good. What room is he in?"

She told him, pointed toward the correct hallway, he thanked her and left for the room.

+ + +

Facts spun through my mind.

Colleen worked for Basque and she was the first victim in this crime spree. If the offenders weren't working together, she could have been how their lives interconnected.

The cases are linked through her.

Two cases.

Two offenders.

One interconnected puzzle.

Someone donated that money to that mission. Someone picked up those mattresses.

The abductor knew the woods, had to have spent time in that neighborhood. The mission . . .

Deep in thought, I glanced past Taci and saw the sign to the hospital's chapel just down the hall.

And then, the facts of the case began to reshuffle themselves before me all over again and everything I'd thought was true turned on its head.

We needed a person who could have met Adele here in the hospital after her car accident and would also have been able to get into the school.

My eyes were still on the sign to the chapel.

When Colleen was brought to the hospital, she had a

rosary with her—which meant she would have had it with her when she was left by the pier. And that meant the killer would've known she had it, could have easily guessed that she was Catholic.

When you were arresting Vincent, he said Colleen's abductor mentioned last rites.

Oh yes.

I had it, or I thought I did.

"Taci, grab that phone book."

She did and I flipped to the right page.

If our guy was the person I was thinking of, he would have known to switch the plates, been at enough crime scenes to know how to frustrate the investigation.

He has a portable phone—

He knows Radar, wouldn't have stuck out at the department when he dropped off the package.

Switching to another line, I punched in the number for the West Reagan Street Mission. I had to know if this guy ever volunteered there. If he did, it would fit, it would all make sense.

Who would think to mention last rites to a Catholic like that? Only someone who—

The mission's director, Reverend Tate, picked up and confirmed what I was thinking. "Yes, of course. He comes in every Friday night. He was here earlier today, as a matter of fact. For a funeral we had."

That was it. That's how he disappeared into the neighborhood after fleeing from the train yards. The people knew him from his work at the mission. He wouldn't have stuck out or drawn attention to himself at the funeral either.

No, he wasn't a cop or a doctor.

Who else could have convinced the secretary at the school to let him see the Walker children?

A minister.

I saw the other line blinking and when I pressed the button, Gabriele came on again. "Pat, we've got the name of the victim. You're not going to—"

"Our chaplain . . ." Honestly, I was still caught up in my thoughts about the kidnapper. "It's Padilla."

"Yes." Gabriele sounded shocked. "How did you know?"

That got my attention. "What?"

"The victim. Sylvia Padilla, she's the police chaplain's wife. How did you know it was her?"

Oh no.

Basque had killed Joshua's wife. It was all tied together in one intricate web.

If Padilla finds out, he'll come after Basque. You know he will.

"Call Reverend Padilla. Find him." I let the phone drop and hobbled away from the counter. "If Agent Hawkins gets here," I shouted over my shoulder, "send him to Basque's room right away."

I told Taci and the doctors to stay there and, as fast as my injured leg would take me, I rushed toward Richard Basque's hospital room.

99

Reverend Joshua Padilla knew the officer who was sta-tioned outside Basque's door: Lyrie. He'd counseled him after he'd shot a gang member last year.

"Thorne told me I'm supposed to go in," he said to Lyrie. "Talk to him. Before his surgery."

"Why?"

"I guess he asked for me while he was at the slaughter-house."

"I'm not authorized to—"

"You know it's protocol to let spiritual advisers speak with victims and injured suspects."

"Yeah." Lyrie rubbed his head. "Alright, look, there's an FBI agent in there. Parker. The guy's strapped to the bed. But she stays in the room."

"I'm supposed to meet with people confidentially."

"She stays, Padre."

The tranquilizer. Use it if you need to. Get in, meet Basque, then get out.

"Alright."

+ + +

I heard heavy footsteps pounding around the corner behind me.

I looked back.

Ralph.

"Radio Ellen," I called to him. "She's at the room!"

He was quickly catching up with me. "I tried already.
There's interference here in the hospital."

"Then let's move."

One hallway to go.

+ + +

Lyrie introduced Joshua to Special Agent Parker and then
left the room.

Joshua looked toward Basque, but his attention was
immediately drawn to the television on the wall. There
was a news report about the woman who'd been killed at
the slaughterhouse.

A name flashed across the screen and the announcer
said, "We're getting unconfirmed reports that the victim's name is Sylvia Padilla."

Joshua froze.

He locked eyes with Basque and knew it was true.

Parker looked at Joshua oddly. "Didn't Lyrie just say
your last name is—"

But then her words were cut off as he jammed the
needle fiercely into her neck and depressed the plunger.
The tranquilizer kicked in almost immediately. He held
one hand over her mouth and with the other he stopped
her from reaching for her gun.

She faded and he lowered her to the floor.

He quickly checked—there was no lock on the door.

He slid her body against it to slow anyone down who might try to interrupt him. After wedging her legs solidly in the nearby bathroom doorway, he turned a cart on its side and jammed it in to lock them in place. Nobody was going to get the hospital room's door open without torquing Agent Parker's spine.

Then Joshua turned to Basque, whose wrists and ankles were strapped to the bed.

The man's jaw was broken so he couldn't cry out for help.

His hands were restrained so he couldn't hit the call button.

"You took Sylvia." Joshua's voice was trembling. "You killed my wife." He produced the necrotome from its sheath.

Voices shouted in his head: *You are beyond redemption, Joshua!*

No! It's not evil to pursue justice!

Basque just watched him. Didn't struggle to get free. Didn't look away.

You took care of your father, Joshua. You did what needed to be done. You're good at doing what needs to be done.

He pulled up a chair beside the bed.

+ + +

Ralph shouted down the hall for Lyrie to open Basque's door, but when he tried, he was able to open it only far enough to get a hand inside.

Ralph beat me to the room. "I got it," he told Lyrie.

But then he looked into the room. "It's Ellen! She's down!"

And that's when I arrived.

+ + +

Joshua heard Detective Bowers shout, "Padilla, stop! Get away from the bed!" Through the crack in the doorway he could see movement. He wasn't sure how many people.

So this was it.

Endgame.

He tightened his grip on the handle of the necrotome, the "cutting instrument of the dead."

Yes, he would do this for Sylvia.

Your father taught you what to do. This is your chance, just like you did in the cellar under the barn.

Bowers called again for him to stop, even as Joshua saw a massive arm squeeze through the crack in the door, clutch Agent Parker's armpit, and begin to lift her from the floor.

+ + +

Ralph gritted his teeth, shoved his other hand through the crack as well so he could get a better grip on Ellen's limp body.

He managed to get her high enough to free her legs, then he leaned heavily against the door.

+ + +

Joshua had the necrotome raised when the door swung open. Lyrie stepped forward to support Parker, and the enormous guy who'd lifted her whipped out a Glock, aimed it at Joshua. "Move away from the bed!"

"Listen to him!" It was Bowers again. He stood in the doorway beside the big guy. "Back away."

The evil which I would not.

That I do.

In an instant, the rest of the passage came to him, the conclusion St. Paul had reached, the one Reverend Tate had mentioned in his prayer at the funeral: "Who shall deliver me from the body of this death? I thank God through Jesus Christ our Lord," and Joshua thought of his wife dying at the hand of this man now lying in front of him, and he thought of redemption and sin and hope and eternity. He had, all of his life, wanted to find God's forgiveness, and now he was sure he never would.

+ + +

"Step back!" Ralph bellowed, moving into the room.

"Get back, Joshua!" I yelled. "Now!"

+ + +

"No murderer hath eternal life abiding in him." Those words raced through Joshua's mind, chased by the ones from Reverend Tate's homily, *"Let us take responsibility for our sins . . . Let us trust in the Lord Jesus Christ, the one whose blood cleanseth us from all sin."*

The blood.

Always the blood.

And that cleansing was what Joshua yearned for, even as he said to Basque, "A shedder of blood shall die," and then he thrust the necrotome deep into the man's abdomen.

But that was the last thing he ever did. Because Special Agent Ralph Hawkins fired three shots in quick succession and Joshua Padilla dropped dead to the floor and entered eternity.

For the reckoning.

+ + +

Ralph lowered his gun.

The knife handle jutted from Basque's abdomen.

"We need a doctor in here!" I yelled. "Now!"

TWO DAYS LATER

Friday, November 21

The Coffeehouse

100

8:31 a.m.

They were able to save Richard Basque.

They stitched up his abdomen, wired his jaw shut, and the prognosis was positive.

I wasn't sure how I felt about that.

We'd stopped Griffin, Basque, and Joshua Padilla. Radar was safe, Lionel, Colleen, Tod, Adele and Mallory had all been through traumatizing experiences, but all were recovering. Agent Parker was fine.

But we'd lost Sylvia Padilla.

All too often endings in real life are bittersweet. We all die, but we don't all find peace before we do. However, when I remembered the look on Sylvia's face as she passed away, I knew there was forgiveness there. And I trusted that God had seen what was in her heart and judged her accordingly.

Inevitably, there were going to be charges filed against Carl, Vincent, and Radar for the crimes they'd committed to fulfill Joshua's demands, but I was hopeful that, considering the circumstances, the judge would be lenient—especially with Radar. Initial indications were that things were leaning in that direction.

Browning had, as it turned out, known that Griffin had killed Mindy Wells and it looked as though he would be spending a long time on the other side of some prison bars. So, the wheels of justice were already turning, working their way through the complex, multilayered case.

My shoulder and leg ached, but they would heal soon enough. People say that what doesn't kill you only makes you stronger. I wasn't so sure about that, but the things that don't kill us do shape who we become. And I knew the events of the last week would shape me forever. Whether in a good way or a bad one, only time would tell.

Agent Parker had flown back to DC yesterday, but I'd offered to take Ralph out for coffee before his ten o'clock flight today. When I'd said that, he'd eyed me suspiciously. "You don't even drink coffee."

"Yeah, well, you were bragging on it so much the other day, I figured I'd give it a shot."

He'd looked pleased, and now we were at a neo-hippie coffeehouse not far from the airport. A sign on the wall announced COFFEE THAT'S BETTER THAN ALTERRA'S!

Alterra was one of the most famous roasters in Milwaukee and if I was going to try coffee, I guess this was the place to do it.

When the ponytailed barista behind the counter asked if I wanted "bold" or "mild," I asked if he was kidding. "Would any guy ever say he wants 'mild'?"

"You'd be surprised," he told me.

Both Ralph and I ordered the bold. He went for the largest size they had, I chose the smallest, which they called a "tall" and I had no idea how that worked. The person who'd named it was either a marketing genius or a complete idiot. I tried to give him the benefit of the doubt.

We picked up our drinks. I grabbed a couple sugar packets, tipped some cream into the cup, and we took a seat near the window so we could watch the gently falling snow drift down across my city.

Ralph went at his coffee right away. One gulp and half of it was gone. He shook his head. "I still can't believe a police chaplain did all that."

A lot had come out in the last two days, including confirmation of what Joshua had told Radar about a place under a barn on some land his family used to own in Colorado. Two skeletons were found down there. Dental records told us that one of them had been Joshua's father.

I thought of a young Joshua partaking in the atrocities that happened beneath that barn.

And I thought of a five-year-old Ted Oswald being forced to watch as his father slaughtered puppies in front of him and then lashed out at him if he showed any sign of emotion.

And again, as I had the other day, I wondered about our choices and the point at which we ultimately become accountable for them.

Can we ever really know when someone else is old enough, or mature enough, or mentally healthy enough to be held responsible for his crimes? An arbitrary age of eighteen? The current definition of mental health? Our motives are so tangled and intertwined that I imagined a person could point to extenuating circumstances for nearly any crime. But there must also be accountability. There must be justice.

A reckoning.

If justice exists, there must be a hell.

If love wins, there must be a heaven.

I had a feeling it was going to take me some time to sort all that through.

There was no way to know for sure, but Thorne, who'd known Padilla the longest, speculated that he'd turned to religion to try to find redemption. Just as Radar had said that Griffin deserved to go to hell, I believed Padilla did too. Still, I wondered if, in the end, anything he'd learned or shared with others over the years about the grace of the Almighty had sunk in when it mattered most.

Ralph drew me out of my thoughts: "You must have swung that meat hook hard."

I stared at my cup. I really did not want to do this. "What do you mean?"

"Broke his jaw. Basque's."

I blinked. "When I swung the meat hook?"

"Yeah. When it hit him. I just heard this morning, he told, well . . ." Ralph smiled a little. "I should say 'wrote out for' his lawyer that that's how his jaw got broken."

Basque's apprehension replayed in my mind: grabbing that meat hook, swinging it at his face, him dodging it. The fight. Cuffing him. Sylvia's death as he mocked her. Then punching him. Twice. Hard. The crunch of bone when I hit him—not when I swung the hook at his face.

Ralph stared at me. "What is it?"

"Yeah," I said distractedly. "No, I did. I swung it hard."

Why did he tell them the meat hook broke his jaw?

I had no answer.

So far, Basque denied any involvement in the death of Sylvia Padilla or anyone else. He claimed he was innocent, that he'd heard screams from inside the slaughterhouse, gone in to see what was happening, and found the woman as she was.

He said he'd pulled the scalpel out of her chest to try to help her, and then when I arrived, he got scared, tried to flee, and shot at me with his legally registered firearm just to protect himself, thinking I was the killer.

It was ludicrous. I could hardly believe that anyone with his IQ would try to defend himself with a story like that. I knew it would never fly with a jury. There's no death penalty in Wisconsin, but I was confident this guy was going away forever.

In the slaughterhouse, we found evidence of previous homicides, including the body of Celeste Sikora, a woman who'd disappeared the night before Sylvia was killed, and DNA of a woman named Jasmine Luecke whose body was found in a trailer home outside of town. All of those cases would take time to sort out. For the moment I was just glad we'd caught the right guy.

Ralph was almost done with his coffee. "So, before I go, I gotta ask you—you and Taci? Any more news?"

I thought about what to say.

You had a year of loving someone special, of being loved in return—that's more than some people ever get in a lifetime.

He waited. "You gonna be okay?"

"She's happier, I think, knowing that I don't have to be in second place. So . . ." I wasn't sure how to put this, wasn't even sure I was ready to say it, but I did: "I'm not gonna brood."

We left it at that. He took one last swallow of coffee to

finish off the cup, then reached into his computer bag and pulled out a box that looked like it might hold an office stapler. It was wrapped in a brown paper bag crudely wound in duct tape.

"What's that?"

He slid it toward me. "A present."

"I didn't buy you anything."

"I didn't buy you anything either, bro. Just open it."

It took me a while to work through the duct tape. "You wrapped this yourself, did you?"

"Yup."

Once I got to the box, I tore off the end and tipped the item onto the table.

"A Mini Maglite."

"My Mini Maglite."

"Ralph, that's—"

"It's not that big of a deal. I've got another one at home."

"Okay."

"I figured you needed one. They come in handy."

"Really, thanks."

He nodded toward my still-untried coffee.

"I'm working up the nerve," I explained.

"You'll want to drink it before it gets cold."

"Why?"

He looked at me strangely as if everyone should know the answer to that. "Coffee changes taste as it cools."

"Oh." I couldn't help but think, *You never know, that just might help*. "So, you said sugar and cream? Helps with the taste?"

"Helps calm it."

"Calm it. Right."

He noticed packets of hot cocoa on the counter. "Hang on." He walked over, plopped down a dollar bill, grabbed one of the packets, and nodded to the barista, who nodded back.

When he was back at the table he told me, "Mix this in with the cream and sugar. See where that takes you."

Double-sugar high plus a caffeine high. Not a bad thought. "I'll give it a shot."

I emptied the sugar packets and pouch of hot cocoa into my cup. While I was stirring it all in, Ralph said, "We never finished talking about coincidences. From the other day. How you don't believe in them."

"No, I guess we didn't." The cocoa was almost dissolved.

"Well, don't you think it was a coincidence that your gun jammed when you fired at Basque? I mean, how often does that even happen? Or that we arrived at his hospital room just in time to save his life? A couple seconds later and Padilla would have cut him apart."

I mulled that over. "Well, if those were coincidences, are they really the kind to be thankful for? Twice saving Basque's life?"

It looked like he was going to reply, but in the end said nothing and seemed to grant me the point.

"Alright." Hesitantly, I lifted the cup to my lips. "Nothing ventured, nothing gained."

Since I was sure it was going to be acrid and bitter, I wasn't ready for what happened next.

The concoction somehow tasted both deeply sweet and bitter—but in a good way. And that aroma, which I had to admit really was enticing, actually became part of the flavor on my tongue.

It really was not that bad.

"Well?" Ralph asked.

"I think I could stand to drink this once in a while."

He offered me a satisfied grin. "Give it a few weeks with the hot cocoa, then move on. Honey's good too. Before you know it, you'll be a true coffee aficionado."

"Well, I doubt that would ever happen."

"Never know." He glanced at his watch. We had just a few minutes before we needed to leave for the airport. "By the way, that FBI jacket looked pretty good on you the other day at the bank."

"Thanks."

"Seemed to suit you."

"Thanks."

He leaned forward. "Why are you getting that master's in criminology and law, Pat?"

The answer seemed obvious to me. "To more effectively do my job."

"As a homicide detective."

"That's right."

"How many homicides do you work in any given year?"

"Depends. A couple dozen maybe."

"You're not gonna believe this, but we get calls at the NCAVC every day."

"I do believe that."

"I consulted on more than a hundred homicides last year alone. You want to make a difference, a real difference, come to the NCAVC. Start helping law enforcement agencies nationwide find these guys, and put 'em where they belong. You're experienced, you're sharp, and with a graduate degree in criminology, you'd be a shoo-in."

"Calvin's sort of pressuring me to study with him."

"PhD?"

I nodded.

"Naw, think about the Bureau, man."

"I will," I told him, and I realized I really would seriously consider it.

"Who knows," he said, "we could work together again. You might not have to be the sidekick anymore."

"The way I remember it, you were the sidekick."

He scoffed.

I finished my coffee-cocoa combination and we stepped outside into the light, whispering snow. "By the way," I said, "you never told me what happened in France."

"France." Just the way he said it spoke volumes.

"Yeah."

The car wasn't far. He trudged toward it. I walked beside him.

"I had a bad experience there with pillow mist. Bought some while I was doing a training for INTERPOL."

"Pillow mist?"

"Yeah. You spray it on your pillow at hotels, you know. To . . . so they smell nice—what are you looking at me like that for?"

"You don't strike me as the pillow mist kind of guy."

"Hey, I like a nice-smelling pillow and I'm man enough to admit it."

I had no idea how to respond to that. "So, what happened with the pillow mist?"

"I had a reaction. Allergies. My whole face swelled up for a week."

"And you held it against France instead of pillow mist?"

"I told you. I like a nice-smelling pillow." He climbed

into the car. "Besides, they use the metric system over there."

I decided what present I'd get him in return for the flashlight—a bottle of pillow mist. And I'd make sure it was measured in milliliters. Just for fun.

Then I pulled away from the curb to take Ralph Hawkins, my friend, to the airport.

2007

Epilogue

Time has taught me some things.

Some people say that, in retrospect, our hard times aren't as bad as they seemed, but I'm not so sure about that. I think they were as bad as they seemed, and the good times were just as good too.

Hollywood glamorizes violence. The media either mutes it or sensationalizes it. But here, in this job, you see it for what it truly is every day. The blood and the gore and the terror.

But you see love and beauty too, if you keep an eye out for them.

Now, I wait in the living room.

Taci has become a part of my story, a good one, a gift no one can take away—shared times of love and beauty that really were as good as they seemed. Over the years I've had a number of other relationships, though none as meaningful as the one with her.

A couple weeks ago, however, I started seeing another woman, Christie Ellis. Already she seems special to me, like she might be the one. Before introducing me to her daughter, she'd wanted to get to know me first, so here I am now, in their apartment, waiting for the big meeting.

She's fifteen.

A teenage girl.

And just the thought of talking with her makes me feel clueless.

Christie brags about her all the time, even though she's warned me that she can sometimes be a bit opinionated and a tad impulsive: "Occasionally," she told me. "Just once in a while."

The doorway at the end of the hall opens and footsteps approach.

Christie's daughter emerges from the hallway. Shoulder-length, raven black hair. A look of innocence about her, but wary and deeply intelligent eyes.

Before I can speak, she does. "So, you're Patrick."

"Call me Pat, if you like." I stand and reach out my hand to shake hers, but she makes no move to respond in kind, and I end up lowering my hand somewhat awkwardly again to my side.

Okay.

"Come here." She nods toward the balcony. As we head that way, Christie gives me a hint of a smile: *See, I told you. She's got some spunk to her.*

We step outside and then the two of us are alone on the balcony overlooking New York City, where I live now, working for the Bureau. As it turns out, Ralph was right. That FBI jacket did suit me pretty well after all. And, actually, Calvin was right about that PhD program too. Both, a perfect fit.

"So, you like my mom?"

"I do."

"Well, you better treat her right."

"I will."

"No, I mean it, she's been hurt before." There's a depth of love in her words I've rarely heard from anyone before. "I swear to God you'd better not break her heart."

A pause. "I won't."

The girl has a gaze that's steady and unflinching. "She raised me by herself, okay? I never had a dad here and she never had a husband. She deserves a guy who's man enough to treat her the way a woman deserves to be treated. Okay?"

"Okay."

"Is that you?"

No matter where things went with Christie and me, I knew the answer to that question right away. "Yes. It is."

Only then does she reach out her hand. "In that case, I'm glad to meet you, Patrick."

"I'm glad to meet you too, Tessa."

And as I take her hand, the city and all that the future might hold here seem to spread out in a wide and inviting circle at my feet.

To be continued in The Pawn . . .

SPECIAL THANKS TO

Liesl, Pam, Todd, Tom, Heather, Matt, Jim, Trinity, Shawn, Darren, Ariel, Brent, and Alan. This book could never have come together as it did, when it did, without you all.

Read on for a special sneak preview of
the latest installment of the Bowers Files,

THE KING

Coming in July 2013

Thursday, April 4
Atlanta, Georgia

When Christopher Wellington woke up at 5:14 a.m., he had no intention of killing himself.

Over the past twenty years the thought of taking his own life had, in fact, crossed his mind many times, but never as clearly, as distinctly as that first time, when he was a junior in high school and Caitlyn Vaughn stood him up at prom and everyone knew about it and it felt like someone had knocked his feet out from under him and hit him with a baseball bat in the gut at the same time.

In retrospect it seemed silly, childish even—feeling so devastated by something so inconsequential—but at the time it'd felt like his entire world had crumbled.

That night he'd gone to his father's den in the basement and taken the key to the gun cabinet from the desk drawer where his dad kept it, where he thought it was safely hidden from his two curious children.

Christopher had opened the gun case, loaded one of the revolvers, and then sat at the desk for a long time with the handgun cradled in his hands. Wonder, dreams, hopes, all those things that make life livable seemed to be slipping away like a stream of spent possibilities. There was nothing he could think of that he looked forward to: not summer vacation or his senior year or seeing any movie or listening to any song or playing any video game or being with any girl.

It was as if everything that lay on the horizon of that moment held nothing but the promise of more rejection and despair without any hope of healing.

Yes, a girl can do that to you. Yes, she can rip out your reason for living, just like that, with one glance, one comment, one prom-night giggle when she blows you off and then jokes about it with her friends.

He'd raised the pistol and slid the end of the barrel into his mouth.

Can you ever really know the reason behind an action? Can you ever really tell for sure why you did one thing instead of another? That, yes, this is why you quit your job, bought the Toyota instead of the Ford, ordered spaghetti rather than pizza, didn't pull the trigger when you had the chance?

Maybe it was cowardice, maybe it was some strange breed of courage that kept him from putting a bullet in his brain that night, but at last he'd replaced the revolver and ammunition in the cabinet, and no one had ever known that he'd had a gun barrel clenched between his teeth and his finger pressed against the trigger on prom night.

In the months that followed, thinking about how close he'd come to ending it all had frightened him, and he'd found a persistent heaviness lurking at the edge of his thoughts. Eventually, he'd started taking meds to quiet the depression and keep those thoughts of irreversible solutions away, but still, over the years, it had stolen one marriage, two jobs, and any number of friends from him.

But not since that night in high school two decades earlier had the thought come to him as overpoweringly as it did today: *Kill yourself, Christopher. Take your life. This is something you can do right now. This very day.*

5:21 a.m.

He found his way to the kitchen, put on some coffee just like he did every day, drew a hand across his head to calm his tangled mop of slightly graying hair, and ate two doughnuts and an apple, the skin of which was beginning to wrinkle.

His thoughts chased one another around in an ever-shrinking circle. *I wonder what it would be like to be dead. To finally be free of all the hardships and struggles and disappointments of life.*

Then another series of thoughts: *What disappointments, Christopher? Your life is not that bad!*

Things at the law firm were good, his health was fine, he hadn't been diagnosed with cancer or received any other shattering news. But still, for some reason, he found his eyes drifting around the kitchen until they landed on the wooden knife block beside the microwave on the countertop.

Yes, yes, he realized that he really did want to commit suicide, or self-murder, as it used to be so aptly called.

Self.

Murder.

It was true that two weeks ago he'd broken off a relationship with a woman whom he'd been seeing for eight months. Maybe that was causing this. Maybe some form of repressed anger or undealt-with loss was to blame, but he'd realized he wasn't in love with her anymore and when he told her, he'd found that, apparently, the feeling was mutual.

He'd dealt pretty well with the breakup, and as far as he knew, his ex-girlfriend was doing all right too.

However, now that he thought of it all again, it was as if part of his mind was trying to use that breakup as a justification for letting him think the final, dark things he was considering.

You can't make a relationship work, Christopher. It's because of who you are. You can't change who you are.

5:29 a.m.

He eyed that alluring block of knives. They were certainly sharp enough; he knew this because he'd nearly cut his finger to the bone last month while slicing a tomato for his salad.

Yes, a knife was definitely a possibility—wrists, neck, inside of his upper arm. He didn't know what that artery in the arm was called, but it was an important one, he knew that, one that was nearly impossible to quell the bleeding of once it was slit.

Maybe.

Stop it, Christopher!

His gaze traveled toward the sink.

There was bleach below it. He guessed that if he swallowed a cupful of that, it would burn through his tongue, his throat, his lungs, kill him from the inside out.

A horrible way to die, to be murdered by yourself, but still he went to the sink, pulled out the bottle, and read the warning: *Harmful or fatal if swallowed! Call a physi-*

cian or poison control center immediately. Do not induce vomiting. Seek advanced medical care at once!

Yes, a good long guzzle of that would do it.

What are you even doing here, Christopher? This train of thought, you can't let yourself—

But think of it, though. No more breakups or pain, no more heartache or questions or fear, not ever again.

He dialed off the cap to the bleach, but as he brought the bottle to his mouth, the sharp, acrid smell drew him up short. He couldn't imagine that liquid inside of him, that chemical eating away at his throat, his stomach, killing him in a way he wouldn't wish on his worst enemy.

But you don't have any enemies, Christopher. You don't! You need to get ahold of yourself here, you need to—

He returned the bleach to its home in the cabinet but found himself unable to drive the urge away, that unsettling discomfort, that gathering of terrible thoughts coming together like a convergence of vultures inside his head.

A convergence.

Of.

Vultures.

Self-murder. Yes. You can do this. This is something you can do. Today.

There was still climbing rope in the basement from the times he'd gone out while he was in college. There was a chimney on the roof of his house. He could use that. Tie a good strong knot, loop the other end around his neck, get a running start—

Get control of yourself, Christopher!

He rubbed his head, then went to the bathroom, took a shower, tugged on some clothes. He checked his e-mail just to do something normal, to think something normal, to try putting things back into perspective again.

But all the while, it was as if this idea of suicide had lodged in his brain and grown roots. It seemed like a temptation that he could think of fewer and fewer reasons to resist, something he didn't simply not want to avoid, but something he consciously wanted to do.

5:52 a.m.

A few years ago his psychiatrist had told him that depression was anger turned inward, but Christopher knew that wasn't right. Anger is a symptom of depression, not its cause. Anyone who's dealt with depression can tell you that.

Depression begins with a small disappointment and spirals downward, inward, out of control, like a blackness circling in on itself, pulling in everything else around it, sucking it all in, funneling it out of sight.

Sometimes anger is your only ally because it gives you something to feel when the rest of your life turns numb. It gives you something to fight against when you feel like giving up. More often than not, it's when the anger dissipates, not when it arrives, that you're in trouble.

And right now, Christopher was not feeling angry, but resolute.

It's just the depression. Fight against it.

No, you'll lose. It runs in the family, Christopher.

Like mother, like son.

Though she'd been dead nearly three decades, he could still remember the desperation he felt whenever his dad would leave on his truck routes, still hear the sound of his mother's sharp words and the *smack* of her slapping the face of his older sister, still see her shuffling from the couch to the kitchen to get to a bottle. "Escape in a liquid dream," she called it.

Sometimes she would lock herself in her bedroom. He could hear her crying in there, often for hours. He would knock on the door and call to her, "Mommy, don't cry. It's okay." He was a seven-year-old, too little to know that he was doing no good.

Though his older sister tried to reassure him and told him everything was going to be okay, in the end she'd been wrong. His mother didn't find escape in a liquid dream. The nightmares that had haunted her for so long won on the day that she swallowed that handful of pills.

5:54 a.m.

Christopher felt his heart race.

An inexplicable sense of urgency overwhelmed him.

You could get a gun like you were going to use in high school. Or use pills like Mom. Or jump from a bridge or a railroad trestle. A cliff. There are plenty of—

Another voice inside him shouted, *Stop it!*

Drowning? Tying a weight to your feet and jumping into Altoona Lake? Suffocation? A plastic bag over your head?

He considered those last two options for a minute but realized that to him, the thought of drowning or suffocating was simply too troubling.

A blade, yes.

A knife really was the best choice.

But not slitting an artery. Something more honorable.

He could stab it into his abdomen—yes, yes—lean forward onto the blade like samurai did long ago. But he would need to make sure that the blade was long and that it angled up into his heart. He didn't know much about stab wounds, but he'd heard enough to know that if he ended up stabbing himself just in the abdomen, it would take him a long time to die. And it would not be a pleasant death at all. He would make sure that he didn't—

Why? Why are you even thinking this?!

Because you're a corpse in the making, Christopher. Just like everyone. But you have control over the moment when you reach your destiny. And, unlike most people, you have the courage to make it happen today. Right here. Right now.

How do people live with the knowledge that they'll be gone so soon? How do they go about their daily lives, watch their movies, sip their cappuccinos, birth their babies, and go to school or work or church with the knowledge that they might stop breathing any second?

Denial.

Constant denial.

It's the only way.

Unless there's something better waiting for you after death, Christopher.

Yes, unless.

He returned to the kitchen, went to the knife block, and removed the longest one.

It's astonishing to visit a mall or a coffee shop and look around and realize that all those people, all of them, regardless of their age or health, will—in the metrics of the universe—momentarily be dead. Notwithstanding their smiles and frowns, their joys and fears, their foibles and fantasies and dirty little secrets or golden, hopeful dreams— none of that matters. All those people, all of them, will die and turn into nothing but a pile of bones disintegrating into time.

Not all of us succeed in this life, but there's one thing

everyone who's ever been born has succeeded at—dying. And the world simply twirls on, the universe forgetting that we were ever here.

Christopher went to the living room, where he could have a view of the forest outside, the woods opening wide and full in the spring. There's nothing like spring in Atlanta.

He would die looking at the blossoming trees.

With each moment the question of why he was doing this felt less and less pertinent, like a blurry memory someone he used to be was having.

Free will.

Free to live, to choose.

Free to die, if we desire it.

Kneeling, he drew his shirt up and positioned the tip of the blade against his stomach just below the sternum.

Like mother, like son.

Get this right. You need to get this right or it's going to be a long and messy, messy death.

When the decision finally came, it was almost a reassurance that finally, now, things could move on, just as they were meant to, a man passing away into his destiny in the grave.

He let out a deep breath to relax the muscles in his abdomen so the blade would slide in more easily, and then he tightened his grip on the knife's handle so it would go in at the proper angle.

Christopher closed his eyes.

And with a swift, smooth motion he drove the blade high into his abdomen, aimed at his heart as he leaned forward and then used the force of impact with the floor to bury the knife in, up to the handle.

He fell limply to the side.

There was less pain than he had expected.

At first.

But based on the position of the handle he guessed the tip had found its mark.

The pain began as a tight circle of warmth unfurling through him, turning hotter and brighter with every passing second until it felt like a strange companion, as if it were something he'd always had close by, but had only now, in this moment, begun to experience fully.

He wasn't certain he'd hit his heart but it must have been close because with each heartbeat, the handle quivered slightly, as if it were choreographed to do so, somehow programmed to move in sync with the arrival of his death.

That's when the pain began convulsing through him, and that's when the questions came.

He wondered if hell was real, whether that's where he would go for doing this, for taking his own life—for this self-murder—or whether heaven awaited him, if he'd ever done enough to deserve it.

A preacher's words came to him from a sermon he'd heard on the radio one time while driving through central Georgia: "It's not about what *you have done for God*, brothers and sisters, but about what *God has done for you*. Amen?"

So, had he believed in that enough to receive it?

Your mother—is she in heaven? Did she go to hell for the things she did to her children on those days when she'd had too much to drink? Will you see her again when you die?

Just seconds after he thought that, he heard the front door click open.

Confused, Christopher turned his head toward the hallway, but with no clear view to the front of the house, he saw nothing.

However, he did hear footsteps coming down the hall; two people, he thought, but it was hard to tell because sound and light were merging with the pain rushing through him, the pain that was overwhelming every one of his senses and then blistering apart inside his chest.

It was confusing. Reality itself was becoming fuzzy around the edges.

And it hurt. It really, really hurt.

He grasped the handle to draw out the blade, but as soon as he moved it just the slightest degree, a new shot of pain ripped through him and he had to let go.

He drew in a weak breath and watched the handle quiver as he did.

The footsteps drew closer.

"Who's there?" He tried to speak loudly, but the words were so soft that he was certain no one could have heard them—not even if they'd been in the room with him.

The pain grew tighter and sharper with each breath. Dying wasn't turning out to be at all like they made it seem in the movies. This was no gentle escape into the unknown; this was more like a terrifying descent into a scream you've tried your whole life to keep from uttering.

"Help me, I . . ." This time the words were even softer, barely louder than a breath—

A voice came from the hallway, strong, masculine: "He's in here!"

A woman and a young man whom Christopher didn't recognize entered the living room and strode toward him. He wanted to tell them that he hadn't meant to do this, any of this, that he just hadn't been thinking clearly and had made a terrible mistake, and if they would only help him, he would be okay and—

The man knelt beside him and pressed a pair of fingers gently against the side of Christopher's neck to check his pulse. "He's still alive."

The woman watched silently. "Give it a few minutes. It shouldn't be long."

A cold gust of fear swallowed Christopher.

The man moved back to his partner's side.

No!

Christopher tried to cry out for help but ended up making no sound at all.

And that was the last time he would try to speak, the last time he would try to do anything at all, because after that, everything that happened was natural and inevitable and no longer a matter of the will. Nature ran its course, the universe claimed its next life, and at 5:57 a.m., Christopher Wellington died in strangled, wet silence as the clock just above him on the wall ticked off the seconds, edging its way into the minutes and hours and years that might have been his to enjoy if only he had not chosen to murder himself.

The couple stood by until his chest was no longer moving. At last the man, who was twenty-five, blond, and well built, checked Christopher's pulse again. "Okay."

"Okay," the woman said. At thirty-six she was still in stunning shape, had short, stylish light red hair, distinctive green eyes, and a steely, unwavering gaze.

The man stood. "Do you ever wonder what's going through their minds when they do it?"

"I don't think that's something you would really want to find out."

"No. You're right. I . . . I just . . . I wonder sometimes."

She turned from the corpse. "Check the medicine cabinet. I'll look in the kitchen and the bedroom."

"Right."

After they'd retrieved what they'd come here for, the man asked his partner, "So, what now? Up to Boston?"

"No. We won't be visiting the importer until next Friday. First, we need to get back to Chennai—pay a little visit to the people at the production factory."

"Back to India? I thought we were going to go to—"

"The time frame has changed."

"I didn't know that."

"Now you do."

Without another word, she led him outside to the car, and they left for the airport while Christopher's still-warm corpse lay on the living room floor soaked in blood, less than an hour after he'd awakened expecting to head to work for another ordinary day at the office after his shower and customary cup of strong, black, morning coffee.